KNOT FALLING FOR YOU

A SMALL TOWN WHY CHOOSE OMEGAVERSE ROM-COM

STARSFALLS OMEGAVERSE
BOOK ONE

WINNIE ASTER

CONTENTS

KNOT FALLING FOR YOU

Persephone is trying to live the simple life as a barista in the small town of Starsfalls. When a chance encounter presents an opportunity for Seph to help her favorite bookstore, she jumps at it.

But things don't go according to plan. Seph is a self-proclaimed beta who has spent her life avoiding alphas, and working with a hunky alpha architect is not what she signed on for.

Unfortunately for her, alphas are like bobby pins. They multiply and show up everywhere. Soon the alpha architect is joined by his packmates, who hang around the bookstore and Seph. This poses a problem because Seph has a big secret that no one would *ever* guess (at least that's what she thinks) and now it's at risk of getting out.

When someone tries to sabotage Seph's new job, she has to decide if she can trust an alpha (or five).

There's the handy architect alpha.

The energetic, fiery alpha with golden retriever energy.

An uptight business alpha who could be persuaded to let loose.

The bookish alpha professor who has a sensitive side.

And the billionaire, brooding alpha with a checkered past.

But no matter what, she's definitely *not* falling for them.

Knot Falling for You *is a spicy standalone why choose omegaverse rom-com. It's part of the Starsfalls Omegaverse, where HEAs are guaranteed in this cozy small town.*

CONTENT NOTE

This is a cozy, spicy omegaverse rom-com, but there are mentions of serious topics and issues.

Below are the spicy content notes and trigger warnings, some of which may be mild spoilers.

Spicy Content

This is paranormal fiction, not a realistic guide to spice.
Why choose MFMMMM
Group fun
Knotting
All holes filled on FMC
DVP
Light breath play from knotting

Trigger Warnings

This is a low stakes book, but there are mentions of serious topics and issues.

There is no pregnancy in this book, and none of the main characters have children.

CONTENT NOTE

This book mentions serious topics and traumatic events, with potential triggers listed here. If you think something needs to be added to this list, please don't hesitate to reach out to me at winnie0aster@gmail.com

This book contains:

References to past trauma, burns, and child neglect, but not described in detail

Mentions of arson

Hurt/comfort, groveling due to a misinformed MMC with the FMC

Depictions of misogyny, but not from adult MCs

Abandonment issues

Mild violence in order to protect a MC

Bite marks and mention of minor bleeding from bites

INTRODUCTION TO THE STARSFALLS OMEGAVERSE

The Starsfalls Omegaverse is a contemporary alternate universe with some fantastical paranormal elements. In this universe, humans have secondary biological characteristics and are designated as either an omega, alpha, or beta. The designations can be any gender. Betas are normal humans, while alphas and omegas have extra non-human characteristics and abilities. People in the Starsfalls Omegaverse are not werewolves, and there is no shifting.

This omegaverse includes knotting, heats, slick, perfume, scent marking, purring, growling, barking, hissing, and instincts are close to the surface.

Alphas are larger than betas or omegas, while omegas tend to be smaller than the other designations. Alphas typically form packs and look for an omega to be the center of their pack. They are extremely protective of omegas in general, and especially their mate(s). They are legally allowed to physically protect their omega.

In the Starsfalls Omegaverse, the bond between alphas forms naturally when they spend a lot of time together. They do not have to bite each other to form the mental bond, it's a slow development as they grow close and desire to be packmates. Mental bonds only occur between pack-mates and mates.

Omegas go through heats, where their bodies crave sex. This can be unpleasant and painful to go through alone, so they typically join a pack as a polyamorous relationship with enough alphas to satisfy their heat. If omegas don't want to be in a relationship, they may find temporary alphas to help them through their heats. Knotting toys can help, but many report they are not as satisfactory.

During a heat, omegas are focused on being knotted and are unlikely to remember to eat or drink. Alphas are responsible for taking care of them and ensuring they aren't hurt. Omegas have heats several times a year, unless they're on suppressants to reduce the hormones responsible for heats. Omegas prefer to be in their nests for their heats, a cozy space where they feel safe and comfortable.

In order for an omega to join a pack, alphas have to bite them, and then the omega bites the alpha back to complete the bond. If the omega does not bite them back, it means they have not accepted the bond, and it is incomplete.

Betas can join packs, but they do not have the biological imperative to do so. They can bond with a pack, as alphas instigate the bond unconsciously on their end, which draws the beta into their mental bond. To bond with an omega, the omega has to bite the beta to start the bond, and the beta bites them back to complete it.

Alphas and omegas have stronger scents than betas. Scents can be used to find compatible mates, and they typi-cally partner with someone who smells good to them. A scent match is a stronger scent connection that occurs when an alpha and omega smell irresistible to each other. This means they are highly compatible, like true mates or fated mates. Betas can be scent matches to alphas or omegas. Betas can smell the scents of alphas and omegas, but they cannot sense them as strongly. So while an alpha can smell an omega from across the room, a beta would only smell the omega if they were standing right next to them.

For everyone who wants a boyfriend with pumpkin spice flavored come. And wants his four friends too.

CHAPTER 1

PERSEPHONE

I'm not sure who is annoying me more, the customer with so many special requests for his drink that it covers half the cup in instructions, or Marlene, who is so busy flirting with a businessman that she doesn't see how behind we are. Probably Marlene, since she's the manager who is leaving the rest of us lowly baristas to deal with the afternoon rush on our own.

"Have you finished my half-hot, non-fat, extra whip, shaken not stirred espresso yet? I didn't come to Quickie Coffee to wait half an hour for a drink."

Well, that decided it. I was more annoyed by the customer. "It's almost done. I'm just finishing up the half-hot part." Which means waiting for the drink to cool to room temp, so the guy doesn't complain about burning his mouth when he chugs it.

Stasia comes back from handing out drinks and rolls her eyes at me. This guy is lucky she didn't take his order. She would've told him off for making up a nonsense drink name. I'm too nervous to start an argument with a customer, so I finish cooling the espresso con panna and hand it over.

"Took you long enough. But if this is good, maybe I'll invite you over to make me one tonight." Then he winks, WINKS, at me.

"Sorry we close at 7. I can't make you anything tonight!" I blurt out and dash back to the storeroom to escape the winking horrors of customer service.

I grab oat milk and sprinkles to refill the coffee bar, giving a few longing glances to the packages of pumpkin spice syrup, pecan crumble toppings, and apple pie spiced whipped cream. "Soon I'll be inviting *you* back to my place," I whisper to the fall stock. Marlene won't let us sample even one of the fall coffees until August. She's a cruel manager. Now I'm back to being irritated with her.

I carry the usual boring ingredients to the front and quickly jump back in making orders. Lost in the groove of preparing lattes and iced coffee with Stasia and Grey, we've served the last customer of the afternoon rush before I realize it.

Grey turns to Stasia and I, and from the look on his face, I wish we were still slammed.

"You're coming out tonight, right?" Grey asks excitedly. His eyes are wide like he's beseeching someone to grant him a tray of pistachio croissants and almond cake. Or at least that's what my eyes would look like if I was hoping to get a pile of baked goods. Like pumpkin spice scones, or currant tarts, or....

When I come to, Grey and Stasia are staring at me with twin looks of expectation. "Sorry, what was that?"

"Were you thinking about food again?" Stasia asks accusingly, but a small smile curves her lips.

"I was just saying you should wear a blue dress when

we go out tonight," Grey repeats. "It'll match your eyes, and you'll stand out in the line to get into the club. The Hypnotist is super popular right now, so any extra oomph would be great to help us get in quicker."

I groan quietly. There's no way I'm going to a busy club, especially not one called the Hypnotist. "Sorry Grey, I already have plans tonight, and I really can't get out of them. I have to water my plants, and—"

"You are not seriously trying to get out of going to a club by claiming you have to water your plants, are you?" Stasia interrupts my attempt to do just that.

"It's not just that I have to water my plants, I also have to..." I trail off, trying to come up with something else important that doesn't make me sound like an antisocial homebody.

I look at Grey to see if he's buying the plant thing. Now his eyes are wide with tears. Maybe he thinks it's great I'm such a devoted plant parent?

"You're going to bail on me again? I thought we were friends and esteemed colleagues. But I guess we're just two baristas who happen to work at the same shop," Grey says with a quaver in his voice.

I guess the plant parent thing wasn't that moving. "It's not like that, Grey. You are very much my esteemed colleague and great friend! I'm not really into clubs and dancing. We could go to that cool bar on 5th Street like we usually do. They have a dance floor too, but we can also hang out and talk without music blasting us. I'll buy you one of those sunrise drinks there," I wheedle.

They both frown at that.

"You're calling a run-down ex-cowboy saloon a great bar?" Stasia asks, giving me the stink eye.

"I didn't think it was run down. It just has, you know, a rustic aesthetic," I mumble.

"Yeah, and you need a tetanus shot afterward. Plus, that bar closed down like a year ago, Seph," Grey says, shaking his head pityingly.

There's no way that's right. It hasn't been a year since I went out with them, has it?

"You're coming to my place after close and we'll get ready for the Hypnotist together. I have a blue dress that will look great on you," Stasia decides.

"Yes! I'll grab my clothes and meet you at your place and we'll pre-game!" Grey is back to doe-eyed excitement. I'm still stuck on plant parenting. How have I not thought of another excuse to get out of going to a club? I want to hang out with them, but not there. It's not like you can spend quality time together at a place like that. Grey and Stasia are squealing over how cool the Hypnotist sounds while I've been running through potential excuses in my head.

"Alright, back to work. You're not at the club right now trying to hop on a disco stick," Marlene interrupts. All the customers she deems worthy of flirting with must have left. I quickly get to cleaning the espresso machine and try to ignore the queasiness in my stomach at the thought of being in a packed club.

Stasia and Grey scoff at Marlene, but they also dive into cleaning. I worry it's because they want to get out of here early to go to the club.

CHAPTER 2

PERSEPHONE

I've just finished the final cleaning on the steam wands when I look up to find no one in sight. Now's my chance to clock out and hurry home without the others realizing. I could claim I was so tired I forgot we were supposed to go out tonight. I hurry to the back to hang up my apron and grab my purse from the locker. My purse strap gets stuck on the locker handle for a second, maybe thirty seconds at most, before I free myself and hurtle toward the exit.

"Where are you running away to?" I whip around to see Stasia and Grey staring me down. Damn Stasia with her eagle eyes and quick mouth.

"What? Nowhere! I wasn't running! I was going out to get some fresh air. And to look at the nice trees out back. You know, enjoy being out in nature after a long day while I water the plants and give them the leftover coffee grounds." There, that's totally plausible. I was just talking about needing to water my plants. I could've meant the plants behind the coffeehouse, too. And they wouldn't want leftover grounds to go to waste.

They don't know for sure that I was trying to run away

from them. Are they buying it? The look on Stasia's face says she isn't buying it. Grey doesn't look upset, but he's usually pretty upbeat. It's hard to tell if he believes me or if he's just not that bothered by the idea that I was trying to skip out on club night.

"I've never seen you water anything back there. I've watched you talk to those trees for like twenty minutes at a time, but never water anything," Stasia counters.

Crap, they're not buying it. And now I'm learning Stasia saw me talking to the trees. Which day did she hear me? Did she hear me tell the trees about That Day I Wore the Red Shirt? Or about the time I fell in a puddle, and they had to call the coastguard to save me? No, she couldn't have heard those embarrassing stories. It must've been another day she heard me telling the trees about something normal and not embarrassing. Good, my secrets will stay between me and the trees.

Grey distracts me from my calculations by getting back to our clubbing plans. "Wait a minute for me and I'll walk you to your car. Then I'll hurry to my apartment to grab my outfit and meet up with you at Stasia's."

"Sure, we'll wait out back near the trees," Stasia agrees before I have a chance to object. She's still talking about the trees. Maybe she's going to ask what else I've told them? As Stasia puts her arm through mine and we leave the shop, I'm frantically thinking of not embarrassing things I can tell Stasia I told the trees.

"So..."

"I ate all the Samhain candy in one night!" I blurt out before she can continue her inquisition.

"What?" Stasia looks at me quizzically.

"Just, you know, that's one of my most embarrassing

stories and I've never told you about it," I say to convince her before she can call me out.

"More embarrassing than when you spilled coffee all over those alphas who stopped by on their way to a wedding?" she asks.

"Shit, I forgot you were there when I did that."

Stasia laughs, and after a moment I join her. "Okay fine," I concede. "That was way more embarrassing. I didn't even realize they were dressed so nicely until I saw the coffee dripping off their suits!"

I felt terrible for ruining their outfits (and hairstyles on some of them), but they were all very nice about it. They said they had other suits they could change into and not to worry about paying for the dry cleaning, even though I kept offering. One of them said their omega spilled things on him all the time, so he wasn't fazed by it anymore. After his friend told a joke about omegas spilling things, and I got them new coffees, they were on their way.

Stasia cheered me up afterward when I contemplated quitting, since I definitely ruined thousands of dollars' worth of suits with a few five-dollar coffees. Without her support and gentle teasing, I might have quit working at Quickie Coffee that first ruinous week. Thinking back on it now, I mostly remember the shocked looks on their faces, and it's a fun memory of when I first started. (Although I do still feel bad about ruining those beautiful suits. One of their jackets had a horse pattern in black velvet with shiny white thread for the horns.)

Our laughter turns into reminiscing. Stasia tells one of her favorite stories about the customer who asked her to make him a banana sundae iced coffee. His request ended up involving almost everyone in the coffeehouse as people made suggestions for off-menu items with innuendos.

While listening to her story, an alpha businessman stops at the end of the alley and watches me. I avoid his stare and focus my attention on Stasia. Eventually, he walks away. I uncross my fingers, thankful he moved on quickly. With my suppressants and descenters, alphas shouldn't notice me, but some seem to have a sixth sense and take too much interest in me. Luckily, Stasia didn't notice this one. It gets harder to explain away the focused attention of an alpha when it keeps happening. Stasia's never questioned it much, so hopefully she just thinks I have an especially appealing scent for a beta.

There aren't that many unmated alphas here in Starsfalls. I know where the single ones tend to congregate and avoid those areas. Since I moved here, I haven't had many close encounters. It's when Stasia and I go to one of the bigger cities nearby that I run into issues. When we visit, I steer us toward places with lower densities of alphas, like bookstores, plant nurseries, bead shops, antique stores, ceramics classes... It might be time to plan another trip to the city.

Grey appears by the end of Stasia's story and laughs as she describes the double banana packed coffee cup the customer ended up with. Grey walks us to Stasia's car, so I don't have a chance to escape, but I'm sure I'll think of a way to get out of going to the Hypnotist.

CHAPTER 3
PERSEPHONE

I couldn't get out of going to the Hypnotist. Why do I always forget how soulful Grey's eyes are and how strong Stasia is despite her short stature? Avoidance was my only hope. Once Stasia had me in her car, it was all over.

Current status: propping up the bar and drinking something coconutty while Stasia and Grey dance their hearts out. The view from the bar isn't so bad. It sits above the dance floor, which is recessed and several feet lower than the rest of the club. From my vantage point, there's a mass of swirling, dancing people that's almost hypnotic. Must be where they got the name for the club, which isn't as alternative or pretentious as I feared it would be. The layout means I'm not too claustrophobic up here above the undulating people.

I've just taken a sip of my coconut and passion fruit drink (or is it mango?). Whatever it is, I'm enjoying the coconut and yellow mixed drink when someone bumps into me, and I choke on shredded coconut.

"Oh my god, I'm so sorry! Are you okay? Oh! I know the Heimlich maneuver, don't worry."

Suddenly I'm crushed to death between two hay bales. Oh wait, that's just blonde highlights on an omega who smells like a wheat field. I manage to gulp down the last of the coconut death drink despite my chest being crushed and clear my throat.

"Um, I'm okay now, you saved me. You can let go!" I squeak out to my brawny savior.

"Oh, good! Lucky I was here to help you. This club is so dark no one else would have realized you were choking until it was too late."

I turn around to see who "saved" me. The tall woman smiles benevolently down at me. "Yeah, must be my lucky —" I start to say, when I notice the tattoos around her collarbones. "Are those the runes from the *Fairy Princes* series?"

"Yes! They're the ones Aleric gets when—"

"When his fiancé leaves him in the third book!"

She grins despite my interruption. "Wow, you must be a superfan of the books to recognize these! Most people get tattoos of the stylized symbols of the elements from the series. I've never met anyone who recognized Aleric's runes."

I smile awkwardly at being called a superfan. Is that another term for nerd? At least I don't blush at being called a superfan. I really hope I'm not blushing. "It's a great series. I've read it a few times, I guess. I have a vivid imagination, so I've spent a lot of time picturing what his runes would look like. You must be a superfan too if you got those tattoos!" I blurt out as I realize.

I shouldn't be embarrassed about loving a fantasy romance series anyway, but it's nice to see other people are just as obsessed. Plus, I've only read them like fifty times.

10

It's not like I got a tattoo of them. That's way more commitment to the fandom. I like too many books to get tattoos for all of them, and there's no way I could choose favorites. Well, that and I'm scared of needles. I start to feel sweaty and woozy. Okay, no more tattoo thoughts.

"I'm a huge fan of the *Princes* books. I just styled a room at work after the aesthetic of that series. It has antique velvet couches and wood bookshelves to look like the princes' castle. I want to add some plants to the space too, like Erikk's greenhouse in the second book. I must have a black thumb though, because all the plants I've tried have died in like a week."

I'm still trying to recover from thoughts of tattoos, so it takes me a minute to process what she's saying. When I finally catch up, my heart pounds. "I know plants! I can help you find some that would work indoors. A *Fairy Princes* themed office? That's so cool. Where do you work that they let you decorate like that?"

I always pictured the office life as bland cubicles with cookie cutter furniture and a coworker named Bob who snuck up behind you to breathe heavily in your ear while he asked if you've finished those expense reports yet. Thank goodness I was able to get a barista job with my history degree. I can't imagine having to be polite to heavy-breather Bob every day.

"Oh, I work at the Pen and Tellem Bookstore on Main Street! Actually, I own it, but I don't like to sound too corporate by introducing myself as a big business owner. I love running the bookstore, but I'm trying to live a slow-paced, cottagecore lifestyle. Minus the plants around the cottage. But if you're serious about helping me out with that, we should set up a meeting at Pen and Tellem. If you can recommend the plants I should get and how to care for them, I'll pay you for the consult." The omega looms over me as she gets more animated in her request for help.

"You don't have to convince me to visit Pen and Tellem. I'm in there all the time," I quickly agree before she gets so enthusiastic that I'm at risk of being crushed again. "You don't have to pay me to visit, I'm happy to talk about plants any time. Did you just buy the store? I don't think I've seen you there before."

"Well, it depends on what time you come in," she laughs. "I like to have a slow start to my day, so I work afternoons and evenings. I've owned the store for about five years now. I'm Belinda, by the way."

"I'm Seph. I usually visit in the morning since I work afternoons at Quickie Coffee. I love the atmosphere in bookstores. If my friend hadn't invited me to work at the coffeehouse with her, I was going to apply to all the bookstores in the valley. Pen and Tellem is definitely the best bookstore around though."

Belinda looks pleased with my praise. It's easy to tell, because her smug face is six inches from mine. She must be a touchy person even when she's not saving someone's life.

"I'm just happy people still enjoy coming to Pen and Tellem with the modifications I've made. You never know how people will react to change. And I'm paying you for the plant consult. That knowledge is going to save me some effort and save plants' lives. I can meet you tomorrow around noon if you're free. For now, I've got to get in some movement. I spent all day looking through expense reports."

Hah! I knew expense reports were a real thing. I totally could've pulled off working in a cubicle. "Sure, that sounds great! I'm not working tomorrow, so I can spend as much time as you want at the bookstore."

"Yes! Now join me on the dance floor, Seph. We can try out the dances they do at the princes' ball in book five!"

Is it rude not to dance with your boss when they ask? Is Belinda my boss if it's just a consulting job, or is she more like a coworker? Is it rude not to dance with a new coworker? I'm not dancing with my coworkers now, but they're not new.

Wait, that's it!

"Oh, I'm waiting here for my friends to finish up out there. We were about to head out for the evening. I don't want to venture onto the dance floor again and lose them." I breathe a sigh of relief and mentally praise myself for thinking my way out of that so quickly and socially acceptably. Belinda doesn't seem disappointed, so my new consult job is safe.

"Next time then. I'll see you tomorrow! I've got to find some people to dance with before I shrivel up. You know how it is as an omega. I've been single for too long. I have to get some human contact in where I can!"

"But I'm not—" I eke out through a tight throat, but Belinda is already moving toward the dance floor, and I don't want to shout in the club that I'm not an omega. Because who does that? Plus, people always get suspicious if you loudly deny something. I decide it's not worth it. I'll wait and correct her if she brings it up again tomorrow. She doesn't *know* I'm an omega, and I don't want anyone to think I am. I turn away from the dancers to finish my death drink. As I take a careful sip, Belinda says loudly in my ear, "Hey, maybe wait until your friends return to drink more of that. You know how that almost turned out earlier."

I sputter to clear my throat so I can deny the allegation that I'm bad at swallowing. Before I can, Belinda walks away again, making it down to the dance floor this time. Wiping the tears out of my eyes, I decide I'm done with the coconut drink.

CHAPTER 4

PERSEPHONE

After rolling out of bed, I reminisce about the night before. I'm so glad Grey and Stasia made me go out with them. When they came back to the bar after dancing, I convinced them to leave early and get midnight ramen before the ramen cart closed. I'm also thankful the two of them only gave me a little bit of shit about never joining them on the dance floor. I did let them try to convince me to dance for about ten minutes before kindly reminding them that I gave them both a black eye the last time we danced together. (To be fair, my dancing isn't that bad, it's just stiff and awkward. The black eye was more of a slipping on a puddle in the middle of the dance floor and falling situation. But still. It's a risk being out there.)

It's not until I'm almost done brushing my teeth that I remember I have a job today. I inhale in preparation to squeal my excitement (at home where no one can hear my omega noises), but promptly decide to finish brushing my teeth before celebrating. I very much do not choke on the toothpaste I inhaled. In fact, I didn't inhale any toothpaste at all, because I can brush my teeth like a normal person, thank you. After spitting and rinsing my mouth off, it's safe to let out my excited squeals.

I'm going to work in a bookstore! I've always wanted to work in a bookstore, or a library, or a museum. Since big businesses do genetic tests to confirm your designation in order to provide the best medical coverage, it's never been safe for me to work at a place like that. But consulting with a bookstore! That's basically like being a librarian or a museum collections manager! Maybe I can keep the consulting gig going on the side. I could tell Belinda I'll come back weekly to care for any plants she gets on my recommendation. Or I can help rearrange things when she comes up with another book theme to recreate. I'd do that for free anyway. It would be nice to be involved in something semi-relevant to my degree without the risk of being outed as an omega.

That reminds me, Belinda already thought I was an omega. Unless she meant her comment as like "Oh, you know how us omegas are, even though you're a beta, I'm sure you've heard how much omegas like me need touch." If she brings it up again and thinks I'm an omega too, I'll use my love of perfumes as an excuse for why I sometimes smell stronger than usual for a beta. If I overexert myself, the descenters can wear off, and not every business has good air filters to clear out scents. No craving for alphas from this gal. No occasional need for mild sedation during heats to avoid begging for knots from any nearby alpha for me. Just regular old beta gal me. Ugh, I know when I start referring to myself as a gal it's time to stop the self-reflection.

I move on to choosing an outfit to wow Belinda with my cool book enthusiast, totally a beta vibe. After rummaging in my closet for twenty minutes, I decide on a mustard yellow sweater over a black midi dress and silver speckled black leggings.

I prepare my coffee for the morning, cold brew with pumpkin spice syrup and brown sugar whipped cream. The Quickie Coffee supplier lets me place a personal order alongside the shop's order so I can buy my own seasonal coffee. I don't think I'd survive the wait for Marlene to let us open the pumpkin products at work. Not with them sitting on the shelves and sweetly tempting me for weeks.

As I sip my pumpkin coffee, I contemplate what plants to recommend for Pen and Tellem. I work my way through an almond croissant and ice water as I wander around my apartment looking at my plant collection, deciding which ones would do well in the low light.

By late morning, I'm mostly through my coffee, and I've collected several plant cuttings to show Belinda. She can use those to visualize what she wants in the space. Maybe I can convince her to sell propagated plants at the store. Lots of book people love plants, right? This way, I could rehome a few of the plants that have been multiplying in my apartment over the years. I look around the living room. The pothos, philodendron, cast iron, and other plants sit or drape across the bookshelves that cover most of the walls. If Belinda lets me sell plants at her store, I could use some of that money to buy a big variegated monstera. Spending a hundred dollars on a plant is fine if the other plants paid for it. It's basically trading goods at that point.

I shake myself out of the plant daze and hurry over to the front door to zip up my brown leather faux lace-up boots (no reason to untie and retie laces every time when zippers exist). I'm going for a country librarian vibe, like I know many things about plants, but also books. After savoring my last sip of coffee, I head out the door.

It's a nice late summer day with a cool breeze, so I enjoy the walk to Pen and Tellem. Even though the bookstore is only fifteen minutes by foot, I usually drive if I suspect I'm going to buy a lot of books that I don't want to carry back. I get red and sweaty pretty quickly, so in addition to the embarrassment of people asking if I have heatstroke, the sweat makes my scent stronger. Best to avoid that. Thankfully the summers in Starsfalls rarely get blazing hot.

Main Street has so many great shops besides the bookstore, and it's surrounded by more streets with the same downtown charm. Since Starsfalls is a small town, it's easy to find parking nearby so I can take my purchases back to the car between stores. Otherwise, most of the streets are walkable, so you can go from place to place without driving or taking the trolley. I could pick up a pastry and a coffee, and walk to the town square to sit in the gazebo while I enjoy them in less than ten minutes.

But not today. Today, I'm a businesswoman with an important meeting. I hold my head high as I aim straight for Pen and Tellem. No deviating to other stores, even if it looks like Old Dusty's Antique store has new wooden shelves in its window. Not distracted at all passing the Petticoat Crossroads Boutique with yellow dresses on the clothing rack out front. That's right, I'm all business as I arrive directly at the bookstore thirty minutes after leaving my apartment.

I push through the dark green wooden door and the bells inside Pen and Tellem jingle happily as I enter. The book smell smacks me in the face, and I breathe in deeply. That has to be one of the best smells in the world. This store carries antique, vintage, and modern books, so it has a rich combination of book scents.

Alice peeks around the giant, old mechanical cash register and smiles. "Welcome back, Seph!"

Alice is so short her head barely extends above the curved wooden checkout counter, but her white and pink bobbed hair makes her easy to spot.

"Thanks Alice. Is Belinda around somewhere?"

"Oh, she's not in yet. Did she special order a book for you? It should be back here somewhere. I can grab it."

"No, that's okay. I'm actually here for a business meeting with her," I reply demurely, keeping my self-important businesswoman feelings from showing on my face.

"That's cool. What are you going to ask her about? Are you going to open a rival bookstore? If you do, you should totally carry more cowboy romance books. The four rows here don't do that genre justice. There are so many more bowlegged cowboys to love out there."

The smug look slides off my face. "Belinda asked me to be a consultant for her, actually." Does my yellow sweater not give the appearance of a knowledgeable executive who can share her wisdom with others? I press on bravely, "She asked me to come by today and help her choose some plants for the store. I grow a lot of houseplants in my apartment, so I should be able to find something that will do well in the low light here. Belinda said she wanted something in the new fairy princes section?" I end with a questioning look. I haven't spotted the new setup yet, but the bookshelves are set at different angles, splitting the ground floor into sections. Plus, there's the upper area, which has its own mysteries.

The upper levels overlook the ground floor like a loft, with the center of the building open all the way to the roof. Gallery balconies on the upper floors surround the opening.

Because of the light placement, t's hard to see the upper areas from below. You can just make out a few bookshelves before darkness covers them and the rest of the floor extends back into the shadows.

Alice's face lights up and she hurries around the front desk. "Yes! There's something missing in there! I'm so glad you're going to help with that. Belinda did a great job, but it doesn't quite say 'well-hung princes live on these grounds' when you enter that room. Plants could be just the thing to bring it all together." She rushes me and drags me along behind her as she zigzags through the meandering stacks of books. I spy new antique books with gold embossing during our dash toward the back of the store. I'll have to see if I can escape Alice's clutches and circle back to check them out later. I make a mental note that I should always bring my car when I visit Pen and Tellem.

We've reached the far corner of the store by the time Alice slows. I'm not sure I've ever visited this distant section. There are so many books on the twisting stacks in here, I must have missed it.

"The furniture is totally on point in here, and the rugs are amazing," Alice continues the conversation. "I hope you know some plants that would look good in here. I think Belinda is right. A bit of greenery could be what pulls this sitting room together."

With that, Alice tugs me through the last row of bookshelves into the princes room. Couches surround the edges, with plush Turkish rugs overlapping across the stone floor. I glance up from admiring the delicately carved flowers on the frame of the pink velvet couch that I appear to be straddling and gasp. There are enormous glass windows along one wall.

"There's full-length windows back here?" I ask,

squinting to see through them. It looks like there's moss and debris collected on the outside of the glass.

"More like walls. There's an adjoining greenhouse in this corner."

I turn to see Belinda has joined us.

I scramble off the couch and hurry over to the glass. "You have a whole greenhouse back here? How have I never seen this. Are there plants growing in there? If you clean off the windows, there should be enough light for a lot of different plants. This opens up our options considerably," I quietly contemplate.

Belinda laughs and follows me. "No plants in there besides whatever's growing on the walls, I'm afraid. The previous owners didn't use it, and I could never get anything going in there. All the plants I put in there died, and I could never figure out how to adjust the humidity. Since you're an expert, I wondered if you might be able to help fix this, too."

My eyes can't open any wider. My mouth probably couldn't open any wider, either. I close it with a snap and blink to clear the stupefied look off my face.

"I would love to!" I squeak. That's not very business-woman of me. I clear my throat and continue at a slightly lower decibel, "Can we get into the greenhouse from here? Once I see what we're working with, I'll have a better idea of what plants will work in the princes room."

"The door is just over here." Belinda leads us to the edge of the glass wall and pulls out a large brass skeleton key. I bounce on my feet as I wait for her to unlock the hidden door.

"I can help clean off the windows," Alice says as she follows us over. "I want to see how the light hits that dark red rug. I can totally picture the Fire Prince laying on it."

"He would love that rug, wouldn't he?" Belinda agrees. "But who's watching the register?"

Alice's eyes widen and she runs back the way we came.

Belinda and I laugh as she pushes on the door. It creaks open and warm air brushes past me as I step inside. I look up at the roof, which must be at least two stories high. It's hard to tell because it tapers to a point along the peak. Moss, dirt, and dust cover most of the panes, so I can't see what buildings border it on the outside. I still can't believe I never noticed the glass peak rising behind the bookstore.

Long wooden tables and benches sit haphazardly throughout the room, with giant stone urn planters and classical romantic statues dotting the open space. I run my hand along a table as I walk around. The wooden furniture seems to be in good shape, and I don't notice any major cracks in the planters.

"If we can get the windows cleaned, this is a great setup," I tell Belinda. "You mentioned the humidity levels might be a problem?"

"There are misters along the metal frame that connect to a humidity meter and thermostat. The controls are supposed to automatically trigger the misters and HVAC. The greenhouse is supposed to maintain a consistent temperature and humidity level," Belinda says as she sits on a bench. "But they never seem to work right. When I turn up the temperature setting, the misters start spewing cold water. I increase the humidity setting and the heater turns on and the misters shut off. I need to find a company with experience in restoring old buildings with integrated utilities like this to fix it. Unfortunately, I've had other projects higher on my priority list.

"For now, we can clean off the lower windows so you can see how much light we'll get in the bookstore and choose the plants for the princes room. After that, if you want to be my overseer for restoring the greenhouse, I can set up a contractor position. It would be a big help if you managed the restoration. Would you be willing to work here part-time?"

Managing a building restoration project? Finally, I can get paid to use my history degree. "I can help with both," I assure her. "I work afternoons four days a week at Quickie Coffee. I'll have plenty of time to oversee the greenhouse work."

"Great! I'll hire an architect soon so you can get started. Now, about the plants for the princes room. I'm thinking ferns..." Belinda leads us back into the bookstore as I pull out my plant cuttings, my mind racing with ideas.

CHAPTER 5

BASEL

S hading my eyes, I crane my neck to see the tip of the Silver Needle. The chrome monstrosity is one of the tallest buildings in downtown Boarwood. I'm not a fan of the modern look, but the view of the sun reflecting off the tower never gets old. I return my gaze to earth and walk to the building's entrance.

I check in with security in the white marble lobby and take the elevator to the top floor. All is quiet when I step out, and I relax as I head toward Nix's office in the back. Before I've taken more than a few steps, a raised voice breaks the silence. I sigh. I'd hoped Nix wouldn't be irritable today since he's only here to catch up on paperwork. I stop in the hallway as I prepare to visit him. Everyone else works normal hours, so there's no one around to see me stalling on this Saturday afternoon. I force myself to move, and Nix's voice gets louder as I approach. He's my pack-mate so I shouldn't avoid him, but it's hard to see him agitated when there's nothing I can do to help. I wait for a lull in the noise to raise my hand and knock.

"You can come in, Basel."

I open the door and peer inside. "Missing me?"

"I know everyone else is busy today, so you're the only one who would be here," Nix replies dryly.

His eyebrows aren't pinched, but his delicately boned face is a blank mask. He must not be too stressed, then.

I enter with a grin. "I know I'm your favorite packmate."

I settle into one of the chairs across from him. Nix leans back and rests his long fingers on the desk. "So, what does my favorite packmate want with me?"

"I'm not interrupting, am I? I thought I heard you on the phone just before I knocked," I can't resist asking.

"It's nothing, just talking through a problem to myself," he responds smoothly.

Talking through a problem shouldn't be loud enough to penetrate 4 inch-thick wooden doors. I keep that thought to myself, and instead say, "If you're overloaded, I can help. You know my work schedule is flexible. We can get caught up on your work together."

Nix waves one of his hands and loosens his shoulders to appear relaxed. "It's just paperwork I wanted to look over myself before it's finalized. It won't take long, and you have your own business to manage. I don't need to pull you into this."

"If you're sure..." he nods after I pause, so I go on, "I'm checking in with the pack to see if you'll need me for anything in the next few months. I was offered a restoration job in Starsfalls, and I'll have to be on site for a little while at least."

"That's great, I'm glad you found a local job. I know you prefer to manage things in person. Starsfalls isn't far, I'm sure we'll manage. What's the building, an old factory?"

I do prefer to be on site. In the past, I was always there to oversee the buildings I restored, whether nationally or internationally. Now that we're trying to settle down, it's been months since I took point on a project. I don't want Nix to stress, though. No matter where we landed, I would have to build a local client list.

As an architect specializing in historic restorations, my work has always taken me to new places. Historic projects aren't as common as new builds. I *could* shift to designing modern buildings, but at this point in my career I've made a name for myself working with older architecture. I can oversee projects from home and send my employees to manage things in person. I knew that was the tradeoff for staying in one place. Plus, there are plenty of historic buildings in this valley between the Fossfell Mountains, so there's still opportunities for me to work onsite. My business isn't the reason we moved here, anyway. We settled in Boarwood for one reason, and that reason is sitting across from me, waiting for an answer.

"It's an old greenhouse attached to a historic building, which may have been a factory at one point. The records aren't very clear. I just got the call about the project yesterday afternoon and haven't done much research yet. Should be an interesting challenge since I don't work with greenhouses or conservatories often," I tell Nix. "The greenhouse is attached to a large bookstore, so I'll have to bring Salem to visit at some point. Maybe once the greenhouse is finished, the pack can visit Starsfalls for a weekend getaway. When there's time in everyone's schedule."

"I'm sure we can find time to visit. I'm glad you found a local client so soon. I look forward to seeing what you come up with."

Nix appears happy for me, but like always, the happiness doesn't seem to reach his eyes.

"Thanks," I reply with a grin, choosing to believe what

he says rather than questioning him. "Since you don't need me around, I'll head out and check with the rest of the pack. If they don't need me, I'll get my things together this weekend and leave on Monday for Starsfalls." I use the armrests to push myself up.

"I'll see you tonight at dinner," I say on my way out.

I try to leave before Nix can come up with an excuse to get out of our weekly pack dinner. Even though the dinners are supposed to be mandatory if we're in the same city, Nix usually skips them. Before I can get out the door, he says, "Take as much time as you need to prep. I'll see you in the morning if you can't make it to dinner."

Does he really think I don't know what he's doing? Or that I'll let him get away with it?

"Since I might miss a few pack dinners coming up, I'll be sure I'm there tonight."

Hopefully that guilts him into attending. Nix hasn't come to the pack dinner in at least three weeks, not to mention any other meals. He barely spends time with us, except for some overlapping workout sessions here and there.

Nix smiles, which leans more toward a grimace, and replies, "Great, see you then."

I keep my answering smile in place as I leave his office, only dropping it after I shut the door. On the ride back to the ground floor, I question again our decision to settle in Boarwood.

Earlier this year, we decided to stop moving around every few months. Most of us travel for work, plus we like to experience new places and cultures, so it made sense to live in different cities throughout the year.

Nix has always been prickly, withdrawing from the rest of us when he's in a mood. He's slowly gotten worse over the years, and we realized recently that he's in a dour mood most of the time. We rarely see him and when we do, he's withdrawn. The pack discussed what we could do to help him, with no input from Nix since he denies anything is wrong.

Nix's business isn't the issue, and it's not like he needs to work. He has plenty of money. He's never been interested in dating, much less finding an omega who could help stabilize him. We've tried everything we can think of to get Nix to open up. The whole point of a pack is to work together to solve our problems. Otherwise, why share a life together if you close yourself off when things get difficult. Nix has been attending therapy since we met, but that's not helping enough. We know his fathers were bad role models, but he doesn't take after them and hasn't seen them in years. There must be something else in his past that's haunting him.

During our pack discussions, sans Nix, we decided that spending more time together might help. Spending less time together obviously hasn't. Nix can't stay closed off if there's always at least one pack member around. We suggested the idea of a permanent home to him, claiming we felt it was time to settle down somewhere. Nix accepted it and didn't have a preference where we moved, so the pack chose for him. We picked Boarwood because Nix seemed less restless here the few times we visited. The pack thought the mix of city life and surrounding wilderness might appeal to him. There are plenty of things to do around Boarwood, no matter your interests.

Since we moved, Nix has been worse than ever. We think he might be struggling to adjust to living in one place, combined with the stress of relocating his business head-quarters. Since Nix won't admit to any problems, we've been waiting and hoping that eventually he'll settle in and loosen up. It's getting harder to hold on to hope, though. If a therapist and the support of his pack can't help, I'm not sure what will. There are doctors that specialize in alpha biology, and treatments for when unstable hormones cause emotional problems or personality changes. We might have to look into those soon.

The elevator dings and deposits me back in the lobby, where the sun now stretches across the marble floors. As I step into the light, I breathe deeply and relax on the exhale. We'll give Nix more time to adjust. It's only been a few months, and it's a big change. I don't dwell on the fact that he's been like this for years. He *has* to open up to us at some point. We're his packmates.

When I get back to my jeep, I force myself to shift focus. The greenhouse will be my first project in Starsfalls, and I want to give it the attention it deserves.

CHAPTER 6
PERSEPHONE

I park my car and walk to the bookstore on my first day as the supervisor of the Pen and Tellem Bookstore's Greenhouse in the Back Restoration Project (working title). I haven't been able to take my mind off the greenhouse all weekend. Grey and Stasia had to prod me out of my daydreams, I mean planning, several times. I should bring them some plants as thanks for putting up with me while I work on this side project. And that brings me back to daydreaming about plants. What species would they like that I haven't already given them? I can grow new types of plants in the greenhouse once it's restored, like vanilla bean orchids or pitcher plants. I run through a list of the finicky plants I haven't been able to grow in my apartment.

I'm still thinking through the new options as I pull the bookstore door open. I freeze with one leg through the opening. The sweet scent of old books hits me hard, but I also detect ink (which I recognize because I went through a phase in college where I only took notes using a quill), and curiously, lemons. Did Belinda start a calligraphy class?

Whatever lemon-flavored treats they have, I need some. I look around frantically for them.

"Did you forget where the greenhouse is already?" Alice says as she pops up behind the counter.

"Gah!" I yelp. Recovering quickly, I ask her about the new aromas, "I smell ink. Where's the calligraphy class? And the lemon scones, or is it lemon tea cakes? Which way are they?"

Alice is momentarily confused by my tirade before she laughs and points to a table near the door.

"You must be smelling our new candles! Aren't they amazing? There's one called Classic Bookstore. That's probably the papery smell you're talking about. There are some fruity and gourmet scents too. I love all of them. The candles are made locally with soy wax, and they burn great or work with a candle warmer if you're interested in getting some."

I stare blankly at the table Alice pointed to, which has stacks of candles in glass and ceramic jars. Some look like they were poured in antique stoneware pots and canning jars. Now isn't the time to get distracted by new old candles. Could those really be the source of this amazing scent? As an omega, I mean a beta with a great sense of smell, I've always been able to pick out the different fragrance notes in a candle. I've never come across a candle scent this strong though, and certainly not one that overpowers everything else. I approach warily, afraid of the power of a candle with this much throw. No doubt it will make my eyes water when I get close.

"Do you know what they used to scent the candles? Are you sure they're safe to burn?" I ask suspiciously.

"Of course they're safe! The labels list the usual

fragrance ingredients. You must have a great nose to sniff them out before you've hardly taken a step inside."

"It must be because they're new. My subconscious noticed the change right away," I say to throw her off the scent of my great sense of smell.

I hold one of the Classic Bookstore scented candles, working up the courage to take the lid off the amber jar. I didn't see any named after a lemon, but maybe it's a layering note in one of them. I close my eyes and brace myself, then unscrew the lid.

I'm not immediately blasted with the scent of a thousand thousand-year-old books. I open my eyes. The candle looks ordinary enough. I risk a closer sniff.

"It does smell good," I tell Alice. "I'm sure these will be a big hit."

The ink and lemon scents have faded somewhat. I must have adjusted to the candle smells. Now I'm not sure why I was so frantic to find the lemon cookies at the calligraphy club. Although I do enjoy a good candle, or five.

"I'll have to smell them later and see which ones interest me. For now, I have a job to get to." I set down the candle and turn back to Alice with my confident business-woman smile.

"Right, it's no good getting distracted by the merchandise while on the job. I know the kind of trouble that can get you into. Just last week I was stocking the new *Big Tex* books, when I happened to accidentally read some of the first page. The book just fell open while I was shelving it. I saw it mentioned driving a big rig, and I had to be sure I was stocking the books in the right section. Big rigs don't necessarily fit the cowboy theme, so I wanted to ensure the series hadn't changed genres. So, I read a little more. Then suddenly Belinda was telling me to get back to work. I told her I was making sure I was stocking the right section, but she wasn't having it. She made me get back to shelving books right then and wouldn't even let me finish reading the final chapter! The rest of my shift was rough, having to wait to find out what happened with Big Tex and his new semi-truck." Alice looks wistfully off into the distance after commiserating with my struggles.

"Yeah, totally not your fault," I respond. Alice really loves cowboys. "Well, I'll just head on back." I edge away and sneak past her while she's daydreaming about Big Tex's adventures.

Once I'm out of sight, I hurry toward the back. I can't be late on my first day.

Belinda is waiting in the princes section, reading something on her phone. She looks up at my casual, unhurried approach.

"Hey, thanks again for agreeing to work on the greenhouse," Belinda greets me.

"Oh, it's my pleasure," I reply with a gracious smile. "I'm happy to play a part in preserving our community's hist—is that the Earth Prince's easel?" I interrupt myself and dart around Belinda to look at the easel in the corner.

"It is! I just found it at Old Dusty's Antiques yesterday. Isn't it the perfect addition?"

"It's amazing," I gush. My nose twitches, but not from dust. It's that lemon book smell again. "Unrelated, but have you been burning some of those new candles back here? The scent seems even stronger now."

"I have the Classic Bookstore on a candle warmer upstairs, but it's not near this section. You know how we pick up on different scents. You must be partial to that type," Belinda says with a wink.

"S-sure. I mean, everyone who visits here regularly

must love the bookstore smell, right?" I stutter nervously. Did she mean "we" like omegas or was that just a general "we?" Does she still suspect I'm an omega? I mean, I am, but no one knows. No one can know.

"I would hope all booklovers love the smell of books! But I meant maybe you should keep your nose out for an alpha who smells like books and oak. Those are the top notes in that candle, and they match Tellem's smell pretty closely, I think."

"Oh, I mean, I'm not specifically looking for an alpha. A beta like me doesn't need one, and it seems like they're usually in packs, anyway. I'm not sure I could handle all that."

Belinda gives me a curious look. "Are you sure about that? Maybe your hormone levels are too low to register yet, but—"

A loud thunk in the greenhouse interrupts her. My hormones are just fine, thank you very much. I certainly don't need, or even want, an alpha.

"That architect better not be breaking anything," Belinda stalks over to yank open the greenhouse door. "How's everything going in here?" she asks sweetly as she steps inside.

I follow until the air wafting from the greenhouse hits me. I choke. My pulse races. I'm buzzing but I can't move. I've never been this turned on. It's the book linen and ink and lemon scent from before, but a thousand times stronger. It's a newly penned love letter. It's lemon scones just glazed for afternoon tea. I'm dizzy from it. Or wait, that may be because I'm not breathing. I force myself to exhale the best air I've ever breathed. When I inhale the smell is just as strong, but I try to ignore it so I can function. I take several steadying breaths before I realize what the smell must be.

Alpha.

CHAPTER 7
PERSEPHONE

It's just my luck that I move across the country and find another scent match. That's why the scent was so strong I could smell it across the store. It wasn't the candles. It was him. The scent matched alpha I smelled years ago wasn't this strong. Maybe I was wrong about him. Have I been hiding for nothing? Or did his scent change over the years?

My mind whirls. Now that the scent isn't overpowering my other senses, I hear a male voice responding to Belinda. He doesn't sound familiar, but I can't hear much of what he's saying. That might not mean anything, since it was so long ago. But I don't think scents can change that drastically.

If this alpha is a second scent match, there's no way he's associated with the first one. We're too far from where I met *him* for them to know each other.

This alpha's scent must be digging its hooks into me because I'm thinking strange things. Wouldn't it be fine for an omega to have a scent matched alpha? Pleasant, even. I think of the hidden nest in my apartment. All the times I've tamped down my instincts and hidden my scent over the years, so no one discovers my secret. I could stop all of that and have a mate, or even a pack. Sometimes I imagine what my life would be like with a pack. Only when I'm alone late at night or during my suppressed heats do I let my mind conjure those thoughts. But just like all those times, I make myself consider the reality behind my fantasies.

Alphas don't want an omega to care for and cherish and be cared for in return. They want an omega to control and own. Even better if it's a scent match, so the omega will be desperately attracted to them regardless of their personality. I know that's the reality, I heard it straight from the source. Despite my fleeting fantasies, I never let myself forget the cold, hard truth. I won't ever let my guard down around an alpha again. I may be alone, but I'm free. It makes no difference that this new alpha also smells heavenly. I know what lurks beneath.

I straighten up and adjust my shirt as I mentally prepare to go in there and ignore that scent trap. From what Belinda said, it must be the architect she hired. This is my big opportunity to give back to the people of Starsfalls and use my passion for history. I won't let some stupid alpha chase me away.

It sounds like they've moved deeper into the greenhouse. After quickly checking that no one is around, I move to a corner of the princes room that's out of sight. I pull out my extra-strength descenter from the secret pocket in my purse and spritz myself all over. With the combination of my descenting soaps, deodorant, and spray, I shouldn't smell any stronger than a beta. The hormone suppressants also dampen my scent, in addition to altering it slightly. This alpha shouldn't be able to tell I'm his scent match, but I'm not taking any chances, especially after the shock of his scent. I don't want to overpower the descenters in my excitement. Not that I was *that* excited by his smell. Certainly not. Mind over matter. My body doesn't control me. I've already decided I don't want an alpha, so my body can just deal with it.

I quickly uncap the descenter and do another few sprays on my lower half. No particular reason, just because. I put it away and wait a few seconds to be sure it's working. Then I rummage in my bag for one of my favorite perfumes from the Clawed Foot Apothecary, pumpkin spice and vanilla cake, and spray liberally. That should muddle my natural scent if any of it peeks through. It will also prevent anyone from getting too close and smelling the real me. This stuff is eye-wateringly strong. I return the perfume to my bag and hike it up my shoulder.

I can do this. I'm businesswoman Persephone. All alphas smell the same to me, a beta, and I don't need one. It's time to restore this greenhouse. I nod to myself and walk resolutely over to join the others.

Inside the greenhouse, I find a dark-haired alpha with blue eyes, which stand out against his pale complexion. He's tall and broad, muscles straining against a brown plaid button-down and dark pants.

Oh, and Belinda is there too. As a consummate professional, I pay equal attention to all of my coworkers.

I pictured the architect wearing construction type clothing, like an orange vest or jeans. I also thought he would be bronzed from working long hours in the sun, but this alpha looks like he rarely goes outside. Maybe he only does interior renovations. As I finish my assessment, I realize Belinda and the alpha have stopped talking. Belinda glances between us with a grin on her face. I look up from my perusal to see the alpha staring at me. I do not blush at that realization. Belinda's smile grows.

I clear my throat to introduce myself, but nothing comes out. I try again, this time getting out a professional greeting, "Hi, I'm Persephone." I'm sure that wasn't as breathy and squeaky as it sounded to me.

The alpha doesn't reply, he just keeps staring. My nonexistent blush doesn't get worse, and my face doesn't feel like it's burning. Stupid Belinda is grinning like a Cheshire Cat now. I don't know what she thinks is so funny. She's the one who hired an unprofessional employee, with his too tight clothes caressing bulging biceps and thick thighs, who gawks at people.

I clear my throat again, but even that sounds breathy now. Breathy, but not like a whine. The alpha responds to that, taking a step toward me. I startle, letting out an eep and backing up. Surely he wouldn't try to kiss me when we just met, and right in front of Belinda? She's an omega too, and I didn't hear him hitting on her. He is an alpha, but still, he shouldn't be so forward.

He stops and smiles. It's a glorious smile, one I can imagine him wearing while writing me a heartfelt love letter.

"Do you not shake?" he asks, his voice deep and soothing, but his words snap me out of my reverie.

I scowl ferociously at him. "No, I'm not a dog trained to follow your commands."

Belinda laughs and the alpha's lips crook in a smile.

"Ah, I usually greet people with a handshake. But we can greet each other however you want," he says as he drops his arm. I hadn't even realized he was holding his hand out. Oh, he was going for a normal business handshake, not commanding me to greet him.

I'm not sure why my first instinct was to do what he said. It must be his alpha presence. It's a good thing I was on my guard and showed him I won't let him order me around. I should play it cool now though, since he wasn't actually trying to order me around. This time, at least.

He's waiting for my approval. I mean, response. Belinda moved to the side, so I still have an unobstructed view of her grinning face. Ignoring her, I reply, "We can just exchange names. No need to shake. I'm Seph, the manager of the greenhouse."

His smile is back. "I'm Basel, an architect specializing in historic building restorations. I look forward to working under you."

My face does not get redder at that. I hear Belinda snickering. I give Basel a curt nod and turn to her. This is all her fault, hiring unprofessional people who smell delicious. I level my ferocious scowl at her. Belinda giggles again. She must not have seen it.

"Now that we're all here, are we ready to get to work?" she asks. Finally, my first business meeting is underway.

CHAPTER 8

PERSEPHONE

We spend about an hour developing a plan for the restoration.

"I'll start interviewing builders," Basel says as we get up from the benches. "They'll likely come by to see the greenhouse to give an accurate estimate, if you want to be there for those meetings, Seph."

As our talk went on, I realized I had almost zero renovation knowledge. Sure, I researched the history of this part of Starsfalls after Belinda hired me, and I learned about historic architecture in school. But listening to Basel discussing logistics like reading blueprints and figuring out what needs to be repaired or replaced, plus the construction itself, left me feeling out of my depth. I don't know the finer details like he does. I don't have a fancy degree and years of experience. Sure, I have *a* degree, but I bet Basel spent like a decade studying architecture and has a master's degree or two.

By the end, I'm deflated. I don't think Belinda needs me at all. Basel can easily take care of the renovation without me. All I need to do is come back once the greenhouse is done and choose plants for it.

Despite not wanting to be ordered around by an alpha, I know my limits. "No, it sounds like you have everything in hand. I'll leave you to find the best workers for the project."

"Are you sure? Like I said before, I'm happy to work under you. You have final approval on everything," Basel says sincerely.

I'm surprised he isn't more domineering. For an alpha, he's very courteous. His offer isn't enough to shift my mood, though. I smile and shake my head, using up the last of my social reserves.

I return to the bookstore ahead of them and go to the far edge of the princes room. I stare blankly at the books on the shelves while Belinda says goodbye to Basel.

"I'll have Belinda give you my number, Seph. Text me with any thoughts you have about the restoration whenever you want. I tend to work all hours on a project," Basel sneaks up behind me to say. My nose is so full of his scent already, I didn't smell him getting closer.

I wave limply at him without turning around.

"I'll see you soon," he adds before leaving.

"Thanks again, Basel, for taking on this project so quickly!" Belinda calls after him.

Since I'm straining to listen to avoid being startled again, I hear her come up next to me.

"It sounds like you two will be a great team," Belinda says, nudging me with her elbow. I think she also throws in a wink or two, but I can't tell very well out of the corner of my eye. I'm still unfocused, facing the stacks.

"Are you always this shy around alphas?" Belinda continues when I don't reply. "I thought you were interested in him, but if you don't like him, I can look for someone else."

As much as I want to avoid alphas, this one isn't a problem. It's me. I can't let her fire him because of me.

I turn toward Belinda but can't look her in the eye. I stare past her shoulder instead. "No, he seems great. I don't spend much time around alphas, so I guess I'm shy, but that's not the issue. I'm not sure I'll be much help with the restoration. I know the historical aspects, but I'm not an expert in the actual construction process. It sounds like Basel can handle that. You don't need to pay me to be involved until after the greenhouse is repaired. Then I'll happily be your plant consultant."

Belinda puts her hand on my arm. "I don't need two experts in construction. I wanted you to be involved because you understand the princes theme I'm aiming for, and you're know about plants and history. Don't worry if you don't have the same experience Basel does. He can take care of the technical details. I want you to oversee things to make sure we end up with the right look in the end. Before you got here, he was talking about replacing some of the windowpanes with purple glass because they were authentic to greenhouses at certain points in history."

I tilt my head and scrunch my nose in confusion. "The Air Prince would never have purple things in his greenhouse."

"Exactly!" Belinda says in exasperation. "See, I need you on this project. I'm too busy with the rest of the bookstore to oversee every step here. I want you involved as the vision consultant to keep things on track. Basel researched the history of this building too, but he's more interested in the 1800s architecture, and we want to bring it back to the 1700s. That fits better with our fairy princes theme and it's still in line with the older architecture in Starsfalls. So don't quit on me, Seph. I need you, and Basel needs you."

My heart pounds at her words. It must be because Belinda is counting on me for this project, which aligns perfectly with several of my interests. My heart isn't racing at the idea that Basel needs me. Well, he does need me, but just for this project.

"You're right," I agree. "I'll keep the restoration focused on the right style and stay on top of Basel to make sure everything goes according to plan."

Belinda giggles and hugs me happily.

I can be confident and professional, even if I have to work with a stupid, delicious alpha. I am a businesswoman, after all.

CHAPTER 9

ROMAN

I'm slicing the roast chicken while monitoring Fynn to make sure he doesn't flambé our steaks again, when I hear footsteps coming down the hall. I look up as Basel walks past the kitchen. "Dinner will be ready in twenty," I call out. He doesn't respond, and I hear him heading toward his wing of the house.

"Is he going back to work later?" I ask Salem.

"I don't know. I wasn't sure he would be home at all tonight," he says, looking up from chopping the fennel for the salad.

"Don't worry, I can cook him a steak real quick," Fynn says with a grin. The light from the gas flame reflects eerily in his blue eyes.

"I think we're good with what we have. Basel prefers chicken and there's plenty of that," I quickly deter him.

Fynn shrugs nonchalantly and returns to watching the steaks, while I keep an eye on the size of the flame. I thought he would outgrow his interest in fire. I should have realized sooner that if getting half of his face burned as a child didn't cure his obsession, nothing would. It'll be a lifetime of ensuring that stoves, fireplaces, and candles aren't burning too high.

I finish the chicken and set another place at the table. I consider getting an extra setting for Nix. Since Basel won't be around to guilt him into coming to the "mandatory" weekly pack dinner, I doubt Nix will come home for any of our regular dinners. Basel has always had the best luck navigating Nix's moods. Or at least he's done better than my efforts. Fynn and Salem have stepped back to let Nix work through things on his own, since he won't tell us what's bothering him, but the hands-off approach isn't working. Nix is the reason we moved here and cut back on business travel. The stability was supposed to ground him and improve his mood. If anything, it just made things worse. We see less of Nix than ever, and he's more withdrawn when we do see him.

Fynn pulls the steaks from the grill pan after blackening them and sets them aside to rest. Salem brings the other dishes to the table. I give Fynn a minute while I help Salem before telling him to turn off the stove.

"Relax, I was just about to," he rolls his eyes at me. Fynn slowly turns down the flame, then runs his fingers through his shaggy red hair, shaking it out of the way when it immediately falls across his eyes. If he's going to play around with fire, he could at least have the decency to keep his hair cut so I don't have to worry about his head catching on fire again. Once was more than enough. Seeing him wrapped up in bandages, so small in that giant hospital bed... I shake my head to clear away the bad memories. Fynn carries over the steaks and Salem fills our drinks.

Basel hasn't come back down, and he never answered me. "I'll see if Basel is going to eat with us," I say, pulling the kitchen towel off my shoulder to drop it on the counter on the way out.

"Tell him I made the fennel salad he likes," Salem replies. I nod and head to Basel's wing.

I stick my head in his office but don't see him. I move on to his bedroom and find the door ajar. I push it open to find Basel walking around with one shoe off and his shirt half unbuttoned. I don't see the other shoe anywhere. His workbag is open on the couch in front of the fireplace, laptop and papers spilling out. Basel doesn't say anything when I come in as he paces and rubs the back of his neck. Is this new project stressing him out already?

"Are you coming to dinner, or do you have to work?" I ask.

"What?" he responds after a minute, although he doesn't stop moving.

"I said dinner's ready. Are you coming?"

Basel finally stops next to the couch. "Uh, sure, I'm coming." He starts toward the door.

"Did you want to take off your other shoe first?" I prompt as he limps toward me. Basel stops and stares down at his feet, before finally taking off the other shoe.

I put my hand on his shoulder to steady him. "Are you alright? Everything go okay with the new project?"

He straightens and tosses the shoe behind the door. "Work was amazing. I mean great. Fine. Typical restoration, nothing out of the ordinary," he says quickly, tapering off awkwardly at the end. I stare at the side of his face, but he doesn't say anything else, keeping his gaze on the floor.

"I don't want to use this card, but I can't handle two of my packmates pulling away. Don't turn into Nix and shut us out. If something's wrong, you know you can tell us," I say quietly.

Basel jerks his head up to look at me. "No, it's not like that. It's just—there's this woman. She's amazing. I felt like I'd been struck by lightning when I saw her. But she barely talked to me and wouldn't even shake my hand. Not that she's obligated to, of course, but I don't understand. How can I feel so strongly about her with just one look, while she was so disinterested? Maybe I stared at her too much and freaked her out. It's all my fault. How do I fix this?" He grabs my arm with a plaintive look.

This is not the direction I expected this conversation to go. I thought a contractor was proving difficult to get ahold of or something. If Basel gets the idea that he needs a specific person or company to work on a project, he won't rest until he gets a meeting with them. But this is about a date? I didn't realize he'd found someone here. Of the four of us, Basel doesn't date often. Fynn and Salem go out more, and I do occasionally. We've tried dating as a pack, but never found someone that fits with all of us. We've mostly switched to individual dates, hoping one of our partners will end up being interested in the rest of us and vice versa. Nix doesn't date at all. But now Basel is dating in secret? He is pulling away, except he's leaving us for other people instead of isolating himself.

I don't want our pack to be pulled apart like this, but I also don't want to see Basel upset. He deserves to be happy, even if it's without us. "Don't panic. How many dates have you been on? It takes time for some people to get comfortable around another person."

"Dates?" Basel scrubs his hand through the back of his hair. "No, I just met her today. She's the supervisor for this restoration job. I would love to date her. I shouldn't, though, right? Since she's a coworker. But I want her to like me, or at least not hate me. Should I bring her food the next time I see her? A blanket? Would that be weird? Is it too much like what an alpha would give an omega as a courting gift?"

I relax as I process what he's saying. He's not hiding things from us. Then I focus on the rest of what he said. "Wait, you reacted this strongly to an omega? Was it her smell, her looks? A scent m—"

"It's not that," he cuts me off. "She's a beta, not an omega. She smells good, like pumpkin pie, but it didn't seem like a scent match. She's beautiful and fierce, but it's not just that. I can't explain it. It was like I was electrified when I was near her. A sense that this person is important. She obviously didn't feel the same way, though."

Basel is subdued by the end of his explanation. However, my heart is racing faster than when I thought he was hiding things. He says it's not a scent match, but beta's scents aren't as strong. He might not have been close enough to smell her properly if she wouldn't let him shake her hand. As a beta, she wouldn't be able to smell him well, so she wouldn't know either. In our pack's combined history of dating, no one has ever described someone like this. The only time I felt a connection somewhat like what Basel described was when we formed our alpha pack bonds. I've heard the mate pull is even stronger than the pull to join another alpha in a pack.

"Since she's your coworker..." I say, thinking out loud. "You'll be working together for a while, right?"

"A few months at least."

"Use that time to get to know her, slowly, and let her get to know you. As you spend more time together, you should be able to tell if she's just shy or not interested. She isn't already mated or married, is she?" I ask in a panic. I don't know why that thought upsets me so much. It's not like I've even met this woman.

"I didn't see a ring or bite marks and I didn't smell anyone else on her. She could be dating someone I suppose."

That startles a growl out of both of us, and we quickly cut them off. I don't want to get too invested in someone I don't know, but Basel has never been this interested in someone before. I need to keep my expectations realistic, but I've always wanted a center for our pack. I don't care if they're an omega or a beta, as long as they want to be with my packmates and share our lives together.

It won't do any good to growl around her, especially if she's skittish with Basel. He's one of the least intimidating of us. I definitely don't want Fynn around her until she warms up to Basel. Fynn has a great heart and is protective of the people he cares about, but he can be intense. If he meets this beta and has the same intense reaction that Basel and I have to her, he might decide instantly that she belongs with our pack and come on too strong. That would be sure to scare her off. We can't get ahead of ourselves, if it isn't too late for that already.

I have all these plans to woo her, and I don't even know her name.

"What's her name?" I ask.

"Oh, it's Persephone. Seph. Isn't it perfect?" he says dreamily.

That is a beautiful name. Clearly, we're both smitten. I rub my eyes with the heels of my hands as I think this through. I want to meet Seph, but it makes sense to wait for Basel to find out if she's even interested in dating. If she doesn't like him or is already taken, there's no point in involving the rest of us.

"It is a great name," I assure him. "Get to know Seph like she's any other coworker. If that goes well, you can ask her out after your project is over. Keep us updated on how things go. Unless we should wait to tell the others about her?"

"I don't want to keep things from the pack, but I don't want to get their hopes up if it turns out to be nothing. It's only been a day, and she's just a coworker, not someone I'm dating. It's probably better to keep this between us for now. I'll let you know how things are going, and we can decide when to tell the rest of the pack later. Or not," he mumbles the last sentence.

"Let's act normally then and go down for dinner before Fynn eats it all."

Basel laughs and finally relaxes. "Right. Let's go."

We join Fynn and Salem in the kitchen. Fynn is halfway through a steak and there aren't any left. Apparently, we were gone for too long. I'll be eating chicken with Basel tonight. We join them at the table, and I push the chicken toward Basel first. He gives me a wry smile and glances at the serving plate that's empty except for a little steak juice.

As I spear a forkful of chicken, there's footsteps again in the hall. Nix joins us a moment later.

"Just in time, Nix. Come eat," Salem greets him.

Nix grabs a plate from the cabinet before joining us.

It's not fair to put this burden on a partner, but I secretly hope that if we find our mate, Nix will finally open up. Then he can work through whatever his issue is in therapy and be happy. I worry about how lifeless he's become these past few years.

At least Basel got him to eat with us again. I focus on appreciating the present moment. I'll make the most of having the pack together now, and deal with tomorrow, tomorrow.

CHAPTER 10
PERSEPHONE

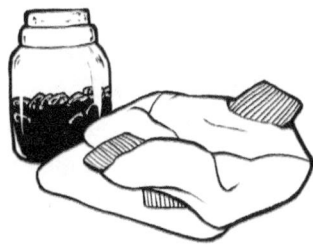

The treetops rush toward me. Just before I can graze the leaves with my outstretched fingers, gravity snatches me away. The ground hurtles toward me, and I close my eyes. When I open them, the sky surrounds me. Back and forth, the pattern repeats. Eventually I realize I'm on a swing.

A faint voice speaks behind me, but I can't tell what they're saying. I try to slow my momentum and look for them, but I can't stop. The swing continues flinging me through the air. When the voice comes again, it's right in my ear.

"I can help you go higher," it tells me. It sounds like a young boy. "We can go further together."

"I'm doing fine on my own," I reply, my voice also childish, "but it might be nice to have some help."

Small hands push me, and I fly higher. Soon I'll be able to reach the trees, and maybe even the sky beyond.

"Of course you need my help," the boy continues, "omegas need alphas. You can't live without us."

That distracts me from my flight, and I try again to look

behind me to see who the speaker is. I only manage to catch a glimpse of wheat blond curls. "That's not true. Omegas and alphas may help each other, but I don't *need* an alpha. I can take care of myself."

He laughs. "Omegas need alphas to guide them. And omegas won't be happy without at least one alpha to serve. They get agitated and irrational without alphas around."

I dig my heels into the ground, my feet dragging roughly through the dirt, but I'm unable to stop the swing. The motion is making me feel sick. Or maybe it's his words.

Society says alphas and omegas are complimentary. Puzzle pieces fitting together to complete the picture. Hormones can become unbalanced and cause stress and irritation if one is without the other for too long. Not to mention the heats. There's medication to remedy those issues, but most omegas plan to settle down with a pack eventually.

Some people have another perspective about how alphas and omegas fit together. A small minority believe omegas belong to alphas. They think alphas can do whatever they want with omegas because they're weaker and simpleminded, existing only to serve alphas. Of course, they believe alphas should be the leaders in all things, the home, businesses, and politics. The scariest part is that you never know who harbors these dark thoughts. I wasn't expecting to hear it from this boy, though I don't know who he is.

"Omegas are strong. We can do things on our own," I argue back.

"Omegas have to serve alphas. The greatest day for a pack is when they find their scent matched omega. Omegas are excited to find their alphas, because they know they can't do things on their own. My fathers said so. Without omegas to take care of things, alphas get angry and yell and throw things. I've seen how my fathers act now that my mother is gone."

I feel bad for him, but I can't let him think such things. Before I can tell the boy he's wrong, he continues in a low whisper, "I can smell you. You're *my* scent match, so you have to do what I say."

Chills run down my spine. As the swing moves toward the trees, I jump.

Soaring through the air, I'm finally free. As my momentum slows, I look for something to cushion my landing, but all I see are more trees. I'm alone.

I wake with a jolt tangled in my blankets. I fight to free myself from the trap, my heart still pounding from the fall. Eventually I make my way out and sit on the edge of the bed. As the grogginess clears, I do know who the boy is. I haven't seen him since we were children, but I remember everything about him even though I've tried to forget. He was the first alpha who smelled good to me. My scent match.

We met the fall I moved to Gaea. I was in a new foster home, and Phoenix visited with his fathers. His parental pack donated to the local charities, including foster and adoption agencies. His fathers went around with the press to show off all the good they did. While they played up their generosity for the cameras, Phoenix played with the foster kids. The swing in my dream was the one in the big maple tree in the field behind the foster home.

I liked Phoenix at first. We had fun running around playing whatever games we thought of, and he smelled so good. It wasn't until the end of his visit that he started talking about alphas and omegas, saying the same type of thing as in my dream. As an adult, I recognize he had issues at home. Back then, all I knew was that I didn't like the way he talked about those things. I knew it wasn't right for anyone to be subservient to someone else.

Sometimes I wonder if Phoenix chose a different path as an adult, rather than following in his fathers' footsteps. I've never tried to find out, because there's one thing that hasn't changed. I can't risk being around a bigoted scent match. I won't be made into a servant, forced to do an alpha's bidding.

After Phoenix's visit, I petitioned the foster system to send me to a group home on this side of the country, claiming my family used to live in this area and I wanted to be closer to them. That wasn't true. My parents died before I was old enough to remember them. But my request was approved, and I moved away from Gaea and from Phoenix. Since foster records are confidential, I escaped Phoenix and haven't heard from him since, if he even tried to look for me. Maybe he moved on to another vulnerable omega.

That encounter affected the rest of my life. At the time I believed what he said about alphas being able to do whatever they wanted, including forcing an omega to join their pack. Now I know that's illegal. Omegas have the same rights as anyone else. No one can force them to mate. As a child, his words scared me (and to be honest, they still terrify me) so much that I hid my omega nature. I didn't want Phoenix to find me, but more than that, I didn't want any alpha to control me based on my designation. Pretending to be a beta and ignoring my omega impulses is safer.

My worry now is that my body will betray me. Since we're scent matched, I can't risk my hormones tempting me into staying with Phoenix despite our opposing beliefs. I can't trust my omega. From what he said, Phoenix's mother stayed with her alphas despite their bigotry. I don't want that to be my life, so I've continued to hide my true nature and avoided alphas. Even after learning Basel is also my scent match, I can't bring myself to trust that he would be any different. By the time he reveals his controlling nature, it could be too late. It's better to stay away from alphas altogether.

I don't need an alpha. I'm doing just fine on my own. I won't let anything push me around, even my own hormones. My mind is in charge, not my body. And my mind has decided that I'll continue working on the Greenhouse at the Back of the Bookstore Restoration Project, and I'll treat Basel like any other coworker. I don't need an alpha, no matter how good he smells, and I won't let one stop me from achieving my dreams. I'm a great asset to the greenhouse project, and it's an honor to help my favorite bookstore. I'm meeting Basel today to discuss things. I can do this.

After going over my decision again, I'm determined to see things through. Now, my mind has decided it needs pastries. I'm hanging out with Stasia this morning before work, so I can tell her how things are going. I text her to meet me at Powder Puff Pastries in an hour.

I make my first pumpkin spice whipped cream coffee of the day while I get ready. I pull on a heather gray tunic dress with mother-of-pearl buttons down the front. That should be professional enough for a historic adviser.

I drive to meet Stasia, since I'm going to the bookstore afterward. I've learned my lesson to always bring my car. It would have been awful if I'd had to carry all those candles home at my last visit.

CHAPTER II

PERSEPHONE

I find Stasia at a patio table at the bakery on the corner of Main Street. She has several powdered croissants, powdered donuts, and powdered beignets in front of her. I sit and examine her selection while she greets me.

"Are you excited about your first big day of work? This history plant thing is so perfect for you!"

I reach for a powdered croissant with pistachios before I reply, but Stasia slaps my hand away.

"No sharing my food until you tell me what's going on," she scolds me. "You've been so excited about working at the bookstore. Hell, I'm excited for you! Grey and I were bouncing around Quickie Coffee with you celebrating your new job. But since you met with the architect, you've hardly said anything about it. What's going on? Do you not think he can handle it like you want him to?"

I look longingly at the croissants. Apparently if I want one, I'll have to walk all the way inside the bakery to order or tell Stasia what dampened my pants. I mean spirits. I sigh and lean back in my chair. I'll have to come up with something. I'm not traveling that far to get pastries when there's some right here.

"I'm sure the architect can do what I want. I bet he's great at handling things. Restoration things. Obviously," I explain eloquently.

Stasia has a menacing twinkle in her eye. Now I'm the one concerned.

I hurry on before she can say anything. "The architect is an alpha, and you know they make me nervous. I usually avoid them, but this one seems okay. He's not overbearing so far. I'll work with him like a professional and everything will be fine. I can handle being around an alpha for a little while." I quickly snatch my croissant now that I've paid for it. I take a bite. Ah, it is pistachio, with powdered sugar and a few curls of lemon zest.

"So, this architect, what's his name? Is he cute?"

My eyes close as I savor the croissant. When I open them, Stasia is smirking at me. I slowly finish chewing and swallow.

"Basel? I mean, he's fine, I guess. He's an alpha and they're always, you know, tall and stuff. I know some people are into that." I pause to clear my dry throat. "I'm not, though. He's just someone I work with. Even if I was into alphas, I keep my personal and professional life separate."

I take another bite to stop the rambling.

"Riiiight," Stasia acknowledges my very normal response to being asked if I think someone is attractive. "I know you're not fond of alphas, but they're not all bad, Seph. Since you'll be spending time with him anyway, it might be good to keep an open mind. You wouldn't be happy if someone thought all omegas acted the same. It's not fair to think all alphas are entitled assholes or something."

I choke on a pistachio. Stasia pushes her coffee over, and I quickly chug it to clear my throat. Mmm, caramel pecan iced coffee. I drink a little more to make sure the food went down. After returning the drink when Stasia snatches it from my hand, I assure her I'm not prejudiced. "I know all alphas aren't bad. Omegas are fine too. That has nothing to do with me," I add nervously.

Stasia doesn't know I'm an omega. She wouldn't betray my secret if I told her, but I don't want her to have to lie for me. It's best I continue distancing myself from omega related stuff so she doesn't suspect anything.

"I've seen happy packs. I'm not bigoted, I swear. I just prefer to be extra safe and avoid alphas in my dating life. I'll be a good coworker to Basel and treat him like I would anyone else. It took me a bit to get used to the idea. That's why I wasn't as excited about the project recently. I'm fine now, don't worry," I finish with a totally not strained smile.

Stasia sighs. "Well, if you're sure. I want you to be happy, Seph. Protect yourself however you need to, but reserving judgement until you see someone's actions is a valid way of protecting yourself. You don't want to cut off a relationship with someone good just because you have some preconceived notions about them. Whether that's a professional or personal relationship. If he *does* try to hurt you, I'll be all over him. So keep me updated, but be open to new experiences."

I stuff the last of the croissant in my mouth and reach across the table to hold her hand. "Thanks Stasia. I'll do my best to keep an open mind. The restoration won't take long, and once it's over Basel will be gone and I'll never see him again. I'll be fine."

I rub my chest. For some reason, that croissant is giving me heartburn.

Stasia squeezes my hand. "Great! I'm glad you're trying new things. I can't wait to see the greenhouse once it's done. I hope you make it look just like the Air Prince's greenhouse. It sounded so romantic in the book."

I grab another croissant while she's distracted. This one is a pain au chocolat with sliced figs on top sprinkled with cocoa powder. After eating a few bites, I ask, "Since we're on the subject of romance. Are you still seeing that guy from the copy shop?"

"No, he said he couldn't date someone who doesn't have a serious job. He works at a copy shop! How is that any more serious than working at a coffeehouse?" she asks indignantly.

I giggle. "I don't know, they're both necessary jobs. Ours is tastier, though."

"Well, he doesn't know what he's missing out on. Anyway, I met another guy while I was leaving the copy shop. He's a professional rock climber and told me about his recent climb up the side of Wisterberry Mountain."

Stasia tells me about her new love interest while I work my way through half the pastries at the table. We get a refill on the food and I get my own coffee, and spend the rest of the morning chatting. When it's time for me to leave for the bookstore, I hug Stasia goodbye. She waves before heading off to learn how to rock climb.

CHAPTER 12
BASEL

I've decided. This is the shirt I'm wearing. Do the pants match? I run my hand through my hair, and the glint from my gold watch catches my eye. Is the watch too much? I don't always wear one, but it shows I'm successful and stylish. I want Seph to like me for who I am, but she wouldn't get close to me when we first met. How can she get to know me if I don't do something to catch her attention?

Normally I'm not flustered by social situations, and I enjoy working with people. I'm the one who is the best at wrangling Nix after all. But with Seph, it's like my mind short circuits. I like her so much already and I barely know her. She was so cute in her little yellow sweater, like a shy librarian. When she thought I was out of line, she didn't hesitate to put me in my place. Not that I would purpose-fully do anything to make her uncomfortable. I would do anything she asked of me.

When we discussed the renovation, Seph was quiet. I wasn't sure if she didn't like my ideas or if she didn't like me. She was straightforward before, so I hoped she would tell me if something was wrong. I want to learn more about her. If I could fix whatever caused her to shut me out and make her happy, she might want to get to know me in return.

Maybe it's the shoes. If I change these brown loafers for the burgundy ones, the rest of the outfit works. This should catch Seph's attention without being too ostentatious. I grab the shoes and my workbag and hurry to the garage. I'll barely have time to get there a few minutes before we're supposed to meet, and I prefer to be at least fifteen minutes early. That's what I consider on time. I already packed the other clothes I'll need for the week so I can stay in town. I sling my workbag onto the passenger seat and start the drive to Starsfalls.

I make better time than I thought I would, so I stop at Quickie Coffee to get a drink and snack for Seph. I order a pumpkin coffee, assuming she likes those since she smells like pumpkin pie. The male barista tells me they're not serving pumpkin flavors yet but the manager interrupts to compliment my shirt and physique. I try to disengage by asking about the other coffee flavors, but she continues her advances. She offers to give me the pumpkin coffee early as "our little secret." The barista rolls his eyes where she's shoved him behind her. I agree to let her get me the pumpkin coffee since it's for Seph. While the manager goes to make it, I place the rest of my order and pay. I get my cappuccino and danishes and wait for the other coffee.

The manager licks her lips as she hands me the cup with her number written on it next to a lipstick kiss.

"Thanks, my coworker will love this," I tell her.

Undaunted, she replies with a wink, "There's plenty more where that came from. Text me any time when you want another treat." Thankfully, she walks away after to help another customer.

The barista hands me an empty cup while she's not looking, and I swap out the graffitied coffee cup. I thank him and add another tip to the jar, then I'm off to meet my mate—I mean coworker—at the bookstore.

As soon as I enter Pen and Tellem, I smell Seph's trail of pumpkin spice even over the pumpkin coffee. I follow her scent after saying hello to Alice at the front desk.

I find Seph in the greenhouse with a measuring tape stretched across the short wall on the side of the building. She's muttering to herself and rearranging the tape. I can't make out everything, just a few words here and there like "strong enough," "crates of them," and most intriguingly, "cook them if they fall." I watch for a bit as she moves the measuring tape in different configurations. Before it gets to the point where it would be creepy to be watching her for so long, I walk over, scuffing my shoes along the floor so she realizes I'm here without startling her.

"Good afternoon."

I was unsuccessful, because she jumps and lets out a squeak. She turns to me with a flushed face and wide eyes.

"H-hey. Afternoon."

Her gray dress reminds me of a buttoned-up librarian again, and when combined with her reddened face, it makes me think of the other ways I could fluster her. I realize it's my turn to say something, so I offer her the food. "I got you a pumpkin coffee and some pastries. Hopefully I picked flavors you like."

I set the food on one of the tables. Seph stares at it without coming closer. I don't know if she doesn't want the food or doesn't want to be near me. She might not like pumpkin. Not everyone likes things that match their scent. I can give her the cappuccino I got for myself. I'm just about to apologize when she rushes to the table and scoops up the pumpkin coffee.

She opens the lid to sniff it. "This is Quickie Coffee's pumpkin recipe. How did you get this? They're not serving fall drinks yet!" She sniffs it a few more times and then looks accusingly at me.

"Ah, the manager offered to let me get it early since I tried to order it. I didn't realize they weren't selling them yet," I clumsily try to explain without bringing up the one-sided flirting.

"Oh. Are you going out with her, then?" Seph avoids eye contact and looks down at her coffee.

I botched that. But does that mean Seph doesn't want me to date anyone else? I feel a brief flare of hope, but it's quickly snuffed out since she looks upset. I quickly reassure her, "No, I'm not interested in her. She was...outgoing, but I only accepted the pumpkin coffee for you."

Her shoulders unbunch, and she beams at me. "Oh, okay then. Marlene is usually pretty strict with the seasonal stuff, so I wasn't sure if you guys were together or something. Thanks for the drink, I love their pumpkin coffees! You said there were snacks, too?" She peers into the bag hopefully.

"Yes, I got several different kinds. Since I haven't been there before, I wasn't sure what was good. I thought we could share them while we go over our first steps."

She makes oohing and ahhing noises as she pulls each pastry out and sets them on the table. I must have picked good ones. I sit on a bench near her and wait to see if she'll join me. After pulling the rest of the food out, she sits next to me while staring distractedly at the pastry options. She eventually chooses an apple butter danish and I take a cherry pie flavored one.

Seph savors the food I brought her, and I swell with pride that I provided for her. Pleased tingles race through my body as she takes another bite. My eyes stray to her lips and the tingles congregate in my cock. I quickly look away and focus on my own food. I take a bite and subtly shift to make my excitement less obvious.

"So, do you have any recommendations for the project? Something to do with the wall you were measuring?" I ask.

Seph blinks like she's coming out of a food trance. "I have an idea for the greenhouse, but I'm not sure if it will be feasible this year," she hedges.

"If you tell me what it is, I can certainly try to meet your deadline. At the very least, I can get you an estimate for how long it will take. The restoration plans we discussed should only take a few months. There's time to adjust things and still finish the greenhouse by the end of the year."

"It will only take a few months?" She perks up at that. "From everything you mentioned, I thought it would take a lot longer. Plus, they say to always expect delays with construction."

"That's true, parts can be out of stock or there's more damage than was apparent. I've already found local contractors that come highly recommended, so we're off to a good start. Just let me know what you want to change."

"I was thinking it would be good if we finished the greenhouse in time to decorate it for the local Autumnfalls Festival. That's when Starsfalls turns into an autumn town, and local businesses and the city council go all out decorating for the season. For two weeks in October, they shut down part of Main Street for a street fair where vendors sell fall things and other booths offer games and food.

"Pen and Tellem always has great decorations. We could have a festival pop-up in the greenhouse and make it look like a farm stand with pumpkins and apples. We could sell apple cider and pumpkin pies and other autumn things. If we had a sturdy shelf, we could fill it with pumpkins as a backdrop for people to take pictures. When they post those on social media and tag the bookstore, it would help spread the word about the new greenhouse. After fall, I can put the plants in here like we planned."

"So you were measuring to see if we could put shelves there for the pumpkins?"

Seph bites her lip and nods. "Do you think we'd be able to build that before the festival?"

Of course I'm going to agree when she's looking at me with those hopeful eyes and asking me to take care of her. I mean, take care of this for her. "I'm sure we'll be able to build extra furniture, it shouldn't take long once we get the materials. I can hire more workers if we need to. I'll have the greenhouse done so you can debut it at the Autumnfalls Festival."

She beams at me, but I don't get to savor her smile for long. The next thing I know, she has her arms wrapped around me and her face is buried in my chest as she straddles me. My cock is thrilled by this development, and it rises to meet her. I don't know how we escalated to this so quickly, and it's not like I can think clearly with her on me. I hold her close, and my purr rumbles out of me. Her dress is hiked up from spreading her legs to fit around me. I grip the back of her thigh to hold her still so I can rub against her but pause when I realize she's saying something.

"Thank you so much! I've always wanted to be more

involved in the town festivals, and designing my own space will be amazing. I can't believe I'll be able to combine my love of history with my favorite season. I'm so glad Belinda hired you for this restoration. You're the best coworker."

Her last word douses me with chills like I plunged into a frozen lake. She wasn't coming on to me. She was hugging me as a friendly coworker who heard good news. My body is confused by the shift from no touching to sudden full body contact, but that's no excuse for trying to rub myself all over her. I choke down my purr to a low rumble and loosen my hold.

"It's no problem. It's part of my job to manage the development in order to meet deadlines. I'm glad you're so passionate about the project. It's nice to work with like-minded people."

Seph pats me lightly on the back and releases me so I can see her face again. It's flushed red with her enthusiasm. I smile at her with what I hope is a polite expression, and not desperate. I also hope she didn't notice my "passion" for our project. She slides back onto the bench and adjusts her dress without mentioning it. I slide my legs further under the table to make sure my cock is out of sight. It still hasn't gotten the memo that this is not the time to make an appearance.

After patting the hair out of her face, Seph asks, "Should we get started with the contractors then?"

"Sure, I'll let them know they can come by and write up the work that needs to be done. Then we'll order supplies. You can finish up the pastries while I do that," I offer.

She grins at that. "If you're sure. Thanks!" She dives back into the pastries.

At least we're past the no touching barrier in our work

relationship, but I'm not sure this is much better. My body isn't listening to my brain that this was platonic contact.

I pull out my phone to message the builders. While I do that, I watch Seph out of the corner of my eye. Seeing her enjoy the food I brought still pleases me. One day, I hope she'll look at me with that much passion.

CHAPTER 13
PERSEPHONE

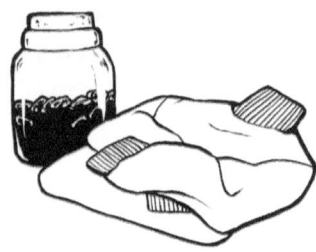

The contractors bustle around the greenhouse like ants, inspecting damage and figuring out what needs to be repaired first. Wiring needing to be replaced, along with the rusted metal framing. Since Basel is in charge of the finer details, I'm only half paying attention to their plans for this copper wire or that I-beam. Instead, I'm thinking about our moment earlier.

Basel didn't feel me rub against him, did he? He hasn't acted any different since our "hug." I didn't intend to sit on him, but I was so excited about our plans that, before I realized it, I was hugging him. And since we were sitting, that hug was more like straddling. His scent was so much stronger up close. I couldn't help rubbing against him a little bit while we were pressed together. Unfortunately, I mean fortunately, with my constricting dress I wasn't able to rub my pussy on him. The suppressants I use lessen the amount of slick I produce, but with the way he affects me, I probably still would have left a damp spot on his pants if I'd been able to sit all the way down.

He didn't push me into anything either, like some

alphas might. I've heard there are alphas so conceited that they think just glancing in their direction means you want them to knot you. Basel *was* purring, but alphas do that when they're happy, and not just for a mate. I tried to cover up my faux pas by saying I thought of him as a great coworker. He seems to have bought it, and believed my clumsy hugging was simply the result of a coworker who was excited about our work plans.

Still, I can't help but replay the moment in my mind. It felt so amazing to be pressed against him, feeling the thick muscles in his thighs and chest and back. To think, a simple hug while we were fully clothed could cause all this slick...

"Did you want shelves up to the top of the wall, or just partway?"

The question startles me out of my reverie, and I look up to find Basel and the others waiting for my response. "I think halfway up would be plenty. I'm picturing it as a product display and photo backdrop. If they go all the way up, it would be too difficult to get things down. Unless we had rolling ladders like in the bookstore."

"That's easy enough," one builder, Yvonne, I think, says. "We can secure the shelves to the metal supports on the greenhouse and add the ladder track as we go."

"Really?" I ask excitedly. I mentioned the ladder as an afterthought. I didn't think they would actually put one in. Who wouldn't want a ladder for their bookshelves? Or pumpkin shelves?

"Sure. Customers can use the ladders for their photoshoots too," Basel says.

"Yes! That will be great," I smile at his idea, but I'm picturing myself in a ballgown on the ladder picking out pumpkins, not the customers.

After figuring out the shelf size, we go through my other

ideas for designing a pop-up for the festival. The builders figure out a timeline for the restoration based on the damage they found. Barring major issues, the greenhouse should be repaired in time.

After the builders leave to order materials and schedule their workers, Basel and I are alone again.

"All that planning made me hungry. It's almost time for an early dinner. Would you like to join me? I'm not familiar with the restaurants around here, so choose any place you want," Basel says.

My heart beats faster, and I think it's because I want to spend more time with him, and not just for work. The promise of food can also make my heart pound, but looking at Basel's smile, I think this time it's because of him.

"That would be great. There's a good hibachi place nearby if you're in the mood for that."

"Sounds good to me."

We close up the greenhouse and head toward the front of the bookstore.

"Did you spend a lot of time at Pen and Tellem before this project?" Basel asks as we walk through the stacks.

"I'm in here all the time! It has a great selection of antique and modern books, and the store is so cozy despite being so big. There's always more to explore." I lean a little closer to confess, "I didn't even know there was a greenhouse back here before Belinda hired me to work there. You would think I'd notice a whole other building with as much time as I spend here. I guess I can be kind of oblivious sometimes." I blush after admitting that. Other people don't notice that about me, so I feel exposed after divulging that information. Hopefully Basel won't think less of me.

"There is a lot packed in this store. It's like a maze, in a good way. I'm sure most people don't know the greenhouse is back there. I wouldn't have noticed it either. Once we get it fixed up, we'll advertise it well," he says.

Basel holds the front door open for me to go through first and then follows me out. We walk to the restaurant since it's not far, and I close my eyes to enjoy the cool breeze blowing my hair back.

"From out here you can't tell that—" Basel continues, before he's interrupted.

"This is what you're renovating? Doesn't look like the building needs much work. Should be a quick project," a cocky male voice says.

I look over to find Basel motionless beside me. I can't see around him to whoever's talking. Basel looks hesitant, like he's been caught doing something he wasn't supposed to. I'm not sure why he would have that expression on his face.

Basel turns to the man but keeps himself between us.

"I'm restoring a greenhouse at the back of this bookstore. What are you doing here, Fynn?" Basel asks.

"I was curious. You didn't say much about your new project before you left. Since you're staying here, I figured I would come visit. You can tell me all about the greenhouse at dinner," Fynn says.

I try to peek around Basel, but he's so damn big, I can't get a good look around him. With the other people passing by on the sidewalk, there's no room for me to move.

"Actually, I already have plans for dinner. I can tell you about it over drinks tonight. I'll text you where to meet me later. Why don't you look around the bookstore and find something to bring back to Salem," Basel says, though it sounds like an order. That stern command has me kind of tingly. He turns back to me and puts his hand on my shoulder. He guides me away while I'm distracted by his authoritarian side before I can see who he's rebuffed.

I try for one last peek, but Basel keeps us moving and the other pedestrians are still in the way. I sigh and give up on identifying the owner of the mystery voice. Maybe it's an annoying contractor he's trying to spare me from meeting?

Something darts around my side. I startle and look up to find a red-haired alpha smirking at me.

"You've already found a local girlfriend, Basel? That's quick for you. What's your name, doll?" He's the source of the mystery voice, so this must be Fynn.

"I'm not his girlfriend. I'm Seph, the supervisor of the restoration project," I reply primly, and not with a squeaky voice. Fynn is so charismatic and striking, with his vibrant, messy hair and tight black t-shirt. Not to mention he's an alpha. They always have that imposing air about them, and it's making me flustered and nervous. I can't have him mistaking me for Basel's date. After my lap hugging earlier, I have to make it clear I only have coworker feelings for Basel.

Fynn raises an eyebrow. "You look close for new coworkers." The wind shifts, eddying around our little group, and I'm hit with the second scent to stupefy me this week.

It smells like the embers in a bonfire, smoky wood and heat, if heat had a scent. There's also something sweet in it, like marshmallows roasting in the flames. I suck in air like I can't get enough oxygen, but it's that smell I can't get enough of. It mixes with Basel's book and lemon scent, like a fireplace roaring in a library while you turn the pages of your favorite book.

I know what this is by now, another scent match. They must be packmates. Basel hasn't mentioned his pack, even though alphas usually bring them up early on when they're talking to a potential partner. We're just coworkers though, so why would he mention them. His pack isn't relevant to his professional life if they don't work in the same business. Clearly Basel has been treating me like any other coworker.

Good.

That's good. Great, actually. He didn't even want me to meet his packmate, and after I gave him a lap dance. Fine. It's obvious he doesn't have any feelings for me beyond professional, so he's keeping me away from his personal life. Whatever. I'm doing that too. No problem. I need to stop grinding my teeth and clenching my jaw. There's no reason for these two to affect me like this. I don't want them to be interested in me, so I shouldn't be hurt or upset. Which I'm not. Obviously.

While trying to loosen my jaw, I notice they're both silent. I look between them, and Basel is staring at Fynn while Fynn stares at me. Fynn shouldn't be able to smell me, so I'm not sure why he's staring. I've kept up with my descenting routine today. I've been told I'm cute, but I'm not attractive enough to have people staring at me literally in the street like this. Was I was so distracted by their scents that I missed something they said?

I'm not sure I can handle being around two scent matches. Basel thinks of me as just a coworker (which is totally great), so there's no reason to hang around him if it's not work related.

"I just remembered I have things to do, so I'll let you two get on with your evening," I say and stop walking.

I've barely taken a step back the way we came when Basel grabs one arm and Fynn grabs the other.

"Hang on," Basel moves in front of me.

I glare down at where his hand holds me loosely. He lets

go and steps back. "I thought we were getting dinner together. Don't let my packmate interrupt us."

"So you are packmates," I accuse. I knew he was trying to keep me away from his pack. Bastard. Not that I care.

Fynn doesn't see my glare, since he's moved up close behind me. He rubs his hands down my arms and leans down to my ear. "I'm sorry I didn't get a chance to introduce myself. Basel gets so focused on work sometimes, he obviously forgot his manners."

I get goosebumps from Fynn's hot breath on my neck and rough voice in my ear. It sounds raspier than it should be, unless he's been sick. There's scarring on his face, up his cheek toward his eyebrow and hairline. Is he hurting still? I feel a pang at the thought of him in pain from whatever caused the scar and injured his throat.

"*My* manners," Basel sputters in response.

My thoughts about an injured Fynn distract me from his proximity enough that I'm able to think. Although it almost feels like he's nuzzling my hair and neck now.

"You still haven't introduced yourself," I remind Fynn as I step out of his arms to face them both.

Fynn grins and leans toward me again. "I'm Fynn, Basel's packmate, and the funnest member of Pack Goldenrod. I'd be happy to prove that to you anytime. I can give you a sneak peek at dinner."

His smile is too good. I feel my face heating. And other parts. I *must* get out of this dinner now. "It's nice to meet you, Fynn. I don't want to keep Basel from his pack more than the job requires. I'll let you catch up." I gradually back away this time. They might not notice I'm leaving if I move realllly slowly.

"He does not have to come to dinner," Basel says, finally collecting his thoughts. "I'll see him later. I already said I would take you to dinner and I don't go back on my word. Please don't let him scare you off."

Basel looks serious, almost pained, like there's more behind his words, before quickly giving me a lighthearted smile. Fynn tenses at Basel's words but doesn't look up at him.

"It would all be good, clean fun, I assure you," Fynn counters with another smile. "Though I don't want to get in the way of your work. I'll see you later, Basel. I hope to see you again soon, doll."

I don't know what that was all about. Fynn seems nice, if exuberant and a bit forward. They're packmates, so shouldn't they want to spend time together? I don't know much about packs, but I thought packmates trusted each other. Is Basel really afraid Fynn would scare me away? How could he?

There's another echoing twinge at the thought of their pain. I don't know the subtext here, but I want to ease the tension. Besides, it doesn't make sense to split up their pack.

"You must be hungry after the drive from Boarwood. The three of us can get dinner and we'll fill you in on the project," I offer.

Fynn perks up and Basel's smile seems genuine now.

"If you're sure about changing our plans..." Basel says.

"It's not a problem. We made the plans like ten minutes ago anyway," I respond confidently. I'm sure I can handle dinner with my scent matches without jumping them.

"Alright! Where are we eating?" Fynn rubs his hands together in anticipation.

"At a hibachi place this way," I tell him.

"Fuck yes," he says passionately.

Fynn must really love Asian food. I lead the way for the two alphas that now follow me to the restaurant.

I'm glad we could smooth things over, but I didn't exactly think through how difficult this would be. I have to endure a dinner with my scent matches without outing my real designation or letting them know I'm attracted to them. Yay.

CHAPTER 14

FYNN

Basel has been keeping his cute little coworker to himself. I can't say I blame him. I also want to take her away somewhere, just us and the pack. We'd take care of her and show her a good time. Since I first saw her, I've been imagining all the things we could do together, and it has me half hard. I've been trying to hide it though since Seph doesn't seem like the type to appreciate seeing my cock right away. I haven't been able to settle down though because I can't take my eyes off her. Plus, she took us to a hibachi place. She's perfect for me. Looking at fire and eating delicious food, it's my ideal date. At least for a first date. I have better ideas for a second date.

Maybe the staring and kidnapping thing is why Basel didn't want me to meet her. I tried to hide those thoughts from the pack bond, so while Basel doesn't know exactly what I'm thinking about, he knows how my mind works. He must have figured I would want to get Seph alone with us in a secluded nest somewhere. I glance over at him, and yeah, he's giving me the "you better behave yourself or else" look. I give Basel my most charming smile and then turn it on Seph.

"Are you from Starsfalls?" I ask. When do I ever ask a fling about their life? I'm not looking for something permanent. I'm out for a good time and some mutual fun with someone I won't see for long. With the way Nix is, there's no way I'll be able to find someone who wants to date all of my packmates, and vice versa. It's better to give off the casual vibe from the beginning, so we both know it's temporary and no one gets hurt. One way to do that is to not learn much about them beyond the present.

Yet here I am, asking Seph for her life story. I don't know what's going on with me. I guess asking where she's from isn't her life story, but that's more personal than I usually get. And I want to know more than that, I want to know everything about her. Fuck, why do I feel this strongly about her so quickly? It's not like she's a scent match or an omega to affect my alpha and get me acting out. She smells good, like a cinnamon baked pumpkin, but there's no omega scent pull.

Despite my internal struggle, I notice Seph is quiet for a beat too long before responding to my question. I almost start to think she didn't hear me, but then she says, "No, I moved to Starsfalls after college because my friend Stasia moved here."

"Is Stasia a historian, too?" Basel asks.

I give him a dirty look. Why is he asking about other women? I want to learn more about Seph. I thought Basel liked her too, so why is he asking about this Stasia?

Seph's eyes light up as she gushes about her friend, "No, she's an aquatic biologist and she's really smart, but so humble about it. She studies the mussels that live in the rivers around here. Stasia says she likes to have a balanced life, so she works two jobs. She does some biology field-work, but most of her biology work is writing reports for environmental studies. In the afternoons she works at Quickie Coffee with me since it keeps her active. That way she doesn't have to sit at a desk all day.

"It's great that we still hang out together so much after college. We had a few overlapping courses in school, and we've been almost inseparable ever since. She's a great friend, always supportive, and she encourages me to try new things even if I complain about them sometimes. Okay, a lot of the time. I tend to get stuck in a rut and she helps get me out of my comfort zone. I hope she thinks I'm a good friend to her. I support all her activities, though I worry about her safety sometimes. I think I help keep her grounded when she wants to try something risky. Stasia is so smart and works hard at everything she does. She inspires me to do my best, but also to let loose and have fun."

I guess Basel was right to ask about Stasia. When you care about someone, you should be interested in their life, which includes their friends. Hearing Seph talk about Stasia revealed more about her, too. I'm not great at getting to know people outside of our pack, so it's good that Basel's here to help.

"Stasia sounds like a great friend. She's right that a balanced lifestyle is important. I'm always up for a good time, so I'm happy to help if you want some fun ideas," I say.

Seph blushes. She must be interested if she's picking up my innuendo. At least I hope that's what it means. She tried to pull away from us earlier, but she could just be shy around new people. I'll have to be careful not to overwhelm her like Basel thought I would. I know I can be a bit much even for my packmates sometimes, but they don't complain. They look out for me no matter what I get up to. (We have a lot of fire extinguishers around the house.)

Seph stops at a red door with a flaming grill painted on it. I haven't been paying attention to anything except her, so I didn't notice we'd arrived. Basel holds the door open for Seph and I follow closely behind to keep an eye on her. I don't help her inside, despite my instincts clawing at me to do so. I ache to put my hand on her back, or my arm around her, or fuck really just put my hands all over her.

I can be patient and wait for her to be comfortable around me. I have a feeling I'll want her around for a long time. I tuck my hands in my pockets as I follow her to our seats. I'm still going to make sure she's safe, even if we're not together yet. It's hard to tell if that thought stems from my alpha, or my past. It's unlikely she'd be in danger in a hibachi place. Except for the fire, and I know how to control that now, so it won't hurt her. I scan the other people in the restaurant, glaring at anyone who looks at Seph for too long. Though I don't trust many people outside our pack, I don't normally eye everyone with suspicion like I am now. Maybe Seph is affecting my alpha more than I thought, because I don't want to let anyone else near her.

Basel holds out the chair for her at the grill. As she sits, I move my seat closer. My leg touches hers, and I drape my arm along the back of her chair. Basel glares at me from behind her shoulder, but I pretend I don't see him.

I lean down to ask, "What's good here? I love anything grilled, but do you have some favorites?"

Her eyes widen and she blushes when she turns to find me so close. It takes a minute for her to answer. I gloat internally that she's so affected by me and I'm not even touching her. Legs touching at the table doesn't count.

Imagining all the ways I can make her flush once she's comfortable with me has my cock fully hard now. That's fine, it's hidden under the table. Seph won't notice unless she's trying to look for it. Or feel for it. Once we're together, I wonder if she'd touch me while we're eating dinner with the pack at home. We could see how long we could play footsie without the others noticing. I'm not sure I could hide it for long with her rubbing me. If I put my hands on her, she'd get slick for me. I'd run my fingers along her lips until she's dripping and squirming in her chair. After teasing her, I'd push two fingers inside. Not enough to stretch her much, just to get her wanting more. At that point, my packmates would notice the wet sounds she makes as her slick coats my hand while I sloppily finger her. Not to mention her moans. Dinner plans would change at that point. We'd clear off the table and feast on Seph instead. Finally, I'd give her what she wants and push my cock inside her. I can practically feel her pussy trying to drag me in. After she comes on my cock a few times, I'd knot her and lock us together. My packmates would have to wait their turn. I know she'd feel so good stretched around my knot, squeezing me while I fill her with come.

As I replay the end of my fantasy, a chill runs through me and deflates my big plan. Seph is oblivious to my thoughts, thank fuck. She's been helpfully telling me about her favorite menu items. I like her excitement about the food, especially the steak yaki udon. I try to remember everything she mentioned while I was zoned out. She explanations why she likes chicken katsu, but only with pineapple fried rice. It's an intriguing combination that I'll have to try.

Meanwhile, I'm still thinking about where my fantasy went so wrong. Why am I fantasizing about knotting Seph when she's a beta? I've been with plenty of betas before and never cared about using my knot. I've been with omegas too, and while knotting them felt good, it wasn't earth-shattering. So why am I obsessed with knotting now? It has been a while since I've been with anyone. I haven't made much effort to check out the club scene after moving to Boarwood. I must be too hard up to think clearly and my alpha is trying to take over. He needs to get a grip. We're not going to knot an unsuspecting beta. I'm not into hurting others.

I focus back on Seph's food takes and do my best to push the other images out of my head. I never thought I needed an omega to be satisfied, and I still don't. I'm not some useless alpha who relies on his knot as the only way to give pleasure. I like Seph as the beta she is. At least the rest of my alpha fantasy was correct. I want Seph to be with my packmates too. Basel is listening raptly to her food critiques, so I assume he's also interested in that. After knowing her for less than an hour, I'm invested, so I'm sure the others will be too. I'm usually the least likely one to date exclusively. Except for Nix, who has his own hangups. I just hope we'll be able to get him on board this time.

My chest warms, and for once, this blazing feeling isn't from watching flames dance. It's all from being near this little beta. She's too cute. I slide my arm down around her shoulders and squeeze her closer. She squeaks and cuts off her food monologue.

"Your picks sound great. I like the unusual combinations you mentioned. Do you make food at Quickie Coffee?" I say.

Seph blinks and leans closer. I let out a short purr and keep holding her. I'll back off if she's not interested, but so far, she seems into me.

"I'm not an expert or a chef, I just love food. I like to research recipes and compare them to find the best version. I also like eating, and I've tried most of the restaurants around Starsfalls. Not that there's that many of them. But I like to try new things in addition to my favorites, so I mix up what I order every other visit.

"We only make drinks at Quickie Coffee. We get food deliveries every morning from the local Powder Puff Pastries and Miner's Diner and serve that. Like the name says, we're supposed to be quick, so there's no time to bake anything. The pre-made food's always fresh, though," she whispers conspiratorially.

I laugh at her secret. "I'm not bothered by a coffee shop that doesn't make the food they serve, as long as it's good. Quickies have their place." She blushes and looks at Basel like she's checking to see if he's upset by our banter. Basel smiles at her and she smiles shyly back.

He leans in with a question of his own and we get to know Seph better as dinner continues. We order several things she recommended. I point out the techniques used on the grill, and how the fire brings out different flavors in the meats and vegetables. Seph listens intently, even when I veer off into talking about the flavors various types of wood impart and the few benefits of gas grills. How smoking meat and campfire cooking open up whole new ways of flavoring food.

She listens as Basel describes his start in restoration and historic reconstruction. He tells her about the buildings he's worked on around the world, and Seph eagerly asks for more details. Eventually they tell me their plans for the greenhouse and Seph's hope to use it as a pop-up shop for the Autumnfalls Festival. The whole dinner, Seph never moves out from under my arm.

Time passes quickly and we're surprised when the server tells us the restaurant is closing soon. We get up to leave and Basel pays the bill, with a generous tip for taking up a table all evening. Once we're out on the sidewalk, we stay close to Seph.

"Can we drive you home?" Basel asks. "I know this is a small town, and it's probably safe, but I don't want to leave you alone in the dark."

"I parked by the bookstore. You can walk me to my car if you want, but you don't have to worry about it," Seph says with a smile.

"We'll walk you to your car." I lean down to whisper, "I don't want to be left on my own either."

She giggles, and we follow her back the way we came.

When we reach her car, I know it's time to say goodbye, but I don't want to let her go. I comfort myself with the fact that she's working with Basel, so she'll be in our lives for at least a few months. Though I hope she'll be around for much longer.

Basel tells her goodnight, and she does the same, holding out her hand hesitantly for a handshake. Basel's smile lights up his face. I forget how striking he is when he's completely focused on something, or someone in this case. He takes her hand gently and places a kiss on the back of it.

Seph ducks her head, but I see her smile through the curtain of blonde waves. Now it's my turn to say goodnight. I'm not suave and sophisticated like Basel. That worked well for me earlier since I spent dinner pressed up against her. I'm more like the scorching sun beating down on you, and you're left to either get out of the way or enjoy the heat. I don't want Seph to run away, so I try to temper myself.

"Goodnight, doll," I tell her.

She grins, but then gives me a playful scowl. "You know my name now. There's no reason to keep calling me 'doll.'"

"I can't help it. You're small and perfect and I want to carry you around with me," I tease back. Hopefully she can't tell how serious I am about that idea.

Seph continues her mock scowl, but her eyes are bright. "I don't need to be carried. I'll see you around, Fynn." She leans toward me.

I slowly bring my arms up and wait to see if she'll move away. When she doesn't, I hug her. She wraps her arms partway around my back, as far as she can reach. I keep holding her until Basel clears his throat, which I take to mean he's telling me to let her go. I ignore him until he does it again. Seph hasn't let go of me either, but I guess Basel's right not to push her. Despite telling us about her life at dinner, I have the sense that Seph was holding back. It reminds me of Nix. Seph obviously isn't ready to share everything with us yet, and I assume that rules out more physical activities.

I sigh and reluctantly release her. Seph slowly pulls back. She keeps her head down, and from this close I can't see her face since she's so much shorter than me. I trail my hands down the outside of her arms to her fingertips and then step back. She gets in her car without looking back, and I close the door behind her. Basel and I move to the sidewalk to watch her go. She smiles and waves before driving off. We wave back and watch until she eventually turns and disappears.

Basel puffs out a breath, and I quirk my eyebrow at him.

"I worried it would overwhelm Seph to meet you because she was so protective of her personal space when we first met. But she seemed to enjoy your closeness, and you got her to open up more than I have. I'm sorry I tried to keep you away. She clearly enjoys your exuberance. At least as much as the rest of us do, anyway," Basel adds teasingly, though he still looks apologetic.

I know what my packmates think of me. With the pack bond, it would be almost impossible not to know. I can be a lot, but they always have my back. I've never questioned that. I'll admit I *was* a little hurt when Basel tried to brush me off at first. After spending time with Seph and seeing how guarded she is, I can't blame him.

I smirk at him. "I'm sure you were worried I'd be so charming I'd steal her away. Conveniently for you, I'd prefer to share her with the pack."

Basel chuckles.

I want him to know that I see how special Seph is. I won't do anything, at least on purpose, to scare her away. We don't even know if she's willing to date a pack. Not all betas are interested in pack life. Not all alphas and omegas are either, but that's less common.

"If she met me first, it might have gone differently. She wouldn't have known if I was safe or just some annoying alpha trying to take her home for the night. I'm sure she warmed up to us because of you."

"I didn't even know if she liked me," Basel admits. "It wasn't until earlier today that she opened up. The first time we met she wouldn't even shake my hand, but today, she hugged me. I don't know what changed, but whatever it is, I'm glad she's getting to know us. You followed me down here at the right time." He gives me a hard look.

I give him my most innocent look. "I missed my pack-mate and I didn't have anything else scheduled. I figured why not come down here and see what my favorite pack-mate is working on. You didn't tell us much about it, and now I know why," I end with a toothy smile.

Basel ducks his head in acknowledgement. "Alright, no more keeping things from each other. Let's go back to my suite at the Fools Rush Inn, and we can call the others to tell them what's going on. I already mentioned Seph to Roman because he saw how distracted I was after meeting her. We'll tell Salem and see if Nix is available. I know he's not interested in dating, but he should at least know if we start seeing her. At worst, he'll just keep hiding away from us like usual." He looks pained despite the flippant remark.

I don't want Seph to join a pack that isn't all in on her. I'll make sure Nix pulls his head out of wherever he's keeping it and pays attention to her. I can't imagine him not being as drawn to her as we are.

I clap Basel on the shoulder. "Lead the way. We'll drag Nix down to meet her at some point and make sure he's on his best behavior. Don't worry about him," I say to comfort him. He takes Nix's isolation the hardest.

Basel nods gratefully, and we head for the inn.

CHAPTER 15

PERSEPHONE

I park at my apartment building and hurry inside. Not because it's dangerous out here, like Basel and Fynn worried, but because I have to get some *alone* time soon or I'll combust.

I rush up the stairs and fumble to unlock my apartment door. I curse as I try to unlock it with the wrong key three times before finally getting it open, stumbling through, and slamming the door shut behind me. I pant as I lean against it for a moment after locking it. Then I drop my purse and keys and hurry to my nest.

I made it through dinner without sitting on their laps or rubbing up on them. Fynn rubbed against me a little, but that was just because there wasn't enough room for the large alpha to fit next to me at the grill. It's the restaurant's fault he had to sit pressed against me.

I'd call dinner a success because I didn't let my omega drive me into the arms of my scent matches. As far as not reacting to their presence at all, that's an enormous failure. I flop into bed and rummage in my nightstand for my knight in shining armor. Or knight in pink silicone.

My pussy still hasn't gotten the memo that these alphas are just as off limits as any other alpha. It was producing slick the whole time, like it was flashing a light to say, "Hey! Safe port in here!" Or whatever it is those lighthouse beacons are supposed to mean. I'll have to ask Stasia.

I don't *need* them, though. I can take care of myself, and I intend to. Even with the suppressants blocking some of the hormones responsible for heats and excess slick, it wasn't enough to keep my pussy in line. Thankfully, these leggings are waterproof. I yank them off and toss them into a corner.

It's time to decompress and forget all about the alphas that caused this mess.

I'm sweaty, sticky, and exhausted, but there's still fresh slick making an appearance. I glare down at my crotch as much as I can while being collapsed spread-eagle in my nest. I'm catching my breath after the I-don't-know-how-many orgasms. It's those alphas' fault I'm like this, not my poor, abused pussy. It's their stupid scents and alphaness and tight shirts and muscular arms and bedroom eyes that caused this. I was just fine before they blew into town. Living my life like a normal person, not getting desperately horny in the bookstore or on the streets. Well, maybe sometimes at the bookstore if I started reading one of the romance books while I was there. But that was never out of control horniness like this. After leaving Basel and Fynn behind hours ago and taking care of things myself, I'm still wet.

I should check my suppressants and make sure I didn't get a bad batch. They say heat can damage them. Maybe I put them close to the oven at some point? Or left them near a sunny window for too long? It can get pretty hot in here with the morning light. It's either the suppressants or I need to get checked out by my doctor. I may have built up a tolerance to the type of suppressant I use and need to switch to another. That would make sense. I've been taking the same brand since I first presented. Now that I'm older, I might need a different type, or a stronger one. I'm sure that's all this is.

Scent matches are compelling, but you don't *have* to be with them. There must be some kind of suppressant that works for unwanted scent matches. I'll visit my doctor as soon as possible and figure this out. I can't be rolling around in bed all day after seeing Basel and Fynn for just a few hours. Especially since I have to work with Basel. We'll be around each other a lot more from now on. Fynn sounded like he was going to stick around too.

First priority tomorrow morning is calling the doctor's office to get an appointment. Or checking the app and scheduling an appointment on there. No reason to make a phone call if I don't have to.

There, that's decided. Now, back to either working off the rest of this slick or exhausting myself enough that I fall asleep.

The trials you go through as an omega.

I make sure my knight is plugged in and get back to work.

The next morning, I rehydrate with several cups of ice water and make an appointment on the app to get my hormones checked. Once I'm less wrung out and can open my eyes more than a sliver, I make my coffee.

While talking with Basel and Fynn last night (don't think about them too much, I don't want to get riled up again), Basel suggested I start planning the products for the pop-up now. He was confident we would finish the restoration in time, so there's no reason not to. This morning I'm going to visit a few vendors in town to see what we can order for the festival.

We'll need tons of pumpkins and gourds and apples, obviously. If I want to serve or sell food, that's a whole permit thing. I'll ask if Belinda knows how to apply for food permits. The bookstore sometimes sells food at events. I can visit the orchards and farms around Starsfalls for the produce and seasonal food like apple cider donuts. Five Pies bakery could provide some of the other offerings, like fig and vanilla bean scones, Basque pumpkin cheesecakes, and quince tarts. The pop-up could have fresh apple cider. It could be served in a big cauldron with a flame underneath to keep the cider hot all day. For cold drinks, a hollowed-out pumpkin could have iced pumpkin juice that comes out of a spigot stuck through the side. If we use fresh pumpkins every day and keep them on a bed of ice, with maybe a little dry ice around that for the aesthetics, the pumpkins should stay fresh until the end of the day. Surely that will pass food safety inspections.

I really need to consult with an event planner, preferably one who has experience serving unique food arrangements. Starsfalls has so many festivals and activities, there must be lots of them in town.

This will be a big undertaking, but Belinda was excited when I texted her about my Autumnfalls Festival ideas. If I work in some Gothic and Victorian-style Samhain decorations for the festival, it will still fit with the fairy princes theme. Belinda was happy to let me set up the temporary pop-up, and afterward I can put in the plants we discussed.

The festival will be a great way to advertise the opening of the greenhouse. People might not notice it otherwise since it's hidden at the back (see, myself for example). The pop-up should attract new customers and ensure the greenhouse was a good investment for Pen and Tellem.

After finishing my pumpkin cinnamon roll coffee and the vanilla scone I brought home from Quickie Coffee the other day, I head into town.

CHAPTER 16

PERSEPHONE

I wander around town visiting the local vendors and come up with a list of supplies for our pop-up. I also bravely call some local farmers, most of whom say they'll have enough stock to supply the greenhouse along with their usual buyers. Everything's lining up perfectly.

I have a spring in my step as I visit Pen and Tellem to check on the restoration. Basel texted me to let me know that the builders are pulling out old wiring and loose metal frames. With my current good luck streak, I bet Basel won't even be here and I won't have to worry about preserving the dignity of my leggings. Last I heard, he was looking for a glass supplier and hoping to find actual antique panes for the replacements.

As I bounce my way through the bookstore, blissfully thinking about my autumn plans, I don't pay attention to where I'm going. By the time I realize I'm nowhere near the princes sitting room, I'm in the medieval fantasy section across the store from where I'm supposed to be. I turn around to make my way back, happy to leave this strange area behind, even though it has an oddly spicy, intriguing smell today. Do some of these authors print their books with weird medieval techniques that make them smell different? I shake my head. Who knows what those types of history people get up to (myself excluded, of course, I'm not a medievalist).

I'm almost free of this peculiar section when I see a pale flash dart down one of the shadowy aisles.

A ghost???

Belinda never mentioned the store was haunted. I've been here thousands of times and never seen a ghost. It could be only this section that's haunted. It must be the ghosts of people from the Middle Ages who are mad that we call them smelly and incorrectly claim they only bathed once a month.

I'm frozen, not daring to look down the aisle in case I make eye contact with a ghost. Or is it bears you're not supposed to make eye contact with? I can never remember. Can ghosts suck your soul out through your eyes, or is it cameras that capture souls? I should've taken more notes from that Victorian witchcraft book I read.

After standing still for a few minutes and not having my soul sucked out, I decide to be brave businesswoman Persephone. I'll simply go down there and tell the ghost not to scare people away from the books. After all, I'm financially invested in Pen and Tellem now.

I'm not trying to chase the ghost away from its home. If it's friendly, I have no problem with it. I don't *know* that it tried to startle me. It may have been spookily moving along, silently drifting between the aisles, and minding its own business.

I hope ghosts have feet. It will *really* freak me out if they don't have feet.

Before I can continue psychoanalyzing the actions of a

ghost and my dislike of feet, yet fear of no feet, I take a deep breath and start down the aisle.

I creep along the shelves. Why does Belinda keep it so dark down here? How are people supposed to read the book titles. I edge along a bookshelf, checking left and right for movement or ghostly eyes. Or feet. I make it to the end of the L-shaped aisle without further sign of the mystical realm. I steady myself with a few deep breaths. It smells even spicier down here. Maybe that's the smell of ghosts. I stick my head into the intersecting aisle and check both ways for specters.

Nothing.

I slip into the next passage and keep looking. It's even darker in this direction, and surely the ghost sticks to the dark. I look down each row of books as I pass. I reach another L-shaped bookshelf and have to move around the short corner to see down that aisle. I lean past the edge of the shelf and don't see anything except for a statue on a bench. It's a human statue made of dark stone for the hair and clothes, and a pale marble for the skin. The statue is bent forward, head in hand, facing away so I can't see its face. I hope the statue has a face. A faceless statue is even worse than a ghost with no feet. In its other hand the statue holds an open book. I'm about to back away to continue my ghost hunt, when the statue suddenly moves and turns a page!!!

"Eeek!!" I squeal and reel backward, crashing into the shelf as I twist around. I thrash as I try to escape the clutches of the statue that's grabbing at me and holding me down. In the midst of my desperate struggle, a warm pair of hands lifts me away from the dastardly statue and sets me on my feet.

"Are you alright?" Pale eyes gaze at me with concern.

I'm mesmerized by them, my rescuer who saved me from the handsy statue. The warm hands leave my waist to brush my hair back and adjust my rumpled sweater. I'm still unable to answer. The spicy smell is overwhelming. It must be from the cursed statue nearby. From this close, I scent pink peppercorns and crumbling leaves blowing in a crisp autumn breeze.

My protector rubs my shoulders after adjusting my outfit. "Did you hit your head? I didn't feel any bumps or see a cut, but we should get you to a hospital to check. Can you tell me your name?"

I finally blink, breaking the hold his eyes have on me. "I-I'm fine. Thank you for saving me. I was so startled I couldn't think, but I'm fine now. I didn't hit my head. I'm Seph."

The eyes retreat, and I'm able to see the rest of my rescuer's face as he leans back. I blink a few more times. It's the statue!! It still has its grip on me. I look around for an escape and see books scattered over the floor and empty spots on the shelf above me. The aisle where the statue was is empty except for the bench and the book it was reading, which is now on the floor.

I look back at the statue that has ahold of me and realize it's just an alpha with inky hair, pale skin, and tight clothes. The sleeves on his button-down are rolled up his forearm, and his arms are ripped as hell and veiny. His pants are tight around his thighs, somehow keeping him constrained despite the muscles flexing as he moves. No wonder I thought he was a statue. Every part of him is well-defined, and his clothes are doing all they can to show that off.

I feel myself blushing and I scramble out of his clutches to stand up before he notices. This is one of the most mortifying things to happen to me, and it's in front of an alpha that smells like the perfect fall day! I step on a book as I stand and wobble, starting to fall again, but the alpha quickly catches me and holds me steady.

"I'm fine. Just clumsy," I say with a fake carefree laugh as I try to worm my way out of this situation. At least he doesn't know I thought he was a statue or that I was hunting ghosts. With the way his skin stands out against his dark clothes, I must have glimpsed him as he walked past and mistaken the flashes of white for a ghost. I can't believe I plunged into a shelf because I thought a statue came to life. I shouldn't have read that witchcraft book so late at night. Those stories obviously got to me.

"Are you sure your head is okay?" he asks again.

No, no, I'm not sure it is.

"I can take you to get it checked out. I'm sure there's an urgent care nearby that will see you quickly."

"Really, I'm okay. I don't need you to take care of me. Thanks for the assist with—" I gesture vaguely behind me to the massive pile of books I knocked to the ground. "I'll let you get back to reading." I sidestep him and avoid tripping this time.

I'll tell Alice I knocked a bunch of books over back here and promise to bring her lots of coffee and treats if she'll reshelve them for me. I don't want to be around this alpha any longer than necessary, even if that means leaving books in disarray. It's because he's overbearing, and not because I'm so embarrassed my face must be glowing. I shuffle away from him, and he steps back finally.

"I'm glad you're alright. It's so dark down here it's difficult to see where the aisles are. Ah, I haven't introduced myself. I'm Salem. It's nice to meet you, Seph."

My heart flutters when he says my name. I halt my

escape and turn back, looking him in the eyes. Mistake. They're so solemn and captivating. He gives me a small smile, and his eyes flash with a golden sheen as they catch what little light exists back here.

I sigh dreamily. What right do his eyes have to be so hypnotic? While I've been staring at him, he moved closer.

"May I at least walk with you to the front of the store where it's brighter? It's eerie being alone back here. I'll ask the woman at the front desk for help putting the books back where they belong," Salem says with an imploring look.

I am going that way anyway, and I don't want to leave him alone here in the dark. Plus, it's not like I'm one hundred percent sure he's the ghost I saw. There could still be one floating around here, footless.

"Sure, let's get out of here together," I tell him. He smiles and it's like the sun shining through the golden leaves on a tree. I'm so entranced that I let him put my hand through the crook of his arm and escort me without even thinking about it.

We make it to the front without further incident, with me stealthily huffing his autumn leaf scent. Only because I really like autumn. It has nothing to do with him as an alpha. Alice looks up from her book as we reach the desk.

"I accidentally knocked some books off a shelf in the medieval fantasy section. Could one of the staff members help me reshelve them? I don't want to put them back in the wrong spot," Salem asks her.

"Oh, don't worry about it, hon. I knock books over all the time. I can take care of it, you don't need to bother," Alice says. She sticks a bookmark in her book and sets it on the counter. I see she's reading *Big Tex and the Long Haul*. She hops off her stool and comes around the desk.

"Sally, can you watch the desk while I go stock?" Alice calls down an aisle.

"Sure thing," echoes back.

"I can do it, Alice. It's really my fault the books fell off the shelf," I pause my sniffing to admit. Since Salem is over here now, I can go back and fix my mess without an alpha hanging around.

I pull away from him to do just that, but Alice stops me. "It's no problem, Seph. I should stretch my legs. Plus, I want to savor the book I'm reading, so I could use a break. You head on back to the greenhouse."

Alice ventures into the dark and leaves me alone with Salem before I can protest.

Salem is giving me a curious look, but I avoid getting caught in his eyes this time. Even if I don't need to pick up those books, I still have to get away from him before my omega gets any more notions. My doctor's appointment isn't until later this week, and obviously my suppressants aren't working like they should. Double the reason for me to avoid alphas right now.

"Thanks again for helping me out back there. I'll see you around," I say, reluctantly letting go of his arm. I mean happily letting go. Of his firm, muscular arm. No, just a regular arm. I'm not interested in him or his arm.

"Are you sure you don't want to sit down for a few minutes? I can check again for bumps or cuts now that we're in the light."

I make the mistake of looking in his eyes and my "no alphas allowed" resolve wavers.

"Well, I—" I haltingly reply, when I'm interrupted by a booming voice.

"There you are!"

For the second time today, I let out a squeal and twist

around, falling backward into something hard. This time I stay on my feet as Salem props me up. My heart is pounding like crazy from the unexpected voice after going up against a ghost just minutes ago. I hastily push my hair out of my face and see Fynn watching me with concern.

Fynn holds his hands out placatingly. "I'm sorry, doll, I didn't mean to scare you. I was looking for you because Basel said you'd be here soon. Then I was excited when I saw you. I didn't mean to yell in your ear."

"Um, it's fine," I tell him and pull away from Salem. This time I straighten my own clothes. "I'm a bit out of sorts today and easily startled."

With Fynn here, I really need to get away from Salem. Together, they smell like the best autumn night spent around a campfire roasting s'mores. Fynn and Basel are a pack, so I can't avoid their combined scents, but I can at least ditch Salem and his amazing smell.

"I have to get going. Thanks for your help. Again," I tell Salem and scoot out from between them to go to the greenhouse.

Fynn's next words stop me.

"You two met already? I was wondering where you'd gotten to. Thought you were going to check out the renovations with us, but I should've known we couldn't keep you away from the books."

I slowly turn back to them in dawning horror.

"I'm not sure why you even bothered to try," Salem replies dryly. "I take it Seph is the project lead you mentioned?"

No.

Salem can't be another packmate, can he? How do they all smell so good? I should be used to Fynn's scent by now, but it still hits me hard. Now there's another one in the mix.

Their pack house must be at least a few hours away, why are they all coming here?? Also, Salem loves books so much he wandered off from his packmates? How cute is that. No, not cute. I don't need to hang around more alphas, no matter how cute they are.

I know what alphas really want. An omega to stay at home and take care of their every whim. They don't know I'm an omega, so their only interest in me would be a brief fling, and I don't want that either. I have got to stop running into members of this pack. How many packmates do they even have. Aren't two mouthwatering, big, attractive alphas enough? I know packs are often three or more, but still, two alphas like that was plenty. Salem must be the last of them.

I comfort myself with that thought. Since I've met all of them now, I know who to avoid. I breathe evenly and try to push away the effects of their mingled scents. (It doesn't work, but hey I tried. Come on, doctor's appointment.)

"That's me," I tell Salem with a game smile. "I take it you're Fynn and Basel's packmate?"

"I am. I hope you don't mind they invited me to see what you're working on," he says with a soft smile.

"Sure, it's a cool building. Come check it out," I say, deciding we might as well get to work.

Fynn hurries over to walk close beside me, and Salem joins on my other side. I tilt my head up to side-eye Fynn for walking close enough to brush against me, but he just grins. Gah, why does he have to have such a tempting smile. I return his smile without meaning to and face forward again. It's best I focus on where I'm going anyway. I don't want any more mishaps.

I drift through the bookstore in a cloud of alpha scents.

103

It's not until we reach the princes section that I realize what else they said.

"Invited *us* down?" I ask in dismay.

"You found her then?" I hear Basel call from the greenhouse.

"Yeah, and we found a tagalong too," Fynn replies, gently guiding me toward the door and away from where I was rooted to the floor.

Sandwiched between Fynn and Salem, I couldn't smell anything else. Now that we're closer and I'm paying attention, I scent another new alpha.

Fynn has to help me through the doorway, where the scent of cinnamon sticks, nutmeg, and crisp apple gets stronger, along with Basel's castle library and limoncello smell. They blend perfectly with the scents of the alphas walking with me.

An alpha with shoulder-length, wavy chestnut hair and green eyes stands next to Basel. His suit jacket and collared shirt make him look like he just stepped out of his penthouse office to tell his assistant he needs a new fountain pen. He has an intercom at his desk but prefers to talk with his assistant in-person, since it makes him seem more approachable. But he does need that new three-thousand-dollar pen delivered today, so if the assistant who makes less than two thousand dollars a month could just get on that...

I jerk my gaze away from the high-powered corporate alpha. I don't know what he's actually like obviously, but that's the vibe he gives off. I hope he *is* an asshole. That will make it even easier to stay away from this pack, assuming he's part of it.

"Seph, this is Roman, one of our packmates," Basel introduces us.

Yep, of course he is.

He continues with the bad news, "I see you've already met Salem, another member of Pack Goldenrod. I was telling them about your plans for the greenhouse and they wanted to see our progress. I hope you don't mind that I invited them down before it's finished."

"It's good to meet you, Seph. I've loved festivals since I was a kid, and I have great memories of attending them with my brothers. Your pop-up sounds wonderful. I'm looking forward to visiting during the Autumnfalls Festival," Roman says.

Damn, he's nice too. Why couldn't at least one of them be an asshole.

Guess I have to be polite back. "Thanks, I'm looking forward to the festival too. I'm glad to have Basel's help so we're ready on time."

Please don't let them hang around long. Their combined scents are winding their way through me and taking hold. If I cross my legs, will it be obvious I'm trying to stop slick from dripping down them? It might be worth it either way if the pressure offers some relief to my throbbing pussy. Though if I'm going for relief, I'm sure the alphas would be happy to help me.

No! Bad pussy! No alphas allowed. Do I need to get that tattooed down there? I move my purse up my shoulder and subtly pinch myself to redirect my body's urges.

It's working!

Wait, no, now I'm in pain and horny. Why did I pinch myself so hard? Luckily they don't seem to have noticed my twitching.

Basel detailed the progress on the greenhouse while I was preoccupied. Now that his packmates have heard about it, they'll leave. Then I'll have Basel all to myself. So we can work on the shelf designs. Not for anything else. I pinch my arm again. Still not working.

The pinching was effective in distracting me from the conversation at least. They're all looking at me like I'm supposed to respond to something.

"Sure, sounds great," I hastily answer. When in doubt, yes is always the right answer, right? Right. That smoothed everything over because they smile at me.

"Great, we can head over now. Unless you want to look around the bookstore some more first," Basel addresses the last part to Salem.

"I can check out the books another time. I'll be in town for a while anyway, so I can come back later," Salem says.

Fuck.

"Do you want to go to Quickie Coffee or Five Pies, Seph? Or is there another cafe in town that's better for talking business?" Basel asks.

At least I was saying yes to going for an afternoon snack, so it's not all bad. I might have agreed to do something really perverted with them and I wouldn't have realized. Why did I think saying yes is always the right answer. My pussy must've taken over my brain. Now I have to spend more time with four, *four*, of my scent matches.

Why couldn't my doctor have seen me today.

"Five Pies is a good place for snacks and chats," I confirm.

I leave Pen and Tellem with my omega in shambles, wanting to touch her mates, but I won't let her. At least the alphas haven't noticed how oddly I'm behaving. Then again, I seem to only act erratically around them, so why would they expect anything different.

CHAPTER 17

SALEM

I never thought I would find someone who could entice me away from books, and she did so without even trying. It's rare for any of us to suggest we may have found a mate, especially after knowing them so briefly. Roman was excited and he hadn't even met her.

Even so, when my packmates first told me they were interested in someone who seemed like a potential partner for all of us, I wasn't optimistic. Despite my love of flowery prose and grand stories, I may be the most sensible alpha in our pack when it comes to romance. Or perhaps I'm more guarded. In any case, I didn't have high hopes coming down here to meet Seph.

While I was reading one such romantic novel, I heard the clatter of books falling and hurried over to save them before they were too damaged. When I saw Seph under the pile of books, all other thoughts vanished. I only cared about saving her. I quickly pulled her out and let the books fall away without a care for them, just hoping Seph wasn't hurt. She looked so precious, despite being shocked and disheveled. I wanted to stand there and gaze upon her, but I had to make sure she was safe first.

If we lived nearby, I think I would have immediately carried her home to see if she needed to be bandaged. She refused a doctor, but thankfully let me check her for injuries. I'm not sure I would've been able to keep my alpha in check if she hadn't. I've never had such protective impulses, except for when it comes to my packmates. Even then, it was never so all-encompassing like it is with Seph. Even the few omegas I've been near didn't make me feel this way. One look at this beta in distress and I was throwing books around like a beast.

I've hardly been able to tear my eyes away from Seph, but when I do, I see my packmates are just as captivated. Roman was right to like her sight unseen. I seized the seat beside her when we arrived at the bakery, and her pumpkin spice scent now permeates me. Fynn was quick to snatch the chair on her other side. I'm glad he's also interested in her as more than a passing date.

Basel said Seph was slow to trust, but that she's been warming up to them. I do hope she'll be interested in me. They said she spends a lot of time in the bookstore, so at least we have a love of books in common. My packmates sometimes tease me for getting so lost in my books that I retreat from the world. Their playful words are all in good fun, but I've always worried a mate wouldn't like that. Seph should understand though, as a fellow booklover. Regardless, I suspect books won't be able to keep me away from her for long.

Instead, I may have to worry about Fynn capturing all of Seph's attention. Since we sat down, he's had his arm on the back of her chair and is leaning so close he's practically cuddling her right here in public. She seems receptive, which is good, but I want her to notice me, too. I lean closer. Fynn is taking up the back of her chair, but I can get close on this side. Seph turns as I shift closer and gives me a tentative smile before focusing back on Basel as he talks about the greenhouse shelves.

Now that she's accepted my advance, I relax. I've always wanted a mate to share with my packmates, but I'd rather have no mate than split up our pack. I enjoy my solitude, and being alone is better than being with the wrong partner.

I hope Seph will want me in addition to the others. I'm not as outgoing and charming as my packmates. I've often worried my quiet nature would put a potential mate off, but Seph also seems to have a quiet side. It's like we're kindred spirits. I never thought I would find a partner so similar to me.

After discussing the shelves, Seph updates us on her progress with festival suppliers.

"I talked to one farm that has fifty different kinds of gourds for sale. Fifty! We'll be able to make an amazing display with that many kinds. We could provide recipe suggestions, so people know they're not just for decoration. They can tag Pen and Tellem in their social media posts showing the food they cooked with our pumpkins and help spread the word about the greenhouse."

She's so animated when talking about the festival. I love watching someone discuss the things they're passionate about. It's admirable how invested she is in making a welcoming place for the community. Some fall events are so energetic and crowded, like the haunted house and carnival games, but Seph's pop-up will be a respite from the more involved activities. She's put a lot of thought and heart into this.

"I heard you have a history degree. Did you always want to use it for public outreach like this?" I ask once she finishes relaying her plans and has taken a breath and a gulp of coffee.

"Oh, I never thought about it like that," Seph says. She blinks and considers my question before answering. "I *have* always enjoyed sharing the fascinating things I learn with people. I suppose I do like public outreach. Though it's a bit selfish, since I mainly like sharing the things I'm interested in."

"I know how you feel. I work part-time as an adjunct professor for Romantic Period and Victorian Era literature. Sharing books and the cultures that produced them with my students is one of the highlights of my life. Though I admit I don't enjoy the grading," I confess with chagrin. "But seeing my students learn and hearing their opinions on the material is worth it."

I'm pleased I noticed something about Seph that she didn't realize about herself. I feel a connection with her, and it's nice to see proof that I'm not reading into things that aren't there.

"It also saves the rest of us from having to hear him discuss books for hours," Fynn adds.

I give him a flat look while Roman and Basel try to hide their laughs. Seph puts her hand on my thigh and leans closer. "I enjoy discussing books. I'd be happy to listen to you anytime. Though no promises that I've read the same books, so I might not have much to contribute to the conversation."

Her face is close enough for me to nuzzle, but I stop myself from doing just that. "I'd like that," I tell her instead.

"I could use some study sessions, too. I'll join you," Fynn somehow presses himself even closer to Seph.

Roman scoffs, and Seph blushes.

"I'll give you one-on-one lessons whenever you want, Fynn," I say. The others laugh, and Fynn smirks at me.

Seph realizes her hand is still on my thigh and quickly pulls it back. The heat from it lingers, like a brand.

Roman ignores Fynn to ask Seph about the book genres she likes. She tells us about her favorite paranormal and sci-fi novels, and the subjects she enjoys in history and nature non-fiction. While I listen, I contemplate my fascination with her.

My body has been showing interest in Seph since we met. Usually it takes time for me to be interested in someone intimately. I need to get to know them before I experience romantic feelings and sexual attraction. I don't want Seph to know how my alpha is reacting. I'd still like to learn more about her before getting romantically involved. I have the sense I would be heartbroken if we dated and she later decided she didn't like our pack.

I suppose I am guarded rather than simply pragmatic. I'm glad Seph seems to think similarly by getting to know us before becoming physical (despite Fynn's advances). I control my body, not the other way around.

At the edge of my vision, I see the strain in my slacks. Well, I control my actions at least. I've not pounced on Seph like my alpha wants me to, except for helping her out of the books earlier. I haven't pushed her back in her cushioned chair and kissed and nuzzled her like I want to. That would hardly be appropriate in public. Though with Basel and Roman sitting across from us, they would block most people's view. They could cover us while I kissed Seph and ran my hand up her thighs. It felt so good having her hand on me before. I should return the favor. My packmates would keep a lookout while I help her feel good. I could massage her wherever she wants, until I feel her clench around me.

Someone in the bakery drops a plate, and I'm jarred out of my thoughts. The connection I feel to Seph is overwhelming my mind now, too. I still don't want to get romantically involved so soon. Do I? No, it's safer to slowly get to know each other.

Fynn is watching me like he heard my thoughts, even though I've hidden them from the bond. They're out of character for me, so he shouldn't be able to guess what I'm thinking. I realize he's also hiding his thoughts, which is unusual. I'm sure he has the same ideas about Seph that I do, as they're more his style anyway. At least Seph and I are on the same page about taking things slow.

I lean closer to ask about one of the sci-fi novels she mentioned, which is one of my favorites. We spend the rest of our time at the bakery discussing books and everyone, even Fynn, chimes in.

CHAPTER 18

PERSEPHONE

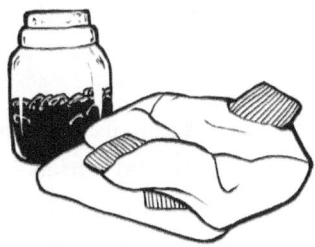

I stretch slowly as I wake for the day. The sunlight streaming across my bed warms me, staving off the early morning chill. I'm glad I installed shutters that are remote activated. I can relax in total darkness, and then let the sun in when I'm ready, without ever having to leave my nest. I mean bed.

My thoughts have been consumed with meeting the other alphas in Pack Goldenrod. We had a slightly shaky start. Okay, a very rocky start, involving a ghost, a cursed statue, and an avalanche of books, but the rest of the time was nice. Great, even. I enjoyed talking to them, and not just because we discussed one of my favorite subjects (books). I liked that they had different perspectives but still fit together as a pack. It's been interesting to learn about them as individuals and then see how they function as a group.

Despite having to change pants immediately after getting home, I kept myself under control. I didn't climb on any of them this time. And although I had to ignore my throbbing clit all afternoon, I enjoyed spending time with them.

I suppose it's not the worst thing to be friends with alphas. After I get new suppressants, I'll be able to ignore my omega impulses again. Then it will be easy to have a normal friendship with them. I won't have to avoid the pack outside of work.

I take a deep breath and hold it for a few seconds before letting it out. I think I will accept a friendship with Basel's pack. It feels good to let go of my bias and accept that an omega like me can be friends with alphas. I'm still not interested in dating them, but that doesn't mean I have to avoid them altogether.

I feel giddy, almost weightless, with my decision. My face hurts and I realize I'm grinning like an idiot, alone in my room. I've also taken another deep breath and have been holding it. I let out a gusty exhale and resume breathing normally.

I'm just a regular gal with casual, platonic alpha friendships. It's normal to be excited about seeing friends often and hanging out with them. It's those friendly feelings that are making me look forward to seeing the pack later today.

With the thought of new friends buoying me, I'm ready to face the day.

After showering, descenting, applying lotion, re-scenting (with pumpkin spice body spray), and getting dressed, I head into the kitchen. I check my phone while eating a slice of rhubarb coffee cake. There's a message from an unknown number and I tap to read it, thinking it's a vendor getting back to me. Instead, it's a text from Roman who says Basel gave him my number, which he hopes is okay since it's work related. Roman has experience planning corporate events and offers to help with the business aspects of the pop-up, like meeting with suppliers and setting up contracts.

I squeal in excitement. Paperwork is the worst!! I would love for him to deal with that part. Roman can ensure I don't overlook any details while I plan the fun parts.

I reply thanking him profusely (but coolly and professionally. I *am* still a businesswoman even if Roman's my friend). I tell him I plan to visit more suppliers today, and he's welcome to come if he's still in town. Roman and Salem said they would likely stick around for a while.

I eat my coffee cake while patiently waiting for Roman's reply, checking my phone after each bite.

After a long minute, Roman texts that he's happy to help me today whenever I want. I squeak briefly, choking on cake crumbs. After taking a swig of coffee, I tell him when to meet me. I hurry through the rest of my breakfast so I can plan where to take Roman for our reconnaissance.

I write down all the questions I have about event planning. I wonder what kind of events he's done. Retirement parties for CEOs or fundraising galas? I hope he doesn't plan corporate retreats. Those sound like their own circle of hell. Well, whatever he's done, he has more experience than me. I'm not sure why Belinda left me in charge of planning the pop-up, actually.

Oh, right, because it was my idea.

Well, all the more reason to bring in Roman and make this the best first Autumnfalls Festival Pop-up in the Greenhouse at the Back of Pen and Tellem Bookstore (working title).

I meet Roman outside Pen and Tellem to begin our mission. Somehow he's gotten even more attractive since the time I last saw him. Or my memory isn't good enough to contain his magnificent visage. Whatever it is, he looks great standing outside the bookstore, the sun shining on his curls. He appears more cherubic than corporate today.

"Hey," I greet him eloquently.

"Good morning. I hope you don't mind that I invited myself to be on your planning committee. I've organized several business events, so I know some things that should help with the pop-up," Roman says warmly.

I consider whether my decision to be friends with an alpha is due to the caliber of the alphas in Pack Goldenrod. Many alphas I've been around in the past, like at school or the coffee shop, have been demanding. I'm sure they'd say they were simply assertive. With Roman and the others, they plan or suggest things, but always make sure I agree with what they're proposing. They're helping me accomplish the things I want and haven't demanded I do what they want. Their pack has offered to help however I'd like them to, and they've done so without me having to spell out every little thing they should do. It's nice to be supported without needing to direct everything. At Quickie Coffee, I sometimes feel like a micromanager when we're busy. The other baristas are great, but things can fall apart quickly during a rush, and not everyone has a sense of what tasks need to be done first.

I don't feel like this pack is pushing me for a romantic relationship, either. Fynn has been a bit affectionate, but that's probably just his personality. Some friends are affectionate like that.

That's the other problem with alphas. If they're not ordering you around the office, they're ordering you onto their cock (so I hear. And not just from those videos I watch online). Especially if you're an omega. Not that this pack knows I'm an omega, but even if they did, I can't imagine they would behave like that.

Although I trust their minds, I don't trust their alphas. Their instincts might push them to see if we're compatible if they know I'm an omega, so I'll keep that a secret. It's not like I've told Stasia or anyone else.

"I'm sure you'll be a big help," I smile up at Roman.

"I'll do my best," he smiles back. "Do you want to grab a coffee before we head out?"

"Yes!" I can always use a coffee. I finished my morning coffee thirty minutes ago, so it's time for an early mid-morning coffee.

Roman clears his throat. "I know this is your town and you know it best, but would you mind if I drive us? Or we can go separately, but I thought it would be easier if we stay together today," he says apprehensively.

Coffee, and I get to be driven around? "Of course you can!" I practically yell. I clear my throat and soften the rest of my reply, "I don't need to be the driver. I'm happy to tell you where we're going and leave it to you."

"Thank you. My SUV is parked just down here," Roman gestures to the side street.

I was so excited about not having to drive that I forgot he looked nervous. Why does he want to be the driver?

"Are you a backseat driver or something?" I ask warily. I didn't peg him as one of those, but I guess as long as he's the one driving, it doesn't matter. I'd prefer to be a passenger, anyway.

His lips quirk. "I wouldn't call myself that. I have some anxiety when I'm not the one driving. I'm mostly used to riding with one of my packmates now, but they still typically let me drive. This has nothing to do with your skill as a driver. It's my problem that I haven't been able to get past."

"Oh, that's too bad. I don't want you to be anxious. You're welcome to drive me around any time." I rub his arm to comfort him.

"It's alright, Seph. Though some of my, ah, dates have been offended when I tell them I prefer to drive. Even after I explain why, some people still think I'm insulting them or trying to control them."

My stomach drops when he mentions his dates and my hand falls away. Does he have a girlfriend now? Is he dating people in Starsfalls?

Whatever. It doesn't matter to me. Actually, I'm happy when my friends find a partner, so good for him. It must be the coffee cake making my stomach feel like it's been stomped on and turned inside out.

I haven't mustered up a response by the time we get to his SUV. Roman opens the passenger door and helps me up. Once he's in the driver's seat, he starts the car but doesn't pull out.

"Are you sure this is okay? You can drive if you want. I'm sure I would be fine with it, just like if one of my packmates were driving," he says quietly.

I muster up the courage to face him and find he's watching me with concern. My silence must have freaked him out. I can't say I was quiet because I didn't like hearing about his dating life. Friends should be happy for their friends going on dates. It's the cake causing this feeling. It's not because I don't want Roman dating other people. I don't want to tell him I have an upset stomach though. I have to think of something else, quick. He's already worried that I'm mad about the driving thing, and he shouldn't feel bad about his anxiety.

"Uh-um. It's not that! I actually like being the passenger. It's just, um, IthinkIatesomebadcakethismorning," I say in a rush.

I realllly didn't want to tell him that, but I couldn't think of anything else.

Roman looks more concerned now. That confession didn't even help!

"We don't have to get food or visit suppliers if you're not feeling up for it. I can take you home if you want to relax instead."

I wonder how Roman would get me to relax. With a massage or something? Does he invite his dates over to "relax" too? I have to get off the subject of Roman's dates. It's making me queasier.

"No worries, the coffee will settle my stomach. Let's go!" I tell him in a fake chipper voice.

Somehow *that* convinces him, and he puts the car in drive.

I flop back in my seat. Crisis averted.

Roman asks about my music preferences as he drives. He flips between radio stations to find a local one that plays good music. He pauses on one reading a farm report about thirty chickens that got loose over the weekend and broke into a hardware store.

"How did they get the register open?" I squeak out between laughs.

"Maybe they pecked the lock," he suggests.

That causes another laughing fit. When I finally settle down and wipe away the tears, we've parked at our destination. Unfortunately, I recognize the parking lot.

"Do you want to go in, or should I order for us and bring it out?" Roman asks.

I'd be fine with going in if it wasn't *here*. I also don't

want to send him in alone where he'll fall prey to Marlene, like Basel almost did.

"I'll go with you. I might pick out a snack too."

Roman opens my door and helps me out. I let him lead us to Quickie Coffee's front door, and quickly scoot inside when he opens it. Once he's through, I follow behind him to the register, staying out of sight of the workers. It's busy enough that none of them notice me.

"Couldn't stay away?" Stasia says next to me.

I jump, stumbling into Roman. If I act normal, she won't realize I'm with him.

"Well, you make the best coffee in town," I reply smoothly after Roman sets me back on my feet.

"I heard you serve a great pumpkin spice coffee," Roman adds.

He isn't part of this conversation. Why is he chiming in?

Stasia smiles at him. "The best. You two are a cute couple."

She's a demon.

"This is Roman, a packmate of the architect for the greenhouse. He's going to help me plan the pop-up," I quickly correct her.

"You're dating a whole pack? That's great, Seph!" Stasia gushes. It's like she thinks I won't tell people about the time she ate a donut off the sidewalk in retaliation for embarrassing me like this.

"We aren't currently courting Seph, I'm afraid," Roman finally helps me out. Where was he before? As my friend, he should've been quick to set the record straight that we're just business partners and friends. Not mates. Or dates.

"Oh, well let me know if you want help with courting gift ideas for her. We've been friends for years, so I know what she likes. You guys will make such a cute pack."

"Do you remember that one really hot summer a few years ago..." I remind her ominously. If she's smart, she'll take my threat seriously. I *will* tell Roman about that donut and embarrass her.

"That's very kind of you. I'll let you know if I ever need ideas," Roman says graciously.

There. Take that, Stasia. Even though she's my best friend, I won't let this stand. I don't want any alphas getting ideas about me, especially my new friends. Roman is slightly behind me, so he shouldn't be able to see my blush. I don't want him to know how uneasy this made me, because there's nothing wrong with his pack. That life just isn't for me, and I don't want to make him feel bad if I'm forced to explain why I don't want to be with an alpha.

On another note, Stasia has a list of the things I like? That's so sweet of her. What a great friend. But still, she knows I don't want a pack. Why is she hassling us like this? A friend should support my decision.

"Well then, I'll go get coffees for you and your handsome business partner. Do you both want the pumpkin coffee?"

"Sure, that sounds good to me. Is there anything else you want?" Roman asks me.

"I'll get snacks for us. Stasia, I'll help make the coffees."

"Are you the owner, to give a customer permission to make their own coffee?" Roman looks at Stasia curiously.

She laughs. "No, definitely not. Seph works here too. Didn't she tell you?"

"I must have missed that detail. Sorry Seph, I didn't mean to bring you into work on your day off," Roman says with a grimace.

"Quickie Coffee has great coffee, I never tire of it. Especially the pumpkin coffee," I reassure him before hustling Stasia into the back.

"So pushy. You should do something to help you relax. I have an idea of what you could try," Stasia waggles her eyebrows at me after I close the stockroom door behind us.

I huff and fold my arms sternly for the lecture I'm about to give. "You know I don't do alphas. Just what do you think you were doing out there, young lady?"

The demon cackles at me.

"What, he seemed like a nice alpha, and he's hot. I thought you'd be a cute couple. Or that maybe you already were a couple, and you came in here to confess that you'd finally gotten over your hangups about alphas," she says after her laughter subsides.

I frown. I do not have hangups about alphas. I have normal, healthy concerns and considerations. And I have carefully considered that being with an alpha or a pack doesn't fit with my lifestyle. No worries or anxiety here.

"I have perfectly reasonable reasons not to date alphas. There's no reason *to* date them, anyway. My preference is betas, I can't help that," I correct her.

"You've been saying that for years, Seph," Stasia tells me seriously. "But eventually you'll probably need to be with an alpha. I've heard that medical intervention can be hard on your body, and medication loses its effectiveness eventually."

I panic internally. What does she mean? She doesn't know I'm an omega, so what is she talking about? What other medical things have I told her about? I told her my dentist said I had great teeth. I told her when that cold medication made me dizzy. None of that has anything to do with alphas, though. What else could she be referring to?

"It's not like I'm an omega who needs an alpha," I titter

nervously. Maybe she wasn't referring to omegas, and I put that thought in her head for no reason. Oh no, should I take it back? How?

Before I can formulate a plan, Stasia pats me on the arm.

"Okay, okay, Seph. Whatever you think is best. I just want you to live your best life and not let anything hold you back. You know I'm always here for you and I'm ready to listen if you ever want to talk things out."

"Thanks, Stasia. I am living my best life. I just haven't found anyone I'm interested in," I say with relief. She wasn't referring to omegas then. She just wants me to be happy and be open to finding a romantic partner. That's fine.

We hug it out. After letting go, she says, "I can't believe you were going to tell him about The Donut."

"You're lucky I didn't! Embarrassing me in front of my new business partner like that," I give her a stern look.

"Whatever. I'm not embarrassed about it, it was a good donut. But I know you wouldn't tell people if it was *you* who ate it. Let's go make your coffees before your coworker gets a poor impression of our store," Stasia says with a toss of her hair and opens the door.

I follow her out. It did look like the perfect donut. Even so, I wouldn't have eaten it after it fell on the sidewalk. And I *certainly* wouldn't tell anyone if I did.

"Is Marlene really letting us serve pumpkin coffee now?" I ask as Stasia pulls out cups and I grab the coffee grounds.

"She just announced it this morning. I texted you to let you know you could stop by and get your fix," Grey says as he sidles up to us at the espresso machine.

"Thanks, Grey. I must've missed your text because I was

consulting with my business partner on the festival preparations," I tell him in my best professional businesswoman voice.

"No problem. I wouldn't be checking my messages either if I had your 'business partner' to 'consult with,'" he says with an admiring look at Roman.

There's a flare of heat in my chest. I must be running low on caffeine. I concentrate on making the espresso. "He's the perfect partner, experienced with handling big things and making sure everyone has a great time," I tell Grey primly.

He snorts and Stasia laughs. I don't know what's so funny about event planning.

While the espresso brews, I pick out some snacks from the pastry display case. Stasia adds the milk and syrup to our cups. I bag up our snacks, keeping an eye on Grey until he finally stops glancing at Roman and goes back to serving customers.

Once our coffees are ready, Stasia and I bring the food and drinks over to Roman's table. He meets us partway to help carry things.

"I'll let you two partners get back to work. I'll talk to you later, Seph. It was nice to meet you, Roman. Don't forget, any time you need gift ideas for this one..." Stasia points her thumb at me.

"I'll keep you in mind," Roman smiles at her.

I say goodbye and Stasia returns to the counter.

"Do you want to eat here or on the road?" Roman asks.

"We could stay here for a bit. Unless you're busy later and we need to get going?" He mentioned dating. Maybe he has a date later. I hope he doesn't, as it would cut into our business time.

"The only thing on my schedule is spending time with you."

I beam (professionally) at him as he pulls out my chair.

Roman compliments the pumpkin coffee, saying it's the best seasonal coffee he's ever had.

"Right? We get the best ingredients for the shop, you can tell. But we also roast and brew the beans correctly, and don't burn or water them down. The pumpkin coffees have the best ratio of coffee to milk, so with the pumpkin foam, it's not too sweet or too bitter. It's my favorite drink at Quickie Coffee. I look forward to it every year, and I'm always sad to see it go. I suppose that makes me appreciate it more when it's available," I say.

"Do you think we could get Quickie Coffee to make drinks at our pop-up? They could offer a limited menu of the pumpkin and other fall products, so we wouldn't need as many supplies. Since you work here, you could make sure the coffee bar has everything we'd need."

My maple pecan croissant falls from my hand as I stare at him in shock.

"That's such a good idea!" I say, half-shouting at him for the second time today. "It would be amazing to serve Quickie Coffee's pumpkin drinks to people who visit our pop-up. I'm so glad you're helping me plan this. You have the best ideas."

"It's thanks to you. You sold me on the coffee here. It makes sense to offer the limited time fall coffees so people can enjoy them while they're around."

"Yes!"

He pats the underside of my arm, which I think is an odd place to randomly touch someone. That is, until I realize I've grabbed his forearms in my excitement, and I quickly let him go. I brush past any awkwardness by smoothly transitioning to picking my croissant up off the table, like that's what I was aiming for the whole time.

Roman talks through the logistics of setting up a coffee bar in the greenhouse and the utilities we would need. I chime in where I can about which coffee machines and milk frothers we'll need, along with supplies like the average amount of beans and other ingredients we use daily.

During our conversation, I surreptitiously look around to see if anyone noticed I dropped the croissant on the bare table. I don't think anyone was looking our way, not even Grey. Did Roman notice I dropped it? Probably not. He was too busy listening to what I was saying and letting me paw at him. I think I can eat the croissant without anyone thinking it's unsanitary.

I take a small bite while Roman talks food permits. No one gasps dramatically in disgust, so I think I'm safe. I'm glad Roman has experience with getting permits. My knowledge in that area consists mainly of knowing that food permits exist and how to follow the sanitary procedures in a restaurant (I wouldn't serve anyone a table croissant or floor donut. I save those for myself).

I finish the last of my snack while Roman reviews the notes he took on his phone.

"We have a solid start for the coffee collaboration," Roman says after checking things over.

"I agree, it's a great plan." I daintily wipe crumbs off my mouth. "I'm ready to head out and meet with the suppliers if you are. It doesn't look like my manager, Marlene, is in, so I'll present our plan to her later."

We wave goodbye to Stasia as we go, who gives me a thumbs up behind Roman's back.

I stretch out in the heated seat in Roman's SUV with my

coffee and extra pastries. I'm fed, caffeinated, and excited to enlist vendors for the pop-up.

CHAPTER 19
ROMAN

I keep glancing over to make sure Seph is really next to me. I'm pleased she's letting me help her with the pop-up. Fall events were always my favorite growing up, visiting pumpkin patches, picking apples, and going on hayrides. Attending things like that were the only times my family pack got together and paid any attention to me. Otherwise, most of the time my parents were focused on their hobbies and my much older brothers were busy with their own lives.

I'm happy now that I have my own pack with pack-mates who actually spend time together. Except for Nix, but he doesn't work overtime to ignore us. He's clearly trying to hide from something, maybe himself, but not us. Regardless, I hope to convince him to spend more time together as a pack, and not just at events.

If we found a mate, that would surely draw him in. It worked for my fathers. Not that I would burden Seph, or any other partner, by using them to "fix" him. I think Nix will be drawn to her just like the rest of us, no coaxing required. I hope we can convince him to visit Starsfalls and meet her soon.

As I drive us to the first supplier, Seph tells me about the best spots in town for a picnic. I note each place so we can take her there in the future. I laugh when she tells me about the picnic with Stasia when bumblebees chased them away from their blanket. When they crept back later, the bees were eating the frosting off their carrot cake. I'm not surprised to learn they brought a whole cake on a picnic for just the two of them.

After meeting with the vendors in town, we're on the way to visit an apple orchard at the edge of Starsfalls. The orchard makes their own cider and vinegar there. Seph said we could sell vinegar shrubs for mocktails along with the regular cider as alternatives to hard ciders, which would require a liquor license. It's a smart plan since liquor licenses can be difficult to get and non-alcoholic drink mixes are popular right now.

I've had more fun working with Seph than I usually do when planning events. Normally I work with cookie-cutter corporate events, where businesses don't want to innovate with the type of food they serve or how they set things up. I'm usually on the security side of things, but I have helped with other aspects, especially when I worked with Nix. Planning with Seph is so freeing. I can be creative and brainstorm with someone who thinks similarly.

Seph points out the good picnic spots all the way to the orchard. We pull onto the road to the main building, which is lined with a low stone fence. I park at the barn that provides admission for the orchard along with a store where they sell their farm goods. After I open Seph's door, she spins in a circle to look at the apple trees surrounding us. Her hair flares out around her, the sunlight making it shine like gold. Seph's happiness is catching, and I feel light and carefree being with her.

"Do you visit the orchards often when the apples are in season?" I steady her as she staggers out of her spin.

She grins up at me, the clouds reflecting in her blue eyes. Her hands rest on my chest, and since I'm holding her arms, it's almost like we're embracing.

"I visit at least a few times. Stasia and I always go together, and sometimes we convince Grey to come with us too."

I hold her closer as she leans in. "I'm glad you have a good pack of friends. Was Grey the one at work earlier?"

"That's him. Sorry I didn't get a chance to introduce you," Seph glances away as she explains.

"I'm sure I'll meet him another time. We should start all our business outings with pumpkin coffee."

She's leaning against me completely now, as close as she can get. Though I do use one leg to keep a little distance between our lower halves, so she doesn't feel how much I'm enjoying this.

"I'd love that," Seph says breathlessly.

I tilt my head closer...

"You ready to pick some apples, Seph? The Pink Pearls are just ripe for the picking!" A rough voice calls to us.

That startles her out of our moment, and she moves away. I drop my arms and turn to see an older man standing in the barn door.

"Really? Those are some of the best apples. Isn't it kind of early for them to be ready?" Seph asks as we walk over.

"It's a few weeks early, but we had some cooler evenings, and they ripened up," he says.

Once we reach him, he holds out his hand for me to shake.

"I'm Brooks Ackerman, the owner of this orchard, along with my wife Nadine here," he nods his head to the interior of the store.

I shake his hand and introduce myself, "I'm Roman with the Goldenrod Pack. We're helping Seph with her pop-up for the Autumnfalls Festival."

An older woman appears behind Brooks, presumably his wife.

"I didn't realize you were involved with a pack, Seph. That's so lovely. I'm glad you found some nice alphas to treat you right," Nadine congratulates her in a kind voice.

Seph looks panicked and replies quickly, "His pack has been a great help with the greenhouse renovation. I'm glad Belinda found them. They're great business partners and I've enjoyed having them as my coworkers." Her eyes dart nervously to me.

I'm not entirely sure if she doesn't want to be seen dating someone she works with, or if it's simply too soon for her to let people know she's spending time with a pack. If we hadn't been interrupted just now, we would have had our first kiss. Seph hugged me and leaned in, so she wasn't trying to keep a professional distance between us. Perhaps she's more traditional and wants us to officially ask to court her. I'll have to talk to the pack later and see what they think. Basel and Fynn have spent the most time with her. They might have a sense of how she wants to proceed. If Seph doesn't want to date a coworker, I don't want to make her feel awkward by asking her about it directly. We can always wait to ask her out until the greenhouse is finished

"It's nice to find so many helpful people to support you," Nadine says.

We move quickly past the suggestion that we're dating, so I don't get any more clues as to why Seph looked nervous.

Seph talks with the couple about the other apple varieties that are in season, and I ask which ones we should expect to be ready for the festival. Brooks says that most of their apples will be ripe then, so it's up to us which ones we want to stock. Seph asks which apples are the best for snacking, and which are used for cider and vinegar. Nadine recommends using Honeycrisp or Pazazz apples for baking. Seph takes notes so she can share the information with our customers.

"Well, those are the basics," Brooks says. "We can adjust your order as we get closer and know how many bushels of apples we have available. Now, do you want to get to picking?"

"Yes!" Seph bounces on her toes in excitement.

I can't help my smiles when I'm around her. When I manage to pull myself away from Seph to ask what tools we'll need, I find the Ackermans already watching me. They give me a knowing look before Brooks gestures for me to follow him to the side.

"We have baskets, ladders, and apple picking poles over here," he says as we walk to the edge of the barn.

I collect the supplies without comment on my obvious infatuation and carry them back to Seph and Nadine, who are in a heated discussion about their favorite apple desserts. When they're done, the Ackermans bid us goodbye and return to their store. Seph leads us to the Pink Pearl apple trees since she remembers the way and I follow with the supplies.

"This looks like a good one," Seph stops at a tree heavy with apples.

"Do you want to pick from the low branches first, or should I set up the ladder?" I ask.

She stands under the tree near the trunk and looks up. I set our things down and join her.

"I think I'll start with the ladder. It's more fun to collect the higher apples," Seph decides.

I smile and place the ladder where she directs me to, setting the basket next to it. Seph starts up the steps and I jump to hold her steady.

"You don't have to hold on to me, you can pick some too," she pauses to tell me.

I'm not going to leave and risk her falling off.

"I'll pick some when you're back on the ground. I'm happy to hold you steady so you can reach the higher ones," I assure her.

Seph huffs at me. "There's like three steps on this ladder. I'll be fine."

I raise my eyebrow at that. "There are four steps. Besides, the ground isn't even, and the ladder could tip out from under you. If you hit your head from any height, you'll get hurt," I tell her seriously.

"Okay, fine." She rolls her eyes, but I see her smile as she turns back to the tree.

Seph picks while I hold her steady and drop her finds in the basket. We collect dozens of them, moving around to different trees as Seph hunts for the "perfect sunset yellow squat apples," which have the best flavor according to her.

I'm enjoying our time together as we work. It reminds me of some of the best times with my pack, when we have a common goal we're working on together. That always makes me feel closer to my packmates. Like the time we built custom bookshelves for Salem rather than hiring one of Basel's contractors. That might not sound like a big task, until you know it's an entire room with floor to ceiling bookshelves two stories high. If that weren't enough, we also carved designs on all the shelves. The project took a while, but I enjoyed the process with my packmates. The project was worth it in the end for the journey alone, not to mention how much Salem loved the library. Salem helped us build the shelves, but he was still so appreciative that we worked so hard for him. With Basel's guidance the shelves turned out perfectly, like they came from an antique library.

When we moved to Boarwood, we had all the shelves removed and sent to the new house, along with the books. Salem loved that room, and it seemed cruel to leave it behind in one of the houses we wouldn't be visiting as often anymore. Now I'm even more glad we spent the money to move his library. I know Seph will love it. If she likes Pen and Tellem that much, Salem's library will be a fun surprise for her. I'm not sure she'll want to live with us in Boarwood, though. Seph seems to love Starsfalls. Well, moving Salem's library from Boarwood to Starsfalls will be a quicker trip than the previous move.

I'm smiling at the thought of Seph living with us as she's absorbed with the apples. Seph is telling me all the things she's going to make with them, and how she's going use them for decoration in the meantime. I listen to her apple plans while I envision our lives together. Not to get too ahead of myself, but I am planning for a future with her. It will be easier when the time comes if I already have options worked out for combining our lives. I'm sure the pack will be happy to move to Starsfalls, or wherever Seph decides.

I'm knocked out of my plans when an apple hits me on

the head. Seph stares at me, horrified, with her mouth fallen open.

"Oh my gosh, are you okay? I'm so sorry, I accidentally hit that apple when I was reaching for another one and knocked it off. I'm so sorry!" She whimpers and runs her fingers through my hair to check for damage. "I'm so sorry. I didn't mean to. Are you hurt? I can go for help. Here, just lay on the ground and rest while I get a med kit from the store. Or, wait, I'll call an ambulance!"

I laugh as she rambles and apologizes. I put my hands on either side of her face.

"Seph. Take a deep breath," I say firmly, and she does. "Now let it out slowly," I add, as she holds her breath. When she's breathing normally again, I reassure her, "I'm fine, I just didn't expect it. I'm not injured. You don't have to worry."

"Are you sure? That was a big apple, and it fell right on your head!" she squeaks out.

I grin at her description. "I'm uninjured. You felt it yourself, not even a bump, right? I don't need medical attention." I lean closer to where she stands on the ladder. "You're welcome to keep running your fingers over me, though," I add in a lower voice.

She blinks, clearly struggling to let go of her worry, but blushes and bites her lip when my words register. I move in slowly. My hands are still on her face, but I hold her loosely so she can pull away. I shift my fingers into her hair and press my lips gently to hers. After a (too) brief kiss, I pull away to gauge her reaction. Her pupils are blown, and she's panting through parted lips. I kiss her again, more firmly this time, molding my lips to hers. She kisses me back, grabbing the front of my shirt to hold me close. I run my tongue along her lower lip. She moans and opens further so I can twine my tongue with hers.

Seph puts her arms around my neck, tilting off the ladder. I lift her thighs, and she wraps her legs around my waist. I press her back against the trunk of the tree that hit me.

I kiss across her jaw and down her neck. When I lick the edge of her neck where it meets her shoulder, she shivers. Her hands clench in my hair as I kiss the other side, gently running my teeth across her skin. When I move back up to her face she tenses. I pull my head back and Seph is still, her eyes squeezed shut.

"What's wrong? Did I hurt you?" I didn't think I was holding her against the tree too hard. I move back to give her room. She lets go of my hair and leans away, so I set her down on the ground and step back.

"I'm sorry I got carried away. Are you alright?" I ask again. I'm alarmed now. I thought she wanted to kiss me too, but she looks upset. Seph finally opens her eyes but won't look at me.

She clears her throat before she responds. "It's fine. I got carried away too. I didn't mean to start this…"

"Of course. It's my fault. We can go back to apple picking. Or if you're tired, I can take you home?" I offer, hoping she doesn't want to leave me. I don't want her to be upset, and she still hasn't looked at me.

"Let's just get back to the apples. There's room in the basket for more," Seph says as she walks around me to the ladder. She stops partway and turns back, finally looking at me again.

"If you're sure *you're* alright to keep going. That apple hit you hard. I'm sorry again about that."

I give her an encouraging smile. "Don't worry about me. I'm fine."

She gives me a strained smile. "Ok. Great."

I hold the ladder as she climbs up. We resume picking apples in silence, except for directions on where to move next. Before our kiss, I kept one hand on Seph while she was on the ladder. Now, I hold the ladder and hover one hand nearby to grab her if she wavers. I'm not sure what changed during our kiss, but she's giving me the cold shoulder and I take that to mean my touch isn't welcome now.

We finish filling the basket with a few other varieties on top of the Pink Pearls. I heft up the apple basket and grab the ladder and picking tool to carry back. Seph attempts to carry something, but I wave her off.

As we walk back to the barn, she keeps her distance. I return the supplies and bring the basket to the front of the store. Seph comes out of the barn with Nadine and a sack to take our apples home. It has the name and logo of the orchard, Ladon's Garden, on it, with a scaled bird twined around the barn and apple trees.

"Could we buy some of those bags for the pop-up to give customers who buy a lot of produce?" I ask Nadine.

"I'm sure we could do that. It would be nice advertising for us. Is he always so full of good ideas, Seph?" Nadine asks her.

"Hm? Oh, yes, always. Good ideas," Seph replies absently.

Despite what she said earlier, it's obviously time to take her home.

We pack our apples, and I make arrangements to email the Akermans paperwork for the pop-up orders. I put Seph's apples in the trunk and open the passenger door for her to get in.

On the drive back, I ask a few questions about the orchard to see if she wants to bring up what happened between us, but Seph responds with one-word answers. I make sure the radio is playing a station she likes and lapse into silence.

I worry the entire way about how I've upset her. Moving too quickly is the only answer I can come up with. I knew I should have waited to make our interest in her as a pack clear, so we could court her officially. I thought she wanted to kiss me, and I let that go to my head, but I should have checked with her first.

When we make it back to town, I ask where she parked. That rouses Seph enough to say more than a few words, and she asks if we're going to visit any more vendors today. I tell her I think we have a good start, so we can resume another day. She doesn't argue and directs me to her car. I park next to it and let her out. I pull out our apple bags and carry them to her car.

"Don't you want some of these?" Seph asks as she watches.

"No, you should have them. You did most of the work, I was just the backup."

She frowns. "No, you were a great help. You even took an apple to the head for your efforts."

I smile and straighten up after setting down the last of the bags. Hopefully that means she doesn't hate me. "It was a glancing blow. I'll get my own apples another time."

"If you're sure..." she trails off and looks at her car.

I have to address what happened earlier. I don't want to leave without making sure she's alright.

"I didn't mean to rush things with you earlier, Seph. I enjoy spending time with you and hope to continue to do so. But if you don't feel the same, I can work on the pop-up remotely. We don't have to meet up."

She looks distressed, and I worry she's going to agree we shouldn't see each other anymore. I slump in relief when she says instead, "I like you too, Roman. I'm happy to keep working with you. It was just a bit much earlier."

"Of course. I won't do that again. I'll behave properly in the future."

I'll tell the pack that we need to ask to court her properly. I won't get romantically involved with her again until we make it clear we want to date her with the intention of becoming mates. I don't want Seph to think I'm a pushy alpha who's interested in anything that moves.

"Good. That's great. I look forward to our future plans, then," she smiles at me.

I grin in return. That means she agrees we need to ask to court her properly. I'm relieved she's looking for a long-term relationship too.

"I'll see you soon," I say as I open the car door for her.

"See you!"

She smiles and waves after I shut it, and I watch as she drives away.

When she's out of sight, I drive back to the inn to tell the others about our day and come up with a courting plan.

CHAPTER 20
PERSEPHONE

I'm relieved Roman took my comment that we should remain just business partners so well. I was worried he would be upset, or maybe even angry, that I rejected him. None of his packmates seem like that type of alpha, but I haven't known them for long. You never really know what alphas are like, and they're bigger and stronger than me, so it always feels risky rejecting one. I didn't want to hurt Roman, and he proved he wasn't a bad alpha with his response. I like his pack so much. As friends. I'm glad he agreed to remain professional so we could keep working together.

I sigh thinking about our kiss. It was the best one I've ever had. Why did it have to be with an alpha? I find myself holding my fingers to my lips and shake free of the memories to get back to work. I'm sketching out plans for the layout of our festival offerings.

I'm unable to keep my thoughts away from the pack for long. I'm just glad I got in to see the doctor before my date with Roman. I mean business meeting. Except the doctor was no help with the suppressants. She said they lose their effectiveness over time, and the hormones can't be repressed anymore. She then had the audacity to ask if I've been around some compatible alphas lately. As if that's any excuse for my hormones to go haywire! She wouldn't even give me extra suppressants to stave off a heat once it starts. I usually take a few days off work and use painkillers and mild sedatives to ride out my heat alone. But with scent matches around, I can't risk my heat-addled omega reaching out to them.

According to my heat schedule, I'm supposed to have one this fall. I decided it's better to push this one off until after the festival, when the Goldenrod Pack leaves town. That way I don't run the risk of making decisions while under the influence (of hormones).

I got the heat suppressants from the pharmacy anyway, since you don't need a prescription to get them. I wanted advice from the doctor to figure out which medication I should switch to, but if she won't help, I don't need her. It's my body to manage as I see fit. I took my doctor's recommendations under advisement, but I have goals to accomplish. I don't have time for a heat until after this autumn. What was she even going on about alphas for, I am *not* falling for any of them. Not even my scent matches.

Despite being distracted, I finish sketching the display cases with the products we'll sell. I finally look at the pictures Basel sent me of the greenhouse yesterday. I was too emotionally wrung out to look at them last night after my day with Roman. I use the first few photos to visualize where the furnishings will go when the greenhouse is complete, and then scroll through the texts he sent.

There are pictures of the builders working, along with Fynn and Salem. In some of the photos, Fynn is helping install the metal framing and moving equipment around. I laugh at a series of images where Fynn talks animatedly with a builder, and in the later photos they're working companionably on whatever they had been arguing about. In many of them, Salem is off to the side, quietly observing. I'm not sure he has much experience with construction besides what he's picked up from Basel or read about the subject. He said he spends most of his time reading or teaching. Fynn didn't mention construction experience either, but he seems like the type to involve himself in whatever's going on.

A few photos later, Salem is helping a woodworker lay out planks for the shelves and in another, he's planing wood. As the photos progress through the day, Salem is there as the shelves take shape. He antiques the wood by creating chips and grooves along the edges. I sweat in commiseration as I see an image of Salem hefting the weighty boards into place, muscles straining through his shirt. Apparently Salem is skilled in woodworking. I examine that picture a bit longer before moving on.

I don't know their pack that well, I suppose. It's only been a few weeks, but when I'm with them, I feel a connection. It's almost like I've always known them. I feel a rush of warmth when I think about getting to know them better. Every new thing I learn makes me more interested. I want to know how Salem learned to use those tools. Have they built things together before? Basel said the pack isn't usually involved in his restoration projects. He traveled often for work, and his packmates have their own jobs. Did Basel teach them about construction, or did they learn elsewhere? Does Fynn even have experience with metalwork or is he just inquisitive and a quick learner? I'll have to visit the greenhouse soon while they're all working. Then I can observe and hopefully get some answers to my questions.

It's not until the last few photos that Basel appears. In one, Basel talks to a couple of the builders. In another, he's looking at blueprints on a table with his eyebrows pinched like he's deep in concentration. I admire him and his dedication showcased in the photo. It's normal to appreciate a hardworking coworker like that. In his formfitting jeans and t-shirt. I gasp at the next image of Basel bent over to look at Salem's progress, who paused to talk to him. The photo is taken from behind Basel...

When I eventually look at the rest of the image, I see Fynn's reflection in the glass walls. He's looking into the camera on his phone with a grin. I laugh at the artistry of Basel's photographer. He has a good eye.

The last photo is a pack selfie, which does a good job of capturing their personalities. Fynn looks wide-eyed and energetic, Basel confident and sure, and Salem is handsome, but unassuming. You might overlook him with the others there, but if you look at his eyes, you can practically see the thoughts swirling around in there. I smile back at them on my screen.

Just as I finish saving the photos to my phone, I get a call from an unknown number. Why does it have to be a phone call? Don't people know they can send a text. I consider letting it go to voicemail, but since it's probably about the pop-up, I decide to answer it. I make sure I have a pen and paper ready so I can take notes if I need to. After taking a deep breath, I answer.

"Hello, this is Persephone."

"I've been hearing about you all over town, Persephone," a feminine voice says.

I don't recognize the caller. "Um. Thanks? Is this about the pop-up at Pen and Tellem?" I ask.

"Oh, it is. I heard you've been trying to take all my suppliers and copy my stall," she responds bitterly.

I panic. I'm not copying anyone, am I? I've taken inspiration from things I've seen at the festival and online, but I can't think of a specific stall we would be similar to. Especially since we'll be in a greenhouse. No one else has a space like that. Plus, it's not even set up yet. She must have the wrong person.

"We're creating a unique pop-up for the bookstore. We're not copying anyone. What did you say your name was? I'm sure this is just a misunderstanding," I say with what I hope is a firm voice.

"Don't act like you don't know who I am," she scoffs. "Usually the local suppliers sell their goods to whoever wants to carry them. But since you're trying to copy me, I'm going to get my vendors to sign an exclusivity contract and prevent you from getting supplies. My relationship with them goes back years. I'm sure they'll be happy to support me and drop you. No one likes a copycat," she says venomously, hanging up before I can think of a response.

I sit motionless, still holding the phone to my ear. My mind is spinning with options, but I can't decide what to do. Should I call the vendors I've talked to? Would that make it seem like I *was* trying to steal the vendors from whoever that woman is? Do the vendors already think badly of me? Should I call her back and try to explain I'm not copying her? I'm afraid if I do that, I'll freeze up again and won't be able to get anything out. Should I go to Belinda and ask her if she knows what's going on?

As my thoughts churn, I melt out of my petrified state and the tears flow. I can't make them stop. That rules out going to see anyone. I can't go outside like this. I hate anyone seeing me cry, and I don't want to be sobbing on the street. Underneath all the thoughts is the urge to call Basel and the pack because they'll fix everything. My mind knows that isn't true. I think.

I don't even know what's going on, so I couldn't explain to them what's happening to get them to fix it. I stop myself from calling them, but as I cry harder, I can't think of much besides not choking on my tears. All that's left is the instinct to call my pack.

I blink the tears away for long enough to shakily scroll to Basel's contact. I tap the call button.

CHAPTER 21
NIX

I have a slow morning at home since my packmates are out. I worked late last night, but when I came back everyone was awake and running around the house. I briefly saw Roman, Salem, and Fynn as they packed to spend a few days in Starsfalls. Basel was there too, picking up more things for his extended stay. I'm glad the town is nice enough my packmates want to vacation there.

Despite the effort I put into avoiding them, I do miss my packmates when they're gone. At least the distance makes it easier to avoid telling them I fucked up our lives before we even met.

Every hour, every moment, I waver between telling them what I've done or letting them live in ignorance so they still have hope. I always come back to the decision that it's best not to tell them. That way, they can find a mate without feeling guilty. It's better for them that I not spend much time with the pack, in case I confess in a vulnerable moment.

I hate myself for joining this pack and keeping secrets, but I couldn't reject the bond I felt with my packmates. I'm not strong enough to sever a poisoned bond, unlike her. I was too selfish to stay away from my pack for their own good. I joined them, and let our bond grow and corrupt. Over the years I've thought about how to fix my mistake but haven't made any progress.

So here I am, another day as a member of the Goldenrod Pack, using my time to avoid my packmates and wallow in self-loathing. At least I have the house to myself for the next few days. I can catch up on sleep, though my unconscious moments are just as haunted.

While waiting for the espresso machine to finish, I hear a faint ring. Did one of them come back for something? I strain to listen, but besides the ringtone, I don't hear anything. I remain hidden in the kitchen, making my breakfast, so whoever it is will grab what they forgot and be on their way.

The phone starts up again. I look down at my steaming espresso, which is slightly too hot to drink yet. I have nothing else to do until it's ready, so I guess I'll see which of them came back. I set the cup on the counter and walk to the front hall. I make it to the entry without seeing anyone, but the phone gets louder.

I look around and determine the ringing is coming from the foyer bench. I feel around and find the phone stuck down the side of the bench. Apparently my packmates haven't returned, at least not yet. It looks like Basel's phone. As I lift it out from where it's wedged in the cushions, I accidentally swipe to answer the call.

I hold it up to my ear and say hello without looking, thinking it's either one of my packmates looking for Basel's phone, or one of his work contacts. I don't want to hang up on either now that I've accepted the call.

Contrary to my expectations, I hear crying on the other

end. I tense and the blood rushes in my ears. Whoever it is sounds extremely upset or injured. The crying sounds feminine, so it's unlikely to be a call from my packmates, but I can't make out much else.

"Are you alright?" I ask. I can't pull the phone away to check the caller ID. If someone's in trouble, I don't want to miss anything they say.

Whoever it is sniffles like they're trying to compose themselves, but then there's a whimper and the sobbing starts again.

"I can help you. Can you tell me where you are? Or share your location in text?" I try again. I realize my voice is rough and deep. Hopefully I'm not upsetting them further, but I can't seem to calm down either. I feel like running straight through the walls between us to get to this person, if only they would tell me where they are.

The phone creaks in my tight grip as I wait for a response.

The crying sounds like it's getting farther away. "Wait, don't hang up! Just tell me what you need, and I'll help. We'll help," I say desperately, hoping they don't end the call. If they were looking for Basel, they may not want to talk to me, but I don't care. I have to help them.

I hear a ding and quickly pull the phone away before I think about it. There's a pin sharing their location on a map. I tap quickly to get directions, and see it's in Starsfalls near the bookstore where Basel's working. I zoom in, and the pin shows it's on the third floor of an apartment building. I put the phone back to my ear.

"Okay, I see you're in an apartment in Starsfalls. I'm on my way now. I can call someone for help in the meantime if you need me to. Do you want to stay on the phone with me?

Or tell me what's wrong?" I ask as comfortingly as I can, which isn't much. I'm not used to taking care of someone.

Usually I can stay calm in tense situations. I'm hands-on with many of the non-profits I donate to and visit them to make sure our money is being used to care for the people who need it. That can mean dealing with combative people who don't want help or who think we aren't doing enough to help. When we send aid after a natural disaster, we provide funding and services. I'm trained in emergency response and often join in to help get trapped people out of collapsed buildings or give medical aid to the injured. I'm always calm and in control in those situations.

Now, after a simple phone call, I can't think clearly. It's like a haze descended on my brain and I can't shake it. I don't even know who I'm trying to help. It's not one of my packmates, but I feel as distraught as if it were.

I rush through putting on my shoes and grab my keys as I wait to see if they'll say anything. It sounds like the crying slows, but they only let out another loud whimper. I feel a jolt and a heavy thrumming comes from my chest. In confusion, I recognize it as a purr. The woman must be an omega, and her distress caused my alpha to comfort her. I've never reacted like this to an omega before, and I've never purred for anyone.

Though the sound staggered me, it has the opposite effect on the omega, and she calms enough to respond.

"I'll wait here for you," she says in a small, scratchy voice. I hear more sniffling before she hangs up.

I take a moment to regain motor function, but when I do, I run out the door and switch to my phone to call for a ride.

On the way to Starsfalls, I try contacting my other packmates, minus Basel. None of them answer my calls or texts. I recall them mentioning they were going to be sourcing supplies around the mountains today. They may not be any closer to Starsfalls than I am, and it seems like they're either busy or out of cell range. It's a good thing I chose to get there as fast as possible and called for a helicopter. By car it would have been a few hours to Starsfalls, but by air it's only half an hour. Since the pack travels so often for business, we have private aircraft to make travel easier and more comfortable. But this is the first time I've really been grateful for a quick trip. Those other urgent business meetings seem irrelevant now.

I grab the first aid kit from the helicopter to bring with me. I don't know if the omega is injured or just upset, but I'd rather come prepared if she doesn't want to go to the hospital. I'm rifling through the kit to see what it includes when a sudden thought hits me.

My head snaps up and I look toward Starsfalls as if I can see through the trees and buildings between us. Was the omega calling Basel because she's in heat and he's an alpha? I don't think he mentioned dating anyone in town, but I haven't been around much. Perhaps they don't know each other well, but she felt safe enough with him to ask for help. He's a great person, so it wouldn't surprise me if an omega thought he was a good choice to help with a heat.

I've never been with an omega, much less one in heat. Normally the thought doesn't do anything for me, but since the idea of *this* omega in heat registered, I've been half hard and ready to help however she wants. She sounded upset, but a heat can be painful if there's no alpha or medication to help.

I'm sure it's just because I don't like hearing an omega

in distress that my alpha is so "eager" to assist. I look down at my lap and try to will my erection away. I don't know that she called Basel because of a heat, and regardless, I don't want to walk in there like a cocky asshole. I'm not that kind of alpha and I don't want to give her the wrong impression.

I try to get rid of these thoughts by shaking my head like a dog trying to shake off water. I do it so hard that my headset almost flies off, and it doesn't even work. Pressing the heels of my hands into my eyes, I try to concentrate on something else. It doesn't matter if she's in heat. I'll get her to a heat clinic or send the helicopter to bring Basel back. I won't help her with that myself. I can't believe I even considered it, or that my alpha considered it.

My chest aches and my insides twist. I could never be with another omega. I've never behaved like this before. Maybe I've been isolating myself too much and my alpha is unbalanced, trying to throw me into a rut. Well, I won't let that happen. Even if it does, I'll get through it alone. Analyzing my feelings helped calm me, though I still have a wrenching feeling in my chest. I have a plan to get help if her heat is the issue, and it doesn't include my involvement.

I'll find out what it is soon enough. The helicopter lowers as we reach a field at the edge of Starsfalls, and I brace for landing.

After disembarking, I get into the SUV waiting for me and quickly drive to the building listed on the map.

When I arrive, I slam the vehicle into park in the first spot I see and jump out. I stride past the people moving slowly on the sidewalk and rush into the building, running up the stairs to the third floor. Now that I'm close, my mind has shut down except for one thought: find the omega.

The location didn't show an apartment number, but the pin hovered on the right side of the hallway. I pound my fist on each door down that side of the hall. After reaching the end, I knock again on every one on my way back after none of them open. I've almost made it back to the first door when the one in front of me cracks open and I hear sniffling.

"Basel?" asks the voice from the phone call.

I can't see inside because the door is barely open. The omega is hidden behind it, except for the edge of a blanket wrapped around her.

"No, I'm his packmate. He left his phone at the house, and I was the only there to answer it. I can help you with whatever you need, though," I answer in my most soothing voice, and my purr has kicked in again. She must not have been able to tell I wasn't Basel on the phone since she was crying so hard.

"His packmate?"

"That's right. I'm Nix."

Confoundingly, at that, she slams the door shut and I hear it swiftly lock.

I wait to see if she'll explain what's wrong, but all is quiet. I knock gently on her door this time.

"I can help you with anything that Basel could," my traitorous mouth says. Didn't I just tell myself I wasn't going to help this omega with her heat? My alpha still doesn't agree, but that's too damn bad.

Although, come to think of it, she doesn't smell like she's in heat. I've heard that without intervention, omegas in heat can fill a building with their scent if they don't have an alpha to help. I couldn't even smell that she was an omega when her door was open. I could be wrong about her designation, but her whimpers certainly sounded like an omega. I haven't been around many of them, but alphas have an instinctual response to their noises and scents. If she is in heat, she may have used strong descenters to avoid attracting unwanted attention.

"If you're hurt, I can help you," I try again.

"You're not Basel's packmate!" She startles me by shouting through the door.

I rear back. That wasn't what I expected to hear. I'm not his packmate? How well does this omega know Basel? Do my packmates not tell people about me because I'm gone so often? They wouldn't do that; pretend I don't even exist. There's a sharp pain in my chest. My pack wouldn't cut me out just because I'm away so much. Would they?

The dark thoughts circle in my mind like vultures.

"I know you're still out there. Go away!" the omega yells again.

No. No one can separate me from my pack. If my pack-mates want me to leave, they'll have to tell me themselves. They always try to include me, even up to last night, when they pestered me to have a late meal with them. If they wanted to get rid of me, they wouldn't keep trying to include me.

I take a deep breath to calm myself and think this through. The omega must not know Basel well if she doesn't know about all of his packmates. He's only been working in Starsfalls for a few weeks, so it's not surprising she doesn't know about the rest of us. It's smart of her not to let a strange alpha in, especially if she's in heat and vulnerable. Pride fills me at the fact that she slammed the door in my face and yelled at me. She can certainly take care of herself. But still, I'm not going to let her suffer if I can help.

"I am still here. And I am Basel's packmate. He accidentally left his phone at the pack house this morning, so I answered it. Basel, Fynn, Roman, and Salem are traveling today to find supplies for the greenhouse restoration. I tried calling them after we talked, but no one answered. They must be somewhere with no service. Since I couldn't get ahold of them, I came myself to help."

Naming my other packmates might prove I'm one of them if she knows the others. Speaking of names, I realize I never looked to see if her name was saved in Basel's phone, and I was so focused on getting to her I never asked.

"What's your name, omega?" If we start at the beginning with introductions, maybe she'll feel more comfortable. I already told her my name, but it was hardly a proper greeting.

She's silent again. I don't even hear sniffling. Did she walk away to try calling one of the others? Just as I'm about to try knocking again, she responds.

"I'm not an omega," she says quietly, sounding nervous.

She must still think I'm an untrustworthy alpha.

"Alright. What's your name then, sweetheart?" I try again.

"I'm not telling you. Go away!" She's back to yelling.

I sigh and drop down to sit next to her door, leaning my head back against the wall.

"I answered your call. I'm responsible for you until you tell me you're okay. I can keep trying my packmates and see if they answer, but I'm staying here until you tell me why you're upset and what I can do to help. I have a first aid kit if you're injured."

Now that I'm here in person, it doesn't seem like she's

physically hurt. I didn't smell any blood when she briefly opened the door, and it's harder for descenters to hide that scent. I still think it could be a heat, but there might be something else that's upset her.

"I don't need help," she replies petulantly.

My lips twitch into a small smile.

"Well, you certainly sounded upset on the phone and when you answered the door. Just tell me what made you cry, and I'll fix it."

It's silent again for a while. I wait patiently, or as patiently as I can at least. I'm still on edge because I know she's upset. I'm glad she's no longer crying, though. It was almost physically painful to listen to that.

"I don't think it's something you can fix," she says eventually.

I close my eyes. It's sounding like the problem isn't heat related, unless she thinks the rest of my pack won't be able to get here in time to help. I wish I knew who was behind the door. I should have paid more attention after Basel and the others started visiting Starsfalls. Is this omega someone they've been dating, or is she someone Basel works with? Would she call him to her apartment if this is work related?

"I'll do my best to try if you tell me what the problem is."

There's rustling behind the door.

"It's—I got a phone call. She said I was copying her, and she wouldn't let me use any suppliers in town for the festival. But I would never copy someone! At least not on purpose. Maybe some of my ideas for the greenhouse are similar to hers? But we haven't even set anything up yet! I could rearrange things if I knew what she was talking about.

"Plus, everyone here shares suppliers! They just set up

155

their stands differently or make different food with the fall produce. I don't even know who called me. How could I be copying her?!" she says rapidly, tripping over her words to get everything out. Her explanation ends on a sob, and she starts crying again.

I shoot up from the floor. Who threatened my omega? I'll stop them. No one will ever bother her again.

"Let me in. I'll use your phone to find her and make her leave you alone," I tell her in a growl.

There's a break in the crying. "You will?" she sniffles.

I have to unlock my jaw to speak, I'm so rigid with anger. It's taking most of my effort not to pull the door off its hinges so I can get in there and help. But she doesn't know me, and I don't want to scare her. So I make the effort to reply with words.

"Yes. I'll tell her she has no right to tell you what to do, and I have lawyers who will back you up. This woman can't have exclusive rights to all the suppliers in town, and I doubt they want to limit their distribution like that."

She sniffs again. "You think so? I wasn't sure the vendors would do that either. But I don't want people to think I'm trying to steal ideas," she says, sounding anxious.

"I'm sure people don't think that. It sounds like this woman is trying to stir up trouble. Once the festival begins it will be obvious that you have your own great ideas and don't need to take someone else's."

"I guess you're right. I'll just ignore her then. You don't need to do anything."

I frown. I'm not so sure about that. I don't want someone spreading nasty rumors about my omega. She sounds too nice to do what this person is accusing her of, which I'm sure is obvious to anyone that knows her. Still, gossip can be hurtful. At the very least, I want my lawyers to send this woman a cease and desist letter so she leaves my omega alone and doesn't interfere with her business.

"I'd still feel better if I could talk to this person and ensure she won't bother you again. Even if it's obvious these are false claims, I don't want her calling and upsetting you again," I respond slowly. I think about asking her to text the woman's number to Basel's phone, but I want her to open the door so I can see that she's alright.

"Are you really one of Basel's packmates?" she asks again.

Clearly they haven't mentioned me at all.

"Yes. I've been busy with work, so I haven't had a chance to visit Starsfalls yet. I know my other packmates have been around. I'm not sure how much they've told you about our pack. Fynn was the first one I met, years ago when we were kids. I ran into Salem and Roman a couple years later at school, and then Salem transferred to a high school for gifted students, where he met Basel. Roman introduced us, and our pack has been inseparable ever since."

I wince as I finish relaying our history. I'm not sure I can count myself as inseparable after all I've done to keep myself at a distance. I love my packmates, but I failed them, and I know I don't deserve to truly be part of our pack. Despite that, I haven't been able to leave, so perhaps we are inseparable.

"How did you meet Fynn if it wasn't at school?" she asks.

Ah, she's smart, she caught that.

"My parental pack donated to a lot of non-profits, including some that help children in foster care. My fathers liked to visit the causes they supported, so we went to a few events the charities held for the children."

So my fathers could be seen as benevolent benefactors and get good press without actually being very involved, I think to myself.

"I met Fynn at one of those events at an amusement park. He was sneaking onto roller coasters that he wasn't tall enough to ride on. He got through by hiding in groups of taller kids. He's lucky he didn't slip out and break something," I say wryly.

Fynn's fortune in life would make you think he was born with a four-leaf clover in one hand and a rabbit's foot in the other. I think a cat may have also granted him a few of its nine lives. Fynn has gotten himself into so many situations that he shouldn't have, but he always comes out the other side unscathed. His only misfortune was that he was never paired with a good foster family. Despite the poor quality of care from his foster parents, and one home in particular, he survived the system.

"I haven't been a good packmate recently," I admit. "Or ever really. I spend too much time working and not enough time enjoying life with my packmates. I shouldn't be surprised that none of them mentioned me. If I didn't constantly isolate myself you would have known who I am, and I wouldn't have upset you further by coming here. I'm sorry."

Another deadbolt slides through the door, and I stand up to leave. I'm sure it's obvious now to the omega that I'm not equipped to help her. I'll track down my packmates in person and send them back here.

Before I can step away, the door swings open.

I turn back to find a blanket enveloping the short omega, the fabric draped over her head and wrapped around her body. When she looks up, everything else fades away, and the only thing I see is her face.

My heart stops and my lungs freeze. I stare, and stare, but no matter how hard I look, it doesn't make sense. Did the helicopter crash on the way here and I'm in a coma? That's the only thing that would make sense. This is what I see every night in my dreams, during the brief periods that I'm able to sleep.

I don't think I ever envisioned this variant, though. When my mind pictured what she would look like as an adult, it was always with the same shoulder-length blonde hair she had when we were children. Now her hair is long, tumbling down her shoulders and disappearing into the blanket. Her eyes are still big and blue, and they hold my entire world. Her heart-shaped face is slightly narrower as an adult. My imagination could never picture her this perfect. Her red lips are parted in an O as she stares back at me.

I'm not sure how this dream will go. Usually, she yells at me for how I treated her. Or looks at me with disgust or horror and runs from me. Rarely do my dreams grant me a reprieve where she smiles and embraces me.

I desperately hope this is one of the good dreams. I wait to see which way it will play out.

CHAPTER 22

PERSEPHONE

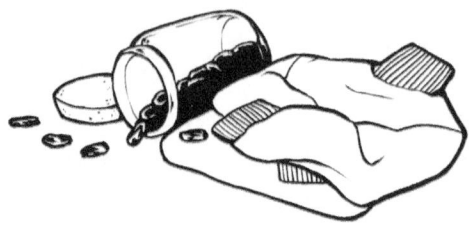

My eyes must be too swollen and irritated for me to see clearly. The growly alpha outside my door is *him*? Despite his rough voice, he was so sweet and caring. He didn't barge in and demand I listen to him, he simply offered his help. The alpha I knew wouldn't do that. He said an omega's role was to obey alphas. I doubt an alpha like that would care about my petty problems, or even let me have my own life where I could work on my passions and be away from the home.

Maybe this alpha just looks similar to the one I knew, with his curly halo of hair and brown doe eyes in a fine-boned, sharp face. The few times I pictured what *he* might look like as an adult it was something like this. Though I hardly spent any time considering what he looks like now. None at all, basically. I certainly haven't thought of him every night since we met.

This alpha is just coincidentally similar to how I pictured the other one. Plus, my eyes are blurry from crying. If I could just clear them, I'm sure I'll see he's not the alpha I knew. That alpha wouldn't care for me like this one has.

At that thought, I close my mouth (which was hanging open) and purse my lips. I blink and squint, trying to see him better. He hasn't said anything since I opened the door, probably because I've been staring at him like a loon. My nose twitches, and I sniff to clear it. With my mouth closed I can hardly breathe, my nose is so swollen and clogged from crying.

I can't resolve the image in front of me into anything distinct. What did he say his name was? Nix? Well, that's clear at least. It's not the name of the alpha I knew. Since Nix is one of Basel's packmates, I need to pull myself together and be polite. Especially since he's trying to help, and he doesn't even know me.

I thought I knew all the members of his pack, but since Nix never visited Starsfalls, I suppose it makes sense they didn't tell me about him. Still, you'd think someone would have mentioned him by now with how much time I've spent with them. Unless there's a reason they didn't mention this packmate.

I eye him distrustfully (and blurrily). Maybe they didn't tell me about Nix because of his bad habits, like he dominates every conversation to talk about trains. Or he hogs all the food at breakfast. I glare at him.

He hasn't made any aggressive moves since I opened the door, and he doesn't react to my glare. I drop my scowl and sigh, breathing in through my mouth so I can get enough air. I was feeling faint.

"Why don't you come in? You came all this way to help me, the least I can do is offer you some coffee and pastries. And *maybe* we could look into figuring out who called me. Just so I know who it is," I hasten to add. I don't want to engage with her if I can avoid it. I'll continue planning the pop-up as I have been since I know it's unique. I'm sure this woman will forget about me soon enough.

I step to the side to let Nix in. He blinks once, and then gives me the biggest smile I've ever seen. It dazzles me so much that after he walks through the door, it takes me a minute to close it. I rub my eyes as I shut the door. They're obviously more irritated than I thought if I was that stunned by a smile.

I turn back to see him still smiling at me, and an image flickers through my mind like déjà vu. I squint at the alpha again.

"What did you say your name was?" I clear my throat after asking. That unstops my nose, and I can finally breathe again.

I only get one inhale before everything stops.

I smell that warm sugar, vanilla glaze, and pumpkin scent for the first time in over a decade. It's like a freshly roasted pumpkin made into pumpkin pie. Or pumpkin cookies with brown sugar frosting. A pumpkin cream that you add to your favorite coffee.

Just like the first time I smelled it, I pause and eagerly wait for my scent match to approach me. Phoenix doesn't do that this time, though. Instead, he moves past me and stands near the kitchen.

While I stare at him, he answers again that his name is Nix.

"It's not Phoenix?" I find the courage to ask.

His smile drops.

"That's right," he says blankly. "Since you left, I haven't gone by my full name. I couldn't bear to hear anyone else call me that after I lost you. I started using a nickname."

His eyes are unfocused, and he looks confused.

Why is he confused? Did he not know it was me before?

162

I thought he would recognize me anywhere. My chest burns like there's a crack in it and I inhale sharply. His baked pumpkin scent fills me, and I notice my scent isn't mingling with his like it did in the past. Ah, that's right, I use descenters now and run a dozen air purifiers in my apartment to keep my scent hidden. I shouldn't be hurt that he didn't recognize me, especially without my scent to remind him.

My chest still aches. It's not like I wanted him to recognize me. I spent half of my childhood and all of my adult life making sure I was hidden from Phoenix and anything that could lead him to me.

Already, he's a different alpha from the boy I met. People change as they grow up. Did he move away from the sexist views of his family? Maybe he just learned to hide them better. It's easy for wealthy alpha families to disguise their misogyny behind money, where the omegas don't *have* to work, so why don't they just stay home and not worry their pretty little heads about it. While isolated at home, no one can see how they're controlled by their alphas.

I tense, preparing myself to run for my phone (which I stupidly left in the kitchen) and call for help. What if he barks at me and tries to make me leave with him?

Phoenix is between me and my phone, but he hasn't made a move yet. His eyes are distant like he's lost in thought.

If what he said about being Basel's packmate is true, including the part about being distant from them, he wouldn't have known who I was until now. Why did he keep himself isolated? That doesn't make sense. He was all about pack life when we were younger.

Phoenix still hasn't moved, so I slowly inch closer. He

doesn't react, still looking down at the floor, absorbed in thought. When I'm close, I reach out and gingerly touch his arm.

"Phoenix," I say when he doesn't respond. I grip his arm more firmly and repeat myself. This time, his head snaps up, and he stares into my eyes. He shifts suddenly, and I squeak in surprise and drop my arm as I prepare to scuttle away. His hands hover around my face.

"Can I touch you?" he asks, eyes haunted.

"O-okay," I stutter out. Maybe this will snap him out of whatever he's thinking and I can get him to leave. He sounded normal outside my apartment (well, as normal as a growly, agitated alpha can be), but now that he knows who I am, it's like he's broken down.

He slowly brings his hands toward my face until he's cradling it. I flush under his gaze and gentle touch and drop my eyes to the floor. I can't handle looking at the reverent expression on his face. If he's changed as an adult and isn't like his fathers, and I've been hiding from him all this time...

The tears return, overflowing and slipping down my face. Phoenix moves his head down to look me in the eyes.

"Don't cry, Persephone. I'm sorry. I'm sorry for what I told you back then. I don't believe those things now, and even then it didn't seem right, but I didn't know any other way to be. I heard you asked to be moved to a different foster home and I knew it was because of what I said. You couldn't endure the thought of your scent match being horrible, like my fathers were to my mother. I didn't blame you. I never tried to follow you because I knew you were afraid of me, but I've thought about you every day, every hour. You were right to leave me. Now that I'm here, I want you to know I'm not anything like the alphas I described when we first met.

"I've wished for years that I could tell you that. But if I tracked you down, how could you believe I wasn't a controlling alpha? The alpha who hunted you to make you listen to what he had to say? I respected your choice and stayed away. I hoped you would find a different alpha to be your mate, a better one.

"I didn't know you were working with my pack now. I'll leave you alone and never bother you again. You can keep working with them without me around, but if you don't want to, I'll explain to them that it's my fault. Since I'm here, I wanted to tell you that you don't have to worry about me forcing a bond on you. Actually, I hope you haven't thought of me at all since you left. I want you to be happy."

He tenderly brushes the tears off my cheeks and releases me.

"Thank you for listening. I'll leave you alone. Please don't be upset because of me."

He steps back and moves around me toward the door. I'm still trying to process everything he said. His words match his actions since he came to my apartment. He's been protective and caring, but not controlling. Phoenix cared about my concerns and wanted to help me with my work. He went out of his way like this for someone he didn't know. It could all be a front to get me to bond with him, except he seemed so sincere.

The front door unlocks.

"Wait!" I quickly spin around, getting tangled in my blanket cape. There's a twinge in my abdomen as I attempt to disentangle myself. Pulling up one side of the blanket yanks it out from under my feet, and I start to fall.

Before I collapse, Phoenix catches me.

I shift around enough to get my hands out and grab his shirt.

"Don't go yet," I plead.

A flicker of hope crosses his face before he schools it into a neutral expression. "I'll stay as long as you want," he assures me before untangling the blanket from my legs while I clutch him.

Once I'm wrested free and Phoenix straightens up, I'm not sure what to do. I flex my hands in his shirt and then release it.

"Um, do you want to sit down? We can talk some more. There's a lot to catch up on." I giggle nervously. Great, way to bring up that you avoided him for years.

Phoenix just smiles. "I'd like that."

He holds the bottom of my blanket up like a train as I lead us over to the couch. He adjusts the blanket around me after I sit, then moves over to the chair next to the couch. I want to tell him to sit next to me, but I don't want to so quickly forget the lesson he taught me. Alphas can be dangerous, and demand that their omegas submit to them. Or maybe I do want to forget. Forget that I spent years avoiding Phoenix and missing out on happiness for no reason.

We could start over now. I've already met the rest of his pack, and they're my scent matches too. If they're as kind and caring as they appear, I could continue to get to know them, and when we're ready, we could bond. I'm giddy at the prospect that I could join this pack, and my stomach flutters.

I beam at Phoenix. Seeing him here in my apartment is so surreal. I've been equal parts hopeful and afraid that this day would come. Even though I was scared of the things he said, I still longed for him.

Now that he's here, I'm not sure what to ask first. I want to know everything, but I don't want to bring up bad memories for him. I don't know much about him as an adult besides the few things he's told me, since the others never mentioned him. I frown. That reminds me, Phoenix said he kept himself apart from his pack. His packmates seem great, so I don't understand why he would do that.

"You said you don't spend much time with Basel and the others?"

He dips his head in admission. "That's right. I felt guilty for never telling them about you. How I found a scent match and lost you by treating you badly. I was ashamed of the way I acted, and ashamed that I likely ruined their chances at another match. I've heard a scent match can change if a pack gains or loses members, and we met before I even had a pack, but I wasn't sure if that rumor was true. I was too cowardly to confess that I'd scared you away, and I didn't want to lose them too," Phoenix says miserably. He leans forward and puts his forearms on his knees, lacing his fingers together. "I'm not sure how you feel about my packmates. If you always use descenter as a way to hide from me, I assume they haven't smelled your real scent. Can you tell if they're your scent matches?"

He shouldn't feel guilty. It's his fathers that should feel bad for telling him how alphas are "supposed" to act. Before I get too worked up on his behalf, I realize he asked a question. As I consider my answer, I my body gets flushed with heat. Smelling Phoenix now while thinking about his packmates causes my slick to go wild, even more so than when I first met Basel. Since then, I've had to double up on descenter and use slick absorbing underwear. I fiddle with the edge of my blanket as I squirm in my seat, causing another twinge in my stomach.

I answer without letting him know how flustered his pack makes me. "Sure, they smell good," I say casually, my voice cracking on the "good." My face is so flushed, I doubt I would have fooled him anyway by trying to play it cool.

I hear him exhale a chuckle and risk a peek at him. He looks pleased as he gazes at me affectionally. It's a better look than his wounded appearance a minute ago. I give him a shy smile in return.

"I like them a lot," I continue, hoping to ease his self-inflicted torment. "They're kind and supportive, and I've enjoyed getting to know them. I've been treating them like coworkers though, since Basel was hired to do the restoration, and the others have joined in."

This next part probably won't help Phoenix feel better, but I think he should know. "I generally avoid alphas, so I've been keeping them at a distance even though we're scent matches. I, um, wasn't sure I wanted to be with any alphas."

My forehead crinkles as I remember something. "I told Roman I wanted to keep things professional between us, and he agreed. I don't think they're interested in me that way."

Now I feel even more rejected than when Roman agreed so quickly that we should just stay coworkers. Meeting Phoenix again and seeing how he's changed has made me reconsider being part of a pack. Well, that and meeting his packmates. I know it's a quick change of heart, but really, I've been eye fucking the rest of his pack since we met. Plus, they've all been so amazing, it's made me reconsider my actions and how I let the words of a confused child color my view of all alphas. It seems like karma that when I finally want to be with my scent matched pack, they only want to be friends.

"When did you tell him that?" Phoenix asks, breaking me out of my swirling thoughts.

"Hm? Oh, I told him yesterday."

"What were you doing that prompted that conversion?"

I flush. "Um, we were, uh, kissing."

He's motionless for a second before breaking into laughter. I give him a moment (like a millisecond) to get it out of his system, then toss one of my throw pillows at his chest. He catches it and keeps laughing.

I huff and lean back on the couch as I wait for him to finish. Just when I'm about to start tapping my foot impatiently, he finally stops.

"So, you were kissing, and you don't think Roman is interested in you romantically?" Phoenix asks in amused disbelief.

"If you paid attention to the story, after we kissed, he said he wasn't interested in me. So either he wasn't interested in me to begin with, or my kissing ability turned him off!" I respond hotly.

Phoenix leans forward and squeezes my knee. "Persephone, I'm sure he enjoyed himself. He likely didn't want to scare you away. My pack will be happy to take things slow if you allow us to court you. Or we can get to know each other as friends before moving to courting. I have no desire to push you into anything you're not comfortable with. I'm just happy to be near you. And I know Roman, he's not one for casual romances. If he kissed you, I'm sure he's interested in you as a potential mate."

My toes curl and I tingle after hearing his words. I try not to let myself get carried away thinking about being with them, but it's hard not to. I feel like I'm being swept away just from the touch of Phoenix's hand.

"You really think so?" I ask to be sure.

"Yes, I do. They've never worked on Basel's restoration projects before, and they all have their own jobs. There must be another reason they're here," Phoenix's lips quirk in amusement, but he refrains from laughing at me this time.

I roll my eyes but can't help my smile. I knew they had their own work and hobbies, but I thought maybe they worked together sometimes so they could spend time as a pack.

"I'm glad they like me back," I confess. "Do you think I should tell them we're scent matches? I guess we'll have to if we tell them how you and I met. I can stop using descenter, too. Or do you not want them to know we met as kids? I don't want them to be upset with you. We can keep our history to ourselves." I quickly backtrack, grabbing his arm in concern.

"I'll tell the pack about our history and what I did, as long as you're alright with them knowing. I should have done that a long time ago."

"We can tell them together. They're not allowed to be mad at you about it, it's not your fault. Plus, I could have tried to find you again when I was older to see if you'd changed. This is just how things played out. I matched with the rest of your pack, and we found each other again. I don't want you to feel guilty or ashamed about what happened anymore," I order him sternly.

Phoenix nods gravely. "Yes, ma'am. I'll try."

We've both leaned forward that our faces are now just inches apart. I'm drawn even closer as I stare into his soft brown eyes. Phoenix moves closer too. My heart pounds and my pussy goes into overdrive. When his lips are a hairsbreadth away, a sharp pain in my stomach makes me flinch away.

Phoenix leans back quickly. "I'm sorry. I didn't mean to push you."

"No, it's not you," I hurry to explain after I catch my breath. "I leaned in too, but then I got a cramp. I must have pulled something when I got caught up in the blanket earlier."

I whimper and double over as a bigger cramp hits me.

Phoenix drops to his knees and wraps his arms around me. He rubs my back and purrs to comfort me. The pain eases, and I melt into him.

"I don't think it's a muscle cramp," he says in my ear, making me shiver.

I'm too relaxed, unable to muster up the energy to respond. It feels so good to be pressed against him like this, I don't want to do anything else.

"I can take you to your nest if you'll allow me. Do you have a pack on call, or do you go to a clinic? Any medication I can get you?" Phoenix continues when I don't reply.

His words confuse me, and all this thinking is making my head hurt, but I figure I need to make the effort to respond.

"What do you mean?"

"Your scent has filled the room and you're having abdominal cramps. I think it's the start of your heat."

That shocks me out of my impression of a limp noodle. I pull away and scoot back on the couch. I pat my cheeks like I can somehow tell my temperature from that. When that tells me nothing, as expected, I panic and immediately go into denial.

"It can't be my heat! I got stronger suppressants to push

it back until after the festival! It's just barely the start of fall now, and even without the suppressants it's not due for at least another month," I babble.

Phoenix brushes his hands over my hair and pulls me back into his chest, purring to calm me.

"Finding a scent match can trigger an omega's heat. You've been around five scent matches now, so it's not surprising this happened. It will be okay, Persephone. I know you don't know my pack very well, and you and I have a complicated history. You don't have to be with us for this. If you have alphas on standby for your heats, I can call them. Since your mates triggered this, I don't think suppressants will be able to stop it now. If you have pain relievers, I'll get them and take care of you until your helpers arrive."

"I don't have any other alphas to call," I say absent-mindedly, still struggling with the idea of my body's betrayal.

He frowns. "Who helps you then? Some betas? I'll call them. You can't go through this alone."

"I've made it through all my heats alone, and it's been just fine," I say defensively. I still don't like being told what to do.

Phoenix stops bristling and tries again, "I know you can take care of yourself, but heats are painful without help. Even with medication, they're unpleasant. Since this heat was triggered by scent matches, I think it will be more intense than usual. I don't want you to suffer through that."

Usually the suppressants lessen the intensity of my heats, and relaxants let me get through them alone (with an electric knight). Phoenix is right, though. We learned in school that potential mates can trigger a heat that's like being hit by a freight train. I don't want to go through that alone. I whimper in fear.

Phoenix hugs me close. "Shh, it's okay, Persephone. We can contact the Heat Seekers matching service. They have vetted alphas on call to help omegas through their heat and they'll send someone over quickly. You can choose the ones you want on their app."

I whimper again and grip Phoenix tightly. I don't want other alphas, I want my pack. Why won't they help me? Why would they leave while I'm in heat? I can feel the slick on my thighs and I'm drowning in my scent, the warm cashmere and smoked tonka beans mixing with Phoenix's pumpkin pie. I rub my face against the side of his neck and hear him stifle a growl. I greedily inhale more of his scent. After several deep breaths, I still don't smell the rest of my pack, and I whine in distress. Where are they? They have to be here for my heat.

"Where are they?" I groan.

"I'll pull up the app and help you pick someone," Phoenix shifts around to get out his phone.

"Yes, call them. Tell them to hurry up and come back here," I encourage him. I need the rest of my pack.

"I thought you said you hadn't used the app before?" Phoenix pauses his tapping to ask.

I moan again. My temperature must have spiked because it's hard to think. Why is he taking so long to call our pack? I don't care what he uses to contact them.

I just don't understand why Phoenix won't help me. If he doesn't know what to do, I'll have to take matters into my own hands.

I lean back to get my legs out of the blanket, and Phoenix shifts to give me room. Once they're free, I wrap my thighs around him and push him onto the floor. Phoenix lands with a thump on my plush fur rug with me straddling his chest. He looks good spread out beneath me, his eyes wide in surprise. I grin at him in triumph and shimmy down so my pussy is over his cock. Phoenix grabs my waist.

"Persephone—" he starts, but I cut him off.

"You have to move at least a little, you don't just lay there," I demonstrate by rolling my hips along his length. His grip on my hips doesn't allow me much range of motion though. It's fine that he doesn't have experience. I can teach him what to do as long as he listens to directions.

Phoenix groans. "Persephone, this isn't—I'm not trying to take advantage of the situation. I don't want to rush into this just because your heat started. You'll need more than one alpha, anyway. Let me show you the Heat Seekers app so you can pick some."

Part of what Phoenix says makes it through the heat haze. I sit up and stop attempting to unsuccessfully grind on him (he still won't let me move my hips!).

"What do you mean other alphas?? I want *my* pack. I don't want any other alphas here. I can't have them around my nest," I glare down at him and cross my arms.

He looks surprised. "Your pack? You mean us? The Goldenrod Pack? We would love to be here for you, but I don't want you to regret it afterward. I'm in this for the long run, there's time to take things slowly."

"I don't feel rushed. I've been getting to know the others for weeks, and I've known you almost my whole life!"

He laughs and finally removes his hands from my hips and cups my cheeks (on my face). "Well, I certainly feel like

I've known you forever. If you're really sure about this, I'll track down my packmates."

Bracing my hands on his shoulders, I smile beatifically down at him and grind on his cock.

Phoenix groans again, but this time grabs my hips to help me rub against him. He presses up into me and I close my eyes and let him move me. He's rumbling under me, growling or purring, I can't tell which and I don't really care as the vibrations travel up into me.

My legs shake, and I whine into his neck. I must have collapsed onto him at some point. Phoenix has his feet braced on the floor and I clasp my legs around him as much as I can with them trembling. All sensation in my body seems to concentrate on my clit, flowing up from my toes and down from my head, before spreading back out in a rush as I come against him. Phoenix grips my ass and the back of my neck as he grinds me through my climax.

The pleasure clears away the heat effects temporarily, and I lie limply as I catch my breath. I'm about to ask Phoenix again to track down his packmates so he knows I want this even without the influence of hormones. Before I can, there's a pounding on my front door (the apartment door).

Phoenix tightens his grip on me and growls menacingly. I pat him soothingly on the shoulder. He holds me in place as he gets to his feet and quickly carries me to the back of my apartment.

"Which way is your nest? Once I set you down in there, lock the door behind me. I'll get rid of whoever's out there," Phoenix says in my ear.

"My nest is through there," I whisper back to him. "It's probably just a delivery, don't worry about it. We can stay in my nest."

I nuzzle his neck while he carries me into my nest. The heat crept back faster than I thought it would. Usually I have a few waves of pre-heat horniness before I have to confine myself to the nest for the full heat. I already want to lock us in now. Well, Phoenix and the rest of my pack.

"Lock the door after me and wait for me to come back before you open it," Phoenix repeats seriously as he sets me down.

I blink at his stern face, and he moves into the hall and shuts the door behind him before I can protest. Without Phoenix in my nose, I can smell myself more clearly, and I remember that my perfume filled the apartment. With me coming on him, there's a lot of slick scenting the air too. Since Phoenix triggered my heat and broke through the suppressants, my scent is too strong for the descenters to cover. The air filters in the rest of the apartment aren't up to the task either. Only the nest has a separate ventilation system to keep scents from leaking into the building. The nest air is vented outside, and the system neutralizes scents on the way out. But we were in the living room for a while, so my perfume could have already seeped into the building. Who knows what kind of alphas I may have drawn in.

I hurry to lock the door after him, and I hear him try the knob to make sure it's locked.

"I'll be back soon. Don't open the door until I tell you it's safe," Phoenix repeats.

"I won't. I'll wait for you," I promise anxiously.

"It will be okay, Persephone," he says, and then it's quiet.

I hold my breath to see if I can hear him open the front door. The nest room has more soundproofing, so it was hard enough to hear Phoenix talking on the other side of the door. I doubt I'll be able to hear anything at the front of the apartment. Unless it's something really loud.

Surely whoever it is will go away without a fight when they see Phoenix. He's big, even for an alpha. Still, maybe I should go out there to help. I don't want to lose him again right after I found him.

I'm not sure how well I'd do in a fight, but I could be the distraction while Phoenix sneaks up behind the other alphas to take them out. Would that actually work, or does that only happen in the movies? I chew nervously on my thumbnail.

I tentatively reach for the lock with my other hand, but before I decide if I should go out there or not, there's a gentle knock on the nest door. I squeak and jump away, crashing softly into the pile of blankets behind me.

"It's Phoenix, you can open up. I think you'll be pleased with what I found at the door," Phoenix says.

"Yeah, we have some big packages you need to sign for."

There's scuffling sounds after that, but I'm hardly paying attention. I'm too focused on the other voice, which belonged to Fynn!

I hasten to fend off the blankets and jump up to unlock the door.

I throw it open and see Phoenix in the front with Fynn shouldered in next to him. Phoenix smiles happily and Fynn has his usual cocky grin. Behind them are Basel, Salem, and Roman, who look more concerned than their other packmates.

"There's my doll," Fynn says as he pushes past Phoenix and scoops me up in a hug.

I giggle and wrap my arms around his neck, dangling off of him since he's so much taller than me. Fynn purrs and I melt on him.

"Are you okay, Seph? Nix texted and called us dozens of times but didn't say what was going on. When we tried calling back, he didn't answer, but we saw his location was in Starsfalls. You weren't answering either, and we've been worried something happened to you," Basel says over Fynn's shoulder.

"Can't you tell what's going on?" Fynn replies before I can. "She obviously wants us to help with her heat," he explains smugly.

I giggle and smush my face further into his neck to get a direct hit of his scent. With all my alphas here, my body is going crazy at our combined scents. Getting a closeup of Fynn's smell is heavenly without the suppressants dulling my senses. I can't wait to get this close to the others, too.

"Did you know you were an omega?" Salem asks me in concern. "Did you know she was?" he turns to the others without waiting for my answer.

"Is that really all that's going on?" Roman says.

Why do they keep talking? Like Fynn said, my alphas should be able to tell why they're here.

"It's kind of a long story," Phoenix answers vaguely.

"How did you meet? Did you go to see the greenhouse?" Basel looks at him doubtfully.

I sigh into Fynn's neck, and he squeezes me gently. Apparently we're still not past the talking stage. I pull back so I can see the others. I'd better involve myself so we can talk through the important things quickly before my heat truly sets in.

"Phoenix is right, it's a long story. We can talk about everything more later, but the short answer is, I was upset about some of the pop-up planning. I called Basel's phone to ask for your help," I say.

"You left it at the house. When I heard it ringing, I answered and offered to come help," Phoenix tells them.

"When Phoenix got here, I realized we'd met before, when we were kids. Back then we suspected we were scent matches."

Phoenix clears his throat before confessing, "When I first met Persephone, I still listened to my fathers' ideas about pack life. I repeated some of those beliefs to her, since she smelled like my omega. As you all know, my fathers' opinions are awful, and I scared her away. I'm sorry I didn't tell you about matching with Persephone before. I didn't see her again after that day, and I was afraid to tell you how I hurt our scent match and lost her."

Phoenix is downcast again, and after I'd just cheered him up too.

"It's not your fault," I reassure him, reaching over Fynn to rub Phoenix's shoulder. "Your fathers are to blame. They're the ones who should know better, that bigoted ideas are harmful to omegas *and* alphas."

Before I have time to worry that anyone will be angry at Phoenix, they jump in to help me comfort him.

"I'm sorry you felt you had to hide that from us, Nix," Salem tells him sadly.

"You were just a kid. Seph is right, your fathers are to blame," Roman says.

"Yeah, fuck them," Fynn says succinctly.

Basel hasn't said anything, and I turn to look at him. He's frowning but doesn't seem mad. As the others quiet, Phoenix looks to Basel too but drops his eyes.

"Is that why you've kept yourself at a distance from us? Why you've been pulling away from the pack?" Basel asks grimly.

"I've been so ashamed of what I did to our mate, and

ashamed of hiding her from you. It made me sick to keep this secret, but I still couldn't bring myself to tell you I lost Persephone because I frightened her so badly she ran away. I didn't feel good enough to be a member of this pack, but I'm selfish and couldn't leave it entirely. I'm sorry."

I squeeze Phoenix's arm and wait for Basel's response.

"From now on, you need to be an involved member of this pack. Your upbringing is not your fault, but we need to work together to function as a pack, especially now that we found Seph. No more pulling away," Basel commands.

"Yes, of course. No more secrets. All I've ever wanted is for Persephone to be with us. I'll be here for the pack and for her as long as she wants," Phoenix says.

I smile at him. I'm glad he's sharing his feelings with the pack, and, selfishly, I like hearing him confirm his interest in me. In the past, I've wondered if Phoenix moved on over the years we spent apart. It was so long ago when we met, and my memories might have been clouded by the years. I couldn't be sure that he felt the same kinship I did. Hearing Phoenix profess his commitment now would be making me swoon if Fynn weren't holding me up. It could be the heat hormones making me want to settle down with my alphas, but I still think I'd be happy to hear that from Phoenix every day.

"Good," Basel turns to me. "Seph, we've been discussing how to ask to officially court you. That was before we knew you were an omega, and now that we can smell the real you, we can tell we're scent matches. I wanted you to know that the pack wants to be with you regardless of our designations. We care about you and love spending time with you. This isn't how we planned to ask, but will you allow us to court you? We would also be honored to help you with this heat if you'll have us. If it's too soon for that yet, we understand."

I wait impatiently for Basel to finish, even though it is nice to know they want me even without the compulsion of pheromones. As soon as he stops talking, I launch myself at him. Basel catches me and hugs me.

Finally, I can rub my face on him too.

"Yes! Yes, I want to be with you, with this pack. For my heat and after," I tell him breathlessly. My heat feels like it's looming over me, waiting to strike. Now that I've reconciled with Phoenix, I'm eager to get them in my nest. Sure, we're in the room, but I haven't gotten my alphas into the sheets and made the bed smell like them.

"You've made me very happy, Seph. Now we can discuss boundaries and what you're comfortable and uncomfortable with. What food do you prefer during your heats, and what temperature do you want the room set to?" Basel asks.

Fynn groans in frustration. "The temperature? Come on, man, you'll cool off her heat with that kind of talk."

"We want her to be comfortable," Roman argues back.

"Boundaries and comfort are important during a heat. Alphas need to keep those things in mind for when an omega isn't able to think clearly," Salem adds.

I happen to agree with Fynn. I'm tired of talking. We can figure most things out as they come up.

"Nothing cold and don't be mean, otherwise I'm open to trying things with you," I rattle off quickly, and try to pull myself up to reach Basel's lips.

Basel leans down (my arms aren't strong enough to pull myself up) and we finally, *finally* kiss.

Basel wraps his hand around the back of my head to deepen our kiss. Someone else comes over to kiss my neck and based on the crackling bonfire scent that surrounds me, it's Fynn. When Basel pulls back, Fynn turns my face to the side and takes over. He gives me a few firm kisses before licking along my lower lip. I part my mouth eagerly for our tongues to meet.

Basel sets me down and holds me steady as he kisses down my neck to my chest. He kneels in front of me to run his lips along my collarbone while his hands massage my hips. Fynn breaks our kiss, and I whine at him. Basel quickly turns my head and kisses me. Their hands move under my shirt, exploring my back and stomach, as they lift it up. Basel pulls away briefly and they tug it off. Fynn strokes up my stomach to cup my breasts. He kneads them with his fingers and gently pinches my nipples. I arch into his touch.

Someone growls behind me, and Fynn growls back.

"You have to share," Roman orders. Fynn grumbles but lets Roman nudge him out of the way to take his place. Basel lets go too, and Roman turns me to face him. He cups my cheeks just like our first kiss and smiles down at me.

"I'm so happy you're letting us court you," Roman tells me sweetly. He leans forward and I close my eyes as I wait for his lips to touch mine. Instead, they brush my ear as he continues, "I'll take you apple picking every year." I moan at his words, and then he kisses me.

It's even better than the first time. I rub myself against his chest and his silk shirt teases my nipples. After a few kisses, he pulls away and turns me.

Salem is there, and he holds me close like when he rescued me in the bookstore. I gaze up and get lost in his eyes. Will that happen every time I look at him?

Salem runs one hand through my hair and holds it back before leaning down to kiss me gently. I press against him, but he holds me in place and keeps our first kiss soft.

Slowly, he tightens his hand in the back of my hair as our kiss intensifies. He reaches down to lift me up, and I eagerly wrap my thighs around him.

Once I'm draped over him, Salem walks us toward my bed. He steps down the stairs to the recessed mattress and kneels to lower me into the nest of blankets and pillows.

Other hands brush my skin and hair now, and I can't tell who they belong to with my eyes closed and our scents mingling in the canopied nest. Salem moves down to kiss my chest, gently unwrapping my legs so he can shift lower. Fynn leans over from the opposite direction, and I eagerly reach for him to kiss me again. While Fynn distracts me, Salem stops his exploration and trades places with someone else.

Fynn suddenly lifts his head away, and I blink my eyes open to see Phoenix kneeling above me, tugging him back by the hair. Phoenix releases him, and Fynn sneaks in to give me one more kiss before sitting back.

Phoenix leans over me now, our roles reversed from earlier, as he bends down to kiss me. Phoenix braces a forearm next to me and trails the other hand up to my breast. I loop my leg around his thigh to rub against him. He growls and bites my lip, and I whimper into his mouth. When he releases it, he moves down to kiss and nip at my breasts.

Phoenix tucks his thumb into the top of my leggings and teases it along the hem. I try to rub my pussy against him again, but his chest pins my hips to the mattress. I whine and wriggle against him, one hand holding his head to me, the other pulling on the back of his shirt. He's wearing far too many clothes.

Suddenly I'm too hot and bothered, and not in a good way. This heat is coming on faster than any of my others.

My eyes snap open and I look around at the others. The light is dim with the curtains drawn around the nest, cocooning us, but it's enough for me to see that they still have their clothes on too.

"Clothes. Off," I demand.

The four of them hurry to shuck their shirts and pants. I watch closely to make sure they're following my directive, greedily looking at every new patch of skin they expose. Fynn is the quickest to take things off, but just as he reaches for his boxers and a strip of hair appears, Phoenix sits up and blocks my view. Since Phoenix also starts removing his clothes, I decide not to complain.

With his shirt off, I examine the light curls dusting Phoenix's chest and trace their path down his stomach until they disappear. I reach forward to run my fingers through them, making him groan.

"I almost don't want to take my pants off, because they're covered in your slick from when you came on me earlier," Phoenix tells me in a low voice.

I pant, and my pussy flutters at the thought that I've marked him.

He slowly unbuttons the top of his pants. "But if you promise to come on my cock and gush all over my lap again, I supposed I could be persuaded to take them off."

I gasp at his dirty words before responding in a squeaky voice, "Yes, yes, I promise!"

Phoenix gives me a wicked smile and pops open the rest of the buttons. "Good girl."

He braces his hand above my head and holds himself over me as slides his pants off. I struggle to decide where to look, up at his smile or down at what he's revealing. I break away from his gaze in time to see his cock freed and straightened up between us. Precum slides along the head, and some drips down onto my stomach. I whimper as it lands. Phoenix leans down to lick it off and then continues moving down to kiss my mound.

I run my fingers through his hair as he nuzzles me. He licks the top of my slit and then pulls my thighs apart to lick the slick from my inner thighs. Phoenix nuzzles my mound again and circles his tongue around my clit, making me clamp my thighs around his head. I squeak as he presses his tongue flat to swipe from my pussy to clit, causing more slick to pour out. I feel him growl and lap it up before going back to teasing my clit. My thighs shake from his undivided attention. Phoenix holds my hips in place so I can't squirm away, and I lock my ankles behind his head to brace myself.

I whine as Phoenix winds me up, tingles spreading to my thighs and stomach. Tears fill my eyes as I get closer and closer, tension building until I almost can't stand it. Phoenix suddenly sucks hard on my clit, and everything bursts. My thighs attempt to smother him in my pussy as they tighten around his head, but he just keeps sucking on me through my orgasm.

When the waves subside, my body goes limp and releases him. Phoenix gently licks my pussy, causing me to twitch with aftershocks. Hands brush the hair back from my face and someone kisses away the tears from the corners of my eyes. That was the most intense orgasm I've ever had, and we've only just started.

Despite thinking my body will need a few minutes to recover, I'm hit with a heat cramp. I wince and try to curl up, but Phoenix is still between my legs. He moves up to wrap his arms around me.

"Are you alright, Persephone? Was that too fast?" he asks.

"No. Cramp. Inside me. Now," I explain as concisely as

possible. I'm afraid if I move too much the cramps will come back faster.

Phoenix doesn't question me again. He kisses me and I taste myself on him, our mingled spiced pumpkin flavors making me whimper and forget about the cramps. I clutch him to me and pull his hips down, his cock rubbing along my pussy. He slides his head against my clit and circles my lips. Once it's covered in slick, Phoenix fits it at my entrance. I tilt my hips up to urge him in, and he slowly pushes inside. The stretch causes tingles to race up my spine, and I feel another orgasm building. Phoenix pushes further, stretching me around him. I look down at our connection, and he's barely inside me. Is it still just the head? Phoenix pulls partially out, and I whine and dig my nails into his shoulders to pull him further in, even though the feeling is intense.

"I'm not going anywhere," he assures me.

And he doesn't, slowly moving forward again to work his way inside. Between his cock stretching me and his fingers rubbing my clit, I forget about demanding he fill me immediately, lost in the push and pull. I bite at his neck as he moves in me. Eventually it feels like there's no more room left for him to go, and his hips are flush to mine on the downstroke. Phoenix growls and nips at my neck, and I quickly arch it to the side for him to mark. He kisses my neck again and gently scrapes his teeth on my skin. I shudder in anticipation of the bite that will bond me to Phoenix and his pack forever.

It never comes, as Phoenix kisses my neck a few more times and then pulls back. I whine in distress that he rejected me. I thought he wanted me, plus we're scent matched. Phoenix groans and leans toward my neck again, and I hold still. This time Basel stops him.

"We haven't talked about bonding, Nix. We can't do that in the middle of a heat. We want to bond with you, Seph, but we need to talk about it when our heads are clear," Basel says.

Phoenix growls.

"I want to bond her too, but she's not thinking properly now," Basel reminds him.

I don't care what they say. I'm the omega, and I want to be bonded to my pack *now*.

Phoenix, however, agrees, "I know. It's hard to think clearly. Help keep me in check."

"I will."

"We'll help each other," Roman adds.

Meanwhile, I'm not getting enough attention. I squeeze Phoenix's cock, and I'm gratified when he groans and returns his focus to me. I grin up at him. He growls and lifts one of my legs around his side for a deeper angle while he fucks me. I whine as I'm bounced between his body and the mattress. My body flushes as another orgasm approaches.

My breathing is shallow and my pussy flexes around Phoenix with the first pulses of an orgasm, when I feel additional pressure at my entrance. He slows his thrusts but the stretch increases, stalling my orgasm. Phoenix curls down to kiss me as he works his knot inside me. My pussy seems to stretch and stretch, far beyond what I thought was possible, as his knot fills me. It locks his cock inside me, pressing into the nerves at my entrance and putting pressure on my clit from the inside, making my body shake before I even realizing I'm coming. I open my mouth on a scream, but nothing comes out. Slick squirts out between us as I come on his cock. He growls and sucks hard on my neck without breaking the skin. Phoenix's cock jerks as his come fills me with heat. Our orgasms feed off each other until we're both wrung out. Ironically, I also feel like I might burst with all the come Phoenix's knot is keeping stuffed inside me.

Phoenix holds me close and purrs, and I can't tell if the vibrations are more relaxing or stimulating. I fall into a doze despite the sensation, the heat activities combining with my rough morning to pull me under.

CHAPTER 23

PERSEPHONE

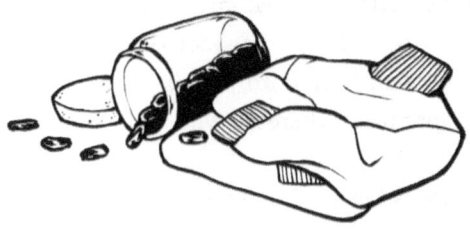

I wake as Phoenix pulls out of me. His knot must have gone down while I slept. I sigh as the pressure releases, some of his come slipping out to mix with the slick on my thighs.

One of his packmates is quick to take his spot, which works for me because the heat is already making me needy again. I blink to clear my groggy vision and see Basel above me.

He smiles and strokes my cheek. "Do you want more?" he asks.

"Yes, I want you," I tell him eagerly. There's an empty ache in my pussy, and he needs to fill it. I tug on his shoulders to pull him down and he follows my directions, leaning down to kiss across my face. Basel cradles the back of my head and wraps his other arm around my waist. I hold my breath as I wait for him to press into me.

I let out a squeal as I'm lifted instead. Basel chuckles in my ear, and there's more laughter behind me. One voice is close as someone slides up behind me.

"Do you want *only* Basel?" Fynn whispers in my ear.

His words cause goosebumps to break out across my skin. Of course not. I want all of them and I want them now. I've never been with more than one person at a time, and normally I might be nervous about being able to keep up. But since it's during my heat, my omega is very sure they'll be the ones who will have to work to keep up with us.

I tilt my head back onto Fynn's shoulder. "I want you too," I whisper back. There's a wild smile on his face before he kisses me.

Basel moves his hand down to play with my clit, and his head nuzzles my breasts. I continue kissing Fynn, but even with two of them touching me, it's not enough. I need more. I press my ass back into Fynn, and he growls and grinds his cock against my cheeks and lower back. I try to push for more, but Fynn holds me in place as he moves a hand down to replace Basel's fingers on my clit. He circles my lips, rubbing my slick and Phoenix's come around, before pushing two fingers inside. I moan at the intrusion, and Fynn adds a third finger to sloppily finger fuck me. I forget what it was I wanted, writhing between Fynn's fingers inside me and Basel's mouth on my nipples.

I whine as I wait for them to coax out my orgasm. Before I reach the edge, Fynn removes his hand. I growl into his mouth and try to slide down to keep his fingers inside me. I feel him smile as he slides his tongue against mine. Before I truly consider biting it in protest, Fynn drags his fingers back to my other entrance. I relax as they massage the outside, teasing at the opening. Basel returns to playing with my clit, just enough to keep me on edge. Fynn slowly eases a finger inside me using my slick, but I want more.

I haven't done this with a partner before, but I've used toys on my own, so I know I can fit more of him inside me. I push back, and he moves his finger a few times before adding another. My legs twitch at the sensations from Fynn's gentle strokes and Basel's teasing. Fynn moves deeper as he stretches me, adding a third finger. My slick keeps his movements smooth, and he pushes in more roughly. I whine and arch my back for more. They oblige, increasing the pace, finally making me come hard while they hold me between them.

As I begin to come down, Fynn replaces his fingers with his cock, pushing his head in with one firm thrust. The new sensation yanks my orgasm back to crash over me again, my body tightening around him. I vaguely hear Fynn groan in my ear. My slick flows between us, easing his way as he pushes further inside.

After several thrusts, Fynn pauses and holds me still for Basel to work his cock into my pussy. Basel kisses me as he does, and I feel him press against Fynn on the other side as they fill me. I run my hands over Basel's shoulders and hold on to anchor myself.

Basel and Fynn move deeper with each thrust, moving me back and forth between them. I'm lost, unable to keep track of how many times I come on them. They keep passing me back and forth, despite my body trying to lock them in place. They alternate kissing and nipping at my neck, and the tension of not knowing for sure if they'll break the skin and bond me heightens everything.

I don't know whose knot swells first, but they both grow rapidly as they expand to lock us together. I briefly wonder if I'll be able to take them both at once. Before worry can pull me out of the moment, the drag of their knots hits the sensitive spots inside me and scatters all thoughts. This time I do scream as I orgasm and their knots lock us together. Basel and Fynn come with me, cocks pulsing as they fill me. With two of them I feel stuffed quickly, but they fill me with more.

When my orgasm releases me, I slump between them. They purr and kiss my face, hair, and neck. I'm limp with exhaustion, so they have to adjust me like a doll for us to lay down on our sides. I settle in to recover while we wait for their knots to release. I'm sure by the time they do, my heat will have me ready for more.

Basel kisses my eyelids and Fynn licks my neck, waking me from my catnap. I whimper and twist, feeling feverish, needing them to fuck me again. Instead, Basel pulls out and gives me a kiss on the lips before backing away. I try to hold on to him until Salem slides in next to me. He meets my lips with his own and I forget about anything else as I taste him for the first time, peppery and earthy.

The kisses on my neck turn rougher as Roman takes Fynn's place, the stubble from his short beard abrading me.

Salem strokes my face before leaning back for Roman to take a turn. I eagerly turn to him, Salem's taste mingling with Roman's apple pie. I savor the scents of my alphas mixing in my nest, my perfume blooming around us.

I slide my leg over Salem's hip and arch into Roman, confident now that I know I can take two of them like this. I'm eager to get them inside me as my heat roars to an inferno, and I whine when they're not quick enough for my liking.

I'm startled out of my pout when Salem rolls back and Roman helps me up onto him. They set me on Salem's cock where it lays across his stomach, gliding me along it. Roman kneels over him at my back to grind against me. I brace myself on Salem's shoulders to rub myself against them. Roman palms my breasts and his cock teases past my entrance as I move. I try to angle my hips so the head will slide inside on his next pass, but Roman grips the hair at the back of my head and holds me up to keep teasing me. My protesting whine turns into a squeak when my nipple is pinched. I blink down at Salem's crooked smile as he tugs on it.

"Don't rush us," Salem warns me sternly, though he's still smiling. I pant at his commanding air. Roman gently bites my ear while Salem holds me under their control. I squeak and moan as they combine pleasure with light pinches as they play with my breasts. Slick floods over Salem's cock and stomach and he bucks up against me.

Salem works his hand between us to squeeze his fingers on either side of my clit. He traps my clit between his knuckles at the same time they close their fingers on my nipples. The orgasm slams into me, the feelings zinging between those points and freezing me in place.

My mouth falls open when I come, and I taste glazed pumpkin cookies. Salem releases my hair for Phoenix to take over as he works his cock deeper. I moan around it, sucking and licking to get more of his taste on my tongue. Phoenix brushes my cheek with one hand and grips my hair with the other as he fucks my mouth.

"Good girl," he growls.

I'm so focused on Phoenix that I don't notice the others have readjusted until Salem pulls me onto his cock, my slick making it easy for him to fully seat himself in my pussy. My eyes roll back and jaw goes slack, and Phoenix takes the opportunity to slide further down my throat. He teases me with his rhythm, fluctuating between letting me get a quick breath or a longer one between strokes. Once I've taken all of him and my nose touches his public bone, Phoenix holds me there. Behind me, Roman uses his thumbs to spread me to take him too. I whine, but it gets caught on Phoenix's cock. Salem is content to lay sheathed in me while Roman thrusts, stimulating both of us.

I'm stuffed full, throbbing around my alphas. Before I start to feel fluttery from lack of oxygen, Phoenix pulls back and lets me breathe, saliva stringing from my lips to his cock. When Phoenix brushes past my lips again, I watch as he fucks me, still stroking my face gently as he does. I'm happy to let him take control. I know he'll stop if I want him to, but I don't. Not until he comes in me at least, then maybe I'll taste one of the others.

While I enjoy my view of Phoenix, which is the only thing I can see anyway, Roman bites along my neck between thrusts. His teasing causes tingles to spread down my spine until I almost can't take it. Roman grips my hips hard, his thrusts getting wilder and rougher, and his bites become more untamed. Roman's teeth linger and press in harder.

My eyelids flutter at the thought that one of them might slip and bond me anyway, even though they're trying to hold back. I enjoy having that power over them, that they know they have to stop their alphas from claiming me right away. My omega wants the same thing, but during brief moments of coherence, I realize I shouldn't push them on it, so I don't beg for it. Much.

I try to tilt my head to give Roman better access, but I can't with Phoenix holding me. My omega is satisfied that my alphas are holding me between them and not letting me get away. I wouldn't want to be anywhere else.

Salem's knot grows, forcing Roman to work harder with each stroke. Salem locks me on his lap, my pussy fluttering with the beginning of my orgasm and massaging his knot as he comes. I whine, the sound cut off as Phoenix pushes forward again. As his cock slides past my tongue, the flavor is spicier than before.

Phoenix moves deep, and his knot swells behind my teeth. The idea of being stuck on his cock makes me come as warmth pours down my throat. After a few more thrusts, Roman's knot fills me too, locking us together. My connections to them blur until it seems like we're one.

I barely twitch as Phoenix pulls out and I gasp in a breath. Some of this come dribbles down the side of my mouth. They lower me onto Salem, since I'm still stuck on two of my alphas. I lay bonelessly on his chest as I catch my breath. Roman leans over us to kiss the side of my head. After a few minutes, they shift us to the side so Roman can lay down too. He curls around me, purring as I drift off to sleep.

This time a deeper sleep takes me, my omega satisfied with getting come from all my alphas. For now, at least. The heat is still several days away from being over.

CHAPTER 24

FYNN

I slam the door in the delivery guy's face. He was using his nose way too much while dropping off our food. I couldn't be more smug about having my omega's scent covering me (and her slick coating my cock), but that guy shouldn't be sniffing around her things. And I count myself as belonging to her.

I turn all the locks on the door, glad Seph takes her safety seriously, and make my way back to the nest with the food. It's been a full day, or maybe two, of Seph's heat. The pack has been keeping her happy, giving her plenty of knots and come to satisfy her omega. In between that, we ate through all the food she had ready in the fridge. We've been ordering takeout whenever we have a spare minute from sleeping or fucking. Not that I'm complaining. For her next heat, though, we'll have to stock up on food beforehand, so no delivery people get near my omega while she's vulnerable. Like Basel mentioned, we'll have to learn more of her favorite foods when we're not preoccupied like this. I wonder if Seph's tastes change during her heat. I'll have to ask her later.

I return to the nest to find Seph has woken from her nap and trapped Nix underneath her. Roman takes the opportunity to slide in from behind. I unpack our food while watching the three of them. Salem has also woken up and is sprawled on his side, watching. Basel is still passed out on his front at the other end of the bed. He's been wearing himself thin servicing Seph in addition to making sure she's hydrated, eating, and resting enough. That doesn't leave him much time to care for himself. It's good he's sleeping now. I might've had to knock him out if he kept that up.

I know he feels strongly about Seph, but we all do. It's not like we'll get lost in a rut and let her faint from hunger. I'm not likely to be the first person you'd ask for help with something like watering your plants while you're on vacation. Just because I play with a little fire on occasion doesn't mean I don't know how to keep Seph safe. Basel will have to learn he's not the only one who's responsible for caring for our mate. Plus, I *have* been taking good care of Seph's plants while she's too busy to water them. I'll have to show them to Seph and Basel later once her heat is over. I'm sure they'll be impressed.

I eat the orange chicken and noodles, chugging water in between bites, while I wait for them to finish so I can bring them food. Salem seems content to watch for now, so I don't make him a plate yet. I refill my own and drink a few more bottles of water.

Seph whines and writhes between Nix and Roman as they knot her. They purr and growl while they play with her. Eventually the group settles, though they'll be locked together for a while still.

I prepare their plates, and Salem helps me carry the food and water over. I bring Basel's plate too, but set it nearby for when he wakes up. Roman and Nix sit up so

Nix can lean against the wall with Seph held between them. I hand over Roman and Nix's plates and hold Seph's so I can feed her. She looks at me with unfocused eyes and I bring a bottle up to her lips for her to drink. She eagerly opens her mouth, making my cock throb. That decides my plans for her once she's fed. After drinking half the bottle, I switch to feeding her forkfuls of beef and noodles. She'll need the calories and protein to keep up with the demands of her heat. I don't want her left feeling exhausted and crashing when it ends in a few days.

I alternate kissing her forehead and wiping the sauce off her face as I feed her. When her chewing slows, I know I've filled her up enough, at least with food. I have her drink a little more water, then kiss the top of her head as I stand to take the dishes away. Salem is already getting seconds. I come back to refill Roman and Nix's plates while Seph rests on Nix's chest.

Everyone finishes eating, except for Basel, who still hasn't woken up. I lay next to Seph and watch her sleep while the others also settle down to rest. When Basel eventually wakes up, I point out his plate at the edge of the nest. He comes over to check on Seph first, who is sleeping deeply on Nix. Their knots released a little while ago, and Roman moved off of her to rest nearby. Basel strokes across her skin and kisses her shoulders as he reassures himself that we haven't exhausted her while he slept for a few meager hours. I raise an eyebrow at him. Basel gives me an apologetic smile but still asks how much she ate and drank. I tell him, and once he's satisfied Seph has been taken care of, he finally eats his own food.

When Seph wakes up later, I steal her off a sleeping Nix. I move us to the side and lay her on her back. I kiss her lips gently as I wait for her to fully wake up. Seph smiles and kisses me back, opening her eyes after I pull away.

"Good morning, doll," I whisper.

"G'morning," she replies with a yawn. "Is it actually morning?" she asks with a cute head tilt. Her movement makes me eye her neck with lust. I almost want her heat to end now so she's thinking clearly enough for us to ask about bonding. Seph wanted to bond already, but my packmates are right. You can't trust that feelings will be the same after a heat. We did only ask to court her a day ago. Or is it two? I still haven't figured it out.

I bring my eyes back to her face to chase the toothy thoughts from my mind. I grin as I answer her question, "I'm not sure. But it's always a good time when I'm with you. So good morning, good afternoon, and good evening." I tell her with a kiss between each greeting. She giggles and kisses me back.

I brush my hand across her hair as I lean over her. "Whatever time it is, do you want me to help you clean up?"

Seph blushes. "Only if you want to. I'm sure I need it, but I can do it myself."

"I'll do it. It will be my pleasure," I tell her firmly.

I slide down to lick across her neck. She squeaks and giggles as I work my way across it. I've tongued my way down to her breasts by the time she thinks to question me.

"Fynn! I thought we were going to shower."

"Why would you think that?" I pop my head up briefly to reply before going back to licking and sucking her nipples.

She moans and wiggles under me before responding, "You said you were going to clean me up."

"I am. Now stay there and be a good girl while I lick the come and slick off you."

She gasps at my words, and I go back to focusing on my task. Seph has no more questions, and I make my way to her pussy without further protest. I do a thorough job of cleaning her to make room for more come. I suppose going through her heat without a bond isn't so bad. I take my time and savor the moans and whines as fresh slick slides down my chin and her hands grip my hair. I feel my alpha leading me into a rut. I'll have to knot her soon. As my brain turns off all thought except for fucking Seph, the last idea to come through is the hope that we'll be bonded before her next heat.

CHAPTER 25
PERSEPHONE

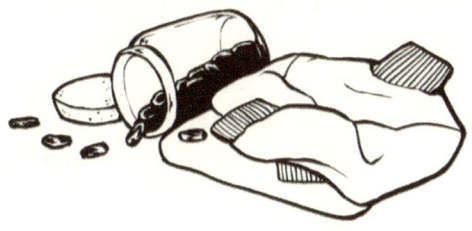

I yawn and try to stretch my legs, but they're tangled in something and don't move much. I give up and relax on the mattress with a sigh. I'm so cozy and warm, but it feels like it's time to get up. I rub my face on the pillow, which is firmer than I remember it being, but it's silky smooth so I don't mind. As my mind wakes up, I think about what I have to do today.

I'll have to stop by the greenhouse to see the progress. I was mapping out the pop-up to show the builders and see if they'll make the shelves I added to the sketch. Did I finish my sketch? I remember deciding where the various products would go, apple cider here, pumpkin coffee there. I don't recall drawing the apple baskets. Did I put them next to the table of pumpkins? I shift as I try to puzzle out what I chose, bumping into another firm pillow. When did I buy all these hard pillows? I'm usually a soft girl. No hard, uncomfortable beds for me, thank you. Though these aren't uncomfortable, they're not what I usually use.

Now I remember, I was just getting to the apple baskets when I got a phone call...

I gasp and sit up, or try to, getting caught in the arms and legs spread across me. I flop back on the mattress with a grunt. As the mattress grunts back, the events of the past few days surfaces. The scary phone call that led to me calling Basel in a panic, but I ended up talking to Phoenix, *my* Phoenix, who came over. The rest of the pack joining us and helping me through my heat.

I blush as I recall our contortions.

"Are you okay, Seph?" Basel asks from somewhere next to me.

I bury my face into the chest beneath me, by the scent it's Salem, and smile. Despite how quickly things progressed after Phoenix arrived, I don't regret agreeing to let them court me and spending my heat with them.

Courting! Me! I never thought I'd let any alphas court me. Now, my scent matches surround me after helping me through the best heat I've ever had. And I guess it's good we didn't rush into bonding during my heat. I know at some point I'll ask them to bite me into the pack when I'm not hormone addled.

"I'm great," I clear my throat, not having used it much for talking recently. Just other noises—and uses—that my throat isn't accustomed to. "I'm very great," I try again. "How are you guys?" I ask into Salem's chest. His chest vibrates with a quiet laugh beneath me.

"We're all great," Fynn says from somewhere near my legs. He climbs his way up my body. "Though I'm a bit dehydrated, I think, since I've been making so much come for you," he finishes with a whisper in my ear.

I blush harder, glad my face is still hidden. I'm not sure I'll get used to Fynn's dirty talk. Or any of theirs, really. They all had some interesting things to say during my heat.

I enjoyed it, I just wish my face didn't broadcast how much their words affect me.

"Well, that was very kind of you," I tell Fynn.

They all laugh now. Fynn squeezes me in a hug as much as he can with the others still wrapped around me.

"I take it the heat has broken?" Phoenix asks at my back. I turn my head to smile at him. I've missed him so much. Despite the unsettling things he said, I never stopped thinking about him and wishing he was with me.

"It seems like it," I say.

"Do you want to get up and see what day it is?" Salem says. "We can clean up and go to the kitchen for a meal. You're not too sore, are you?"

"I don't feel any worse than I do after a long hike. But getting cleaned up would be nice. In the shower," I add, to clarify for Fynn. He just laughs.

We disentangle ourselves and get out of the nest. Phoenix helps me sit up, and Fynn carries me to the bathroom. Luckily this apartment building is pack friendly, so the shower is big enough to fit three of us. The others leave to use the shower next to the spare bedroom.

Phoenix turns on the water and adjusts it. When it's the perfect, almost scalding temperature, he motions for Fynn to carry me inside. Fynn sets me on my feet, and they hold me between them while we rinse off. They wash and condition my hair, and I do the same for them. Fynn washes my legs and feet, while Phoenix steadies me. Fynn reaches around to wash the back of my thighs, and as I squirm at the ticklish sensation, I feel Phoenix's hard cock behind me. I don't know how he isn't out of stamina by now.

While Phoenix distracted me, Fynn pulled my thighs apart, ostensibly to clean them, until I feel his tongue between my legs. I grab his hair to tilt his head back, but he doesn't follow my gentle tug and I don't want to yank on his hair. I can't shift my hips backward with Phoenix behind me.

"Fynn! I said we were only in here to clean up!" I tell him in a stern tone, that's not breathy or needy at all.

His tongue leaves me, and he tilts his face up just enough that I can see his eyes.

"No, you said you'd get clean in the shower. And that's what we're doing," he says, voice muffled.

His eyes crinkle at the corners in amusement, and he returns to tonguing me. I moan and give another half-hearted attempt at wiggling away. They don't have to keep making me come, my heat is over. I thought they would be worn out or maybe even bored of doing this.

Phoenix chuckles and holds me in place for Fynn's ministrations. The steam from the shower swirls around us and rivulets of water run across my skin. I suppose we *are* getting cleaned up this way. I relax and let myself get swept away.

Thirty minutes later, we're out of the shower and dried off. Salem helps me look through my clothes for whatever soft and cozy outfit calls to me. The guys put on their clean clothes that they ran through the wash at some point.

I've looked through half my clothing rack and I'm on the third dresser drawer when I find my stretchy white knit sweats. I make a noise of appreciation as I pull the cozy pants on. Salem helps me stuff the other clothes back in the drawer so I can close it. I return to the closet and find a gray sweatshirt buried in the back. I'm already wearing long fuzzy pink socks, so the sweatshirt completes my ensemble.

We venture out into the kitchen where the rest of the pack has gathered. They're having a whispered conversation that cuts off when Salem and I enter. Before I worry that they're having second thoughts about me, they welcome me over.

Basel stands up to hug me, then leads me to sit on one of the stools at my kitchen island. Roman sets an opened bottle of water in front of me and Phoenix is close behind with a plate of cinnamon apple brioche donuts and bacon croissant sandwiches. I drink some of the water and start on the donuts. Just as I think about asking if anyone made coffee, Roman sets a cup in front of me that smells like pumpkin and has whipped cream sprinkled with pumpkin pie spice. I give him a grateful smile and take a sip.

Heaven. Thank goodness the heat hormones overpower the withdrawal I'd normally get from suddenly not drinking coffee for days. That first sip post-heat is always amazing, but this one is better than the best. It's made perfectly with the finest whipped cream and spices, and it was made by my alphas. My pack!

It's hard to believe I have a pack now. They're not *officially* mine yet since we haven't bonded, but they are officially courting me, so I'm counting it. I grin as I take a second sip, some of the coffee tickling down the corner of my mouth. Fynn is quick to lick it away. Will he ever run out of energy? I look forward to finding out. I eye him speculatively, and he eyes me back, and before I know it, he's leaning in again. Basel pushes him back with a warning look. The spell broken, I resume eating my food before I try to eat something else.

I work my way through breakfast (apparently it's 10 am, so a good time to start the day), while the others check on what we missed during my heat. Basel says work at the greenhouse is progressing well in our absence. He was able to send some directions during heat breaks. The others check on their work and the news, reading the important or interesting headlines out loud for us.

One article says a giant Flemish rabbit got loose in Starsfalls on Thursday and terrorized a grocery store. It had a standoff with police for hours before they lured it away from the produce section and into a cage to return it home. I almost choke on a piece of bacon when Salem reports that the rabbit took down two officers before the standoff ended. The officers were taken to the local hospital to treat minor injuries and bruised egos.

After finishing the food, I sip my coffee while they read the rest of the news. I'm busy savoring a mouthful of the dark roast with a dollop of sweet pumpkin cream when I notice they've gone quiet. I open my eyes to see everyone looking serious. I set down my coffee and prepare myself for whatever's weighing on their minds.

Basel starts, "Nix filled us in on the details from your call. Is there anything you recognize about the woman who contacted you? Roman can look into her if you give him the number she called you from."

Fynn wraps his arms around me from behind and purrs comfortingly. I lean into him, but I don't really need the soothing effects. Now that a few days have passed since the phone call, or now that I've been fucked silly, I'm not as upset about the woman's accusations. Obviously I'm not happy someone thinks I'm trying to copy them, but it seems like the best thing I can do is continue with my plans. This woman will see that our pop-up is unique once it's open.

"I still don't recognize her voice," I tell them. "You can pull her number from my phone, but I'm not as worried about it now." I look at Phoenix with chagrin. "Sorry I freaked out on you and made you rush over." I frown as I remember how quickly he seemed to get here. Do tears affect how you perceive time? "How did you get here so fast? Were you already bringing Basel's phone to Starsfalls?"

"I called one of our helicopters to take me over so I could get here quickly. And I'm glad you called. You can come to us for help at any time. Besides, that was the best phone call of my life since it brought us back together," Phoenix says sweetly, reaching over to hold my hand. It sits limply in his, as I'm too busy gaping at him to respond.

"Did-did you say you took a *helicopter* to get here?" I squeak out.

Phoenix grins and continues rubbing his thumb along the back of my hand. "I did."

He doesn't say anything else. What. The. Fuck. Who just has a *helicopter* on speed dial? Do they have a yacht on speed dial too? Or an airship? Wait, I could get behind an airship. So steampunk.

"We're not asshole billionaires who have our own space program or something. We have business meetings across the country and internationally, and sometimes need to get to them quickly. So our pack has a small fleet of private planes and helicopters," I hear Roman say.

I tune back in to the conversation, which I realize has continued without me while I was daydreaming about what I'd wear to travel on my airship. And where would I go? I could bring Stasia and visit the castles in Acock-upon-Hunipott. The airship would fit in perfectly with the architecture there. My alphas are starting to look worried. I need to respond to the whole helicopter thing.

"It's fine, I just didn't expect it. I mean, I knew when we

were kids that your family pack was rich, Phoenix, but I haven't thought about it much. Um, as long as you're aware I'm not super well off. I can take us out on date nights and stuff, but we'll probably have to drive." I giggle nervously.

I didn't need to worry though, as my alphas practically trip over themselves to reassure me it doesn't matter how much money I have. They also argue that they would prefer to pay for us, anyway.

"I know it seems 'traditional,' but the thought of providing for you makes us feel good. We don't want to control the money, we want to share what we have with you. But if you don't like that, we can discuss other ways of splitting things," Basel says.

"If you're sure, that's fine with me. I know most alphas prefer to provide for their omegas. I just wanted you to know I don't expect it. I have my own money to pay for things, and I want to treat you guys well, too."

"You already are a treat, doll," Fynn says while nuzzling the back of my hair. I roll my eyes at him even though he can't see it.

The others agree they're happy to share what they have, no strings attached. Now that we've settled that, we return to the issue we were discussing before they distracted me with airships. I ask them to hand me my phone. I see it plugged in on the kitchen counter, so one of them must have put it on to charge. Roman hands it over, and I unlock it and pull up the number of the mystery caller. I look it over, but don't recognize it. Not surprising, since I don't have many phone numbers memorized. I give my phone back to Roman for him to copy the number.

"Assuming the number wasn't spoofed, it belongs to Lili Kuragari. Her address is listed in town. Do you recognize the name?" Roman looks up to ask me.

"No, it doesn't sound familiar," I reply in consternation. I didn't recognize her voice, so I guess it's not strange that I don't know her. Starsfalls is small, but not that small. I don't know everyone who lives here. Still, I thought her name would be familiar at least. I don't even know anyone with that last name.

Roman goes back to checking something on his phone, then holds it out for me to see. "This is her social media account. She has pictures of herself at the Autumnfalls Festival over the years. I don't see anything in her stall that stands out compared to the booths nearby."

I take the phone from him and flip through more of her photos. She has long, straight black hair and a cheerful smile as she sells candles to customers. I don't know how I haven't seen Lili at the festival before. I bought candied pecans and vanilla pumpkin lotion from the booths on either side of hers. Lili's booth has tons of candles in antique tins. I would have bought dozens of those if I'd seen them. Roman is right, her booth is nice, but it's nothing out of the ordinary. The other products she sells, like apple cider and wool scarves, are sold by several others. We're not selling anything like her candles, so I don't know how we could be copying her.

"I don't know what she thinks we're trying to copy. Our setup will be completely different since it's in a greenhouse. Maybe she's confused me for someone else, because I don't think we've ever met in person," I say, returning his phone.

"Maybe so. We'll call her back and let her know she's made a mistake," Roman assures me.

"I don't think we need to do that. She didn't leave any messages while we were busy. I'm sure we can ignore her and move on. Lili will see for herself at the festival that we didn't copy her," I repeat. I know it's good to stand up for yourself, but this seems like an unnecessary confrontation I can avoid.

"She greatly upset you with her accusations. I think it's best to let her know that what she said was unprofessional and inappropriate," Phoenix says.

"I don't know," I hedge. Maybe she's already forgotten about me and calling her will make her mad all over again.

No one says anything, but a few of them shift subtly, and they're avoiding eye contact with each other.

I narrow my eyes at them (minus Fynn, since he's still busy nuzzling the back of my neck).

"What is it?" I demand.

"I received messages from the builders that a woman tried to stop them from working on the greenhouse. They didn't get her name, but I'm assuming it's Lili. They said she told them they couldn't build the shelves the way they were laid out. The builders called Belinda, and she kicked the woman out and forbade her from coming back. Since Lili threatened to stop the vendors from working with us, I think we should contact them to make sure she won't be able to interfere with our business," Basel says.

I tense at his words and Fynn purrs harder around me. Will the vendors ignore Lili like the builders did, or will they listen to her? I turn my worried gaze to Roman. He was with me when I visited many of the vendors. Does he think they won't work with us anymore?

"I'll call around and make sure we're still set to order from the vendors we liked. I didn't want to call without talking to you first and deciding how we wanted to handle this," Roman says.

"You can call and make sure our orders are still in place. Maybe wait to bring up Lili though and see if they mention her," I say.

I'm sure the vendors won't start selling exclusively to one person this year, but it will ease my mind to call and make sure. I gently dislodge Fynn and get up to find my notes with the vendor list. Fynn follows me back and forth as I carry my notebook back to the kitchen island. I write out a cleaned-up list of the vendors and the products we're ordering from them and give it to Roman.

"These are the vendors we'll definitely want to use. We could contact a few to see if they heard from Lili. If she hasn't said anything to them, then she probably hasn't tried to blacklist us," I say.

"I'll say I'm calling to check that they're still taking orders," Roman says while looking through my list.

"Later this week we'll pay Lili a visit and tell her not to bother you," Fynn says while Roman dials.

I turn my head squint at Fynn. "There's no reason to threaten people. I don't want you guys getting in trouble," I whisper to him.

"We can see what the suppliers say before we decide, but she did try to obstruct my workers at the greenhouse. It would be fair to warn her away if she keeps interfering with our work," Basel says quietly.

I frown but don't respond, listening in with the others on Roman's side of the call.

"We wanted to make sure you still had supplies available for the fall festival," Roman says, pausing while they reply. "That's good to hear. I have a purchase order for the festival ready to send over." He talks about logistics like the delivery date before ending the call.

"So? Had Lili called them?" I ask uncertainly.

"She talked to them about us. The vendor said they don't do exclusive contracts for the festival and that's what they told Lili. She didn't seem happy about it, but they aren't going to limit their business like that," Roman says.

I let out the breath I was holding, but it's hard to take another one. I'm glad the vendors don't want to be exclusive, but I can't believe someone I don't even know was trying to cut me out of the festival! How many people has she talked to about this? Surely no one I know would believe what Lili's saying.

"We'll get her to stop," Fynn repeats.

I chew anxiously on my lip.

"I can talk to Lili myself and tell her to leave our business alone, or we can go through our lawyers," Basel says.

That sounds cool and professional. Just two businesses in disagreement, working things out as they set up their "competing" storefronts. This isn't about a person spreading rumors about me and trying to hurt me personally. I can deal with that. I relax at the thought that it's not personal. Yes, the lawyers can handle it.

"Wait, we have lawyers?" I ask.

Basel smiles while Phoenix and Roman chuckle.

"Yes, I have lawyers on retainer for my business contracts. The pack has lawyers for personal matters, and there are lawyers for several of the other's businesses too. You don't have to worry, we'll get this taken care of. We'll do everything within our power to help you, Seph. Between the five of us, we have contacts who can get almost anything you could ask for," Basel assures me.

"Like helicopter pilots?" I ask teasingly.

"Yes, like helicopter pilots," he says with a laugh.

Other things in my life are going well, so I don't need the pack to sweep in and fix everything. This Lili situation is the only problem I have that needs to be taken care of. Well, that and my issues with alphas and omegas and no longer being able to suppress my heats. But my pack has already taken very good care of that. I'm tingly again just from the thought of the last few days, and a wisp of my perfume sneaks out. Fynn growls and rubs his cheek against mine.

"I'm sure Seph wants to check on the greenhouse now that her heat is over," Basel reminds him.

"We don't want to put her life on hold," Phoenix adds.

Fynn grumbles into my hair while I blush.

"Fine," he agrees, but turns my face for a deep, licking kiss. That does nothing to lessen my perfume cloud.

Fynn sets me on my feet, and I stagger off to grab my things. We'll visit the greenhouse together, as a pack. I grin as I collect my purse and stuff my notes inside. It's a comfort to have supportive alphas who are helping me achieve my goals.

CHAPTER 26

PERSEPHONE

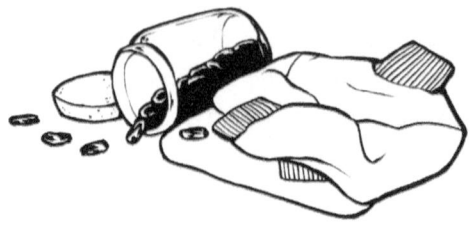

W e pile into one of the pack's large SUVs, since it fits all of them plus me, pressed between Salem and Basel in the middle seats. Fynn leans close in the back seat, while Phoenix is in the front seat and Roman drives. They offered to let me take the front, but this way several of my alphas can sit close to me. Omegas need reassurance after a heat, and it's nice to be close to alphas now after spending my life avoiding them. Damn omega hormones were right that alphas and omegas balance each other out. Pack life really does suit us.

We arrive at Pen and Tellem without incident (by which I mean Fynn was prevented from pulling me into the back seat to continue the kiss he gave me before we left). When we enter the bookstore, I wave to Alice as we pass by the front desk. She waves back distractedly, barely looking up from her book. I peek at the cover and see it's another one in the Big Tex series, *Big Tex and the Boots with the Spurs*.

I lead the way back to the greenhouse to see what we missed during my heat. I hear hammering and metallic clangs as we approach. Sounds like the builders are hard at work despite our absence. Roman holds the door open, and I gasp as I step inside. The sun streams through the glass roof, making the dark wood furniture gleam and the concrete planters glitter. I walk to the center of the room and spin to take it all in.

The windows are clean and most of the broken ones have been repaired or replaced. Currently the builders are fixing the metal braces on the roof. Others are setting up a shelf next to one that's already anchored to the wall. I spot several new wooden chairs of different styles. Some are thick and sturdy, like they belong around a Viking's dinner table, while others are small and ornate, more at home in an old palace with golden walls and velvet furnishings. I stroke along the different chairs, trying to determine if they're antique or modern reproductions.

"Do you like them?" Roman asks.

"They're amazing! Where did they come from? I love the different styles, we can mix and match them around the long tables. I never thought of styling different periods together like this."

Roman is pleased by my praise. "I found them at antique stores here and there when we were out sourcing materials around the valley. I had them sent over to see if you like them. Since they're wood, I thought they would fit with your style, but if you don't like some of them, we can take them out. Or if they don't fit here, we can move them to your apartment."

I launch myself at him almost before he's finished.

"Thank you, thank you! This is so nice! I love them all, they're perfect here," I say into his chest as I squeeze him.

Roman chuckles and rubs my back. "Good, I'm glad you

like them. I was planning to offer them as a courting gift. I didn't have time to arrange them here myself, so they're not wrapped or anything. I hope you'll still accept them as a gift, though."

"Of course I will! How would you wrap a chair, anyway? They're great, Roman, I love them. Thank you," I tell him sincerely.

"How *were* you going to wrap the chairs?" Fynn asks sarcastically.

"I was going to tie bows on them or something. I hadn't decided yet," Roman mutters and hugs me tighter.

When we separate, I blush and straighten my clothes. I'd forgotten the builders were here. I'm not usually one for public displays of affection. I'm so used to hiding that I'm an omega, I've always avoided doing anything that could draw attention to me, like PDA.

Oh shit.

I'm an omega. I forgot to use my descenting soap and sprays today! I discreetly sniff myself and stiffen as I smell my actual scent under the alpha smells covering me. There's no need to hide my designation anymore, but I didn't even think about it before we left this morning. I just waltzed through the bookstore without a care as to who could smell me. Alice didn't say anything, but she was pretty engrossed in her Big Tex book. I should have told Stasia about this first. I don't want her to hear it from someone else. It's usually big news when someone's designation is revealed, especially if they're a late bloomer like people will think I am.

I take a few steps toward the door and then back as I decide if I should go to the coffee shop right now to tell Stasia or not. Is she even at Quickie Coffee today? I'm not sure what day it is. I make little progress in determining the best course of action as I pace back and forth.

"Are you alright, Seph?" Roman asks, following along with me to rub my back. Fynn paces with us too, stroking my hair. They're watching me with concern, but I'm too focused on my thoughts to respond.

"That cat's out of the bag, I see," Belinda booms as she strides into the greenhouse.

"It's not! My cat is covered. Nothing's been in my bag. I mean, what cat? What's going on?" I fumble to deny. How does she know I slept with them? Their scents *are* all over me, but that just means we've been close. It doesn't necessarily mean we had sex. I showered after the last time, so she couldn't be smelling that. Belinda is asking about my cat, though. Unless she was talking to one of the builders about their cat, which seems inappropriate for a boss to mention to their employee.

One builder scoffs and another smothers a laugh. I glare in their direction, but none of them are looking our way. Meanwhile Fynn snickers right next to me! Isn't he supposed to help me if I'm trying to hide something?

Belinda's lips quirk in a smile, but she doesn't laugh. "I thought you said you weren't an omega. It's obvious by your scent now that you are. Did you just present? I've heard that happens sometimes when the hormones are slow to kick in. There was a guy who presented as an omega by perfuming while playing in a professional football game. There were a bunch of alphas on the field, it was a mess. Plus, presenting that late must be a real mindfuck. Maybe I should have started off by asking if you're doing okay, but you look pretty happy."

I relax and stop giving Fynn a dirty look (not that kind) out of the corner of my eye.

217

"I am happy. I've actually known I was an omega for years, but hid it well to avoid dealing with unwanted attention. I'm sorry I didn't tell you the truth," I explain awkwardly. I hope my friends aren't too upset I omitted the truth.

Okay, I lied to them. It's not that I don't trust them, I just didn't want the omega part of me to influence my life. Now that I've accepted good things can come from being an omega, I'm okay with letting the cat out of the bag, as Belinda put it.

It almost looks like Belinda smothers a laugh before she replies, but I don't know why she would be.

"Well, you did a great job hiding it. Totally had no idea you were an omega using scent blockers. I'm glad you feel comfortable enough to come out now." Belinda turns to my alphas. "I assume that has something to do with your handsome alphas here? Glad to see you and Basel are getting along so well."

"I'm not sure you've met the rest of my pack," Basel introduces the others.

"We asked to court Seph, and she agreed, so we're officially dating," Roman says.

"Congratulations! You make a cute pack, I'm so happy for you. And just in time for fall! You can do all the fun fall relationship activities, like apple picking, going to a pumpkin patch, and, of course, attending the Autumnfalls Festival. I've always wanted to go on a hayride with a date so I could act out a historical peasant romance in the back of a wagon," Belinda sighs wistfully.

That's an interesting fantasy. Hay is too itchy for my taste. Now, if there were some nice plaid blankets over the hay bales, that could be fun ride...

"We've already been apple picking at Ladon's Garden,

so we're working our way through the fall things. We're helping with the greenhouse, but once it's done, there will be plenty of time still to enjoy the festival and all the other autumn things," Roman says.

"That's sweet, it's a pack effort. How is the pop-up planning going?" Belinda asks me.

I gulp. This is my opening to ask about Lili and see if Belinda knows her.

"Well..." I hesitate.

Roman jumps in when he sees me struggling. "It's going well. Seph has great ideas with something for everyone to enjoy. We checked out several vendors and we're finalizing our supply orders. Although, we heard a strange story from the builders, that a woman was trying to stop them from working in here?"

Belinda rolls her eyes. "Yeah, Lili came by the other day while you were on leave."

I blush, not used to people assuming I was on heat leave. It is the obvious conclusion when alphas and their omega disappear for days. Guess I'll have to get used to it. At least that means I don't have to come up with an illness to hide from Stasia and get out of work several times each year. I smile after realizing I'll never have to go through a heat alone again. That's worth people knowing we've been fucking for days.

With the thought of my alphas buoying me, I'm emboldened enough to ask about Lili, "Do you know her?"

"I don't think she's been in the bookstore before, but she looked familiar. I've probably seen her around town."

At least Belinda didn't have to ban a paying customer. As long as Lili doesn't get Belinda's actual customers to boycott Pen and Tellem, it sounds like this shouldn't affect the bookstore.

"I don't recognize her either. Hopefully she stays away now," I say

"I've told my employees to keep her out, and Alice got her to leave quickly when Lili tried to come back yesterday," Belinda assures me.

"She came back already?" I thought after she was kicked out the first time she'd give up, or at least not come back to the bookstore. I barely hold in a distressed whine. My pack shifts closer, and Fynn wraps his arm around me. I guess the guys were right, we'll have to confront the situation with Lili directly.

"Hey, don't worry. Maybe Lili came by for the books that time, they have a way of drawing you in. I don't know that she was coming back to complain about our pop-up," Belinda backtracks.

I'm glad I don't have to deal with this alone. Belinda, Alice, and the other bookstore staff will keep Lili away. It sounded like the vendors are ignoring her too. Stasia and Grey will back me up once I tell them. Ugh, I might have to mention this to Marlene in case Lili tries to find me at Quickie Coffee. Stasia would have texted me if someone came by the cafe looking for me. That might still be a safe place.

"We'll keep going with our current plans for the pop-up. Basel and the builders are on schedule so we should be ready in time for the festival. I brought my notes so we can discuss my ideas for the pop-up and get your input," I tell Belinda while digging in my purse for my notebook and pen.

"I'd love to go over it. I can't wait for the town to decorate for autumn." Belinda clasps her hands against her heart in longing anticipation.

We leave the builders to their work and head into the

princes room to sit on the comfortable chairs while we discuss our plans.

I finish taking notes of Belinda's ideas for the festival, along with a few suggestions from my alphas. I smile after updating the sketch of what the space will look like with the new furniture and shelves. Everything is coming together with the support of my friends and alphas.

Belinda recommended more sellers to check out for things like soap and wool products. Her suggestions have been a big help, and she seems to know all the businesses in town. It must be because she coordinates with the town council and other businesses for the festivals. Quickie Coffee decorates and sells seasonal products too, but the baristas aren't more involved than that. Marlene was the only one who went to the town planning meetings and local business association groups.

Except for a slight hiccup named Lili, I feel good about our pop-up plans and timeline for the restoration. Every construction project and big event has one issue to overcome. This was ours, and it wasn't that bad.

Despite the added pressure, I've remained a consummate professional throughout. I sit up and straighten my sweatshirt, brushing off the crumbs from the breakfast croissants. I went from being an interior plant decorator to restoring a historic building and planning the grand opening to coincide with one of the biggest festivals in Starsfalls. At the same time, I overcame my nervousness around alphas. That last issue is more about my personal life, and it *may* have been caused by my own stubbornness and denial, but still. I've had a lot of personal growth these past few weeks. I deserve to be proud of myself. I brush a few more stray crumbs off my sweatpants and listen as Belinda tells us about the upcoming events at the bookstore.

"I have some fantasy authors coming to promote their new books and do signings. Their series are amazing and they're really popular on social media. Honestly, I'm excited for them to come just so I can meet them. I know we'll have lots of local booklovers come to the events, and I think we'll be able to draw a crowd from the surrounding cities too."

"I'm sure you will. Boarwood has some great bookstores, but Pen and Tellem is unique. It's worth the drive even when there's not an author signing," Salem tells her sincerely.

He's so sweet, and I'm glad there's a fellow booklover in my pack. I smile dreamily at him. He sees me staring and responds with a smile and a wink. Is it too soon to drag them back to my nest?

"Thank you, that's great to hear. I like visiting bookstores with different aesthetics. It makes the book hunt more interesting while you search for new books to love. I want Pen and Tellem to be a place where people are happy to spend hours browsing, reading, or relaxing. That's another reason I'm looking forward to our pop-up. I want people to hang out and enjoy the space."

"They will! Everyone who visits loves this place. If we draw in people who haven't been here before, I'm sure they'll turn into repeat customers. Pen and Tellem is a special place," I say. Who wouldn't love a bookstore like this? There's always more to discover, especially with the addition of the greenhouse.

"I bet the bookstore is even more special for you now.

Can I brag that this is the place where you met your alphas?" Belinda says with a chuckle.

"Tell everyone that comes in! 'Seph found her mates here.' You could get a plaque and everything. We're great marketing. Don't all booklovers have a soft spot for romance?" Fynn teases, though he has a possessive look in his eyes. My heart (and other areas) throb at his claim.

"This place will always be special for our pack," Basel says more seriously.

"I can never thank you enough for bringing us back together," Phoenix adds. I melt into his side, and he wraps his arm around me.

"Awww," Belinda coos while I stare into Phoenix's eyes. "Wait!" Belinda slaps the arm of her chair, startling me out of my romantic staring contest. "What do you mean, *back* together? Did you know each other before? Is that why you were staring at Basel when I first introduced you? I thought you were just really into him," she questions me rapid fire.

I'm flustered by the numerous questions and her telling my pack that I was staring at Basel like a creep when we first met. How can I keep up my appearance as a suave businesswoman with stories like this circulating?

"No, no. I didn't know Basel," I rush to explain before anyone asks about the staring. "I had only met Phoenix, and that was years ago when we were kids. I didn't know he was part of their pack until a few days ago."

"That's so amazing you found each other again. I love stories of childhood friends becoming lovers when they're older."

I'm not sure how to respond. I could just smile and nod, avoiding saying anything. I didn't know Phoenix for long, but I suppose we were friends briefly. I don't want to mention Phoenix's upbringing without his permission. That's his story to tell.

I also still feel guilty for never trying to find Phoenix as an adult. I could have at least looked him up to see if it looked like he'd changed. Even though Phoenix said he doesn't blame me for what I did, it's hard to let go of what could have been. I am happy Phoenix grew into an amazing alpha despite his fathers, and that we found each other again. Belinda's statement is close enough. I decide to go with the smile and nod response. While I'm in the middle of my nod, Phoenix responds instead.

"It might be more accurate to say we went from enemies to lovers. I didn't have the best upbringing in regard to alpha-omega relations. Persephone rightfully didn't want to be friends with me once I told her the bigoted things my family pack believed. As I got older and started thinking for myself, I realized how harmful my fathers' ideas were, and I stopped behaving how they wanted me to. I'm glad I found Persephone again as an adult so I could show her the kind of alpha I actually am. I'm even more grateful that she let me stick around long enough to show her that I didn't turn out like my fathers," he explains, spilling the beans anyway.

What happened to my smile and nod plan?? I know he can't sense my thoughts yet since we haven't bonded, but still. Didn't he see me nodding?

Oh well. I don't mind if others know. I just hope he doesn't feel obligated to explain himself to the people in my life. If he wants to tell them of his own volition, that's fine.

"That's a fun trope too. In real life, it must be harrowing. I didn't realize you've been dealing with so much, Seph." Belinda looks at me with concern.

"It was a surprise to see Phoenix again, but it wasn't as

shocking as I thought it would be. He quickly showed me he was a good, caring alpha, and we've both changed so much since we last saw each other. It's basically like starting from scratch," I say.

I don't want anyone to judge Phoenix based on his family. It's not his fault that's the pack he was born into. I can see the alpha he is, and it's nothing like the "ideal" alpha he described when we first met. Phoenix smiles at me and squeezes my hand.

"I'm glad you worked everything out, especially before your heat. Our bodies like to conspire against us and cause issues at the worst possible time. I missed out on a field trip to a book bindery in high school because my pre-heat cramps were so bad. Biology is a bitch," Belinda commiserates.

"It *was* rude of my body to break through all the suppressants. I tried to plan my heat for a better time, but since we're scent matches, that apparently makes the suppressants less effective."

Belinda shrieks, startling me so much that I almost fall off the couch. Fynn and Phoenix barely keep their arms around me, but they prevent my flail from ending with me on the floor.

"You found your scent matches randomly!? Without using a matchmaking service? That's so rare! I can't believe it. And finding and losing one only to find him again as an adult! It must be true that scent matches draw each other together. Why didn't you say they were your scent matches before? How did you not climb Basel when you first met? No wonder you were staring at him for so long. Aren't scent matches supposed to be like a magnetic connection?" Belinda bounces on her chair in excitement.

I blink, trying and failing to keep up with all the questions she threw at me. "Um, yeah, I guess it is rare to find them accidentally. I never really thought about it since I found Phoenix so young and never went looking for any others. I'd already met a scent match and knew what it felt like, so I guess that's why I could control myself and didn't jump Basel?" I think that answers her interrogation.

"I'm so happy for you! You found your scent matches!" Belinda says before bursting into tears and launching herself at me. Her embrace is like a vise as she traps me in a bear hug and sobs into my hair.

I awkwardly pat her back. "Ah, thank you?" I didn't realize she felt so strongly about scent matches.

The only response I get is incoherent babbling. I keep patting her back and look to my alphas to see if they have any idea what I should do. They just give me sympathetic smiles in return. Well, at least Belinda was satisfied with my answers.

I sit back in the passenger seat and close my eyes, letting Basel buckles me in. Roman starts the car and turns on my seat warmer. The days are getting chillier. I can't focus on enjoying the weather right now, though. I'm still reeling from Belinda's reaction to our scent match. Is everyone going to react this intensely when we tell them? I know Stasia will be happy that I'm dating, but I can't imagine her crying about it. I haven't known Belinda for long, maybe she always feels things deeply.

"Do you want to go to Quickie Coffee for a drink and see if Stasia is there? We'd like to come with you to tell her and your other friends the news that we're together. Unless you prefer to tell them privately," Roman says.

"I don't know. Do you think she'll cry too?" I ask balefully.

I appreciate that Belinda cares, but that was a lot of emotion to deal with, and my own hormones and emotions are still a mess after my heat. I don't want to avoid my best friend, but surely I could wait one more day to tell her about my pack.

Salem reaches forward to rub my shoulders, and some of the tension leaves me as he massages me.

"We don't have to tell anyone else about our courting today. We can let you can catch up with Stasia alone since you've been out for a few days. You should have some friend time," Basel says as he slides into the backseat.

"I don't want to hide you guys. It's just a lot of emotions to deal with. I want Stasia, and Grey, and everyone to know about us. I'm glad we're together," I squeeze Salem's hand.

Roman leans over to kiss the top of my head. "We're proud to be with you, too. We'll follow your lead in telling people. There's no rush from us, we aren't going anywhere," he says while stroking my hair.

"Let's go to Quickie Coffee so I can tell Stasia and the others our big news," I sit up and tell them decisively.

Fynn cheers from the far back seat where the others relegated him, citing the fact that he has to take turns sitting near me. The others chuckle or murmur their support.

I am excited to tell Stasia about my alphas. She'll be thrilled, she's always encouraging me to go on dates. Plus, it's always a good time for coffee.

On the way to the coffee shop, I contemplate texting Stasia to warn her I have big news. She's seen me with a few of my alphas already, so it might not be a surprise that we're together now. Stasia knows I don't spend much time with alphas, or any guys really, so it was already obvious things were different with them.

Roman parks on the street next to the coffee shop and I'm out of time. Salem helps me down from the car. It still makes me feel all bubbly when they do that. Also, their SUV is tall as fuck. Without their help, I'd be scrambling to climb in and leaping to get out. Salem sets me gently on the ground and holds my hand as we walk to Quickie Coffee.

CHAPTER 27

SALEM

I give Seph a parting kiss on the cheek after depositing her at a table with pumpkin coffee, apple scones, and Stasia. We leave them to it, Seph saying she wanted to talk to her alone since they have a lot to catch up on. Our pack doesn't go far, sitting a few tables away so we can keep an eye on her while giving her privacy.

I can hardly take my eyes off Seph no matter the situation, and when I'm not with her, I'm thinking about her. I adjust my wool pants to make it less apparent that I'm yearning for her.

Even after her heat, I can't stay away. I thought alphas would be tired of sex after helping an omega through their heat. It must be different with a mate.

I ache for the day when we'll bond, then Seph will be with me all the time. I have no intention of rushing her decision to join our pack, but I already know she's it for me. Forever.

I want her to be just as sure about us, so we'll court her as long as she wants. I just want her to be happy, but I hope we'll be the ones that make her the happiest she's ever been.

For now, it will be interesting to learn about each other without a bond. With alphas, a bond forms on its own if they're compatible and they spend a lot of time together. The bond with my packmates gave me insight into their inner workings while our pack developed. Trying to understand Seph's thoughts and feelings without a bond will be like reading a mystery novel where you don't learn all the pieces until the end. Once we're bonded, I'll be able to feel what she feels and see the world through her eyes, like a book with a descriptive first-person narrator. I sigh wistfully.

Nix gently nudges me out of my rumination, and I return my focus to our conversation.

"We want Salem's thoughts on this as well," Nix tells the others. I study him briefly, surprised he's making sure we're all involved in a pack discussion. It will take time to reframe his actions in my mind now that I know he's been acting out of guilt. Nix is finally acting like a member of our pack instead of having one foot out the door. I smile at him before turning to the others.

I review what I caught of the conversation while I was distracted. My packmates were discussing how we should approach Lili to get her to leave our omega alone.

"I agree with Basel that a conversation should be our first approach," I respond after organizing my thoughts. My alpha rages that Lili has upset our omega, which is a new feeling for me, but I'm still in control. The other suggestions mentioned, namely the ones involving Fynn's predilection for fire, are an overreaction at this point. We should engage with Lili ourselves to gather information and convince her to leave our pack alone without escalating things.

We could start out more forcefully with lawyers or a restraining order, but this is a small town, and I know Seph is worried about the gossip. I don't want to hurt her relationships with the people here, some of whom might view us as unknown alphas coming here to threaten women. I wouldn't let that happen either if I saw it. If people know why we're trying to warn Lili away, they'll understand our actions. However, gossip tends to spread faster than the truth.

The calm, logical approach is obviously the best initial strategy. I will concede to keeping Fynn's ideas as a backup plan. I'm in agreement with my alpha, if Lili won't be reasonable, we'll protect our omega by whatever means necessary.

Basel nods to me while Fynn huffs and leans back in his seat. He's also been keeping an eye on Seph, and smiles watching her animatedly tell Stasia something. Hopefully he'll realize it's in Seph's best interest to solve this calmly and quickly.

Turning back to Nix, I ask for his thoughts. The others gave their opinions already, with Roman favoring the aggressive approach and suggesting we counter by asking the vendors not to work with Lili.

Nix considers for a moment before answering, watching Seph as she laughs. "My instincts are like Fynn's, telling me we should protect our omega by removing the threat immediately."

Fynn leans forward again. "Yes! That's three of us, we have the majority."

Nix shakes his head slightly. "It's not a civilized approach though. We should talk to Lili and see if she really thinks Persephone is trying to steal her festival ideas, or if there's something more going on. Her actions seem disproportionate, and attempting to physically stop Basel's workers is a step up from telling the vendors they shouldn't work with us. Since she hasn't escalated further, there's a chance we can sort this out without turning it into the town drama."

Fynn scoffs and slumps in his seat. He puts a hand in his pocket, where I know he keeps a lighter. He doesn't argue any more, though.

"Fine, we'll try to talk our way out of this. I know Seph doesn't want anyone gossiping about her," Fynn grumbles.

I hide my smile in my cup as I take a sip of the caramel pecan cappuccino. Seeing Fynn's care for Seph is sweet. He's always cared deeply. That's part of what made it so difficult to watch his childhood unfold. Fynn wanted someone to care for him in return, but the foster homes failed him again and again. He wasn't the most docile child, but he wasn't a bad kid, just energetic. Unfortunately, his foster families never looked after him. Fynn hid how hurt he was by the constant rejection and let those suppressed emotions out in unhealthy ways, developing a predilection for fire.

Once we met, our pack helped Fynn connect in healthy ways, and he's come a long way from the neglected boy he was. I'm thankful Seph sees him for who he is and cares for him in return. He's a handsome guy even with the scarring, but I know that's scared some people off in the past.

"That's settled then. We'll have to ask Seph if she wants to go with us to talk to Lili. We should plan for either scenario," Basel says.

"Seph should *not* go see Lili," Fynn responds hotly.

"I agree. Persephone was extremely upset after Lili's call. I don't want her going through that again," Nix says.

"Seph doesn't have to confront her if she doesn't want to. But we should give her the option, even if we also recommend that we take care of it for her," Basel says.

"Even if Seph talks to Lili, we'll be there with her. We won't let Lili bully our omega," Roman adds.

"Damn right we won't," Fynn growls.

Seph glances over like she can sense Fynn's agitation, she's too far away to have heard him growl. I send her a reassuring smile and nudge Fynn under the table for him to do the same. She smiles back at us and returns to her conversation.

"If she chooses not to meet with Lili, which of us will stay with Seph, and who will visit Lili?" I ask.

"Fynn's not going to see Lili," Roman answers immediately.

That incites Fynn instantly.

"What! Of course I'm going to tell her off in person!"

Seph looks over at us again and I smile and shake my head at her. She doesn't need to worry, we'll deal with him. She still looks concerned, but Stasia pulls her back into their conversation.

"We're trying *not* to escalate things, Fynn. You're the backup in case the reasonable option fails. Besides, this way you get to stay close to Seph. I'm sure you don't want to leave her so soon after her heat, and we should resolve this situation with Lili as soon as possible," Roman tells him.

"You and Salem can stay with Seph while the rest of us talk to Lili. There will be enough of us that Lili will take us seriously, and the two of you can take care of Seph," Basel reasons.

I like my part in this plan. It's easy to stay composed

and reasonable in a discussion, but I'm not one for arguing with someone behaving erratically, and it sounds like the conversation with Lili could easily go in that direction. This way, Seph and I can have some personal time together. As long as Fynn doesn't monopolize her too much.

"Are you sure Salem shouldn't go with you? He teaches literature, he's good at examining people's opinions. Besides, I'm sure he can convince Lili how wrong she is with citations and a bibliography," Fynn says with a smirk in my direction.

He's already attempting to get Seph to himself. Fynn shared well enough during her heat, so I know he's capable of it. At some point we'll sort out times for individual dates with her, but for now, I don't want to be away from Seph so soon after the start of our relationship and her heat.

"He can come with us if he wants to. I didn't want to have too many alphas show up at this woman's door, but..." Basel looks to me.

"I'd prefer to stay with Seph. I'm sure you'll be able to reason with Lili just as well as I can at this point. We don't know much about her or why she thinks we're interfering with her stall," I tell them.

Fynn accepts defeat fairly gracefully, only grumbling a little under his breath, something about "nosy" and "learn to share."

Basel doesn't comment on Fynn's huff. "Let's split up after this, unless Seph has other plans for us. We can take you three back to her apartment. She should rest since she's still recovering from her heat. The rest of us will go visit Lili."

"I found Lili's work address. It's a boutique at the other end of town. We can try there first and see if she's in today," Roman says.

Nix, Roman, and Basel come up with a plan for talking to Lili. We check our emails with the pack lawyers, who gave us options for stopping Lili if she won't willingly leave us alone. Fynn interrupts occasionally with ideas more suited for our backup plan. I listen, but most of my attention is on Seph. I love reading the expressions on her face as she talks with Stasia.

Seph finishes her chat with Stasia, who seems to have taken the reveal that Seph is an omega well. I'm sure it was a shock for her. I know it was for me.

Afterwards, Seph introduces us as her pack. Stasia told us she always knew we were the right pack for Seph, and not just because we were the only alphas Seph let near her. Stasia said she could tell we were considerate and a good fit for her, and quote, "weren't boring guys trying to get Seph to settle down and be boring too, like we're too good to eat a donut off the sidewalk." I'm not sure what she meant by that, but I assume she was referring to Fynn's lively energy. I'm happy to be a homebody, which some might describe as boring, as long as I have my books. I can even teach virtual classes from home. Now that we found Seph, I look forward to many cozy evenings at home reading next to her.

I'm always up for a visit to a bookstore though, and Starsfalls has one of the best. I've visited hundreds of bookstores and libraries all over the world. I've been in a baroque mansion with a library four stories tall, a modern glass bookstore where even the floors between levels were glass, and a bookstore in a historic castle with fireplaces taller than I am. Still, nothing is better than the local bookstore that's welcoming and feels like the owners want you to settle in and spend the day there. Pen and Tellem is the epitome of that, not to mention it also has unique architecture and a wide variety of books and other eclectic items. I haven't even visited the second floor yet. Tellem is striking in its own way, different from the glass bookstore or gold trimmed mansion. I do think I saw a giant fireplace in there, though. I'll have to investigate with Seph at some point.

My admiring thoughts about Seph and bookstores bring me back to the half-formed idea that's been developing since we met. Where will Seph want to live if, and hopefully when, we bond? Our pack is used to traveling and living in different cities throughout the year for work, so we're not set on living in Boarwood. We only chose that city because Nix seemed more stable there when we visited in the past. Now I realize he must have sensed Seph was nearby. It makes sense that after we moved to Boarwood, his alpha was agitated because he felt his omega nearby but was unable to find her, causing Nix to become more agitated.

Which brings me to my point, that I presume our pack will move to Starsfalls if Seph wants to stay here. We'll have to look for a house since we won't all fit in Seph's apartment. I wonder what kind of home she'll want. We could build her one if she doesn't find anything she likes. Basel would be thrilled to design a house for her. We can make her custom bookshelves if she doesn't like the style of the ones we built for my books. And if she agrees, we could combine our books into one library. I feel a thrill at the thought of merging our books together. I watch as Seph finishes up her conversation with Stasia and wonder if I can sneak away with her for a while after we leave.

Seph introduces us to Grey and the rest of their coworkers, who are thrilled that Seph found a pack. I'm glad she's surrounded by good people. Lili's accusations are obviously completely out of character for Seph. I can't imagine anyone would listen to Lili's lies, but I hope we're able to clear things up with her today.

We say our goodbyes and Seph's friends go back to work. Basel and Nix ask Seph if she wants to go with them to talk to Lili, or if they can act in her stead. Seph purses her lips in thought, but after a few tense moments agrees she doesn't need to be there.

With that decided, we return to the car. Fynn attaches himself to Seph like an octopus, and I reluctantly dismiss the idea of stealing her away, at least for now. I know we all want her attention, so I can't blame him.

Fynn tugs Seph into the middle row with him. I slide in on the other side of her while my packmates take their seats around us. Fynn is asking for a list of her favorite sprinkles, inspired by the story Grey recounted about Seph choking on a sprinkle shaped like a turkey, causing her to swear off turkey-shaped sprinkles forever. Seph argues that leaf-shaped sprinkles are the best. As Roman drives us back to her apartment, Fynn teasingly asks her about other sprinkles, getting her riled up in defense of leaf sprinkles.

"What about those shiny round ones I've seen on Jumbl cookies?"

"Those aren't actually sprinkles, they're dragées. That's a totally different category. You can't compare them to actual sprinkles," Seph lectures Fynn, moving her hands around as she explains the differences. "The giant gold ball dragées are the best though, so you're right about that."

Fynn listens intently as Seph describes the best dessert toppings. When we park, she's telling him about streusel and espresso.

Everyone gets out of the SUV so Basel, Nix, and Roman

can give Seph kisses goodbye. By the time they're done, Seph is ruffled and red faced. I contemplate how much rest she really needs, and if she might have enough energy for other things. I'll ask how she feels when we get upstairs. The three of them leave to find Lili while Fynn and I take Seph up to her apartment.

I hold the building door open as Fynn walks Seph inside and up the stairs. When we get to her floor, I notice construction workers at the other end of the hall. Fynn notices them too and stops Seph near the stairs, distracting her by asking her if sugar counts as a sprinkle. I slip past Fynn and Seph to see what the construction crew is working on, reaching them just as a man comes out of a nearby apartment.

"It's like I said, you can easily take out these walls, they're practically made of plywood. You can knock them all down in a day," I hear him order as I approach.

"Excuse me, did you say you're renovating some of the apartments?" I ask him.

He turns and looks me up and down disdainfully before answering. "What business is it of yours? You don't live here." The man puffs himself up. "This is a construction area. Are you wearing a hardhat? No? Then you better get out."

He isn't wearing a hardhat, and neither is the construction crew. I refrain from commenting on that.

"You're correct that I don't live here. My mate, who is standing down the hall, lives in an apartment across from these. I was asking so I can warn her if there's going to be construction noise on her floor in the coming weeks," I reply calmly.

He leans around me to look at Seph. I don't like him

looking at her, but I did mention she lives here, so he might be checking to see if I was telling the truth.

I need to know if there's going to be workers coming and going outside Seph's apartment. She should stay at the inn with us if that's the case. Omegas are sensitive to loud noises and crowds, especially after a heat.

The man finally looks back at me. "Right, that's 3C. She'll be clearing out of here too. This demolition isn't any of your business." He turns to resume talking with the workers, who don't seem any more eager to deal with him than I am.

"You sent her a notice that she'll have to temporarily vacate her apartment?" I ask, trying again to get more information. Seph didn't mention any of this to us, but we did just start courting recently. Most of our time together has been consumed by immediate issues like her heat and the situation with Lili.

"That's what I said, isn't it? You deaf?" He scoffs and rolls his eyes before looking at the workers for support, who remain uninterested in engaging with him.

"How long will she be unable to stay in her apartment?"

"I'm not going to waste my time talking to someone who doesn't even live here. *No one's* going to be living here soon enough. It's not my problem that your girlfriend doesn't tell you anything. Talk to her if you want to see the notice from the owner," he says before turning his back on me.

"What do you mean, no one will be living here?" Seph asks quietly behind me, having walked up with Fynn who is glaring at the man's back.

The manager is ignoring us as he tells the crew they don't need to do more safety checks, and to start knocking down walls without checking for load-bearing beams. He doesn't give any indication he heard Seph's question, but I know he must have. Fynn leaves Seph next to me as he steps up to the manager. I wrap my arm around her waist and pull her close to comfort her.

"Are you going to answer her?" Fynn snaps. The manager twitches and quickly cuts off his conversation to round on him.

"What question?" he sputters. "I'm busy here! Call the owners if you have questions about the apartment closure."

"How can you close an apartment building when there are people living here? I saw other residents coming and going, I know Seph isn't the only one on this floor," Fynn says, angling closer and closer, until he's backed up against the wall.

"It's not my decision. The owners are rezoning the building for commercial use and gave residents notice that they have to move out by the end of the month. Inspectors found mold in the basement, so they'd have to clear out while it's treated anyway. Residents usually complain mold is a health hazard, so it's better if they move out," he explains nervously, avoiding eye contact. The manager looks over at the construction workers for backup, but they're busily readjusting things on their tool belts and seemingly not paying attention to us.

Fynn growls. "What do you mean, they're kicking everyone out?"

"I didn't get a notice about this," Seph says anxiously at the same time.

I squeeze her gently in support.

The manager sidles away from Fynn's wrath and finally responds to Seph, "The owners gave me the final notices a week ago, and I posted them to all the apartment doors and mailboxes. They also emailed the residents, stating they have until the end of the month to move out." Fynn growls again and he cringes. "Like I said, it's not my fault. And—and the mold. It's better for you to just move somewhere else."

"I didn't see any notices on my door, but I haven't checked my mailbox or email since we've been *busy*," Seph whispers to me.

I lean down to kiss her forehead. "It's okay Seph, we can go look now. We'll help you move if this checks out. I'm sorry you might have to leave your home, though," I whisper back.

She stares up at me with wide, worried eyes, like I'm the life raft that will save her. I intend to do so. I move my arm up to curl around her shoulders and lead her away. I don't imagine the manager will be of any more help.

I hear Fynn growl something else as Seph and I walk back to her apartment. While she fumbles in her purse for her keys, I keep an eye on the others. Fynn finishes whatever he's saying and joins us.

Seph eventually gets her keys out, but her hands are so shaky she can't get the key in the lock. I gently take them from her and unlock the door. I hold it open as they file in, Fynn following close behind Seph.

With Fynn out of sight, the manager plucks up his courage to spew more stupidity. He's loudly complaining to the workers that people are too busy looking at social media these days to pay attention to the real world. I ignore him as I follow the others inside where I can shut out his voice.

"And when *that* kind isn't busy with social media, you know what they're doing. Always looking for the next knot to jump on. I've seen videos of it, they're literally gagging for—"

The manager stops talking abruptly. His jaw is no longer working properly, which would explain why he's gone quiet. The construction workers have backed away from him and are edging toward the stairs. Looking closer, the manager may be unconscious. Another reason he didn't finish his sentence, I note absently. Something else is bothering me, but I can't quite put my finger on it. The workers are long gone now, so I can't ask them if they know what's wrong here.

I stare at the manager as I attempt to figure out what's troubling me about the situation. This time, I notice I've been hearing a loud rumbling sound. I'm not sure where it's coming from, but it's like someone is revving a motorcycle engine in the hallway. I look back to Seph's door to make sure she's safely inside and hoping she didn't hear what the manager was saying. Fynn is leaning in her doorway with the door partially closed, so I can't see past him. His arms are folded, and he lifts an eyebrow when he sees me looking. He's no help in figuring out what the noise is.

I'd better wake up the manager so I can ask if they've started working on this floor already and see if that's what's causing the noise. I reach down to pull him up, but pause as I notice something red covering the back of my hand. Did I spill something on it at the coffee shop? I release him to get a closer look.

Oh.

Now I smell the blood.

That's right, *he* was the problem. I look down at the manager again. I must have hit him to prevent him from further disparaging omegas, especially *my* omega. I sigh, which ends the rumbling sound. It must have been my growl. I can't recall the last time I growled at anything, if I ever have. I grab the manager by the collar and haul him up to lean against the wall. I tap him lightly on the side of the face to wake him. After a few taps and a quick shake, he finally opens his eyes. When they focus on me, he tries to get away, but I keep a tight grip on his shirt.

"You won't talk about omegas like that again," I command. My voice is deeper than usual, like I'm talking through a growl.

He nods rapidly like a bobblehead.

"And don't talk to Seph. Ever. We'll work with the building owners directly to sort things out."

The rumbling is back. I compose myself enough to release him and step away. The manager slides down the wall before righting himself and getting up to stumble off down the hall. He glances back at me fearfully a few times before rushing down the stairs where the construction workers disappeared. I hold myself in check and let him go. After a moment, I force myself to return to Seph's apartment.

Fynn is still leaning in the doorway, and he doesn't move as I approach. He just stands there smirking at me. I step closer to brush past him and get to Seph.

"That was quite a show," he finally says.

I don't respond with words, my growl reverberating between us.

"I thought it would take a lot to make you speechless, and even more for you to start a fight. Don't get me wrong, the way that guy was insulting our omega, all omegas, was terrible. But I still didn't picture you stopping him like *that*, and so quickly. You got there before I could," Fynn continues.

I try to get past him again, but he grabs the door to stop me from opening it and I snarl at him. No one will keep me from my omega. My packmate shouldn't be keeping her from me.

"You can come in when you've calmed down. While I'm sure Seph will appreciate that you stood up for her, I don't know how much of his rant she heard. I don't want you coming in growling and upsetting her, making her wonder what he did to get *you* riled up like this."

It takes a second, but as his words register, I step back. I hold my breath to cut off the growls and shake my head to clear it. I need to get my alpha instincts aligned with my mind. Fynn is right. I don't want to scare Seph with my demeanor or make her think the manager said something worse than he did. I don't want her to think I'm a violent alpha, although I *will* protect her when necessary.

I close my eyes and take deep breaths to compose myself. Once I've calmed down, I wait for Fynn to let me through. He looks me over and finally steps back to let me in.

"Thanks, Fynn," I pat his arm as I walk past.

"No problem. We should probably take care of that hand too before you see Seph," he says, locking the door behind us.

I look at my hands again. Only the right one is bloodied.

"Right, of course. Where is she?" I don't see her in the living room or kitchen, and my alpha starts to get agitated again.

"I suggested she check her email, so she's in the back room at her desk. Let's rinse your hand off in the bathroom and I'll look for a first aid kit."

I follow Fynn's instructions and inspect my hand while he searches the cabinets.

"I don't see any cuts. I think all the blood is from the manager," I tell him. Fynn hasn't found a first aid kit, and I don't want to ask Seph for one if we don't have to. I don't want her to worry.

Fynn stands up after checking the last cabinet and I hold out my hand to show him. He brings it up to the light to look it over.

"I don't see any cuts either, and nothing looks broken. It will probably just bruise. Guess you had good form and didn't catch his teeth. You'll have to thank Roman for making you take those alpha defense classes," he tells me with a snicker.

I rub my eyes with my free hand. Roman was so pushy about making us take that class. I tried to get out of it by citing the boxing and Muay Thai classes I've attended. I didn't need to take a street fighting class. Roman made us all go though, saying it's better to be prepared for any situation where you have to defend your omega. I thought the standard fighting advice would be enough, like avoid a fight where possible and get your omega to safety. Or if you have to fight, don't tuck your thumbs. I wouldn't credit Roman's classes for my little fight just now, since I already knew how to punch, but I'm sure he'll be happy to take credit. Like I couldn't figure out how to defend my omega without learning all the dirty fighting tricks they taught us in those defense classes.

I drop my hand and pull the other one back from Fynn since there's no doctoring to be done. He laughs at the look on my face.

"Come on, let's help Seph figure out this apartment mess," Fynn says.

We eagerly set off to join her, getting stuck in the doorway as we try to dart through. Fynn pops out ahead of me, and I follow quickly on his heels.

CHAPTER 28

PERSEPHONE

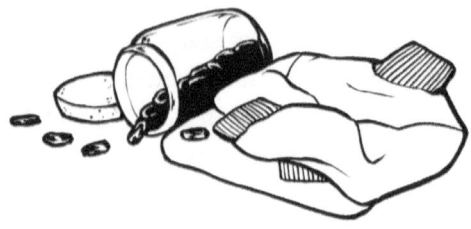

I read over the email for the tenth time, chewing anxiously on my fingernail. Why didn't I check my emails this morning? Instead of making sure I hadn't missed anything important during my heat, I was gallivanting around town without a care in the world. Meanwhile, my apartment is about to be demolished and I'm going to be homeless. And on top of that, someone is trying to destroy my festival plans (which I guess I did give a care about earlier, but still).

It's not like I don't have anyone to ask for help. Stasia and my other friends, along my alphas, will help me apartment hunt, I'm sure. I should be able to find a new place easily enough. Packing is always a hassle, but again I can ask for help with that. I'll have to move my nest carefully. I only recently started calling it a nest instead of my bedroom, but really, it's been my nest all along, and destroying an omega's nest is a huge emotional blow. I'll have to keep a close eye on it while it's packed up so I can set it up perfectly in my new place.

What if there's no omega friendly apartments available? I could make do with a regular one, as long as there's a small room I can make cozy. But it can't be too small, I have alphas now. They all need to fit in my nest.

I have too much stuff to move it all myself and I can't ask my friends to carry this much stuff in exchange for plant cuttings. I'll have to hire movers. I have some savings so that should be fine, but what if I run out of time to pack and have to pay the movers to box up my things too? Or what if I have to put some of my stuff in storage until I find a new place? Moving can get expensive. Are the apartment owners going to pay us anything in compensation for kicking us out? The email didn't mention it. I still have another seven months on my lease. Surely there's something in the contract about being reimbursed if the apartment becomes uninhabitable and I'm forced to move out.

I whine but choke it back. I don't want Fynn and Salem to hear me freaking out. I'm not sure where they've gone to. I thought Fynn said they were going to look around the front door to see if the notice fell behind something, but they've been gone awhile.

They shouldn't have to hold my hand through another crisis. We just started courting and they already have to deal with a bunch of drama. I hope they don't think my life is always this much of a mess. I don't want to scare them away.

So far, they've been eager and willing to help, but I don't want them to burn out or decide it's more trouble than I'm worth. This is a lot to deal with all at once. I don't even want to deal with it, and it's my life.

I should go out and see if they've found the notice, but I can't stop staring at the screen. What does it matter if the manager also put a note at the door. From this email, I can see that what Hogan said is true. They're selling the building, and I have barely a week to move out. I bite my finger-nail harder as the screen blurs.

A hand on my shoulder makes me jump and squeak. At least that breaks my staring contest with the display of doom.

"Sorry, doll." Fynn smooths his hand down my hair. "I didn't mean to startle you, I thought you heard us come in. It looks like you found the email. What does it say?"

Salem comes up to stand on my other side and squeezes my shoulder. I feel steadier now that they're with me. I take a deep breath and read it out for them.

"So, that's that. I did get notified that I have to move out. I need to look at apartment listings and find a moving company *and* see how much it will cost to have them pack for me. Actually, I should get boxes and start packing now, it's going to take a while. Plus, I have to figure out how to safely relocate my plants to the new place." I stand up to get started on all the things I have to do.

"You don't have to worry about that. We have a moving company we use for our moves. They're reliable and careful. They'll move anything, even food and plants. We can call them to pack and move your things, unless you want to choose a different company. Whatever you want to do, we'll help," Salem says, keeping a hand on my arm so I don't rush off to start throwing things in boxes.

Fynn rubs his cheek against my head, scent marking me. "That's right, we have people for anything you need, remember? Don't stress about this. Plus, there's a silver lining, you get to pick a nice, new place to live. We have realtors who can find suitable listings for you to check out."

I stroke Fynn's jaw while I consider their offers. It would be nice not to have to vet a moving company. If the pack already has reliable movers, why shouldn't I use them? I'm not sure about the realtor part though. It doesn't sound worth their time to help me look for an apartment to rent. I can search online like I did when I moved to Starsfalls. I remember seeing a few omega friendly apartments near downtown. I only chose this building because it was closer to Quickie Coffee.

I take another deep breath, inhaling more of their woodsy spiced marshmallow scents, and relax. I know I can handle this, but I appreciate the moral support. And practical support. My alphas always help calm my overactive mind (and not just when we're having sex). Maybe this is what being safe and supported feels like.

I lean into Salem as he massages one side and Fynn rubs the other.

"I'll start looking at listings online in a few minutes, after I rest for a bit. I'm happy to use your movers once I find a place."

After decompressing with cuddles, we move out to the couch with my laptop to search for apartments. Salem sits next to me while Fynn goes to the kitchen to find us a snack. I show Salem the apartments downtown that I've always thought looked nice.

"This one has an ornate wrought iron fire escape that I admire whenever I go by. If you're going to be running for your life, you might as well do it in style," I tell him.

Salem laughs softly. "Of course. If you're going to do something, do it with panache."

"Oh, and this one has a great view of the Fossfell Mountains. I heard someone say on a clear day you can see the waterfalls from this building. All the guidebooks say you have to climb the mountains to get a view of the falls, but I bet if the conditions are right, you can see the mist rising off the water from a vantage point like this," I say, pointing to another listing and showing him the location on a map.

"That building is in line with some of the bigger waterfalls. Do you visit the mountains often? It looks like a nice area to hike."

"I love to walk the trails there! I'm not out there every week, especially now that I'm busy with the greenhouse. Otherwise, I try to go every few weeks, either with Stasia and Grey, or on my own. The falls are magical. At night, with the sky reflecting in the water, it looks like the waterfalls are overflowing with stars. Some drop into pools so deep there are only a few ripples, and the water is calm enough to serve as a reflecting pool. If you stand close, it looks like the water is falling straight from the sky. It's what makes the falls here so special.

"You may have already heard that version of how the town got its name, people here love to share the local lore with visitors. But there's at least one more credible theory for how Starsfalls was named. A few centuries ago, some hunters were traveling looking for game, and they set up camp near a river in the Fossfell Mountains. One night, they were woken by bright flashes outside their tents. When the hunters stumbled out to see what was happening, they found dozens of stars falling onto the mountain, crashing through the trees to the earth and plummeting into the rivers. The stars plunging into the water sent clouds of steam billowing up, and their sight was quickly obscured. Disoriented, the hunters took off in different directions as they tried to find shelter from the falling celestials.

"In the morning, after the steam had cleared, their party reunited and explored the new landscape. They found craters where the stars fell that had cut so deeply into the rivers, they formed the waterfalls we see now. One hunter recorded the event in his journal, which now resides in the Starsfalls Town Museum. His account describes the places they visited and mentions other verified historical events so accurately that many believe the falling stars incident is also true, despite how fantastical it sounds. Of course, others claim the hunters had too much to drink or ate some bad bread. But the hunter mapped out and described the geography of the mountains when they first set up camp, and again after the stars fell. He recorded the changes and drew a new map with precise measurements that closely match modern maps. Seems like a lot of work to fabricate a fake map alongside a real one, especially for someone hungover or sick. I'm not sure what *I* believe, but it's an interesting story, and I love hearing about the new evidence people come up with to prove or disprove the origin of the Starsfalls name."

While I recounted the legends of Starsfalls, Fynn returned with the snacks to listen.

"That's a great origin story," Salem says.

"I could listen to you tell stories all day, doll," Fynn agrees.

I blush and tuck my hair behind my ear. I've never gotten a compliment on my storytelling abilities before.

"That's sweet of you to say. I'm happy to tell you stories whenever you want."

"Really?" Fynn asks. A grin slowly stretches across his face, different from his usual cocky looks. This one makes his face glow, like the first kindling catching in a fireplace, the flame reaching up to light the darkness. This smile reminds me of the one he gave me when we first met. The intensity of his feelings stunned me just as much then. It dazzles me so, that it takes me a moment to realize that wasn't a rhetorical question.

"Of course! If I can't think of a story to tell, I can always read something to you. If you'd like that."

Fynn kneels in front of me and leans forward to hug me, resting his head over my heart.

"I love listening to stories. I can never concentrate long enough to read a book, even if it's interesting. I listen to audiobooks and podcasts, and they're good, but it's not the same as being in front of someone telling a story. Salem reads to me sometimes, but I know he has a lot of books to read, and he can get through them faster on his own. I'd love it if you read to me, Seph," Fynn says into my chest.

Fynn's admission makes me tear up. It's kind of heart-breaking, but also sweet. I can picture Fynn listening intently as Salem reads to him. They're such good pack-mates. I imagine myself reading Fynn a story on a snowy day in winter. We'd be snuggled up next to a fire, with Yule lights strung up around the room. I purr as I hug Fynn tightly. I'm glad there's a way I can give something back to my pack after all they've done for me.

"I was always happy to read to you, Fynn. It doesn't matter how quickly we get through the books. I agree Seph is the better narrator, but you can still ask me to read for you whenever you want," Salem says.

Fynn nods, giving his thanks in a tight voice.

After a long hug, Fynn joins us on the couch and Salem passes out snacks. They help me look through more apart-ment listings while we munch.

"What about those loft spaces downtown." Fynn points to the photos of large, open rooms. "Do you want to move into a house at some point?" he casually asks.

"I'm not set on apartment living, but they're usually

cheaper than renting a house. Housing prices in Starsfalls are fair, but the utilities cost more, and you have to mow the yard and everything. Mowing is so not my thing. I'd rather save money with an apartment than pay to rent a bigger space where I also have to pay someone to mow the lawn that I don't even own," I say, waving away the question. I've seen a few cute rental houses around town, but I can't justify the expense when I could save toward buying one. We found several big, omega friendly apartments, so I shouldn't have to resort to a rental house.

"But if you could afford it, you'd prefer a house?" Salem asks.

"Sure, I figured I would buy a house at some point. I've lived in Starsfalls long enough to know that I'd be happy living here forever, or at least for a long time. I love the small-town vibe, while still having plenty of stores and events. Plus the festivals throughout the year. Then there's all the outdoor activities."

I pause as I consider all the reasons I love Starsfalls. It has everything I want. Well, except my alphas, who live in Boarwood. I choke on a gasp.

"I'm open to moving to other towns, though! I'm sure lots of places offer the same things. I've been to Boarwood a few times, it was great. Lots of cool stores, and it's also near the mountains. I should look for apartments there too," I quickly add.

I don't want them to think I'm not planning to stay with the pack. It's just that I'm not used to coordinating with others like this. I haven't dated much, so I never had to consult with a partner about where we would live. Hopefully Fynn and Salem don't think I'm trying to force them to live where I want.

Neither seem upset. Actually, they're smiling.

"We're not attached to Boarwood. We are ready to settle down in one place, but we aren't set on staying there in particular. You're welcome to move to Boarwood, but we'd also be happy to move here. We like Starsfalls too, and we're already invested in the town," Salem reassures me.

"I don't care where I live, as long as it's with you," Fynn adds.

"Are you sure? I like Starsfalls, but if you want to live somewhere else, we can talk about it."

"The pack already discussed it and decided we'll follow wherever you want to go. I already know you have great taste," Fynn stretches out on the couch and poses provocatively, nodding down at himself, "so I trust you to pick a good town."

I scoff, but his cockiness makes me smile. He grins at me in return.

"We discussed our plans for the future when we decided to court you. If you want to live in Starsfalls, we'll move here. The question now is, do you want a house? Since you have to move anyway, we could look for a permanent home. The pack will pay for it," Salem says.

"I don't expect you to pay for big things like that, and it's still so early in our courting. How could I ask you to buy me a house? I like having you here, but I don't want to rush you guys into living together."

"I presume you have an idea of the kind of wealth Nix comes from. He inherited little good from his fathers, except for a small fraction of their money. He used that to invest in several businesses and donates large amounts to philanthropic causes. He filters much of the revenue from his companies into charities, and even after that, there's plenty left over to support the pack. The rest of us have decent jobs as well, so we can easily afford a house. We'll put it in your name, so you can do what you want with it. We know you can take care of yourself, but the pack wants to take care of you and spoil you. You deserve it," Salem says.

"We can look at a few houses that might suit us, but I'm not sure if I want to get one just yet," I tell them shyly. The thought of picking out a house and living together makes my omega happy, and I feel all warm and fuzzy, but I try to stay logical. We haven't been together that long, and it sounds kind of crazy to buy a place together.

"House hunting will be fun," Fynn whispers in my ear like the devil tempting me into bad decisions. "We can set up a meeting with our realtor to tell them the things you're looking for, unless you already have a place in mind."

"I'm not too picky. There's just a few things I really want, like a fireplace and room for a garden."

"I'll send them a message then. We'll help you sort out this move, Seph," Salem says.

"Thanks. It's hard to worry with you guys around," I admit.

"Good." Fynn kisses the top of my head.

Though several of the recent events in my life have been unwanted (and unwarranted in my opinion, why would I steal someone else's festival idea??), at least they spurred personal growth. The terrible phone call from Lili led to me reconnecting with Phoenix and working through our childhood issues. I finally accepted that I'm an omega, and it's okay to want alphas. Getting kicked out of my apartment will hopefully prove that my alphas are trustworthy and supportive, not controlling. We'll learn more about each other as we house hunt, and I wonder how our ideas will knit together into a home.

This all started with Stasia and Grey making me go to

that Hypnotist club. From there, I met Belinda, who hired me to restore the greenhouse. I mayyyy have to thank them sometime for forcing me out of my comfort zone, as much as their assured gloating will pain me. It's not like I would have met my alphas while sitting around at home.

Not all change is bad. Even working with my scent matches when I wasn't sure if I could trust alphas turned out to be a good thing. I thought the greenhouse project was just a chance to be a professional businesswoman, I didn't realize it would also give me the opportunity to sleep with my coworkers.

Wait.

CHAPTER 29

PERSEPHONE

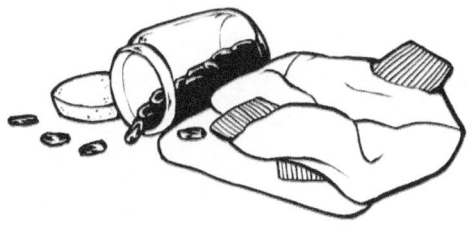

S alem sets up a video call and we talk with their realtor about finding houses for sale in Starsfalls. He mentions that they could remodel a house if it's missing a few of the things we want, and that location and foundation are the most important factors.

Afterward, Fynn and Salem tell me about building the bookshelves for Salem's library, which was a lot of work to make enough to fit all his books (which was a lot! If I hadn't already fallen for him, I'd be swooning. Actually, I did still swoon. I've always wanted a giant library. I didn't realize how attractive it would be to find a guy with an enormous library). But it sounded like they had fun together despite the laborious task. It makes me look forward to our future even more. There will always be challenges in life (ex. my life currently), but getting through it together with a smile is a solid foundation for a pack.

When they described how they built the library, Salem hinted that we could create a larger one with plenty of ladders in our new place and combine our books. It's sensible to have one library room rather than two, but it's still exciting to think of organizing our books together. I played it cool when I told Salem it would be nice to have a shared library. It's not like I have that many books, only a few bookshelves worth, so I don't need a full room just for my stacks.

With a dedicated library room though, I could grow my collection. I always have my eye on more books. I'll be giving Pen and Tellem lots of business once we have a house.

Fynn says if we have to renovate the house, he'll help gut it so we can design it the way I like. He'll show me how to use a sledgehammer so we can do it together. It sounds kind of fun to smash through a wall. When Fynn explained that it's easier to burn the things we remove so there's less to haul away, Salem cut in to say they could hire professionals if there was that much to be redone. That started an argument over whether it was more cost effective for Fynn to burn down part of the building versus hiring construction workers with years of experience to tear down and rebuild a portion of the house.

Salem tried to end the argument by reasoning that it won't save money if the fire gets out of control and burns the whole thing down. Fynn said he knows how to do a controlled burn. I said I'm sure we could find a place that didn't need that much work, which seemed to settle the argument. At least for now.

During our conversation, Fynn mentioned Basel could design a house for us, but I don't want to put that on him. I'm sure it's a lot of effort to design a house from scratch. I told them we should see what's available in Starsfalls first.

Fynn and Salem helped me schedule movers to pack up my things and take most of them to storage. They have a pack suite at the Fools Rush Inn which includes a nest room, so I can stay there until I find a place. My omega is settled now that my alphas made plans for us to stay together, and I feel less anxious about the move.

That was one reason finding alphas just for my heat unsettled me. Afterward they would leave, and I would feel abandoned, even if I didn't want to be in a relationship with them anyway. The hormone fluctuations from a heat cause intense emotions, which are difficult enough to deal with. I don't want to add in feeling like an alpha was just there for a good time.

I still worry it's too soon to move in together, but people say that scent match matings progress more quickly than packs who are just scentually compatible. Scent matches mean people are basically made for each other on a biological level and soul level, and they almost always end up being compatible personality-wise.

There *are* stories of scent matches with incompatible lifestyles who don't stay together, like the pack that lived on a boat, but their scent matched omega got seasick. The body can't overrule the mind completely, as evidenced when I ran from Phoenix. I'm not sure what that means for why most scent matches end up being compatible, but I have wondered if it's some kind of magic finding your soulmates like that.

After doing all we can to sort out my life, we end up talking about whatever comes to mind. Salem and Fynn tell me more about their travels and I ask how they've adjusted to staying in one place. I tell them about my childhood and moving to this part of the country. They love my story about meeting Stasia when we bumped into each other at our university's cafeteria. We were both smuggling bread rolls out, and when we ran into each other, the bread spilled out of our jackets and rolled across the caf floor. Stasia and I ran for it, and after we got away from the scene of our crimes, we discovered we had more in common than just our love for buttery, soft rolls.

Before I realize how late it's gotten, there's a knock at the front door. Fynn goes to check it, opening it to let in the rest of our pack. I jump up to welcome them back, and they surround me in a hug.

Phoenix leads me into the living room and sits me on the couch. He takes the chair next to me and holds my hands in his. I finally notice the serious look on his face, as well as Basel and Roman's, and remember why they've been out. I'd forgotten about Lili and the pop-up during the last few cozy hours spent hanging out with Salem and Fynn. I try to prepare myself for what they have to say, because based on their expressions it isn't happy news.

Roman starts, "It took us awhile to find her, but we talked to Lili in person. The good news is, we determined there's no reason to suspect that your pop-up plans are similar to her stall. There are clear differences in your designs."

"How do you know for sure our designs are different? And if they are different, why is she accusing me of stealing her ideas in the first place?" I interrupt.

"She showed us the mockup of her stall for this year," Basel says. "It's obvious they're nothing alike, besides being on theme for the autumn festival. We showed her your early designs for the pop-up to prove our plans are different. Lili agreed they were nothing like hers, however..."

"She still thinks you're going to replicate her stall in the greenhouse. She said the mockup wasn't proof we're going to follow through with a unique design," Phoenix squeezes my hands as he tells me gently. His touch reminds me to take a breath. I've been breathing quickly and was beginning to feel faint. Salem leans close and starts his low purr.

"Lili also said she didn't know who you were before last week. She supposedly has a 'source' who knows you, and the source heard you asking vendors about Lili's festival orders and requesting the same products."

"Who's her source?" Fynn growls.

"But that's not true!" I say at the same time.

If I'd gone with them I could have told her none of that happened! If we talked face-to-face, she would see I'm telling the truth. This would all be resolved if I'd been brave enough to see her. Now it's like playing the telephone game, words pinging from me to my pack to Lili and her "source," losing meaning as they go.

Phoenix answers me, "We know it's not true, Persephone, and that's what we told her. We offered to set up a meeting with all of us, including her source, so we could figure out where this 'miscommunication' came from."

"Lili declined," Roman says. "I haven't figured out who her source is yet, but I've been looking through all the records and social media posts I can find about Lili and her business." Roman pulls out his phone to show me Lili's socials. "Do any of these people look familiar?"

I take his phone and carefully look through each photo. I don't really remember if there were other people nearby when we visited the vendors, so I'm not sure how much help I can be. Roman pulls up the pages of followers who comment frequently on Lili's personal account and her store's page. No one stands out.

It's like we took several steps backward. When this started, Roman quickly found the name of the woman accusing me. Now, there's an unknown person lurking somewhere in town spreading rumors about me. It could be anyone, and I wouldn't know they were the "source" even if I talked to them on the street or served them at Quickie Coffee.

Maybe someone has a vendetta against me and is using Lili to hurt me. I pale at the thought. It's not a stalker, is it? I haven't noticed anyone following me or received weird calls besides Lili's. Wouldn't I know if I had a stalker? *Someone* must have a grudge against me if they're making up lies. Now everyone in Starsfalls is a suspect. This is so much worse.

I can't see or move, except to breathe in the scent of pumpkin cheesecake with rapid pants. I press my nose further into the scent and fabric slides across my cheek. Phoenix's chest rumbles in a purr as I press my face against it. He says something over my head, and I hear the others talking too, but can't focus on their words. I keep breathing Phoenix in to have something to redirect my thoughts. I know that panicking won't fix anything, but it's hard not to spiral when there's proof that someone is out to get me, and I don't even know why or who it is. Before I get caught up in the panic vortex again, I concentrate on how secure my alphas make me feel. They'll keep me safe and help me figure this out.

As much as I don't want people to think badly of me, I can't control people's thoughts. It should be enough that there are many people in Starsfalls who know me, and know I wouldn't do what I'm being accused of. Even if the source keeps spreading rumors, my friends and alphas will be there for me.

Some of what my alphas are saying starts filtering in. Phoenix tells me to keep taking deep breaths. Roman promises they'll find whoever the source is, and I shouldn't worry. Basel says no one will interfere with our work. Fynn is threatening anyone who has hurt me, vowing he won't let them near me. Salem is quiet except for his purr rumbling loudly at my back.

I force my hands to unclench and release Phoenix's shirt, and then work on relaxing the rest of my muscles one limb at a time. Eventually, I'm no longer tensed up like I'm about to make a mad dash to get the last cookie before anyone else takes it.

I wrap my arms around Phoenix. "Thanks for helping me calm down."

"I'm sorry we scared you. From now on, we can take care of this without involving you," Phoenix says.

"It's not your fault, but I do want to know what's going on since it's my life. It's just the thought that an unknown person has a grudge against me that scared me. Omegas are always warned to beware of rogue alphas or betas, plus there's the cautionary tales about omega stalkers. I know there's no reason to assume this source is interested in me like that, but it reminded me of those nightmare stories, and I panicked."

Phoenix looks more upset, and I worry he's going to say that they're going to shut me out of this.

"That's not what we meant," Basel says beside me. They must have surrounded me while I was freaking out. "We're not trying to coddle you and keep you ignorant of things. We don't like seeing you upset," Basel clenches and unclenches his teeth before continuing, "and we've all heard the stories of bad alphas. There aren't enough police to look after omegas, but since we're officially courting you, we have the right to protect you. That includes going after someone who hurts you. We don't have to wait for the police to investigate or go through the court system. We'll still notify them, but packs can eliminate threats to their omegas before they get too close, since you're an at-risk, protected designation."

I release Phoenix to hug Basel and blink back tears. My emotions been wild enough already, I don't want to get caught up in a crying fit. Basel is so kind, and it upsets me to picture him hurting someone because they threatened me. I don't want him to be forced into doing that. An alpha's instincts urge them to protect their omega and pack, which is why it's legal for them to physically guard them if there's a credible threat. It still saddens me that one bad person could force my alphas to be aggressive.

That's the balancing act of alphas and omegas. They call to each other, alpha instincts driving them to find and protect their omegas. Omega perfume attracts alphas, and heats are painful without their knots, so their instincts urge them to find a pack. But I don't want to take away my alphas' choices. I can't do much to stop my heats, but at the very least I don't want to force them into things they wouldn't do otherwise. I know it's not my fault some stupid person is spreading rumors about me, but it sure feels that way when my alphas talk about needing to protect me.

Basel squeezes me back. "Don't worry Seph, we'll keep you safe."

"I know. I just feel bad that you've been forced into this position," I whisper back.

"It's not your fault," Roman says. "Besides, it's our honor to protect you. Like Basel said, I would worry if you only had the police to rely on. The justice system is often too slow or overworked to prevent crimes. I'm glad we're here to keep you safe. I'll do more research and see if I can narrow down Lili's source. I know several good private investigators that I can bring on too. We'll update you when we find anything. In the meantime, at least one of us will always be with you, so you don't have to worry."

"Thank you," I tell them again, keeping my face buried in Basel's neck.

"Well, since we don't know who we need to fuck up yet, why don't we move on to telling them the good news," Fynn says.

I sputter at the abrupt change of subject, choking on a laugh.

"You have good news, Persephone? Is it about the festival?" Phoenix asks.

"Seph is moving in with us," Fynn interjects gleefully before I can reply.

Basel freezes, and Phoenix pauses my backrub. Basel unwinds my arms from his neck so he can look at me. "Is that true? You want to live with us?"

"Um, I mean, of course I want to. We don't have to move in together right now. I know it's early and I don't want to rush things. But, um, when we got back to my apartment earlier, there was a notice that they're selling the building and I have to move out by the end of the month, which is just a week away. Fynn and Salem said I could come stay with you guys at the inn until I find a new place. We got to talking and thought it made sense to check out some houses that would suit all of us, since we're heading in that direction. Is that okay? We don't have to look at places together if it's too soon," I stumble through explaining.

Basel, Phoenix, and Roman didn't have much of a reaction to Fynn's statement, so I'm not sure if they're interested or not. I'm startled when Basel suddenly pulls me back into his arms and Phoenix squeezes me between them.

265

A second later, another pair of arms surrounds us. Basel, Roman, and Phoenix start talking at the same time.

"Yes, we want to live with you."

"I wanted to move in together right away, but didn't want to pressure you."

"That's amazing news, Persephone."

I grin and hug them back. Salem chuckles somewhere outside our huddle, and I'm sure Fynn is out there looking smug.

After our celebration, they immediately want to discuss the logistics of my impending move.

"I'm sorry you're being forced out of your home. Our suite at the inn has a nest room, so you should be comfortable there until we find somewhere permanent. We'll buy the perfect house for you to decorate however you want, and we don't have to move in until you're comfortable with it," Phoenix says.

"We'll be thrilled to move in whenever you want, and we're happy to take our time," Basel adds.

"The apartment thing is rushing my move, but I already want to be with you all the time. It will probably take a while before we close on a house, so we could plan for that as our permanent move-in together date. Until then, I can stay with you at the inn and we'll see how we like living together outside of my heat."

"That works for us. I want to be around you all the time too, Seph," Roman strokes my cheek.

I look away and blush. I've been through a heat with these alphas, but I'm still shy around them. Maybe it's because I'm not used to accepting affection and care like this.

I bite my lip as I think back over my halting explanation to make sure I didn't forget any important details.

"Are you willing to move to Starsfalls?" I ask hesitantly. I know Fynn and Salem were happy to move here, but I know Phoenix moved one of his major business headquarters to Boarwood, and I don't want to interfere with their work.

"I'd love to move here. Starsfalls has great small-town charm," Basel says.

"Most of my business is conducted on the computer or phone, so I can easily shift my office here, and take brief work trips if necessary," Phoenix assures me. Basel side-eyes his response but doesn't comment on it.

"My work is virtual too, so I can move anywhere," Roman agrees.

I sigh with relief. I'm glad we can stay in Starsfalls. The town has a lot to offer, and I think my alphas will enjoy living here.

Now that all of my alphas have said they want to live with me, the excitement sets in. I squeal and hug everyone in reach. They laugh and return my hug.

We're getting a house!

CHAPTER 30

PERSEPHONE

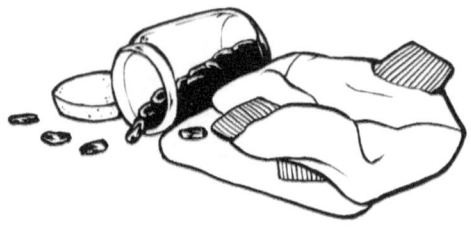

O ver the next few weeks, we fall into a routine of checking on the renovation and planning for the pop-up in the morning. In the afternoons when I'm not working at Quickie Coffee, we visit the houses the pack's realtor found for us. Even though we haven't found one we love, it's been interesting seeing so many different houses.

The moving company packed up my things and took most of it to storage. We moved my plants, food, books, and other important things that I'll need for the next few months to the inn. It's a bit of a tight fit with all my plants plus the six of us. Fynn has been smacked in the face by a leaf more than once. None of my alphas have complained though. They're thrilled to be spending so much time together, as am I.

Roman is still looking for the source of Lili's rumors, though she hasn't bothered us since they talked to her. Roman gives me brief updates on the search, which is enough for me. I trust him to take care of it.

Thanks to my alphas, I haven't been dwelling on the situation.

In between our obligations, we've been having sex whenever we can. We set up my nest at the inn and it's been very acceptable for our activities. The SUV has also been utilized on back roads after visiting vendors. It's a good thing all the seats fold down. Our desires seem as insatiable as they were during my heat, but at least now we're able to take breaks for pesky things like going to work and sitting down to have a meal.

I'm finally living now that I'm not hiding who I am and suppressing what I want. I enjoyed my life before meeting the Goldenrod Pack, with great friends, hobbies, and a fun job. But with them, it's like the final missing piece was put in place and I'm whole.

Looking at my calendar one morning, I'm surprised to find that the Autumnfalls Festival is almost here. Most of the greenhouse has been restored, with just a few finishing touches left. The new shelves are in and the pack helped me find more antique tables and chairs. Everything is going according to plan. Still, seeing how close it is to the festival gives me a jolt.

Soon we'll receive the vendor shipments and start setting out products. Once the festival starts, we'll stock fresh food and drinks daily. Marlene agreed to collab with us, so we'll have a Quickie Coffee bar in the greenhouse. Stasia, Grey, and some of our other coworkers will be there, working around their shifts at the cafe. I planned to work some shifts at the coffee bar, but Roman advised me I would likely be too busy running the pop-up and wouldn't have time for barista work. It was still difficult not to add myself to the schedule, but Roman is right, I'll be plenty busy making sure the greenhouse stays stocked and organized.

I still apologized to Stasia for not working the coffee bar

and taking myself off the schedule at the cafe for the duration of the festival. I feel like I'm abandoning my coworkers. Stasia called me an idiot and said I have enough to do without also working at Quickie Coffee, and she was proud of me for organizing this. Stasia also said she expected me to make this the best pop-up the greenhouse has ever had, so I'd better give it my full attention. I reminded her this is the only pop-up the greenhouse has ever had, but she argued we didn't know that for sure, and that was beside the point anyway.

I'm not sure how I got lucky enough to have the best friend you could ask for, and now the best pack. However it happened, I'm thankful for the amazing people in my life. I'm also thankful for Starsfalls, and I look forward to decorating the greenhouse for all the town's festivals.

At breakfast in the suite's eating nook, I look up at Salem from my spot on his lap. "I'd like to spend awhile at the greenhouse today taking pictures of the shelves. Then I can draw in the products and decide how to arrange them before they arrive. You don't have to hang around all day if you don't want to. With the builders and bookstore staff, I'll be safe from Lili."

"I'm happy to spend the day with you. I can help measure things or rearrange furniture. If you want to focus on your own, I can sit and read while you work," Salem says.

"I like spending time with you too. Once the festival is over, I'd like to join one of your classes and see you teach. It would be fun to delve into classic literature again, I haven't done much of that since college."

Salem brightens up. "You'd really like to join one of my classes?"

270

"Yes! I want to see that side of you and learn more about the books you like."

Salem hugs me and whispers his reply, "I would love to share that with you. I never expected my partner to be interested in literature, but I am thrilled that you are. I want to learn every facet of you too, so I hope you'll keep sharing your favorite books with me."

"We could have our own book club, just you and I," I whisper back.

Based on the hardening of my seat, Salem is very interested in that idea.

We slowly trickle out of the suite for the day. Salem, Fynn, Basel and I head to the greenhouse. Phoenix and Roman have a new lead on Lili's contact, so they peel off from us to investigate.

I don't see Alice at the front when we arrive at Pen and Tellem, but I hear her talking in the mystery fiction section. She's helping someone pick out a book, and I wave as we pass by. She smiles and waves back before returning to convincing the customer that mysteries in seaside towns are more interesting than mysteries set in big cities. The customer still looks skeptical by the time we pass out of view.

When we enter the greenhouse, we find Belinda there along with all of the builders. Usually there are only a few people working at a time since it's a small space. I briefly worry that something has gone wrong, but after a quick glance around, I don't spot anything amiss. In fact, everything looks great. Not a pane out of place and all the furniture is where it should be.

If I needed more confirmation that nothing is wrong, Belinda turns to us with a beaming smile. "I was just getting an update from your team. I hope you don't mind repeating what you told me."

Kas, the glass expert, says, "I'm happy to repeat. My team is finished repairing the walls and foundation."

Yvonne, the lead woodworker, adds, "We built the tables you requested, and the wall shelves are anchored in place. Unless there's something you want us to adjust, that completes the furniture commission."

Belinda grins at us. While Yvonne gave their update, I was admiring the beautiful furniture their team put together. Everything is perfect.

I'm sure I'll rearrange the smaller furniture pieces a few times before the pop-up opens, but that's just how I am. Due to my admiring gaze, it takes me a moment to process everything they said. Basel is on top of things, though, already thanking the builders for their great work and verifying that the plans have been completed, when it finally dawns on me.

"Wait, so does that mean it's done? The greenhouse is finished and ready to use?" I blurt out, interrupting Basel's compliments on sourcing the historic glass panes to replace the damaged ones. He doesn't seem to mind my interruption, chuckling at my outburst.

"That's right, it's done," Basel confirms. "They'll do a final inspection to make sure everything is in place and up to specs, and then the teams will sign off on the work."

I squeal in excitement and jump on Basel in a hug. He catches me and laughs, spinning me around. Belinda laughs too, and I remember I'm supposed to be a professional, so I disentangle myself from him and straighten my outfit.

I thank the builders and follow the team leads around as they show us their work. After the walkthrough, I make eye contact with Belinda, and this time we both squeal and hug each other.

"It looks amazing! I'm so glad I hired you and Basel to fix this space. I can't wait to see how you decorate it for the festival," Belinda tells me.

After our hug, we return to the others, who are discussing their next projects.

"Will your next renovation be in Starsfalls, or are you moving elsewhere?" a builder asks Basel as we approach.

"I don't have anything planned yet," Basel says. When I'm close, he puts his arm around me. "I'll be taking some time off as we move to Starsfalls and settle in here with Seph."

I smile and lean against him. "Well, if a really cool project comes up, you'll have to take it. We could all go with you to check it out," I tell him. I don't want him missing out on doing the things he enjoys because of me.

"I like to take a break between projects, anyway. Plus, we have a pop-up to run and a house to find."

"That's true," I agree.

I just want to make sure my alphas are happy too. Like the stories of alphas controlling omegas, there are some alphas who give up everything to do whatever their omega tells them to. I wouldn't want to be in a pack like that.

"When we found our omega, I hardly worked for months, and we weren't even relocating. I applaud you for still working on the greenhouse while courting," Paz, the metalworker guy, says.

Some of them laugh while I blush.

"We manage our time well," Fynn says, which makes

everyone laugh. I gently elbow him and glare, causing more laughter. He grins and kisses the top of my head.

After the builders leave, Belinda and I briefly discuss the pop-up. She's enthusiastic but doesn't want to know the finer details so she can be surprised once it's done. Belinda will be busy decorating the rest of Pen and Tellem, anyway. The bookstore always has great décor and special sections with autumn and Samhain themed books and sundries. Speaking of which, I'm looking forward to finding new books to get me in the autumn spirit. I want to read cozy novels and peruse the fall cookbooks. A few autumn themed mysteries wouldn't go amiss either.

After I take pictures of the completed greenhouse for my pop-up planning, Basel pulls up the houses we're going to view this afternoon. We've looked at a lot of different places already, including Tudor, brick Colonial, farmhouse and cottage inspired, and historic Victorian houses. I liked elements of many of them, but none of them really spoke to me. I had hoped finding a house would be like building a nest. Once it's the right shape, you just know.

There's a twinge of worry that we haven't found a house yet after this many viewings. Basel's list for today includes another Colonial, some Victorian revivals, and a stone castle. The last one intrigues me, but I'm not thrilled by the proportions of the turrets in the listing photo. The stone also looks a little too dark. Maybe it's a bad photo and the castle will be better in person. Everyone knows if a camera catches you at the wrong angle, you end up looking like you're a lizard in a human suit attempting to mimic human expression. It could be the same for the castle, maybe the sun was in a bad spot when the photos were taken. You can't help it if the sun is against you, just try again another time.

As we trek back through the bookstore, we almost run into Alice down a narrow aisle. She's looking at her phone and doesn't hear me when I apologize for almost running her over. I exchange looks with the others and try to slide past without disturbing her. I don't get very far before she looks up.

"Oh, Seph, how's the greenhouse coming along?" Alice asks.

"It's done! Well, the restoration is done, so now I can decorate for the pop-up!" I tell her enthusiastically.

"That's amazing! I know Belinda originally wanted it to match the fairy princes sitting room, but I'm glad you can decorate it for the holidays too. The *Princes* books cover all the seasons, anyway. I still think about the Winter Ball in book two. I hope one day I'll have someone to spin me around the ice rink in the town square." She ends with a dreamy sigh.

"I'm sure you'll find someone to ice skate with. I'll skate with you this winter if you want," I offer. I know she probably meant a romantic partner, but it's also good to have fun with your friends.

"I'd love that! We'll definitely skate together at the Winterfalls Festival," Alice gives me a quick, tight hug. "I won't hold you guys up any longer, I'm sure you're busy with pop-up prep, and I have a great book to get back to," she holds up her phone.

"They let you read on your phone in here? I thought you book people only liked paper books," Fynn teases Alice, but glances at Salem. Salem gives him an unimpressed look.

Alice, however, isn't bothered. She laughs and says, "Pen and Tellem staff are allowed to read eBooks, even in the bookstore. We sell eBook readers here. Besides, 'book people' know you can't always wait to start the next book until you can get to the bookstore. Sometimes you need a book, stat, so eBooks are the way to go."

"That's right. When you have to start the next book in a series at 2 am, you don't always feel like getting dressed and coming down to Pen and Tellem," I defend. Even though it's open 24/7, sometimes you don't want to leave the nest and brave the cold for the next *Interview with the Space Vampire* installment. I love the feel and smell of physical books, but eBooks are often more convenient than buying or borrowing the paper book. Plus, I can purchase the physical book later to reread if I like it that much.

"As I've told Fynn, physical books and eBooks both have their place. Convenience, space, and time are all factors in book buying and borrowing. Fynn just likes to rile people up about their interests so he can hear an impassioned lecture," Salem explains.

Fynn grins and shrugs. "I like hearing about people's hobbies."

"You could try asking people politely to tell you about them," Salem says in a long-suffering tone, implying they've had this conversation many times before.

"That's less fun," is Fynn's predictable reply.

Alice and I laugh at their exchange.

"I didn't realize I was stepping into something here," Alice says, "Otherwise I might have skipped past the defense of eBooks by telling you that the novella I'm reading is online only. It's a short autumn themed story in the *Big Tex* series. It's a special release, this author doesn't usually write short stories, and I've been devouring it. I finished the new *Big Tex* book recently and thought I would have to wait months for another. Then, surprise! There's a new story on the author's website. I heard she's going to write an winter novella, too. I love seasonal stories, and so far, *Big Tex: Taillights and Autumn Nights* hasn't disappointed."

I smile at Alice's love for the series. I like western elements in home décor and fashion, but never really got into the cowboy western genre. Maybe I'll check out this series at some point. There are already several books on my "must read ASAP" list. I'll have to add *Big Tex* to my "future reads" list.

"We're off to view some houses, but then we'll be doing pop-up things like picking up the fall soaps from the Slippery When Wet store," I tell her.

"Ooh, I'll be buying several of those! You should put some of our autumn scented candles in the greenhouse too. I remember how much you loved the fragrances from that brand when we first got them in, you were practically drooling over them."

I'm flustered at the mention of my delirium when I scented Basel for the first time. I know my alphas were also stunned when my scent blockers wore off and they smelled my actual smoky, nutty, amberish scent, or whatever it is, for the first time (I have a hard time figuring out my own components). But when I smelled Basel, it was like I was possessed as I tried to find the source of the lemon meringue and old book scents. Before my alphas can ask about that, I hurry to assure Alice that we'll have candles at the pop-up. She's satisfied with my answer and lets us pass, the sphinx.

CHAPTER 31

PHOENIX

Roman is quick to get out of the car when we reach our destination, but I follow more slowly.

"At least we're having better luck with this search," he says after I join him at the gate.

"Are you sure about that? We can't even drive down the road to the property because it's so overgrown. That doesn't bode well," I respond with a lift of my eyebrow. Roman doesn't turn to see the disapproving look on my face, so it's wasted on his back. I sigh and step up beside him to help get the gate open.

Roman finds the padlock but has to untangle the vines wrapped around it. I pull more vines away from the gate, but can't unwrap the thicker branches that are strangling it.

"I'll hold the lock while you open it," Roman says and hands me the key, angling the padlock up as much as possi-ble. I put the antique key in and, with a mental apology to the old thing, use some force to get the lock to spring (groan) open. We unwind the chain and get the gate open just enough to walk through, stepping onto the shadowed path beyond.

The entrance is interesting, to say the least. Fynn, who almost exclusively watches horror movies, would love this, but I'm not sure this is the right place for our future home. We've toured so many places in Starsfalls and haven't found a single one that we love. Our half-cocked idea of getting Basel to design our house is sounding better and better.

Which led us to looking at empty lots to find a suitable property to build on. The one we're visiting now is at the edge of Starsfalls, close enough to easily drive into town, while also having sufficient privacy. It has plenty of trees, which is apparent, and it's supposed to have great soil and a large stream.

The dirt path onto the lot obviously hasn't been used in a long time. I worry that we'll have to contend with cleaning up the land and installing utilities before we can even begin building. With the frustration of house hunting and our inability to find Lili's source, I've been feeling like we're letting Persephone down. Roman and I fight our way through the tunnel of trees, and I work out my frustrations on the impeding branches.

The trees at the edge of the property were decorated with yellow and red leaves. Here on the path, it's too dark to see whether the leaves blocking the light are red or green. I consider the most efficient way to clear a path and snort when I picture what Fynn would suggest.

I look at Roman out of the corner of my eye. His face is determined as he pushes through. As upset as I am about not finding the person responsible for Persephone's harassment, I'm sure Roman is taking it even harder. It's his job to do investigations, and now when it matters most, we haven't found anything. If there's an employee stealing corporate secrets or someone wanted by the police flees the country, Roman will track their movements. In a town as small as Starsfalls, you'd think it would take hardly any time at all to find the culprit.

We don't blame Roman for not finding Lili's source, but I worry that he's blaming himself. I may be projecting based on my past behavior, but regardless, I'll keep an eye on him to make sure he doesn't take this personally.

I quickly turn my head, narrowly avoiding getting whipped in the eye with a small branch, and it hits me on the cheek instead. I curse at the sting. Roman looks over and laughs as he sees me rubbing my face. He steps forward without looking and gets a face full of leaves when he turns back. I laugh while he spits out leaves. Once he's done, he grins and presses forward. As long as we're together, we'll make it through.

The road we've been following, which seemed more like a game trail to my estimation, disappears, ending in more dense forest. Roman and I look through the trees for the clearing that's supposed to be here. Turning slowly in a circle, I don't see an end to the woods.

"The path may have worn away. If we continue in the same direction, we should find it eventually," Roman says after consulting the property paperwork and compass app on his phone.

I pull up the plot information too. "The last time this map was updated was fifty years ago. I'd be surprised if the clearing hasn't returned to the woods just like this 'road' has."

"We still have cell signal, so we might as well keep

searching. If we get lost, we'll be able to find our way back with the GPS," he replies.

Roman keeps his phone out and takes the lead as the nonexistent path narrows.

"Did the realtor say if anyone had been maintaining the land? Or has it been left alone for decades?" I ask as I carefully watch the face-height branches.

"He wasn't sure, but if the cleared section has been overgrown, we'll still be able to find it. Most of the trees here are way older than fifty years, so the new growth will tell us where it was."

"New," I scoff to myself. I suppose fifty years is young to most of these trees. There's maple, hickory, pecan, and spruce, most of which look at least a hundred years old. I hope Roman is right about being able to find the newer trees in this crowded wood.

The vegetation is denser the further we go. I know the trail faded, but I still didn't expect it to be this difficult to walk through. I'm not even sure deer could get through here easily.

After another twenty minutes of huffing and puffing through the seemingly never-ending forest, we stop to take a break. While we catch our breath, I look at the property map again. If the GPS is tracking us accurately in here, we're not there yet. Having to battle through the vegetation makes the distance seem to stretch endlessly. It's more difficult than the mountain hikes I'm used to.

"Ready?" Roman asks after we've caught our breath.

I nod back. "Ready."

After another stretch of walking, I consider suggesting we turn back and get the road cleared with machinery. The wind has picked up, and the branches above creak and groan. Few gusts make it down to the forest floor, but when they do, dead leaves eddy around our feet. I trade point with Roman so he has a break from forcing our way through the branches.

I focus carefully on each limb as we crunch through the debris. After bending back a pair of golden boughs, I pause before taking my next step.

Sunlight slants across a glade, red and yellow leaves fluttering down to dance with the tall grasses dotted with goldenrod flowers. I lean forward to look around. At the far end, a river winds through, coming off the Fossfell Mountains and curving across the valley. On the right side of the clearing, the land slopes down to give a clear view of Aurefirth Sea in the distance.

I can picture Persephone here, going on a walk through the grass or sitting on a picnic blanket with us on a pleasant afternoon like this one. I smile as I envision a hazy outline of the house that Basel will design for us.

"I can hold the branches if you're having trouble getting through," Roman says, startling me enough that I almost let go of the limbs.

I look over my shoulder and grin. "Close your eyes."

"Listen, I got a mouth full of leaves earlier after laughing at you. I think we're even," Roman says, eyeing my smile.

"Just close your eyes. You'll be fine," I say with a laugh.

Roman grumbles but obeys. I step out of the woods, keeping a firm grip on the branches, and direct Roman through until he's standing next to me at the edge of the field.

"Okay, open them." I watch for his reaction. I hope he pictures our pack living here like I am.

Roman blinks a few times and looks around before slowly smiling.

"You think this is it too?" I ask.

He turns to me, the sun shining on his face. "This is the one."

We meet with the local wizened realtor before heading back to the Fools Rush Inn just as the sun is setting. I text the rest of the pack that we'll pick up dinner from Tacobout Gyros on the way.

When we enter the suite, Persephone is talking about the different types of gourds she's going to stock in the pop-up. I didn't know there were that many varieties of squash and pumpkins. We set the food in the kitchen and join the others in the living room. Persephone's audience listens with rapt attention until she runs out of steam. We let her know we're back with dinner, not wanting to interrupt her lecture by telling her earlier. Persephone rushes over to hug us.

Basel and Salem unpack the food while Roman and I lead Persephone to the breakfast nook, Fynn following behind. As we eat, we fill each other in on our days, although we don't tell them about our last visit yet.

After eating, Basel and I clean up and the others return to the living room. As we load dishes in the dishwasher, I surreptitiously check to make sure Persephone is distracted by my packmates.

I sidle up to Basel. "Are you still good with designing our house?" I ask quietly.

"I'd love to, as long as Seph doesn't mind waiting for it

to be built. Does that mean you've given up on finding a house around here?" Basel whispers back.

"None of the places we visited have been right for us, until today. We found an empty lot in the perfect location. The entrance leading into the property is a bit overgrown, but it has a clearing with plenty of room for a house. The property isn't far from town, and it includes several acres of good soil, so Persephone can have a big garden. I think it's the perfect place, but we still have to check with her."

"I've been working on some sketches based on what Seph liked at the houses we visited. It shouldn't take long to come up with the blueprints and get started. After you ask her, I'll show everyone my designs."

"What are you whispering about?" Persephone says behind us.

We jump and spin around. She's standing almost toe to toe with us, her hands on her hips.

"Nothing," we reply simultaneously. Not suspicious at all. I wanted to make sure Basel was still on board before we presented the idea to Persephone. I don't want to overwhelm her while she's busy with the pop-up. We can do most of the house design and planning without involving her, but decorating and furnishing the house may still be overwhelming. Persephone tilts her head and lifts an eyebrow skeptically.

"It's a fun surprise, but we're not ready to show you yet. Can you wait a bit for us to tell you?" I ask, trying to recover from our dodgy behavior. Hopefully she won't mind that I spoiled the surprise part of the surprise.

Persephone drops her arms, and her eyes widen. "You have a surprise for me?" she asks breathlessly.

"Yes. Do you like surprises?" Basel asks, trying to gauge her response.

"I love them!" she squeals and launches herself into our chests. We return the hug, and I exhale in relief, letting out the little bit of air that she didn't already knock out. Persephone stops squeezing abruptly and looks up at us. "I love surprises as long as they're not in public," she warns sternly.

"This won't involve an audience," I assure her. She grins and resumes squeezing us.

CHAPTER 32

PERSEPHONE

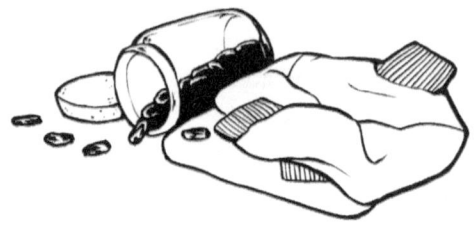

Basel and Phoenix must have shared their secret surprise with the rest of the pack, because my alphas keep going off to talk privately a lot recently. As long as it's a happy surprise I don't mind waiting (slightly im)patiently for them to share. I could use a good surprise for once.

I can't figure out if my surprise is related to the festival, our house hunt, or something else. At least I'll have the pop-up to distract me from my impending surprise.

This morning I rummaged through my boxes to find my hiking boots. Phoenix thought we should take a break and decompress with fresh air and exercise by going on a hike in the Fossfell Mountains and do some leaf peeping on the autumn adorned trees. We planned to leave earlier this morning, but my workout leggings distracted my alphas. After putting on my leggings for the third time, I lace up my boots. I think we'll be able to make it out the door this go round.

Roman is packing trail snacks and lunch while Salem fills water bottles when I return to the kitchen. There's a woven basket and a stack of plaid blankets near the front door. We must be having a picnic too!

Fynn slides up behind me after redressing in the bedroom. "Good, there's plenty of blankets. I don't want you laying on the hard ground," he says, wrapping his arms around my middle.

"We wouldn't have her *sit* on the ground for our *picnic*," Basel emphasizes while tying his boots. I giggle. It sounds like Fynn and Basel have different ideas about what we'll be doing on this picnic.

Fynn doesn't comment other than to say, "Of course," with my favorite crooked smile. Basel holds his stern look for a few seconds until Salem interrupts to ask if he should pack anything else to drink besides water. I request bottles of sparkling apple cider and Salem adds them to the ice chest.

We finish packing and load the SUV, by which I mean I am escorted to the car while my alphas load our picnic supplies. Roman buckles me in the middle seat and Salem hops in on my left just ahead of Fynn. Before Fynn makes it around the car to take the seat Roman was blocking, Phoenix sits on my right. Fynn puts his hands on the doorframe to lean in and glare. Phoenix claps him on the shoulder and gestures to the back row with his head. With a last, lingering glare at his packmate, Fynn climbs in behind me and nuzzles my hair. I sigh and melt as he starts massaging my scalp. *This is the life* is my last coherent thought before succumbing to Fynn's kneading fingers.

"We're here," the white rabbit tells me, pointing to the craggy peaks in the distance. I squint, trying to see through the clouds and flashes of light. Another rabbit rubs my arm, rousing me, and I slowly blink my eyes open. Roman looks back at me with an amused expression.

"We're here," he repeats. By the way he says it, I wonder if that's not the first time he's had to repeat it. Fynn is no longer rubbing my scalp, but I can feel him purring since his face is pressed into my hair.

I sit up and confidently reply, "Okay, I'm ready."

"Then let's go," Roman says with a chuckle.

I don't know what's so funny. I was just resting my eyes and conserving my energy before a big hike. It's the smart choice. Salem kisses my temple, and Phoenix gently wipes the side of my mouth before kissing my cheek and getting out. I squint and quickly run my hand across my mouth to make sure there's no more drool. Not that I was drooling to begin with, obviously. I furiously scrub my face before Phoenix turns around to help me out. I take his hand, and he sets me down in the parking lot at the edge of the trail.

I take a few steps toward the path, which zigzags up the edge of the mountain, and look out across the valley below. I trace the path of the river where it lazily flows down to the Aurefirth Sea. This side of the Fossfells has a stunning view. I rarely hike the trails over here, but I've been to the river and sea to swim. I look back the way we came and can just make out some of the buildings in Starsfalls.

If the trail is good, I'll have to hike here more often. I wonder if there's any good spots to hunt for fossils and minerals. On my usual trails, I stop at the waterways and cliff edges to hunt for specimens. It's a good workout hauling a backpack full of crystals and ammonites out of the mountains.

Salem joins me and holds my hand, distracting me from my dirty thoughts (of digging for crystals). The others have unloaded our picnic supplies and strapped them to their backs. Salem squeezes my hand, "Ready?"

I smile up at him. "Ready."

We join our pack at the trailhead and start the climb.

"Are you sure you're alright?" Basel asks again.

"My offer to carry you still stands. In fact, I'd prefer to carry you no matter where we are," Fynn says.

"I'm fine," I puff at them. "My face just gets red quickly. It doesn't mean anything is wrong. It's genetics. I hike these mountains all the time."

Out of the corner of my eye, I see Salem's lips curve up, but he's smart enough not to keep commenting on how I look like a frizzy hamster. At least hamsters have fur to cover their flushed cheeks. Since I don't want to use my hair to hide my face like I'm the monster in a horror movie, I have to deal with being asked if I have heatstroke. I don't like the heat, but I'm not any more at risk of overheating than anyone else. Omegas can handle higher temperatures than betas, anyway.

It's a cool fall day, my face just reflects any physical exertion. Why doesn't anyone get that.

Fynn says something else about wanting to carry me, but since his interest seems to be for romantic reasons, I don't complain. We continue our hike with frequent breaks, ostensibly to admire the view. I think my alphas are mostly making sure I rest and get enough water. The view *is* spectacular, so I don't mind the chance to admire the leaves and take pictures. The scenery seems to grow more impressive the higher we go. The forest on the opposite mountain looks like a golden blanket, draping down to the oranges and reds on the valley floor below.

After we start up again, Phoenix leans down to whisper, "We can go slower if you want. Our legs are longer, so let us know if we're moving too quickly."

I stop and poke him lightly in the chest. "Listen, I told you I'm fine. You've all had sex with me. You know my face gets red easily. If I survived a heat with you, I can survive a hike just fine." I'm speaking loudly in my zeal, and my voice bounces back off the mountain.

I hear a stifled laugh to my left, but Phoenix is apologetic. "I'm sorry, I know you know yourself better than we do. I just wanted to make sure we weren't pushing you. This is supposed to be an enjoyable, scenic hike, not a training exercise."

Salem is behind me rubbing my back, so I can't see him, but I can see Fynn on my left and my other alphas on the right looking contrite. Wait, was Fynn the one who laughed at my outburst? Before I can ask, movement behind Phoenix distracts me. I look past him to see another hiking group walking up the trail. The fit group of men and women are all smiling. When they see me looking, they wave. My alphas nod and wave back, but I'm too surprised to respond. Once they pass around the bend out of sight, I hear more laughter.

I sigh and slump in defeat. At least my face can't get any redder than it already is.

"Now we have to follow them for the rest of the trail," I moan to myself.

"There's a different path up ahead that we'll take so we can have a nice, private picnic," Basel assures me.

"It's still so embarrassing," I mumble as I turn back to the path.

"What's embarrassing?" Basels asks.

"This!" I wave my arm, gesturing vaguely to where the group disappeared. "I was yelling about our sex life."

This time, it is Fynn who laughs. "Is that what you're worried about? You weren't that loud, and you hardly said anything. But you made a good point. The rest of your alphas should remember how much stamina you have before asking if you're okay every hundred feet."

I sputter at his stamina comment, though I agree with the sentiment. "Well, still. Those other hikers were obviously laughing at me," I reply not at all sulkily.

"I'm sure they were laughing at us, not you. Alphas are protective, which sometimes leads us to be overbearing. They were probably laughing at us for taking you on a hike and trying to carry you the whole way," Fynn comforts me.

The others agree with him.

"Fine, I guess you could be right. And you aren't overbearing. I'm glad you care this much about me, but I'll let you know if I get tired," I say to settle this. They'll have to get used to looking at my red face forever. The thought of forever with my pack perks me back up.

I hug Fynn and then Phoenix.

"We'll stop asking, Persephone. Let us know if you change your mind," Phoenix says.

After the unscheduled break, we go just a bit further before reaching a fork in the trail. We take the opposite path from the eavesdroppers, who I hear chattering as they climb the trail that leads deeper into the mountain.

CHAPTER 33
PERSEPHONE

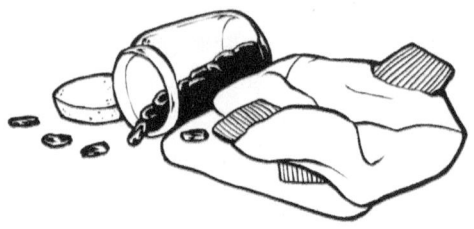

I lay back on my elbows and enjoy the breeze blowing through my hair while my alphas spread out the food and drinks on the picnic blanket around me. They offered to set up the picnic while I rested, and since they've been worried about me overexerting myself, I decided to be magnanimous and let them.

The blanket shifts and I open my eyes to Roman lounging next to me. I smile as he offers me a slice of aged cheddar wrapped in salami. I sit up and take a bite. The others choose a spot on the blanket and start dishing out food.

"The view here is great, don't you think?" Roman asks me. We're facing away from the mountain to look down on the valley.

"It is amazing," I say on a sigh, referring to the food and scenery. "I don't usually hike this side, so it's nice to see a different perspective."

"Do you not like this part of the mountains? I thought it was convenient to get here from Starsfalls," Phoenix says casually.

"It is close, and I definitely like it now that I've been here. It was just habit to go elsewhere. I like collecting fossils and minerals, so after finding some of the best spots to search for them, I kept using those trails."

"Good, I was afraid we picked a bad spot," Phoenix says. "You'll have to show us your usual trails sometime. I'd like to go rock hunting too, if you don't mind me tagging along."

"Yes, that would be fun! And I'll let you carry our finds back," I say teasingly.

He laughs and agrees to my terms. Yesss. I'll always let people help me carry rocks home.

We work our way through the picnic. Periodically, one of them will point out some part of the scenery, like the sun shining on the distant sea, or a hawk flying over the mountain. I didn't realize how much they loved nature. I love climbing around the mountains and going to the beach, but haven't had much free time recently to do those things.

After eating, we lay back on the soft plaid blanket and turn to cloud gazing, pointing out the different shapes we see. So far, I've found a maple leaf and a pumpkin. Salem points to a cloud shaped like a quill, and Roman thinks my pumpkin cloud is now an apple. I smile and agree. Fynn says the clouds above the opposite mountain look like a campfire.

"That one's a castle," Phoenix points out beside me. I look his way, but don't see which cloud he means.

"Where is it?" I ask curiously. I want to see the castle in the sky.

"Down that way, hovering over the valley." He shifts closer, turning my head to follow where he's pointing.

"It is a castle!" I say, sitting up abruptly to get a better view and almost bumping my head against his. Phoenix leans back just in time.

"Looks pretty fancy. I know someone else who loves castles in the air." Fynn pats Salem's knee.

"I do enjoy them," he agrees. "Though I also appreciate things in the real world." He nudges Fynn back.

"The castle picked a good spot to settle," Roman muses.

"Would you live in that castle?" Salem asks me.

"Sure, why not," I laugh. I'm not sure that counts as Salem living in the real world. That sounds more like a dreamland.

"It wouldn't have to look like that castle. We could build any style you want," Basel adds.

"What, like cumulus or cirrus?" See, I still remember some of the cloud types we learned about in grade school. Lucky I do, otherwise I wouldn't be as good at daydreaming with my pack. Everyone knows fantasizing is better when it's backed up by scientific facts.

Basel laughs. "No, like stone or wood. Since we haven't found a house we like, I was thinking I could design one instead."

"Then we just need to decide where to build it. There are plenty of empty residential lots in and around Starsfalls, so if you're open to building a house, we could arrange that," Phoenix says.

I stare at them.

"If that seems like it would be too much work or take too long, we don't have to. But we could oversee everything so you're not burdened with it," Roman says after a pause.

There's more silence while they wait for my response. I try to formulate a reply, but there's so many thoughts running through my head it's hard to string any together into a coherent sentence.

"You—you would design us a house?" I ask Basel.

"I would love to design your dream home." Basel takes my hands in his.

No more words will come, so I launch myself at him and start sobbing.

"Are these happy tears?" Basel sounds uncertain as he rubs my back. The others move closer to rub my back and pet my hair to comfort me.

I nod into Basel's neck, where I'm clinging to him and crying. I'm not sure he understands my answer though. The rest of my alphas offer soothing words, sounding strained, so I don't think they understood me either. It's hard to focus on their quietly murmured words. I hug Basel tighter.

When I compose myself enough to catch my breath, I release my stranglehold to properly reply.

"It would be so so *so* amazing if you designed our house. That alone will make it the perfect home," I say.

"Good. You're happy. That's good." Basel sags in relief.

"Yes! Obviously no other houses would work for us, since we have our own architect who can create our dream home," I praise Basel before strangling him in a hug again.

"We have an idea for the location," Phoenix says.

"If you'll direct your attention back to the cloud castle that now looks more like a duck..." Roman says as he looks over the valley.

"Just west of the river, there's a glade down that way," Phoenix adds.

Salem pulls binoculars out of his bag and hands them to me. I point them to the spot where they want me to look.

"The forest is very scenic, and the river is nice," I tell them. Are they asking me to live out here in the forest rather than in town? It would be nice to be so close to nature, and there'd be plenty of room for a garden.

"Near the bend in the river, you should see the clearing," Roman says.

I pan the binoculars over slightly and adjust the focus. "Oh, I see it!"

"We viewed some of the empty lots around Starsfalls, and that clearing and the surrounding land is the best place we found. The entry road needs to be cleared because the land was sitting unused for so long, but we can take you down for a closer look if you want. We thought this hike would be a good way to get the lay of the land since it's impossible to drive into the property currently," Phoenix explains.

I stare down at the clearing through the binoculars. It's the perfect little secret glade in the woods.

"That land is for sale? We could build a house there?" I ask in disbelief. It's so nice. I'm surprised anyone would sell it or that there's not already someone living there.

"Yes, it's a good area, and we could start developing it as soon as we close," Roman says.

"It seems perfect. Let's drive down there. I want to see it up close even though we can't get to the clearing," I say breathlessly.

"So, we're building a house there?" Fynn asks.

I put down the binoculars and grin. I never thought about custom building a house, but now that they mentioned it, it makes perfect sense. I'm giddy at the thought that we found the spot for our pack home, and nod happily to Fynn.

Fynn grabs me in a hug. "Awesome. I'll tell you where to put the fire pit," he tells Basel over my head.

"We're not building a fire pit," Roman is quick to reject his idea.

"It's a custom build, of course we're including a fire pit. Why wouldn't we? And maybe a smokehouse."

"There's not going to be a fire pit because you'll spend all your time out there testing how things burn. I don't want to lose any more of my shirts to your 'experiments,'" Roman says.

Fynn rolls his eyes. "Aren't you supposed to encourage research and experimentation? And anyway, I'm not going to spend *all* my time out there. I have someone new to hang out with since my last experiment with your clothes." He squeezes my thigh as he argues.

"You're supposed to encourage those things in kids. You're not my kid," Roman responds in exasperation. "However, a smokehouse for meats and cheese isn't a bad idea. See if you can work that in, Basel."

"Yesss," Fynn cheers quietly and grins at me like he won the argument. I laugh at him.

"We can drive down there on our way back if you want," Salem says.

"Yes!" I squirm out of Fynn's hold and jump up to start back down the mountain.

Phoenix laughs and grabs my hand before I get far. "We don't have to rush back. We have time to walk down and drive to the lot before it gets dark."

"Oh, right," I reply with a blush.

They chuckle but get up to pack away the picnic. I bounce on my toes while I wait, staring down at our clearing.

We make it down with fewer breaks than we took on the way up. I'm slightly breathless by the time we reach the car, but still full of energy at the thought of seeing the place where we'll build our home.

CHAPTER 34
PERSEPHONE

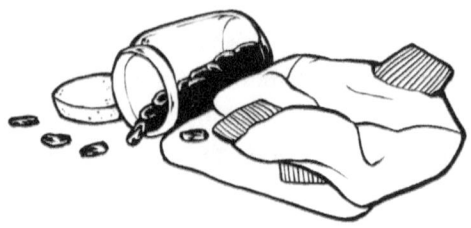

Despite being busier than ever with deliveries and setting up the pop-up, I feel calmer than when I first started the greenhouse restoration. Now that we found a spot for our house, I have the sense that everything is going to work out okay. This pack and the land for our house are everything I could ever want, yet never thought I could ask for.

Our new relationship enthusiasm is still going strong, taking up the rest of the time when we're not working. Some days I don't want to leave the nest, but after I've been brought my coffee, I'm happy to get up and go to work. I appreciate that my alphas support my life outside of them. They don't try to hold me back or keep me from my responsibilities (even when I sometimes want them to).

Stasia has had a few short-lived boyfriends who turned out to be not so much passionate as they were controlling. They tried to keep her from having a life outside of them or stop her from performing better in school or work than they did. When she saw those guys for what they were, she dropped them faster than if she had accidentally picked up a crab (she really hates crabs).

I don't have as much dating experience as Stasia, but I learned from her dating adventures, as we figured out how to navigate the dating scene to avoid the sharks in the water. I may have also avoided some friendly fish over the years because of my past, but it worked out in the end since I reunited with Phoenix and found my pack.

Basel kisses my neck again as I check my work emails and make a list of tasks for the day. His hair tickles me as he leans forward to kiss my jaw.

"I thought you were going to the town hall this morning to get building permits," I tell him breathlessly, setting down my notebook as his hands start roaming.

"That's not until later," he says, turning me around to fit himself in between my legs.

I lace my fingers behind his neck but lean back before he can kiss me. "Are you sure? I don't want to make you late," I ask playfully, fluttering my eyelashes.

He growls and pulls me in for a kiss. My laugh quickly turns into a moan as his tongue sweeps past my lips to tangle with mine. All thoughts of teasing desert me, and I grind on him as his hand slips up the back of my shirt. I clumsily try to unbutton his without breaking our kiss. As soon as I get a few buttons unfastened, I greedily run my hands over his chest. Basel mimics me, lifting my shirt up to cup my breasts. I gasp into his mouth as he pinches one. He growls again and pulls my shirt off. As soon as it's over my head, I'm kissed again as Salem quietly takes over where Basel left off. Basel moves his mouth down to join his hands.

Salem was smart enough to remove his shirt before joining us, and I eagerly run my hands up his biceps and over his back. He kisses down my jaw to my shoulder, sprinkling in gentle bites. I dig my nails into Salem's chest as Basel moves back and forth sucking on my breasts.

It's not enough, and I hurriedly try to unbuckle Salem's pants while they play with me. I'm distracted from my mission by a particularly hard bite from Basel, making me see stars as slick leaks down my thighs. When my vision returns, Salem is pushing off his pants. His cock leaks precum, dripping down to trace along the veins. I grab his hip and lick up his cock, savoring the spicy sweet herbal taste. After I lick away all the precum, he gently tugs my hair and tries to pull me up. I ignore his silent request and run my tongue along the ridge of his crown before covering him with my mouth. I hear him inhale sharply as I suck, and he floods my mouth with more of his taste.

Salem readjusts to hold my hair as I work my way down, and I see his eyes dilate as he watches me. Basel moves out of the way to watch me pleasure his packmate while his hands roam my body. He periodically makes me gasp and constrict around Salem as I pull him deeper.

Salem groans as more precum slides down my throat. His hold on my hair becomes firmer, and he directs my head while flexing his hips forward. I relax my throat, pulling on his hips to encourage him. My pussy flutters as my perfume surrounds us. I close my eyes as he moves faster, focusing on the feel of him, so I'm unprepared for being lifted off my chair.

I open my eyes, but Salem keeps his grip on my head so I can't see who's moving me. My leggings are stripped off and I'm lowered to the floor with a cushion under my knees. Salem moves my head down his cock as other hands grip my thighs. A tongue licks up my pussy to circle my clit, and I squeak around Salem. I just make out a hint of red underneath me before closing my eyes as Fynn licks my clit. My slick drips onto him, and I grind on his face as he moves under me. I jolt when his lips close around my clit and he sucks hard, forcing an orgasm. I shake and whine around Salem, who holds me close as he comes down my throat. Fingers work their way between Fynn's face to slide into my pussy, prolonging my orgasm. Salem pulls away after finishing but keeps his grip on me since I'm too unsteady to hold myself up.

I lean against Salem as Fynn continues his attentions, fingers moving in and out. I whine into Salem's thigh and press my hips back for more. A hand wraps around my throat, and I turn to see Roman behind me. I watch his arm move and realize it's his fingers inside me. He bends down to kiss me and pushes a third finger in. I clench around him as he finger fucks me. My thighs tingle and I already feel like coming again. I cling to whoever I can reach, digging my nails in for leverage to push down on Roman's fingers and urge them deeper.

Before I can, I'm lifted again. I whimper as Roman's fingers are taken away, leaving me empty. I'm not left wanting for long, as Phoenix sets me on his thighs and pulls me down on his cock. I moan as the head slides in, my slick letting him push halfway in with one thrust. I brace myself on his shoulders as he bounces me, his cock rubbing against every sensitive spot inside me. With each thrust, he grinds my clit against his body. I whimper where I've fallen forward onto his chest, my legs shaking and useless.

When I come on Phoenix, my slick coats his lap, and he works me over his growing knot. My pussy stretches around it until it pops inside, locking us together. Phoenix growls as his cock pulses and kicks, filling me while I squirt around him.

The orgasm eventually releases me, and I slump limply in his lap. Somehow, he's able to purr while we catch our breaths. Hands rub my shoulders and massage my back. When I muster up the energy to open my eyes, I see Basel kneeling behind me. He leans down to kiss my temple and whispers, "I saw your schedule. You don't have to be anywhere for another hour." I shiver as his hands wander down to my ass and circle the spot where I'm not connected to Phoenix.

Basel is right, I'm in no hurry this morning. I relax and let him work his fingers inside. Besides, he's the one who started this. I won't let him leave until he finishes.

CHAPTER 35

BASEL

Seph directs the delivery people as they place the giant pumpkins in the greenhouse. Several other types of pumpkins, gourds, and apples have already been dropped off. This current delivery may be my favorite though.

There's just something satisfying about a giant, perfectly grown pumpkin. It's a natural feat of engineering that fruit can grow that big and still be well-formed and stable, and even more astonishing that the pumpkin doesn't collapse in on itself since it's hollow except for the seeds. I appreciate the architectural elements of it.

Plus, the giant pumpkins remind me of that fairytale with the pumpkin carriage. I'm not really a car guy, but I do like some of the original antique cars with hand cranks and the strange and unusual carriages prior to those. Which leads me to thinking we should get a sled for the house and rent horses in the winter to pull us around in the snow. Actually, there's room for a barn on the property, I wonder if Seph likes horses.

Before I get too far with mentally designing our barn, Seph's excited squeal distracts me. She does a happy dance as the last of the giant pumpkins are delivered. I grin at her enthusiasm and the festive atmosphere of the greenhouse now that the pumpkins have arrived. The shelves are filled with an assortment of gourds, squash, and pumpkins that she said would be the perfect backdrop for selfies.

There are tables and bins around the room stacked with more gourds and apples for sale. We bought coffee machines and frothers for the mini Quickie Coffee bar. Other items have been stocked too, like fall scented soaps, candles, and perfumes, plus autumn themed quilts and scarves. Soon we'll bring in the fresh food and open the pop-up.

After Seph signs off on the delivery paperwork, I put my arm around her. "The pumpkins look great. It was a clever idea to bring pumpkin vines to the greenhouse and use them as decorations. It's like the pumpkins were grown right here," I say.

Seph draped the vines along the edges of the room, trailing toward the center and around the pumpkins. With the tiny and giant pumpkins, the greenhouse reminds me of a strange wonderland where objects aren't what you expect.

"They do look great, don't they? Since we dug up the roots and potted them here, I hope they'll survive until the end of the festival," Seph says.

"They look healthy so far, but we can always replace them if they wither. The vines in the fields will die soon, so I'm sure the farms won't mind donating more for your cause."

After a kiss, I follow Seph to unpack and arrange the smaller gourds. We talk as we work, sharing stories about our autumn activities in previous years. I tell her about the fall when Fynn fell out of the cart at a hayride because he tried to grab the head off a scarecrow as we rode past. After assuring her that Fynn wasn't injured, she laughs. I describe the scene after he fell out, the rest of us yelling for the driver to stop so we could get Fynn back. We couldn't see him, and when we jumped out of the cart to look for him, he suddenly popped up from the ditch with the scarecrow's sack mask on his head. Roman was startled and stepped backward, tripping on something in the road and falling into the ditch on the other side. I can't continue the story because Seph and I are laughing so much that it's hard to breathe.

"Nix paid the farm extra for disturbing their operation and the 'accidental' damage to their scarecrow. It's lucky no one was injured, at least physically. Roman's pride may have taken a dent." After considering for a moment, I add, "I think Fynn still has the scarecrow's head somewhere." That sets us off again.

Voices approach from the bookstore as Seph and I settle down and return to sorting out gourds. Belinda enters with an elderly man, and she brings him over to introduce us.

"Gerald here stopped by to see if he could get a sneak peek of the greenhouse. When he was a boy, this greenhouse was in use, and he remembers coming here to pick produce! The greenhouse was part of the festivals back then, too. I thought you might want to hear some of his stories."

"I'd love to! Was the greenhouse connected to a building then? Do you know who owned them?" Seph asks eagerly.

The man rests his hands on his wooden cane as he considers. "I'm afraid I don't remember who the owner was. I'm not sure if I ever knew. I was very young when the greenhouse was open, and it was abandoned by the time I was a teenager. This adjoining building was a bookstore then, and I remember some of the owners. I can't rightly say if any of them were the greenhouse gardener. It's a strange arrangement, a greenhouse in the middle of downtown. I imagine it was built long before I was born, as part of a residence or more relevant business that's no longer here. Although my great-niece loves plants and books, so perhaps a similar book-loving horticulturalist built this place."

Seph nods at him in enthusiastic agreement. "Yes! I also love plants and books. I'm sure there's many of us. Basel found the names of a few previous owners, but we didn't find the original architect or owner. Most historic city directories listed it as a florist or seedsman business. The restoration crew said the building materials predated the directories we found, so we don't know what it was originally."

Seph and Belinda continue peppering Gerald with questions about his memories of Starsfalls. Seph jots down inspiration from the old festivals he describes.

"You remind me of Lilith. When I was a younger man, an enterprising woman bought one of the old, abandoned buildings downtown. She restored many of the original features and turned it into loft apartments. When I heard about your greenhouse project, I said you were just like her. Lilith's restoration turned out beautifully, and those apartments are still highly sought after," Gerald says.

"That's so sweet of you to say. I hope my work is also remembered as a successful preservation of Starsfalls's history. I'm impressed her lofts have been kept up over the decades. Unfortunately I have personal experience with apartment owners not maintaining the building properly. I was evicted recently because inspectors found mold and the whole building has to be gutted and refinished. I'm glad some businesses care about their properties and the people who live and work there. Like Belinda taking the time to restore the greenhouse, rather than tearing it down or refurbishing it into something cheap with no character."

Gerald pats Seph's shoulder. "You poor dear. I hope you've found somewhere decent to live. I can see if Lilith's apartment building has any openings."

"Thank you for the offer, but it worked out for the best that I had to move out of the apartment. I recently found my pack, so we're moving to a bigger place. We're going to build a house just outside of Starsfalls," Seph tells him, smiling as she talks about the plans for our home.

"I'm an architect, so it made sense to design the perfect home for my omega," I say.

"Of course, you want only the best for the ones you love," Gerald agrees.

"Basel and his pack are definitely the best," Seph looks at me with adoration.

Gerald stays a bit longer, until Belinda takes him back to the bookstore to continue their tour. Seph wanted to go with them to hear more of Gerald's stories, but another delivery arrived. I console her with the thought that Belinda can share the stories with her later. That mollifies Seph, and I help her sort out the different varieties of apples and stock the apple cider, apple butter, and dried apples.

The last of the pop-up deliveries will arrive this week, so we'll open before the street fair starts. It will be a good test run and give us time to adjust things after receiving customer feedback. Seph said there are larger crowds during the street fair, with more visitors from out of town. By then, the pop-up will be perfected.

Once the pop-up is open, I'll focus solely on our house.

I've designed renovations for our pack houses before, but I've never created one from scratch. I thought I might be anxious to design something that everyone will like, but when I sat down and started drawing, it took shape almost without thought.

I can't wait to give Seph a home.

CHAPTER 36
PERSEPHONE

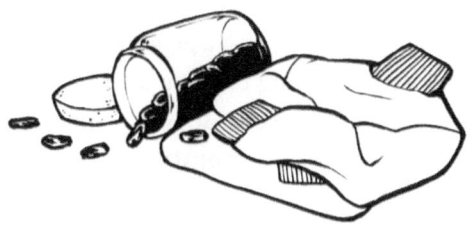

"Which one of these would my head look best in?" Fynn asks, hands on his hips as he looks at the rows of squash and pumpkins.

I laugh, his question reminding me of Basel's story about their hayride. I glance at Roman, wondering if he was reminded of his tumble into the ditch, but he doesn't look perturbed by Fynn's comment. Salem takes my hand, and we join Fynn near the edge of the pumpkin field.

I wasn't sure I would have time to visit a pumpkin patch for fun this year. I didn't have any deliveries scheduled today, so we took the day off to appreciate the crisp autumn morning. I'm glad the three of them came with me. Basel and Phoenix stayed in town to work on our house plans.

"Well, I think red is your color. Why don't you go with the red kuri squash?" I say after looking over Fynn's head-wear options. I'm sure he'll actually carve a pumpkin to wear on his head. He grins and begins sorting through the squash, holding different ones up to his head to compare.

"Where are you going to wearing this?" Roman asks the pertinent question.

"Around town, at the inn, to the festival. You know, wherever. 'Tis the season," Fynn answers smoothly, weighing two squash against each other in his hands.

Salem and I laugh as Roman rolls his eyes.

"How am I supposed to kiss you if you're going to be the headless horseman?" I say with a giggle.

"Don't worry, I'm going to carve a face in it. I can stick my tongue through, you know it's long enough to reach." He sticks his tongue out to demonstrate.

"Eww!" I say with a squeal. "I love pumpkins, but not enough to tongue one!"

Fynn takes a step toward me while holding a squash. I dart away before he can bring it closer.

"I thought you loved fall. Don't you want to support my celebration of the season?" he asks, rounding a table of pumpkins to follow me.

I laugh and hurry down the aisle. "I support your fashion choices! I just don't want to wear them."

Fynn drops the squash and chases after me in earnest. I squeak and run toward the pumpkin field. I don't get far before he snatches me and lifts me off the ground. I yelp and he laughs before turning me in his arms to kiss me. I tangle my fingers in his hair and kiss him back.

"If you want to do this sort of thing, you'll have to wait until we're on our own property. There are other people around and some of them are coming our way," Roman says in an amused voice.

Fynn breaks away to grumpily reply, "Fine. But I was just having a discussion with our omega about the different ways to enjoy autumn."

"Sure, that's what it looked like," Roman replies.

Fynn stands up and sets me on my feet. It's only then that I realize my legs were wrapped around his waist and

Fynn was kneeling like he was about to lay us down on the ground. I blush and dust myself off. It's a good thing Roman was paying attention. I do not want to put on a public show.

I'm breathless from our kiss and my short run. I look around to see if anyone noticed. The only people nearby are a small group, and they're not paying attention to us. Fynn puts his arm around me, and we walk back to the table we'd been looking at.

Salem holds up the squash Fynn dropped. "It didn't break."

"That's a contender, then." Fynn grabs the kuri and tucks it under his other arm. We move on to the next aisle to look for more potential heads. Salem laughs softly and joins us, Roman trailing behind.

We're looking at the Rouge Vif d'Etampe pumpkins when a group of people approaches us.

"I thought that was you, Seph. This is the young woman I was telling you about. Seph renovated the greenhouse downtown and is making it a spectacular contribution to the Autumnfalls Festival," Gerald tells the cluster of adults and children with him.

"It's great to see you again!" I greet Gerald. "I'm not sure about spectacular, but we're doing our best to create a fun pop-up," I tell the others. Based on their similarities, they must be Gerald's relatives. Maybe one is the great-niece he mentioned.

"I'll be glad to boast about you if you're too modest to do it yourself." Gerald takes my hand and pats it in a grandfatherly way. "The greenhouse is perfectly restored, just how I remember it, and the decorations are lovely. Some might say they have an antique flair, but it's what was popular when I was young, so I prefer to think of it as a classic style. As with cars, it sounds better to call the old ones 'classic' rather than old-fashioned or broken-down. Even if the latter might be a more accurate description," he says with a self-deprecating chuckle, thumping his cane on the ground.

"I agree, many older styles are timeless, I think they resonate with an older and younger audience. I took a lot of inspiration from old photos of Starsfalls festivals," I say.

"It shows! Now that I've bragged about you, I must remember my manners and introduce you to my family," Gerald introduces us to his great-niece and other family members, and I introduce my alphas. Gerald's family is just as friendly as he is. They listen attentively as Gerald regales us with tales of festivals past, even though I'm sure they've heard them several times before.

Gerald tells us about the year that the giant Yule tree destined for the city square broke loose during transportation. It slid several blocks down Main Street because of ice on the road before it finally stopped. As he describes the attempts to wrangle the tree, I'm distracted when, out of the corner of my eye, I see something dart past the nearby rows of pumpkins. I turn to look, but don't find anything out of place. Fynn looks around too and then tilts his head questioningly at me, but I give a small shake of my head. Deciding it must have been a kid running around, I concentrate on Gerald's exciting tree story. I catch the end, involving snowshoes, candy canes, and a state of emergency declaration by Starsfalls's mayor.

We stroll through the rest of the pumpkin patch with Gerald's family. Fynn picks out a few red pumpkins and squash to use for his costume, and I fill our wagon with dozens of pumpkin varieties to decorate our suite at the inn.

Due to the greenhouse work, I haven't had time to decorate my home like I usually do. That was fine since I ended up moving anyway, but now most of my things are packed up. I won't be putting out my usual décor, like the pumpkin-shaped mugs, ghost welcome mat, stuffed fabric pumpkins, and leaf garlands, but at least I got to decorate the greenhouse. I still love buying real pumpkins every year, so I'm glad we're doing this. Maybe next fall our house will be done, and we can get tons of pumpkins and apples and hay bales and cornstalks to decorate. Actually, I hope I'll be able to grow tons of pumpkins and corn myself. I'm not sure if there are any apple trees on our property, but we could buy some and transplant them to start our own small orchard.

Roman rolls our cart to the checkout table. The cashier rings up the many, many pumpkins I chose, and we walk through the hay bale arch to exit the pumpkin patch. As we're saying our goodbyes to Gerald, a dark-haired woman runs up to us.

"I told you I wouldn't tell you who my source was, but here you are harassing him! Leave him alone. You can't stop people from telling the truth!" the woman shouts and gestures wildly at Roman.

When she rushed up, Fynn and Salem stepped in front of me, and I tuck myself in closer to hide behind them. I'm so startled by her sudden appearance that I can't make sense of her words.

Roman doesn't have the same problem. "Who's your source? No one here has anything bad to say about Seph. I think you've made up this whole vendetta."

"Made it up! I'm not making anything up. You've been talking to the man who told me all about her. If he hasn't said anything to you, it's probably because he's being polite and doesn't want to mention your unprofessional business practices," she sputters angrily.

"It's a nice day here at a nice farm. There's no reason to argue like this. I'm sure if everyone takes a deep breath, we can calmly discuss whatever is bothering you," Gerald says to diffuse the situation.

"We don't need to discuss it. I already heard the truth from you weeks ago," the woman tells him.

Gerald frowns and Roman looks at him in surprise.

"I'm not sure what you think you heard, young lady, but I haven't said a bad word about Seph or her pack. In fact, I just met them the other day, so I don't know what you think I said about them weeks ago," Gerald says.

I peek around Fynn to get a closer look at the woman. Her voice is familiar, and she matches the social media posts Roman showed me. This must be Lili.

Like Gerald, I'm confused. I didn't know he existed until the other day. Gerald knew about the greenhouse restoration, but didn't know me personally. Even if he did, he seems too nice to spread malicious gossip. He only ever has kind things to say.

"I heard you at Triptolemus' Farm talking about the greenhouse pop-up. You said the person in charge was copying me," Lili says.

"I did visit that farm and talked to Mr. Willoughby about the greenhouse. I was pleased to hear it was being restored to its original form. I'm afraid I don't know your name, dear, so I wasn't talking about you. The only person I remember mentioning was my old friend, Lilith."

Lili's mouth was open to continue her rant, but she snaps it shut, looking stunned. I wait impatiently for her to respond. Now that we're finally getting to the bottom of the rumors she spread, she stops yelling.

"No, no. You said Lili, that's my name. Well, whatever name it was, you said the greenhouse was copying someone. And copying someone's work is wrong," Lili recovers enough to counter smugly, folding her arms and looking down her nose at Roman like she won.

"Oh my. I'm afraid you really have the wrong idea. It sounds like you only heard part of my conversation. I said that the woman responsible for restoring the greenhouse was just like Lilith, who restored another historic building downtown. The greenhouse restoration mirrors Lilith's accomplishments, but that doesn't diminish either of their work," Gerald explains patiently, like he's teaching a child an important lesson.

I look back to Lili for her response. This has been like watching a ping-pong game, except the game is battering my reputation back and forth. If this has all been based on a misunderstanding because Lili misheard "Lilith" as her name, I'm not sure if I'll be relieved or incensed. Roman has been quietly observing their back and forth too, becoming more tense as they go on.

"That's not—" Lili pauses, "what I heard. You said the greenhouse was copying me." Her eyes dart around like she's looking for answers or hoping someone will back her up.

I was so upset by the phone call that started this, but Lili's rumors haven't impacted our business. Her call brought Phoenix and I together sooner than if I had waited for his packmates to introduce us. And if that had happened, I might have run away from Phoenix without giving him a chance to prove he's changed.

If this thing with Lili *is* a misunderstanding, I'd like to move past it as soon as possible. That's why I decide to involve myself, despite my alphas trying to keep us separated.

"As Gerald said, I'm not copying your stall. Why don't we forget about this silly misunderstanding. I hope you have a good time at the festival, and we'll see you around," I peek around my alphas to tell her.

Lili looks shiftily around again but finally realizes no one is paying attention to us. No one is watching and cheering her on for telling us off. Hopefully this time she recognizes that we're telling the truth. Or at the very least, realizes no one else would care if our booths are similar.

Customers don't mind if they can buy the same pumpkin candle at a few different stalls. In fact, I like it when several places sell the same product. I often have trouble deciding what to purchase, and later regret not buying another scent or color. When I find those things again at another booth, it's a happy surprise because it means I can buy the item I missed out on. And maybe a few other things. Not that I think every booth should sell the exact same things, but it's never been an issue before that vendors supply goods to several sellers.

"Even if what he said was vague, the rumors are hurting my business. I can't have you spreading gossip about me like this," Lili says.

Roman growls and steps in front of where I remain tucked behind Fynn. "You're the one causing all the trouble. Now that you know this was based on nothing, it's time for you to leave Seph alone and never speak about her or contact her again. She's been far too kind in not pursuing any legal action against you, but I won't let this slide anymore. If you don't drop this now, you will hear from our lawyers and the police about your harassment. Do you understand?" Roman grits out while staring her down. Since his growl, Lili has been slowly backing away.

"Fine, whatever. It's not like I want to be around you anyway!" Lili says in a snit, storming off into the parking lot. I hope that means she'll drive off into the sunset and we'll never see her again.

I blow out my breath in a puff of air and step around Fynn and Salem to go to our car. They don't let me get far, Fynn putting his arm around me to keep me next to him and Roman moving to stay between me and where Lili walked off.

"We'll leave once we're sure she's gone," Roman says.

"Okay, I'm sure she'll be gone soon. She rushed off pretty quickly," I say and lean against Fynn while we wait.

Gerald clears his throat, and I notice his family is still standing nearby. I'd almost forgotten they were there.

"I'm sorry. It sounds like I got you in a spot of trouble. I didn't think chatting about what's going on in Starsfalls would upset people like this," Gerald says with a sad look on his face.

"It's not your fault. It was Lili's misunderstanding because she was eavesdropping," I duck out from under Fynn's arm to reassure him. "It's cleared up now, anyway."

"I should correct the rumors. Lili told people negative things about you and the greenhouse because of what I said."

"No one believed the rumors. We'll open soon, and then everyone will see for themselves that our pop-up isn't like her booth," I say.

"Seph is right," Roman says. "We talked to the people who heard from Lili, and they didn't believe we did the things she accused us of. Most thought she was exaggerating or blowing off steam. You don't need to worry about her, and it sounds like we don't either."

"It's not your fault, Uncle. Anyone could see she was only cross because she took your words out of context," Gerald's great-niece adds.

"You're sure I can't do anything to help?" Gerald asks one last time.

"We're fine. You should go enjoy the day with your family," I tell him.

He finally agrees and we say goodbye. Roman goes to check the parking lot and make sure Lili is gone. He pulls the car up to the curb and Salem helps me in, and then Salem and Fynn load our pumpkins in the back. Despite my bravado earlier, my emotions and adrenaline are all over the place after the confrontation, and I'm not sure how I feel. Instead of sitting with my worries, I look back over the seats and watch as they carefully pile in the gourds. When I see Fynn stack his red pumpkins in the trunk, I smile. As long as I have my pack, I'll be fine.

CHAPTER 37

PERSEPHONE

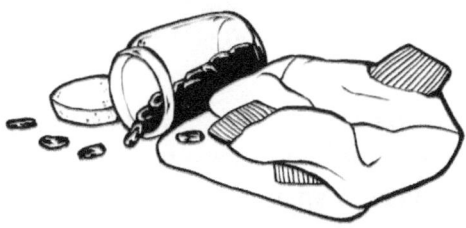

"Put the honeynut squash next to the Pink Pearl apples. No, not those, those are butternut squash. The honeynuts are over there and need to be moved here," I tell one of the bookstore employees.

I'm rushing around making sure everything is in place up during our final preparations before the pop-up opens this morning. The Quickie Coffee bar has espresso machines, fridges, a sink, cups, and, of course, all the coffee beans, syrups, creams, and spices necessary to make the best fall drinks in town (the best anywhere, if you ask me). The pumpkin cinnamon roll coffee can't be beat, and the apple pie spiced tea tastes like you're sitting in an orchard and eating a fresh apple pie. I don't let visions of caffeine waylay me for long, moving on from the coffee bar since it's ready to go.

The baked goods are being unpacked, so I hurry over to arrange the food in display cases. Once the vanilla pumpkin brioche donuts, pecan sticky buns, and other doughy foods are out, I scurry along to the next thing. My alphas are all here to help, managing the deliveries and directing the staff who are going to run the pop-up once it's open. Today's shift at the coffee bar includes Stasia and Grey, who are brewing coffee and mixing the syrups for the day. Belinda and Alice are buzzing around too, making sure we're ready to open at eight a.m. on the dot. It's just a little after seven and the last of the food has been delivered, so I think we'll make it.

I hustle over to where Alice is unpacking a delivery from Ladon's Garden. She's been putting the Opal apples next to the Blondee apples, and they're blending in with each other. I show her how to rearrange them while I unpack the fresh apple cider and apple butter. Belinda and Salem stocked the Powder Puff Pastries and Five Pies apple products, like the apple butter puff pastry tarts and caramel apple danishes, next to this table earlier so customers could find inspiration for using the apples they purchase. I love to buy specialty food but don't always know what to do with it, so hopefully this helps other customers too. Plus, they can buy the apple pastries to eat while they shop.

We step back to admire the apples spilling out of their baskets onto the table, and on the floor below are large antique metal jugs and stoneware crocks filled with even more apples.

"It looks great, thanks Alice."

"Right? So cute!" She moves closer to whisper, "I've been distracted thinking about the *Big Tex* news, so I'm afraid I haven't been at my best with the decorating. Thanks for your backup, cowgirl."

Wow, she definitely has those books on her mind. Can't say I mind being called cowgirl. Maybe that will be my thing. I should get cowboy boots. Fall is the perfect time to wear them, after all. When I last talked to Alice about *Big*

Tex, she was happy about his autumn story, but I'm not sure why she would still be preoccupied by that.

"Is there a new *Big Tex* book coming out soon?" I hazard a guess.

Alice gasps and tears up. I put my arm around her and ask, "What? What's wrong?"

Whatever the news is, it doesn't look good.

"They're—this is—this is going to be the last *Big Tex* book!!" Alice eventually gets out despite being choked up. Then she grabs me and starts crying into my upper arm (she's really short).

I wasn't expecting this. I pat her back and try to comfort her. "I'm sorry, Alice. At least you can always reread the books. It's better to go out on a high point rather than dragging out a series until it's no longer good and ruins the books."

"But it's such a good series. It could never turn bad!" she sobs.

I'm not as good at cheering people up as I thought.

I feel for her. It's hard to say goodbye to a great book. The characters stay with you no matter how many years it's been since you read about them. Great, now I'm tearing up. I keep patting her back so she knows I'm here for her but remain silent since I can't think of anything comforting to say. That seems to help, or Alice just tires of crying, and her tears stop and she pulls away. I grab some napkins off the table and hand them to her. She dabs daintily at her eyes and nose and smooths out her sweater.

"There, how do I look? Can you tell I was crying?"

Her face is red, eyes are swollen, and there's mascara running down her cheeks. I take another napkin from the table to fix the running makeup. Alice stands still as I wipe the mascara off her cheeks.

"There. You look great," I tell her truthfully. She does look great, but she also looks like she's been crying. At least her makeup is where it's supposed to be now.

Alice smiles. "Thanks Seph, you're the best."

"Anytime." I smile back, feeling slightly guilty. It's not like there's a way to make it look like she wasn't crying. It takes time for your face to go back to normal, so no reason to point it out. "Maybe I should start reading *Big Tex,* so I'll be there for the big finish. Then we can commiserate together."

Alice perks up slightly. "You totally should! It's such a great series. The final book comes out early next year, so there's plenty of time to catch up. You'll love *Big Tex and the Nights of Steel* and *Big Tex and the Virgin Roads.* The series starts with a bang too, in *Big Tex and the First Rodeo (It's Not His First Rodeo).* Oh, you'll also love *Big Tex Does Disco.* Actually, they're all amazing. I can't pick a favorite," she gushes.

"I'll start on them soon, then. I've been too busy with the greenhouse and everything to read much lately. It will be nice to have a new series to get into when I have the time."

"We can chat about the books as you finish them! But that reminds me, we should get back to setting up. It must be close to opening time," Alice says, glancing around for what's next.

I look around too, but it seems like almost everything is in place. I check my phone and it's just fifteen minutes before we open.

I decide to do one last walkthrough, but before moving on I remember to ask, "Oh, what's the name of the last book?"

"It's *Big Tex and the Last Ride.* A fitting name at least," Alice says valiantly without tearing up.

I pat her on the back again as we walk to the front to help hang the final ribbons.

"Alright everyone, it's just about time," Belinda says after clapping her hands to get people's attention. The delivery workers are gone, so it's just my pack, Stasia, Grey, and the bookstore staff left back here. Belinda continues her pre-opening pep talk, "I hear voices out there, so I think our customers are ready and waiting. On behalf of Pen and Tellem, I want to thank Seph, Basel, and the rest of their pack for restoring the greenhouse and making the pop-up a beautiful addition to the Autumnfalls Festival. I also want to thank my staff for helping with this new venture, and our friends from Quickie Coffee for joining us."

We all clap for each other like we're getting a class award, and I giggle. Phoenix squeezes me against his side in a celebratory hug. Fynn pats the top of my head, and I roll my eyes at him.

"Thank you all. Now I'll let Seph say a few things as the head of this project," Belinda finishes.

Everyone claps again as they wait for me to step forward.

I gulp, and then hope no one heard it over the clapping. I didn't know there would be public speaking! I would have said I had a sore throat and couldn't talk if I knew she was going to call on me. No, wait. I'm a professional business-woman who just completed her first big project. I can do this.

"Like Belinda said, thanks for your hard work, every-one," I squeak out. I clear my throat and try to channel the strong omega businessboss inside of me. This time my voice comes out more normally, "The pop-up wouldn't have come together so well without your help. Thanks to Belinda, who hired the best contractor for the restoration, and Basel and his workers for finishing the greenhouse in time. We have great local businesses and farmers who provided our products. Thank you to Alice and the bookstore staff, and my longtime coworkers at Quickie Coffee for joining us. I had a lot of support and assistance from my pack, both professionally and personally."

That elicits a few hoots and whistles, which makes me blush. I didn't mean it like that! I meant my alphas supported me personally by doing things like bringing me food when I was too busy planning that I almost missed a meal or reassuring me I *did* order enough varieties of pumpkins.

I quickly move on before I lose my nerve and start stuttering, "So, thank you all for working so hard to make our first year in the greenhouse a success."

I finish my speech with a pounding heart and slightly out of breath, but I did it! I don't even have a chance to overthink what I said as people cheer and then Belinda says it's time to open. She waves me over to the front, and I dutifully follow.

A rust-colored velvet ribbon is stretched across the greenhouse doors. Belinda hands me a pair of antique sheep shears and steps aside for me to cut it. Stasia hurries over to take pictures as I get ready to officially open the greenhouse. I give her a demure smile and hold up the clippers.

"Whoo!" Stasia yells, and my pack and the workers join in with whistles and cheers. I laugh and smile for real. Stasia keeps playing photographer as I cut the ribbon in half with one good squeeze of the sheers.

Stasia makes Belinda and Basel pose with me for a few more pictures before I shoo her away. I don't want to keep our customers waiting any longer. *I* can hardly wait any longer.

Basel and Salem wait to the side, ready to latch the doors to the walls after I open them. I tug on one of the heavy metal doors and throw it open (meaning, I grab the handle and lean back, putting all my weight on the door so that it slowly creaks open a few inches until Fynn comes over to pull it open the rest of the way) for people to enter. As I stalwartly tugged open the door, I was pleased to see several people waiting to come in. Some sneak through before Fynn has the door fully open, and more stream in as Basel opens the other one.

I watch in shock as the people keep coming. There are way more than the ones I glimpsed in the princes sitting room. They must have been lined up in the bookstore waiting to get in. Belinda records a video of our first customers and Stasia takes a few more photos before hurrying into position at the Quickie Coffee bar.

Once I find a break in the traffic I sidle over to Belinda, who is typing on her phone.

"There, posted," Belinda says, and puts her phone in her pocket. "We have a lot of customers already! If we transition right into the Winterfalls Festival after this, and then into plants in the spring, we should keep a steady flow of visitors. That is, if you'd like to stay on as the manager throughout the year. I know I originally just asked you for plant advice, but this all turned out so well I would love to keep you around."

I barely hold myself back from interrupting her. I wait until she pauses long enough that I don't think it's rude to cut in. "I'd love to manage it! I'll be here for as long as you'll have me. Oh, and I came over to thank you for handling the advertising and social media. I'm sure that's a big reason we have so many customers already."

"I just took photos of your work, you're the reason everyone is here. I actually don't have as much time to devote to advertising as I would like. I think Gerald also helped in that regard," Belinda says and nods to someone behind me.

I turn and see Gerald looking at the wool scarves. He notices us looking and gives us a smile and an approving nod. I wave back enthusiastically. I'm glad he came to the opening; I was afraid things with Lili would scare him away.

I think I'm moving on, too. I no longer look over my shoulder when walking around town, worrying that a secret stalker lurks nearby.

"Seems like the pop-up meets his expectations," I say.

"Of course it does, it's amazing in here. Now go mingle so you can see how much everyone loves it. We'll meet back up in a bit and decide if we need to adjust or restock anything. For now, enjoy it and hang out with your pack," Belinda says.

"It would be good to see this place from a customer's perspective," I concede.

Belinda laughs as I skip over to my pack.

CHAPTER 38

PERSEPHONE

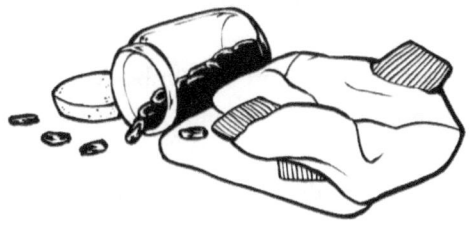

I admire the shoppers who are admiring my pumpkin wall, watching them line up to get their photos taken in front of the pumpkin backdrop. I sigh happily, glad that people are enjoying the autumn activities I put together for them. I move on to observe the customers ordering coffee, ladling apple cider out of the cauldron, dispensing pumpkin juice from the pumpkin keg, and eating pastries.

It's been a few weeks since the greenhouse opened, and people seem to love it. The street fair started last week, and we still get steady business even with the other fall booths open.

Phoenix and Fynn wander around the greenhouse with me while I savor the autumn fruits of my labor. After I tire of people-watching, we buy some pumpkin spice donuts and apple cider. We're sitting on hay bales to eat our treats when Alice suddenly appears through the crowd and rushes up to us.

"Did you hear, did you hear?" she asks breathlessly, grabbing my hands and jumping up and down.

Good thing I just set down my drink, so she only ends up shaking around my half-eaten donut.

"What was I supposed to hear?" I ask.

"It's not the end for *Big Tex*! This is just the beginning of his big adventures!" Alice shouts.

"What do you mean?"

"There's going to be more *Big Tex* books! The *Last Ride* is just wrapping up the first big plot line, it's not the end of the series."

"That's amazing! I've been enjoying *Big Tex* a lot, I'm glad there will be more books. What's the next plot line about?" I say.

"The author hasn't revealed much yet, just that Big Tex is going to explore new places and venture further west than he ever has before. The first book in the new series is *Big Tex Rides Again*. It should come out in the summer next year," Alice says.

"I'll mark it on my calendar."

"I already wrote it in on mine. Oh, I see another cowboy fan over there. I have to tell them the good news!" Alice says before flying off as quickly as she came.

"Do you really put book releases on your calendar?" Fynn asks.

I blink at him in confusion. "Yes. Why?"

"Book nerds," Fynn says as he shakes his head and ruffles my hair affectionally before putting his arm around me.

I huff but let him pull me into his side.

"I think it's adorable," Phoenix says and kisses my temple.

I smile and lace the fingers on my non-donut holding hand with Phoenix's.

Fynn asks about the other books I've read recently, and I

tell him about the *Victorian Werewolf on Mars* series that I sped through. When I'm done, I glance around and consider what snack I want next. I obviously need to try all the food we sell so I can give accurate recommendations if people ask what's good here.

Fynn tells Phoenix he should read things besides business reports so he can join our book discussions. Phoenix says work is important, but he's trying to do more things outside of it. Fynn continues teasing him, something about how most of his meetings could have been an email. Their banter makes me laugh while I scope out the snack situation.

I spot some croissants that look like my next victims. I ogle the varieties I can see from here, Seville orange, matcha and pistachio, rhubarb, and apple pie. While deciding if matcha and apple pie would taste good together, I notice a woman next to the display shoveling a croissant into her mouth. I try to figure out what flavor it is, since it must be good if she's eating it like that. I squint and think I see green powder on her face. I'll have to get the matcha croissant for sure.

I tug on Fynn's sleeve, interrupting his suggestions for out of office messages, to ask if they want to try the croissants with me. When I open my mouth to ask, only a croak comes out.

"What's wrong?" Fynn tenses and looks around for what's upset me.

Phoenix moves in front of me and scans the crowd. They must not see what I saw, because after searching, they turn back to wait for my answer.

Maybe I was wrong. I peer around Phoenix to look at the bakery table again, but with all the people milling between us I can't see it clearly now. *I'm* not even sure I saw what I thought I saw. I don't want to freak them out if I was wrong, and I do still want croissants, so...

"Let's go check out the pastries over there. The matcha and pistachio croissants look really good," I say evasively.

They relax and Fynn laughs.

"Alright, let's go," he says and takes my hand.

Phoenix leads the way through the throng of people. We make it to the pastry display cases, and I look at the other baked goods options. Ooh, fig and rose croissants. Phoenix and Fynn peruse the pastries too, and, remembering my mission, I look around while they're distracted. I tilt my head up to look just beyond the food and make direct eye contact with Lili.

Her cheeks are bulging with what I assume is another croissant, since she demolished the matcha one I saw her eating before. Her eyes are round, and she looks guilty now that she's been caught. I'm not sure if the guilt is because she was told to stay away from me or because her arms are overflowing with croissants, and she feels bad for buying so many. My sleuthing skills aren't the best because I didn't mean for her to see me, but at least I was right that I saw her.

My alphas look to see what I'm staring at since I didn't answer when they asked what I want. They spot Lili right away this time and growl. It looks like Lili tries to make a noise of alarm, but nothing comes out around the food in her mouth, and she almost drops some of her dozens of pastry bags. Clutching them to her chest, Lili turns and flees through the crowd with her hoard.

Fynn starts after her and Phoenix corrals me in the opposite direction. I let him move me a few feet before I gather my wits and dart around him to follow Fynn and Lili.

"Persephone! Wait—" Phoenix says, but I don't stop to wait for him to catch up. I speed after the others, who are getting away. I see Fynn's hair weaving around people, but Lili is too short to see over the mass of people. I keep after Fynn, assuming he has an eye on her.

Just as I'm rounding a barrel of pumpkins to follow Fynn to the right, Lili runs past to the left with a croissant in her teeth. I make a sharp turn and race after her alone.

She makes it through the bottleneck at the greenhouse entrance and pops out into the main part of the bookstore. I keep after her, and her eyes widen when she turns back to see me following. Lili picks up speed, moving faster now that there's fewer people in here. As I run after her, I once again lament that the bedroom activities with my alphas haven't improved my stamina in other areas.

Lili turns into the wizard detectives section. I grin as I hurry to get there before she leaves the aisle. I make it to the entrance just as she gets to the other side and realizes it's a dead end. She looks left and right, but there's nowhere to go. I wait smugly for her to realize I've got her. Lili whips around and sees me standing here. The croissant falls out of her mouth.

I wait quietly to see what she'll say. Silence can be a strong intimidation technique. It's not because I'm trying to catch my breath.

Lili straightens up from being hunched around her pastries and looks resigned to the fact that she won't get past me. I didn't have to say anything and I have her quailing before me.

Lili clears her throat before saying, "I just came here to tell you I'm sorry."

Now I'm unsure. My arms drop from where they were cockily folded, and I shift uncertainly.

"You came here to apologize?" I ask to be sure I heard her correctly.

"Yes. After meeting you at the pumpkin patch, I thought things over. I realized I was wrong about how I handled this. I know now that I misheard what that man said, but I shouldn't have gone after you like I did even if what I thought he said was true. I would be freaked out if someone called to yell at me and showed up at my work. I know your alpha said to leave you alone, and I will, but I thought you would want to know that I realized I was wrong, and I won't be bothering you again," Lili says resolutely. "After this apology," she tacks on awkwardly at the end.

"I'm glad I don't have to worry about you holding a grudge. But why did you run if you came here to talk to me?" I ask apprehensively. Lili seems sincere, but she did manage to corner me back here.

"I wasn't expecting to see you at that moment. I had food in my mouth, so I couldn't tell you why I was here. Then your alphas growled at me, and I was nervous because they already warned me to stay away, so I ran," Lili pouts in embarrassment.

She did have a mouthful back there.

"Thank you for the apology. You're welcome to stay and enjoy the pop-up. I'll let my alphas know you won't bother us anymore," I say magnanimously. I'm great at this business thing. I turned a rival company into a customer.

Lili looks relieved and then happy when I say she can stay. "Really? You don't mind if I check out the rest of the place? It looks amazing in there, by the way. Nothing like how I set up my booth. Obviously." She laughs awkwardly before continuing, "Your design is great, and I love all the food options."

Lili hugs the croissants lovingly, and the bags crinkle as she squishes them.

"Thanks. I'll have to check out your stall when I visit the street fair. We have some tote bags if you want to put your pastries in one to carry around. Unless you planned on eating them all now?" If she can eat that many at once, I'll be impressed.

"That would be great, I collect totes. I'll save these for later, there are so many other things I want to try," she says.

We walk back to the greenhouse together. I'm telling her about the other food sections when Fynn and Phoenix run up to us.

"Get away from her," Phoenix barks.

Lili and I spring away from each other. Fynn steps between us and Phoenix pulls me back.

"I didn't mean you, Persephone. I meant for Lili to get away from you," Phoenix ducks his head and tells me apologetically, throwing in a glare for Lili at the end.

I shake off my reaction so I can diffuse the situation. I grab each of their sleeves. "Listen, Lili just came here to apologize. Everything's fine."

"We told her to stay away from you. If she wanted to apologize, she should have contacted one of us," Phoenix says, watching to make sure Lili doesn't make any sudden moves.

I can't see Lili around them, but I hear crinkling and assume she's clutching her croissants protectively.

"I know I wasn't supposed to bother you, but I wanted to fix this. Starsfalls is a small town, so we might run into each other. I thought it would be better to tell you I realized I was wrong and won't bother you again," she says firmly, though there's a slight waver in her voice.

"You think she's telling the truth?" Fynn asks me.

"Yes, and I already accepted her apology. We were on our way back so she can try more of our food," I tell them.

"It's one thing to forgive her, but we don't have to let her stay at the pop-up you created despite her attempts to stop us," Phoenix protests.

"I know, but I don't want to have a vendetta against her. Lili upset me, but she never actually harmed our business. As a fellow autumn lover, she should get to enjoy our part of the festival, and then I can visit her stall too." I lift my chin stubbornly, so my alphas know I mean business.

Phoenix's lips to twitch into a smile before he looks sternly at Lili. "You swear you won't cause any more trouble?"

"I promise! And I *would* like to see more of the greenhouse, but I don't have to. I can go," she offers quickly.

"If Persephone wants you to stay." Phoenix looks back at me to double check, and I nod aggressively. "Then you can stay, but we'll be watching you."

"That's fine," Lili agrees.

Phoenix moves aside and gestures for her to walk in front of us. Fynn looks at me to see if I'm really okay with this. I smile and take his hand, pulling him along as I catch up to walk with Lili.

"We can let her browse on her own," Phoenix says quietly.

"I already said I would show her around. And we need to get her a tote for her snacks," I say firmly, and he doesn't protest any more.

I walk Lili around the greenhouse, chaperoned by my alphas. After we get her a tote and I get a matcha croissant, we browse the tables. Eventually the tension eases, and Lili relaxes enough to laugh with me and my alphas stop watching her every move distrustfully.

Our rounds end at the ice cream section, where we all get different flavors of ice cream served in hollowed out tiny pumpkins. I have the pumpkin cheesecake, Lili gets brown sugar and fig, Phoenix the Satsuma orange, and Fynn the toasted marshmallow ice cream. Lili sets her new greenhouse tote next to her as we lean against the wall and eat with our tiny spoons.

"This ice cream is amazing. You can really taste the caramelized fig," Lili says.

"I know right. The Magic Beanery Creamery makes good weird flavors," I agree enthusiastically, but sloppily, since my tongue is numb.

"I don't know how they did it, but this tastes exactly like a marshmallow roasted over a bonfire," Fynn says admiringly. "I wonder if we could figure out how to make it at home, but with more of the bonfire taste."

"Just mix some charcoal into the ice cream," Phoenix jokes.

Fynn, however, points his spoon at Phoenix and agrees, "Yes. Let's do that."

"I was kidding," he sighs.

"You know, sometimes you have good ideas," Fynn continues like he didn't hear him.

Lili and I laugh.

"I think it's been too long since I told a joke. I'm out of practice," Phoenix whispers to me.

"Fynn just likes fire too much," I whisper back. Phoenix's eyes crinkle as he smiles.

Once we finish our ice cream, Lili gets ready to leave. "Thanks for showing me around, I loved it."

"Of course, come by any time," I say.

"Do you mean that?" Lili asks me, but glances at Fynn and Phoenix.

"You're welcome here as long as there are no more misunderstandings," Phoenix answers.

I gently elbow him, but Lili smiles brightly and says she'll be back. We say goodbye and I wave as she walks out.

"I didn't expect that Yule miracle today," Phoenix says once she's gone.

"Right? But I'm glad she came by."

"You've handled things so well, doll," Fynn praises me.

"Well, I did my best, but it's not like I made her to listen to reason," I reply modestly.

"You're so cute and friendly, I'm not surprised she gave up her crusade," Fynn says with a wink. "I also meant that you did a great job with this whole greenhouse event. You worked hard to create this, and it's doing great. I'm proud of you."

"It wasn't just me. I couldn't have done this so well without you and the rest of our pack," I say.

Thanks to my alphas, all of my efforts to rigidly control my life by being hyper-independent and denying my omega failed spectacularly. And I'm so glad they did. Life is unpredictable, but with my pack beside me I know we can weather anything and enjoy the ride.

CHAPTER 39

PERSEPHONE

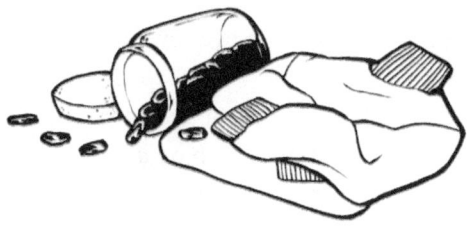

I flop backward onto the nest with a sigh of relief. The fall festival is winding down and the days are getting colder. Soon I'll have to get my extra thick sweaters out of storage. And my taller boots. I guess the weather change isn't so bad if I can pull out the cozy clothes that I've forgotten about since last year. I'll have to see if my alphas will get my winter decorations out of storage so we can decorate the suite. Hopefully they won't mind sorting through dozens of boxes to help me find them.

I'm not sure why I even questioned it, I know my pack is always happy to help me. I just wish I knew for *sure* if they're truly happy to do things for me, or if they feel obligated to. That may be my insecurities talking, but some reassurance from my pack is always nice.

There is one way to be sure we're all happy with our relationship. I've been thinking about it more and more recently, and not because I feel insecure in our relationship, but because I want to be connected to them. My alphas have been courting me for a while now, and we're still taking things slow despite being scent matches. Except for, you know, the whole moving in together and building a house thing. Otherwise, we're taking our relationship one day at a time, moving practically at a glacial pace even though I know they're the pack for me.

They're it. They're all I want. Forever.

I grab a pillow and pull it over my face, squealing into it and grinning like an idiot. I need to decide when to tell them how I feel. Should I make it a big deal and plan a fancy date night? Do I casually slip it in on a regular day, like hey we're together forever now, deal with it? I mull over my options, trying to figure out what each of my alphas would prefer.

After I start to feel woozy, I pull the pillow off my face to get some fresh air. Before I can come up with a plan to tell my pack how I feel, the bed bounces and I open my eyes as Fynn joins me.

"What are you doing in here without an alpha to keep you company?" Fynn asks, brushing the hair out of my face.

"I didn't realize lying around required an alpha's attendance," I quirk an eyebrow and tease back.

"It's not *required*, but it would be more fun," he says with a grin.

"What he means is, we like to be near you, but we understand everyone needs alone time. Right?" Roman says from where he's leaning in the doorway, directing the last question to Fynn.

"Sure, sure," Fynn replies flippantly as he tucks himself around me. I giggle and pat his cheek.

Roman shakes his head in exasperation but joins us on the bed.

"Should we move to the living room to talk about this?" Basel murmurs in the hallway.

"No, she looks too comfortable." Comes Phoenix's barely audible reply.

I assumed Basel wanted to talk about something that didn't involve me, like business stuff, but Phoenix's response doesn't make sense if that's the case. Before I can get up to see what this is all about, Salem reclines on my other side and Phoenix and Basel sit at the end of the bed.

I tilt my head to get a better look at them. They seem serious, but not like whatever they have to say is bad. I relax in Fynn's hold.

Phoenix squeezes my ankle and rubs my foot. "We wanted to check in with you and make sure you're happy with our courting, like a pack meeting. We've never been good at scheduling regular group meetings to discuss things. I know this is last minute, but I thought we could meet now while everyone's here."

"We've had plenty of pack meetings, but not everyone could make them," Roman says mildly, while I struggle to unwrap Fynn's tentacle arms and sit up. This is an upright type of conversation.

"I know I missed out on a lot of things, but I'm going to do better and be more involved from now on," Phoenix acknowledges.

"You've been great since we found Seph, but we went through a lot trying to connect with you. I know that's in the past, but it's still hard to think about sometimes. I'll work through it. Just keep doing what you're doing now," Roman says.

I'm still struggling to get into a sitting position until Fynn sits up and pulls me back against his chest.

"Thanks for always standing by me, even when I wasn't looking," Phoenix replies.

I'm glad I'm up in time to see this moment. It's obvious

from watching them that they're sharing their feelings in the pack bond, like an undercurrent to their words. It must be nice to truly know how someone feels, especially for important things like this.

After another moment, they finish their heart-to-heart and turn back to me.

"That unplanned example should give you an idea of what pack meetings are for. We can discuss anything, good or bad," Phoenix says.

"That's a great idea. I've never been part of a pack meeting before," I say giddily. It sounds so official, like I'm already connected to them.

"Welcome to the first official meeting as the complete Goldenrod Pack," Phoenix says. The others add similar sentiments, and Fynn squeezes me. It quickly turns into a pack hug with lots of purring.

While in the group puddle, we discuss pack affairs. Basel gives us a progress update on the house. I tell them about my new work goals, how I'll still work part-time at Quickie Coffee in addition to managing the greenhouse.

Our conversation meanders into reminiscing about our courtship and checking in on our relationship to see if there's anything we want to change. Basel brings up that Fynn needs to share my shower time with the others. There's not room for all of us in our current shower, so they have to take turns showering with me, and Fynn tends to hop in with me more often than the others. Fynn says he'll try to share, but Basel needs to make sure the showers and baths at our new house are big enough to fit all six of us. To which Basel agrees, and that item is resolved.

Fynn airs his grievances, saying he would like Salem to read to him even more often than he has been recently. That is also resolved satisfactorily as Salem is quick to agree and suggest that he could read to Fynn when I have to shower without him.

Pack meetings sure are productive.

"Is there anything else you want to discuss?" Basel asks me.

"I just wanted to say how happy I am with our pack. I'm so glad I got over myself and my issues with alphas so I could have you in my life," I tell them earnestly.

I should have tried to get over my hangups with alphas before I met them, and improved myself for myself, but I can't change the past now. At least when it mattered most, I was open to letting my mates in. "This pack has been the best thing that's ever happened to me. That's all I wanted to add."

I'm smothered in another mass hug.

Now that I've accepted who I am, I'm ready for more, but I'm not sure if they are. This is supposed to be a safe space, but I'm too afraid of the rejection to bring up the idea on my own.

Basel gives me one last squeeze before releasing me. "We're glad you're happy with how things are now." He pauses and shares a look with the others. Phoenix nods in encouragement.

What was that about? Now I'm starting to sweat. There's obviously something else they want to discuss that they've already talked about amongst themselves. Maybe they're upset that I took the last slice of pizza the other night. Except they said I could have it, so it must be something else. I'm so busy wracking my brain that I almost miss what Basel says next.

"We were thinking, now that we've been together for a while—well, I know it's not even been half a year yet, but it's been long enough that we know our desires aren't clouded by instincts or hormones. We want to be with you for *you*, not because we're scent matched. We love having you in the pack and wanted to know if you felt the same," Basel explains, almost sounding nervous.

Or rather doesn't explain, because I still don't know what he's getting at. Didn't we just go over this, more or less? I frown in confusion. That response isn't what Basel hoped for, because he's definitely nervous now and he looks to the others for help.

"What he means is, do you have any thoughts about our relationship going forward?" Roman tries to clarify.

"Things have been going well as they are?" I say questioningly.

Fynn grunts in exasperation and turns me around to face him. "What they're trying to ask is, will you officially join the pack? Will you accept our bites and bond with us as our mate?"

I blink. This isn't what I thought Basel was asking. I thought he was—"Oh. OH! Yes! Yes, I want to bond with you. All of you." I look around at the others in a daze. This is what I've been wanting, but I didn't think my alphas were ready for it yet. We haven't talked about it since my heat.

Phoenix is the first to gather himself. "Really? You're ready to bond with us?"

"Yes! Let's do it now!" I say greedily and tilt my head to the side so they have access.

Basel laughs in relief. "I'm thrilled that you want to, but we didn't mean right this second."

"Speak for yourself," Fynn says as he leans toward my neck.

I let out a burst of perfume as he gets close, and he growls and darts forward. I open my eyes when there's no bite to see Fynn's arched neck in front of me. Roman pulls

Fynn's head away with a growl, using the grip he has on his hair.

"Don't rush this. Don't you want this to be special for her?" Roman says menacingly.

Fynn's eyes flash in irritation, but he doesn't fight Roman's hold.

"Of course I do. But I also want to feel her inside me." Fynn thumps his chest over his heart in emphasis. "It's not fair alphas form the pack connection without a bite. It's great to feel you guys and all, but I want to feel Seph too. She's obviously part of this pack, but I can't even feel her!"

I tear up at Fynn's words. I don't want him to feel desperate, but it means a lot that he wants to be connected to me this badly.

I press my head into his chest and wrap my arms around him. "I want to be with you, too. I don't care how it's done."

Roman must let go of him, because Fynn kisses the top of my head and purrs. I sniffle into his shirt.

"Roman is right. There's no reason to rush it. That wasn't very romantic. I love you and just wanted to show you that," Fynn rumbles in my ear.

I gasp loudly and pull back to look at him. "You love me?"

Fynn is momentarily confused, but then gets a serious look on his face that I've never seen before. He takes my face in his hands before saying, "Yes, I love you, Seph. I think I was half in love with you the first day we met, and I've fallen more deeply in love with you every day since. It's been hard to contain myself, like my edges are burning with how much I want to bond with you. I thought you knew how I felt because to me it feels like my love is practically visible. I see now that I'm not as obvious as I thought, and I should have told you before. I love you, Seph. I want you at the center of my pack, forever."

I think I would have gasped again, but I haven't let out the air from my first gasp. I stutter out a shaky exhale after he finishes.

"I love you too, so much. You make every day better. I never thought l would find people who could be my best friends and my partners. My love for you also feels like it's trying to spill out of me. I've been wanting to bond with you, but I wasn't sure if it was too soon. At least after we bond we should get better at figuring out what the other one wants," I end on a teary laugh.

Fynn seems younger with the look of awe on his face, like he's been given everything he's ever wanted. I understand that, because I feel the same way. When I was young, even before I met Phoenix, I never thought I would have a pack of my own. How could I imagine I would be loved unconditionally when I'd never experienced it? My birth parents left me, and no pack or parents ever adopted me. I'd already moved through multiple foster families and group homes by the time I found Phoenix, and at least his words gave me something to latch on to. If that's how packs were, then I didn't want one anyway. It was a way to cope.

I was happy to find Stasia, Grey, and my other friends. I know they'll always be there for me, but there was still something missing. My alphas make me feel...not complete, but like I'm greater than I would be alone. Like I can do more and be more because they're part of me and I'm part of them. Together, we're greater than the sum of our parts.

Fynn hugs me fiercely, then hands me into Roman's waiting arms.

"I love you, Seph. I feel like our lives have been building toward finding you. I know I'm not perfect, but you make me feel like I'm both strong and protected, and I hope I make you feel the same way. I know all our days will be better together, and I want forever with you. We may be a pack in name, but we won't be complete until we're bonded to you," Roman says.

"I feel the same way, like I'm invincible when we're together. I love you, Roman." I hug him and try to keep my tears to a minimum. I'm not sure how I'll keep it together long enough to tell all of my alphas how I feel about them.

Roman turns me to Salem next. He takes my hands in his and smiles without saying anything. I happily gaze back at him.

"I should be better with words," Salem eventually says.

I frown and open my mouth to reassure him, but he gently squeezes my hands, so I wait for him to continue.

"With all the literature I've read about love, I thought I knew what it would feel like when I found my mate. Now I know that nothing could have prepared me for finding you. The way you make me feel every time I see you, and when you look back at me with the same feeling reflected in your eyes, I can't put it into words. So, I can forgive all those books for not getting it quite right. You are everything to me. I know I existed without you, but now I think I would cease to be if I didn't have you. You're always in my thoughts, and I can't wait to have you inside me forever after we bond. I love you, Seph," Salem says.

I nod jerkily back at him, since my throat is too tight to say anything yet. I squeeze his hands as he waits for me. After a moment I'm able to reply simply, "I love you, Salem." Looking into his eyes, I can see that he understands the depth of my feelings for him. He pulls me in for a hug and I bury my face in his neck.

When we part, Basel is waiting for me, picking me up to sit on his lap.

"When I first saw you, I felt a jolt, like you were calling to me. That feeling has never gone away. I'm still being called to you, your soul reaching for mine, and I'm trying to answer. As we grew to know each other, the rest of me feels the same way. My mind, heart, and body yearn for you. When we're apart, I think of you, and when we're together, I want to be even closer still. Every part of me loves every part of you, Seph, and soon my soul will tell yours the same," Basel says.

Basel is the one to finally render me speechless. He's right, every part of me loves every part of him, from my omega to his alpha, my heart and mind to his. I pour my feelings for him into a kiss. We linger and exchange a few more kisses before Basel ends with one on my forehead.

He lifts me off his lap and sets me on the edge of the bed where Phoenix kneels in front of me.

"Persephone," Phoenix pauses to smile at me adoringly. "Thank you for always being honest with me. I'm so lucky to have found a mate who is strong, confident, and assertive. I'm glad you were brave enough to turn me away when we first met. I needed time to grow into a man who knew his morals and stood by them. I'm sorry I couldn't stand up for you back then, but I'll never let you down again. I'll care for you and support you as an equal, like an alpha should with their omega."

"You were always the hope in my heart, that I had a mate out there who was my perfect match and the center for my pack. I know hope can't be controlled or caged, and just like hope, I'll never try to contain you. You'll soar far in life, and my only desire is that my love bolsters you throughout our lives. Thank you for not giving up on me and letting me show you who I am and how much I love you. Persephone, will you accept our bites and bond with our pack?" Phoenix asks.

"Yes, of course I will," I sniffle out. "Thank you for coming back to me and being brave enough to try for a second chance at us. You've been in my heart all these years, too. I'm glad letting you go back then was the right choice, because it was the hardest thing I've ever done. I love you so much, and I never want to be apart again."

"We never will be," Phoenix promises. I wrap my arms and legs around him as we kiss. He stands up, lifting me without breaking the kiss, and moves us so we're both kneeling in the center of the bed. When he pulls back, my other alphas surround us.

"Do you want to bond now?" Phoenix asks, running his thumb down my neck. I shiver, breaking out in goosebumps.

"Yes," I whisper, and tilt my head to the side. He kisses my neck, fisting his hand in my hair to hold me there. My heart pounds in anticipation. As many times as I've daydreamed about being bonded to my alphas, I haven't considered the actual biting part much.

I spent most of my life avoiding omega things, so I've only heard a few descriptions of the mating bite. It's usually described as a brief intense sensation just on the edge of pain, similar to an alpha's knot before that intense feeling becomes pleasurable. With the mating bite, it should quickly be overshadowed by feeling the bond lock in place. I try to regulate my panting breaths. My alphas have knotted me plenty of times now and I've always enjoyed it. I'm sure these quick nips will be no problem.

I grip the sides of Phoenix's shirt and brace myself, but he kisses away from my neck back to my lips. My other alphas touch and kiss me too. By the time Phoenix pulls away to lift off my shirt, I'm no longer tense. He resumes kissing me, making his way down my chest where he meets Fynn, who is sucking on one of my breasts. Phoenix takes the other and they alternate sucking and nipping them. Roman tilts my head back and scrapes his teeth along my arched neck, making me moan. A thought flickers briefly, telling me to brace again, but a firm pinch on my nipple chases the idea away before I can catch it. I whimper and slick dampens my thighs. Someone growls and my leggings are partially pulled down before they're suddenly gone to the sound of tearing fabric.

Roman is kissing me so I can't see who parts my legs, and I jolt as a thumb circles my clit. I try to angle toward it, but my legs are being held open so I can't move. They must realize what I want though, because the thumb is replaced by knuckles trapping my clit and squeezing. I shake as I come, my mouth open in a silent scream. Roman takes the opportunity to explore me with his tongue. I dig my nails into his arms as I gush around the fingers plunging into my pussy.

I pant as I catch my breath. I must have been out of it for a second, because Roman is no longer kissing me. My thighs slide over skin, and I flutter my eyes open as Phoenix lowers me onto his cock. I hold on to his shoulders and he grips my ass to lower me down. The head slides in, and Phoenix slowly bounces me up and down, moving deeper while I do my best to help by gushing slick on him. My pussy pulls him in, and I come again as his cock rubs deep inside me. Phoenix growls and tugs me down harder with each thrust.

When I finish, he grinds his knot against my entrance without pushing it inside. Hands run between my thighs and up my cheeks, spreading my slick around, and I turn my head to see Basel behind me. My pussy clenches around Phoenix as Basel fingers me, teasing me until he finally replaces his fingers with his cock. Phoenix continues to grind against my clit as Basel works his way in.

I whine and twist as they pass me back and forth, pulling me onto one cock and off the other. After driving me crazy with their opposing rhythm, they sync up and the sudden fullness makes it hard to breathe. When they pull out, I'm able to catch my breath, and then they start the cycle all over again. Finally, the pressure breaks. Basel wraps his arms under mine to hold me against his chest while I come. Phoenix bends down and kisses me. I sloppily kiss him back as I quiver through my orgasm. Before I finish, he grips my chin and tilts my head up to kiss my neck.

There's a strange sensation as his lips touch. It's like Phoenix is entering me again, but he's still inside me. Before I can figure out what's causing the feeling, a dam bursts open in my chest and Phoenix floods in. He's everywhere, flowing through me and lapping against my edges. Tears trickle down my cheeks as Phoenix stretches out like an ocean inside me, beyond what I can comprehend. I wade in, trailing my fingers through him as I marvel at everything that he is, his love sparkling on the waves around me.

Phoenix settles inside me, a calm sea on a still day, but I can feel everything he feels beneath the surface. At the edges of our connection, like islands in the distance, I sense the other alphas in our pack, Basel, Fynn, Roman, Salem.

I open my eyes to see a dazed Phoenix licking a trace of blood off his lip. I want him to feel me just as clearly, so I pull him close. He follows my demand easily, and I strike, sinking my teeth in over his heart.

The tide flows in reverse this time as I rush into Phoenix, the bond between us snapping into place. Our oceans collide and mix until I can't tell the difference. The waves roll between us, letting my love for him roll in like he did for me. Since Phoenix already has a place inside me, I feel his awe and then delight as my bite connects us. Our souls settle into their new expanse, and I release my jaw to lick at the mark I left on his chest.

When I'm done, Phoenix tilts me back to do the same, tending his bite on my neck. I shiver as his tongue moves over the newly sensitive spot. It causes a cascade of tingles through my body and my pussy gives a reflexive squeeze on his cock.

With a few last tantalizing licks, Phoenix pulls me forward to rest on his chest. As he does, I feel Basel's cock twitch inside me, reminding me I have more alphas to bond with. Basel nuzzles the back of my neck, his exhale tickling my hair and making me shiver. He runs his lips down the right side of my neck, opposite Phoenix's mark on the left.

I eagerly wait for his bite, no longer nervous about the mark that will connect us forever. Basel cradles my head in his hand as he kisses my neck. His other hand slides down my front, brushing my breast and coming to rest across my stomach, before he gently sinks his teeth in.

Basel rises like a craggy peak inside me, suddenly cresting the surface of Phoenix's ocean, my rock and my champion. He promises he'll always be with me, there to help me reach new heights. Being with Basel and joining this pack are already the loftiest things I could have wished for. His love rumbles through me, like a low, rolling earthquake that never ends, as the bond settles in.

I revel in Basel's care as he cleans my neck, but I don't let him linger for long. I direct Phoenix and Basel to help me turn around, and they pull out and readjust me. I stretch up for a kiss from Basel, enjoying the way I can feel his pleasure now in addition to my own. I stroke his cheek, and he smiles, eagerly waiting for me to complete our bond. I kiss over his heart and return his gentle bite.

I stream in across the core of who Basel is, solid and sure. I promise to always be there for him and buoy him up throughout our lives together. I know we'll change as we grow older, but we'll always fit together like this. I focus on my love for him so Basel feels it surrounding him as the bond ties us together.

I languidly release him and clean my bite. He shudders as I finish. I lean against him, his heart beating under my ear and inside me.

I'm worn out, like how I felt after my heat with them. Adjusting to the bonds must take more effort than I realized. I drift between sleep and consciousness, feeling the joy of my two alphas.

CHAPTER 40

PERSEPHONE

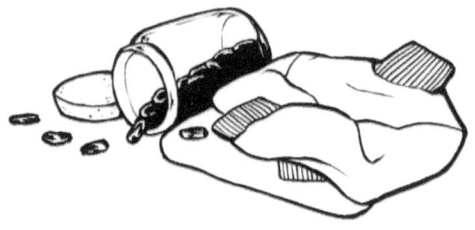

Phoenix and Basel surround me in my dreams, and when I wake, I remember they'll always be with me. I smile and open my eyes to find them waiting for me. They take turns kissing me and I don't want to stop, lost in the sensations bouncing between the three of us. I almost protest when they pull back and sit me up, until I see Fynn.

They pass me to him, and Fynn grins before diving in for a licking kiss. I didn't mean to take a nap after bonding the others, and I'm glad Fynn doesn't seem disappointed by the delay. It surprises me when he stops and allows Salem to turn my head for a kiss. I still half expected Fynn to bite me quickly, even though he agreed a slower approach was better. Instead, he shares me with Salem. Fynn kneels in front, and Salem behind, and with the two of them working together, I'm a panting mess in no time.

Fresh slick coats my legs by the time Fynn slides his cock in. He only thrusts a few times before pulling out and letting Salem take his turn. They trade back and forth, working me into a frenzy since I can't get enough of either of them. They tease me in different ways, at different angles, until eventually I come on Fynn's cock.

Fynn stills, and there's more pressure at my entrance. I think he's going to knot me until I feel fingers spread my lips. I whine as Salem's cock attempts to join Fynn's inside me. Salem kisses the side of my neck, making me quiver when he brushes over Phoenix's bite. "Do you want me here too?" Salem asks. Lost for words, I nod, tugging his hair to urge him closer. More slick flows out, easing Salem's way as he slowly works to fit his head in. My legs tremble, body unsure it can stretch any more. Fynn rubs my clit, distracting me from my impossible task.

The pleasure and pressure build, until I can't feel anything else. Fynn pulls out to push back in with shallow thrusts. Salem follows one of his upward strokes, and with a push, they both pop inside. I lose control, only staying upright because they're holding me. My pussy twitches, stretched around their cocks, and I can't feel anything but them. Salem and Fynn rub against each other as they move deeper. When Fynn pinches my clit, my vision fades and I squirt as I come, my body shaking like they hit me with a lightning bolt.

The light blinds me as the heat beats down from above. But as my senses return, I see only pinpricks of light dotting the darkness that envelopes me. Fynn and Salem are twin weights on my neck as they bite me together. Fynn is a sunbeam, his love shining over me as he shares himself in the bond. I see now how sensitive he is and how intensely he feels emotions. His need for an outlet for the feelings he can't contain, a way to burn off the excess emotions that sometimes fill him to bursting.

Salem is the velvet that envelopes us, his essence reserved, hidden in the distance. His wit, humor, and love shine through like stars if you're lucky enough to get to know him. Somehow, Fynn and Salem blend well together, slipping in to fit neatly inside me with Phoenix and Basel. I shouldn't be surprised, Salem and Fynn's banter reflects the draw between them. Despite their differences, my alphas are like complementary pieces that fit together. I sink into the bright darkness as they share their love for me.

When they let go to soothe their bites, Fynn and Salem carefully slide out of me. They lay me on the bed, as I have little control over my legs after their double feature. Fynn props himself up on one side of me and Salem leans in on the other.

"I don't think I'll be able to bite both of you at the same time," I puff out.

They laugh.

"We don't expect you to. You can bite Salem first," Fynn says.

Salem glances at him in surprise before saying, "You can bite us in whatever order you want, whenever you feel ready. There's no rush."

"I want to complete our bond right now, but this is an important occasion for you too. It should be special, which is why I'm not asking you to prop my head up. Give me a minute to rest so I can bite you without assistance," I say.

Fynn chuckles and lays down with his head is next to mine. Salem smiles at us. I have just enough energy to reach for each of their hands before I fall asleep.

I wake up with my head turned to the side, facing Fynn. Even though he said I should bond Salem first, I don't want Fynn to wait any longer. I love my alpha's equally, but Fynn has always been clingier. Now that I have his bite, I sense the hurt he's buried deep inside himself. Without prying too much into it, I only sense that he felt unwanted or neglected for so long that it permanently scarred him. I assume that stems from his childhood spent in foster care, because I know our pack wouldn't treat him like that.

I strain to reach Salem through his bond, which is difficult since I have yet to complete the connection, but it's enough that he senses what I'm asking. He reassures me he doesn't mind if I bond with Fynn first. Salem won't have to wait much longer, anyway.

I squeeze Salem's hand and let go, rolling to face Fynn and pulling him in for a kiss. I go slowly, feeling his happiness and pleasure rising like steam inside me, making me smile. I'm sure it will take time to adjust to the bonds and being able to feel five other people's emotions, but so far, I'm loving it.

Fynn grows hotter as our kiss gets deeper. I lean into him, and he pulls my hips flush with his. Before he can distract me from my aim, I pull away, and his lips try to follow. I give him a quick kiss on the cheek before he can catch me, and then shimmy down so I'm eye-level with his collarbone. I readjust to get the right angle for the bite, but Fynn grabs my shoulder before I can.

"Salem is supposed to go first," he reminds me.

"I'll bond Salem in a second. You're going first," I say firmly.

"But...are you sure?" His eyes flick to Salem.

"I'll be just behind you," Salem says.

I feel a brief flare of feeling from Fynn, there and gone almost before I notice it, like he's still not really sure I'll bond with him. I want to reassure him, and the best way to do that is to show him that I want him and always will.

I gently move Fynn's hand off my shoulder. Leaning forward, I glance up and wait to see if he's ready. Fynn opens his mouth to protest again, but I feel his emotions wavering, and after a moment, he quirks his lips and nods. I smile and then bite over his heart like I did with the others.

Fynn barely has time to register surprise and relief before I push my affection for him through the bond. Now I can show him how much I love him, how amazing he is, funny, charming, spontaneous, and caring. Fynn hovers around me like a heat haze as I reassure him that the rest of our pack loves him just as much as I do, and he'll never be alone or unwanted again. Fynn still harbored these doubts despite being bonded to his packmates, but I hope our connection will help him recognize his worth as he sees how amazing he is through my eyes.

His happiness bubbles through our bond and scatters his thoughts, which bounce between diving in further to get to know me, to thinking about future plans with our pack. As Fynn's thoughts bump into mine, they pop and dissipate in the steam. Despite the many ideas floating around, most of Fynn's focus is simply on how much he loves me.

After releasing Fynn and cleaning my bite, I hold him. He purrs as we settle into knowing each other. I've read that you can learn to control how much you sense from the other end of the bond. Likewise, you can regulate how much of yourself you share at any given time. That way you're not overwhelmed by someone else's, ahem, pleasurable thoughts when you're somewhere inopportune. When mates are together, they can open the bond and feel the pleasure of the other person alongside their own. However, Fynn feels things so strongly and shares himself so openly that I'm not sure there will ever be much separation between us.

I subtly reach for Phoenix and Basel in the bond to see if Fynn is always this expressive. They quickly send their amusement back and confirm that, yes, Fynn is always this open in their bonds. They've learned to tune some of his exuberance out when they're busy.

Apparently, I'm also not good at limiting what I share, because Fynn agrees that he's fine with them blocking him when they need to concentrate. He hurriedly adds that he can work on restraining himself so he doesn't bother me, and I feel him (unsuccessfully) trying to pull back. I grab at our bond to stop him. I'll learn to focus on my thoughts and leave the others in the background when I need to. Fynn pauses and then untethers himself again as I reassure him that he doesn't have to hold back.

I pull Fynn down for a kiss, his energy making me feel like I've been dropped into a glass of champagne. When we part, I look for Salem waiting patiently beside us. I'm refreshed after my rest and have Fynn's energy bolstering me. Fynn and I sit up, and I lean against his chest before pulling Salem toward me. He kneels in front of me to cup my face in his hands and kiss my forehead, and then straightens up to wait for my bite.

I place my mark on Salem's heart and float into his space, fitting myself between the sparkling points of his intelligence, care, and love. My bond spreads through like mist, my love sinking in as far as I can reach. Our bond is a safe space, soothing and invigorating, like it could calm an anxious mind and facilitate clear thinking. There are definitely times I could use a calming presence, although I like to think I'm not a very anxious person. I hope I can provide the same refuge for him, so that when life gets difficult, we'll be a safe harbor for each other.

Our bond in place, I soothe my mark and hug Salem tight, glad to feel his comforting presence inside me. After a final hug from Fynn and Salem, they hand me off to my last alpha.

Roman crawls across the bed to join me. Once we bond, our pack will be complete. Roman had to wait the longest, but he'll have me all to himself for our joining.

He sits back on his heels and pulls me onto his lap, straddling his thighs. I reach up for a kiss, and Roman lifts me, rubbing his cock along my pussy. I squeeze my legs around him for leverage to grind on him. He keeps one hand on my thigh to help and uses the other to play with my breasts. Roman rolls my nipple between his fingers, and I whimper when he pinches it. Fresh slick makes my bouncing erratic as I slide across his lap.

I dig my nails into his shoulders as I try to come, my kisses turning sloppy. I pant as I get close, and Roman growls and sucks on my tongue. He pulls me onto his cock just as I come, and I clench around him, slick tickling down his shaft as he fucks me with rough thrusts. I claw at his arms, trying to hold on as I shake.

His strokes drag out my orgasm, so that I'm gasping by the end of it. I'm boneless as Roman spreads my legs wide to pull me onto his knot, forcing me to come again as it stretches me. My slick gushes around him and with one last thrust, Roman locks us together. His cock kicks inside me as it fills me with heat.

Roman runs his hands up and down my thighs as I sit droopily in his lap, the side of my face smushed on his chest. When I have the energy to move, I shift to unsquish my face but don't get far, the movement tugging on his knot and making me moan and Roman growl. He pauses his soothing movements on my legs and I still and wait for the aftershocks to settle.

When I think it's safe to move without setting us off, I gingerly sit up. Roman puts an arm around my back to hold me. I rest my hands on his arms and notice the scratches I left, and subtly try to rub them away.

"I suppose it will be a bit until we can bond," I say, since I don't think Roman is flexible enough to reach my neck while I'm stuck on his lap. He chuckles, making me clench around him.

"Actually, I was thinking I would put my bond mark somewhere else, if that's alright with you?" Roman says.

"Oh, sure! Wherever you want is fine. Did you want me to bite you somewhere different?"

"I'd like to have your bite on my chest, too." He lifts my right hand up and kisses my palm. "I want to leave my mark your palm, so you can see that we're always here for you. We're your biggest supporters, and I want my bond to remind you of that every day."

I hug him with my free arm. "That's the perfect spot then," I sniffle into his chest.

"Can I bond you while we're knotted, or would you prefer to wait?"

"Let's do it now." I wonder if it will feel any different to be connected like this while we bond.

"Are you ready?" Roman asks softly.

"I'm ready." I nod, rubbing my cheek on his chest.

He lifts my hand and I watch in anticipation. After one more kiss on it, Roman bites the lower part of my palm.

I almost worry the bond hasn't taken until I realize Roman is already there, like a gentle breeze you don't notice at first. Then he gusts in, mixing with his packmates to fill the rest of the space in my heart. His presence grows as the bond sets, and his love is like a gale, inescapable and all-consuming. It blends with his protectiveness and meticulous care for everything he does. I trust him to catch me if I fall and dispel anything that gets in my way.

Like the breeze that you notice by its absence, longing for it to return and chase away the still loneliness, Roman blows away the lingering isolation I felt after being alone for years without a family or a pack. He replaces it with the surety of his love and safety of his respect for me as an equal. I don't have to worry that I'm trading in my freedom for a pack.

With Roman's bite, my alphas are all settled inside me. He releases my palm to lick away the sting. I peek at the mark, which doesn't look as sore as I expected. When he's done, he ends with a kiss.

I press my hands to his chest, flexing the right one when the bite rubs against him. Roman runs his fingers through my hair, and more hands join him. Phoenix, Basel, Fynn, and Salem circle around us. I feel their anticipation pulsing alongside my own as they wait for me to complete our pack.

Roman runs his thumb along my cheekbone. I smile up at him and lean forward. I take a bracing breath and bite over his heart. I drop suddenly into him as he drifts around me. I flood Roman with my love and admiration for his care, his intelligence, and his tenacity. I fill him with my appreciation for everything he's done to keep the pack together so that we could find each other.

My connection to Roman completes our pack. After tending my final mark, my alphas surge around and within me. We celebrate with hugs, kisses, and "I love you's" as I'm smothered in the middle of our celebratory huddle. Their feelings are like fireworks exploding and echoing inside me. It's even better than I thought it would be, sensing their emotions and knowing they're just as happy as I am.

As my *other* connection to Roman settles down, I slide off his lap. I reach for each of my alphas in turn, to kiss them all again as a newly bonded pack.

The celebration of our union turns into a physical appreciation of each other, and we don't leave the nest for the rest of the day.

CHAPTER 41
PERSEPHONE

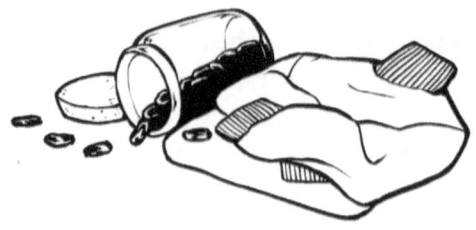

"You haven't mentioned how you chose our pack name," I contemplate lazily the next morning. My head rests on Phoenix's chest, and I absently trace the ridges on his abdomen with my fingers.

"We never told you how we first formed the pack?" Phoenix asks.

I tilt my head up to smile at him and shrug. They've told me how they met over the years leading up to becoming a pack, but not when they made it official. My pack isn't named after any of its members like some are, so I don't know how they chose their name.

"It's not like it's an interesting story," Fynn grumbles from where he's laying across my legs.

Despite his seeming disinterest, I sense a brief spark of pride and then embarrassment from him. I don't understand what that means, but I don't want him to feel bad. I rub his arm and send comforting thoughts. He brightens up and grins, pleased at my attention.

"It's an important moment and shows our strength as a pack," Salem reminds him.

"We are better together," Fynn agrees, but based on what I'm getting through the bond, he's not thinking about platonic pack stories. He winks at me.

"Did you want to tell the story then, Fynn? Or Nix?" Basel asks.

"Nah, someone else can," Fynn is quick to say.

"We knew each other for years before forming our pack," Phoenix says, "but only came up with our pack name the day we made it official. That day, Basel finished his biggest restoration project to date."

"I wrapped up that morning on a four-story brick building. The project was out of town, and right after I signed off on it, I headed home," Basel says.

"He texted us the good news and wanted to meet up later when we were free to celebrate," Salem says. "I hurried to finish my research for the day so I could join them."

"Someone was eager to get the party started," Roman says with a pointed look at Fynn, "and came to hang out with Nix and I while we waited for the others."

"Were you and Phoenix working together then?" I ask curiously.

"I helped him a little early on by setting up his business accounts and websites. As his work grew, he hired more staff who took over."

"He's being modest," Phoenix tells me. "Roman helped me tremendously when I started out on my own."

Phoenix sighs before continuing. "The day we became a pack was also the day I broke away from my parental pack. By the time I was a teenager, I was arguing with my fathers almost constantly about their designation biases. In college, I finally told them I would never be like them. We had nothing in common besides blood. Since my fathers limited their true views to private discussions, I began to see them only at public functions. I'd known Basel, Fynn, Roman, and Salem for years by that point, so I didn't miss the lack of a decent parental pack. If I didn't have my pack-mates, I'm not sure I would have managed a clean split from my family."

"The last time I saw my fathers, I attended a board meeting with them for one of their charities. Afterward, I told them I was cutting all ties with them, personally and professionally. I couldn't stand to be around their conserva-tive ideals any longer." Phoenix's eyes are unfocused, and his story tapers off.

"I attended the board meeting with Nix, but he asked me to wait outside while he told his fathers off," Roman picks up the story for him. "One last family moment, I guess."

Phoenix snorts a laugh and his expression eases.

"By the time that was over, Basel, Salem, and Fynn were almost there. I let them know what was going on, and they met us at the office building where the board meeting was. Nix had talked about cutting out his fathers for a while, but only told me just before the board meeting that he was going to do it then. We were glad he'd finally chosen to take that step, and the others would have been there if they'd known. Even if Nix said they didn't need to be," Roman says dryly.

"I knew you would be there for me afterward. I wanted to close that chapter of my life on my own," Phoenix says with a shrug.

"We met the others in the cafe at the base of the build-ing, and Nix filled us in on what he'd done," Roman says.

"After that, it seemed like the right time to ask if we wanted to make our pack official," Basel explains.

"We agreed, of course. We'd already sensed each other

as the pack bonds formed. All that was left was to register our pack, so we had to choose a name," Salem says.

"No one had any ideas, though. Nix didn't want to use his family name for obvious reasons, and we don't have strong ties to our families or surnames either," Roman says. "We thought we would have to wait to register until we picked out a suitable name, but then someone came up with the perfect one."

I wait with bated breath to hear more, but they stop there. I look around to see who's going to pick up the story, but they're all watching Fynn. Fynn is ignoring them, picking at a thread on the pillow beside him where he's moved to lean against the wall. Eventually Salem nudges Fynn's foot to prompt him.

"It wasn't some clever idea. I just saw some and thought they looked nice. Since no one else had any ideas, I figured we should just pick something and be done with it, and make our pack official," Fynn says sulkily.

I smile and pat his leg. "So, you saw goldenrod nearby?" I ask.

"Yeah, the cafe had a glass wall that overlooked a field. It was the start of fall, so it was full of those yellow flowers."

"It's a fitting name, no matter what inspired it," Basel says, giving Fynn a reprieve. "It was the beginning of new things for us, new careers and a new family. It was also the end of our old lives and the things holding us back. Autumn is the death of one season, but the start of a time of abundance and prosperity, just like we wished for in our lives."

"I didn't tell them this then," Phoenix leans over to whisper conspiratorially to me, although it's loud enough for the others to hear, "but I knew it was a fitting pack name for you, Persephone."

That makes me tear up, but I smile through the tears as I wrap my arms around Phoenix and hold him tight. I thought about him constantly over the years since we met in that field of goldenrod flowers outside my foster home. I love that Phoenix was also thinking of me, and I'm glad he wasn't alone all that time. He found our pack for us.

"It's the perfect name. Thanks for coming up with it Fynn, and all of you for choosing it," I say, my voice muffled in Phoenix's chest. They echo my sentiments and hug me. Fynn gets over his bashfulness from all the praise and comes over to join us.

My love for them swells in the bond, and their love fills me in return. It feels so good to be connected to my pack like this. My pack. We're really a pack now. Bonded. Together forever.

"I love you guys," I choke out around the happy tears.

"We love you too," Phoenix responds for everyone.

"Welcome to Pack Goldenrod, doll," Fynn says.

"Welcome home," Basel adds.

Home. With my pack surrounding me, I'm finally home.

Thank you for reading!

If you want to see spicy character art, sign up for my free newsletter!

You will get an email asking you to confirm you signed up. If you don't see it in your inbox, please check your spam/junk folder. That confirmation email will give you the link to the art!

www.winnieaster.com/subscribe-newsletter/

Signed copies and other merch are available in my store
www.winnieasterauthor.etsy.com/

Support me on Patreon to see art and updates first!
www.patreon.com/WinnieAster

Follow me on social media @WinnieAsterAuthor
www.winnieaster.com/links

If you have any questions or concerns, you can contact me at
winnie0aster@gmail.com

Also by Winnie Aster

Starsfalls Omegaverse

This is a series of standalones, which can be read in any order

Knot Falling for You

They Love Me Knot

Knot Hot for You

A dark omegaverse

Coming April 2027

Preorder now, and follow me for updates and character art!

www.winnieaster.com/links

KNOT FALLING FOR YOU

Persephone is trying to live the simple life as a barista in the small town of Starsfalls. When a chance encounter presents an opportunity for Seph to help her favorite bookstore, she jumps at it.

But things don't go according to plan. Seph is a self-proclaimed beta who has spent her life avoiding alphas, and working with a hunky alpha architect is not what she signed on for.

Unfortunately for her, alphas are like bobby pins. They multiply and show up everywhere. Soon the alpha architect is joined by his packmates, who hang around the bookstore and Seph. This poses a problem because Seph has a big secret that no one would *ever* guess (at least that's what she thinks) and now it's at risk of getting out.

When someone tries to sabotage Seph's new job, she has to decide if she can trust an alpha (or five).

There's the handy architect alpha.

The energetic, fiery alpha with golden retriever energy.

An uptight business alpha who could be persuaded to let loose.

The bookish alpha professor who has a sensitive side.

And the billionaire, brooding alpha with a checkered past.

But no matter what, she's definitely *not* falling for them.

Knot Falling for You *is a spicy standalone why choose omegaverse rom-com. It's part of the Starsfalls Omegaverse, where HEAs are guaranteed in this cozy small town.*